GRAY EAGLES

Duane Unkefer is an artist and a licensed car
racing driver who lives in Los Angeles, having
moved there from New York where he was an
advertising executive. *Gray Eagles* is his first
novel.

Duane Unkefer

GRAY EAGLES

Pan Books
in association with
Macmillan

First published in Great Britain 1986 by Macmillan London Ltd
This edition published 1987 by Pan Books Ltd,
Cavaye Place, London SW10 9PG
in association with Macmillan London Ltd
9 8 7 6 5 4 3 2 1
© Duane Unkefer 1986
ISBN 0 330 29331 1

Printed in Great Britain by
Richard Clay Ltd, Bungay, Suffolk

To my father, Dudley Fred Unkefer, who
lived his life in the perpetuation of good. He
would have liked this book.
And to Helen Grace Mischler, a loving pilgrim
who found her shack by the sea. She would
have liked this book, too.
And to all eagles fallen.

AUTHOR'S NOTE

This is a work of fiction and all incidents and characters are imaginary. There are, however, such places as Chino (California) Field, home of the Planes of Fame Museum; Rebel Field in Harlingen, Texas, home of the Confederate Air Force; Williams AFB and Luke AFB near Phoenix.

All details, historical and mechanical, concerning the Messerschmitt 109 and North American P-51 Mustang fighter aircraft, as well as all references to aerial combat operations over Europe during World War II, are true and accurate.

We are what we pretend to be, so we must be careful about
what we pretend to be.

—KURT VONNEGUT, JR., *Mother Night*

NAVY 2
LIBYA 0
—Badge worn by USAF fighter pilots at Van Nuys,
California, airshow after incident during August 1981
when U.S. Navy fighters shot down two Russian-built
Libyan fighters over the Mediterranean.

A pilot of an Air Force F-15 must confront 300 controls
simultaneously and sometimes is so saturated with
information that he cannot react fast enough, according to
a new government-funded study.

—(UPI) LOS ANGELES TIMES, April 4, 1982

ACKNOWLEDGMENTS

During the solitary journey of this novel there are special people who were helpful, supportive, and caring. Without them, *Gray Eagles* could not have been what it is, and perhaps might not have been. It is small tribute to list them here:

First, my mother, Madalyn, for forty-seven years of faith in all its forms.

My admirable IS typist, Debra Buccello, for her blind confidence, generous support, and a fine manuscript.

My family, who held their breath, sister Linda and Dr. Bob Maurer—for support, brother Dan—the whole way, brothers Dean and Lynn, Mrs Ribbit of Santa Barbara, and my son, Dan, for his contribution, at age eleven, of the term "brain-blinding."

Good friends and readers Jack Redmond, Alice Price, Maureen Redmond, Jean Huber, Helen Scungio, Hugh and Helen James, Tisha Le Rose, Kristen Kuester, Kathleen Wallace, and Elisabeth Bersin. And especially Di Ann Turek and the Holt (Michigan) Literary and Drinking Society; Monica De Young, Donna McGiveron, David Courey, Sarah Szuba, Karen Hiner, Ann Hoven, Kris Garcia, and Joan Kemper.

Those who contributed their expertise to research: Henry A. Pfeiffer, Col. USAF (ret.); Edward T. Maloney, author and president of the Chino Planes of Fame Air Museum; Don Lipsey, M.D., Marlene Schilffarth, Linda Maria Unkefer; Confederate Air Force Colonel(s) Ralph Royce, Carl Payne, Walt Wootton, Dick Baird, Bill Popejoy, and CAF Deputy Commander Wm. L. "Bill" Connell. And those pilots, German and American, who chose to remain anonymous.

Those who saw the manuscript through production; Gail

Myers, Patricia Rau, Beth Olsen, and Wayne Hansen.

Those editors who showed me the excellence that editors do; Dan Wickenden—for encouragement from the start; Toni Dorfman Valk, and Pat Irving Frederick. And two who rolled the dice quickly: Jim Landis at Beech Tree Books and agent Peter Livingston.

The Mary Roberts Rinehart Foundation, for their recognition and support for my first novel. And especially Loretta Trezzo, for—among other graces—typing the manuscript.

Finally, I wish to acknowledge the influence of the late John Gardner—though we never met—through his body of work on the writing of fiction. It needs to be said that *Gray Eagles* would have been a different novel had I not been guided by his precepts.

PROLOGUE
GERMANY 1944

It was as if Hell itself had somehow broken free from the earth and ascended above the clouds into the cold crystal blue. Hundreds of silver B-17 bombers from the US Eighth Air Force churned east in seemingly endless box formations, leaving miles of long cotton vapor trails in the icy air. At 26,000 feet, in a temperature of forty-two degrees below zero, these streams of frozen condensation from each engine exhaust became deadly giveaways, plainly visible in the empty sunlit atmosphere. There was no hiding place.

Each of the bombers, laden with five tons of incendiary and high explosive bombs, bristling with twelve .50 caliber machine guns, plowed steadily forward, locked tenaciously on target courses, stolid and massive in their howling determination to destroy Germany.

Each of the crew of ten, bundled against the bone-chilling cold in fleece-lined suits, braced for the gauntlet of defending German fighters. Gunners crouched in the clicking metallic coils of their ammunition belts, eyes sweeping their quadrants of sky. Pilots cursed the contrails that marked their passage, wrestling the controls to stay straight and level, knowing that death was on the way, knowing there was nothing they could do but fly on. Many prayed.

Above the B-17s, shining echelons of protective escort fighters – lean aluminum-skinned P-51 Mustangs – dropped empty auxiliary fuel pods and peeled off to do battle.

Hurtling up from airfields scattered across France and Germany came swarms of gray-green Messerschmitt 109s and Focke-Wulf 190s. Most of the Luftwaffe pilots were young and hastily trained, their more experienced comrades by now the victims of attrition, casualties of the relentless air battles that were breaking the back of the war in Europe. Fueled by this horror, this proximity to defeat, the Luftwaffe pilots launched themselves with desperate fury against the bomber formations.

Cannon and machine-gun fire hammered and laced across and back and forth and over and under the bombers. Bullets flew like hail, spattering across wings and fuselages, snapping through aluminum skin, piercing fuel tanks, shattering windscreens and turrets, ripping through flesh. Shells arced in countless lethal patterns from aircraft to aircraft, scattering steel shards in explosive convulsions that blew away gun blisters, severed electrical and oil arteries, ripped propellers clean away, chewed off entire tail sections, and slammed through everything that flew.

Entire aircraft, from the smaller Me-109 to the great B-17, frequently erupted in a flashing ball of orange-white fire, flinging away pieces, and self-incinerating in the simultaneous combustion of fuel, bombs, bullets and shells. Stricken engines shuddered and self-destructed. Wings folded and fell away. Fuel tanks ruptured and ignited, releasing boiling sheets of flame along wing surfaces. Some craft miraculously flew on, absorbing impossible amounts of gunfire, their wings shredded, fuselages ripped and peppered. Others fell quickly. Inside, men died in ungodly gore; chewed in half, eviscerated in showers of lead, immolated in fuel and phosphorus, atomized by direct hits. Some of the less fortunate were catapulted into space conscious and afire, conscious and spewing blood, conscious and without parachute. Or, healthy and whole, were trapped by G-forces that pinned them paralyzed in the downward-spinning, somersaulting wreckage of their craft.

This grim debris rained down upon the spring countryside of Germany. Flaming hulks crashed into the damp farmlands. Random showers of spent shells pattered over rooftops. Scorched scraps of fabric and aluminum fluttered down into orchards. Whole engines slammed like smoking meteors into the dark rich dirt.

The survivors also came to earth, the pilots and their planes, wounded and spent, seeping life fluids of blood and oil. Three of the Luftwaffe pilots, in crippled Messerschmitt 109s, searched out their home field. Like great awkward metal birds, the yellow-nosed 109s floated below the gray cloud cover in a misty cool rain, trailing pale smoke from burning oil, leaking coolant as they lined up for approach.

Hauptmann Rudi Felbeck watched his wingman, 200 meters ahead and below, tip crazily towards the runway, landing gear extended. He could see that Hans' 109 was nearly in shreds. Rudi throttled back, his own 109 yawing and swaying. Smoke swirled in the cockpit. The fighter's Daimler-Benz engine sputtered and missed, gasping for fuel. Still watching Hans, Rudi struggled to keep on line. The rudder response was erratic, and the landing gear was so shot up that he could not lower it. He would have to crash land.

The ground rose up. Cool damp air poured in through the shattered canopy as he prepared to shut down and brace for the impact. He had no fear of the concrete rushing up now. He was still numb from what he had experienced in the previous hour. To have survived that storm of steel and carnage was the greatest victory of his twenty-four years. With nothing worse than cuts on the face and one round through the left thigh. Safe now, he thought. Hans down, now me, and Theo right behind. Just hang on. Keep the nose up . . . steady. He shut down the engine as the runway slipped beneath him. Forty feet . . . thirty . . . the battered aircraft settled silently.

Then, as if struck by a bolt of lightning, he felt the 109 lurch and shudder as bullets cracked and ripped through it. Sparks danced off the propeller, the windscreen exploded away, the metal surface of the engine cowling buckled and tore. Struck in the shoulder and arm, needles of glass lashing his face, Rudi shriveled in his seat against the armor plate behind his head. *Not like this*, he thought, *not like this*.

Then the bullets passed him and chattered ahead down the runway after the first 109. Hans had set down, trailing white smoke, rolling about a hundred meters ahead. The bullets chewed into his rudder and then forward, hosing the entire fuselage from tail to nose. Like an animal the Messerschmitt seemed to quiver under the barrage, shedding chips of metal as it collapsed on shattered landing struts and veered off into the grass.

Just before Rudi's 109 made contact, the attacking P-51 passed like a roaring freight train over his head, raining a glittering shower of spent brass shells over his wing surfaces and slamming his plane into the runway with the violent turbulence of its passing. The impact jarred him nearly senseless, jerked his head forward, whipped his gloved hands against the instrument panel. To his dull astonishment the 109 never even bounced. As if already lifeless, the plane skidded straight ahead, metal shrieking on concrete, leaving a wake of dull orange sparks as it slewed around backwards and came to rest in the grass beside the runway.

Another shadow flashed over. Rudi recognized Theo's 109, landing gear reaching for the earth. Theo was level, but the mottled gray-green fuselage was holed aft of the cockpit where it let out a stream of soft black smoke.

As he watched Theo land, Rudi saw anti-aircraft tracers in the distance and, about half a mile down the runway, caught a glimpse of the American P-51. The tracers were following it. The Mustang sparkled with hits, spewed white smoke, tried to climb away, and then slid off to one side and went down level beyond a line of trees. There was no explosion.

Rudi shook his head. Blood sprinkled the instrument panel, dropped on his thighs in shining cold-red globules. *Get out,* he thought, fumbling for the release buckle of his seat harness. He tried to lift the canopy frame and it came apart as he shoved it up and over. He was trembling now and he twitched uncontrollably when more anti-aircraft tracers popped in long sailing arcs of scarlet fire across the field. Were there more Mustangs coming behind? *Please God no more, please.*

He struggled up, crying out in pain. Burning pieces of airplane littered the runway, smoked in the wet grass all around him. He saw Hans' 109 about eighty meters away. It seemed wilted, as if it were beginning to melt internally from the small fires eating away underneath. Rudi could smell the burning rubber and singed paint in the damp air. Thankful he had no fire, he lifted his good leg over the side and, hanging by one arm from the aerial post, slid down to the wing root. Dazed, he clung to the flank of the plane, staring at the ripped metal, at the winged crimson dragon insignia of Fighter Wing 26 painted below the battered cockpit. The engine cowling was loose, contorted. From underneath he heard the hot metal ticking and hissing in a cloud of bitter smoke.

He could not feel either of his feet and his arm was numb. Wiping sweat from his face, his gloved hand came away wet and red. He pushed off his goggles and leather helmet and staggered towards Hans' plane. He was conscious of ground-support vehicles moving across the airfield but he knew he would reach his wingman before they did. He shuffled up to Hans' 109. The fire was growing, feeding on tires and oil lines and wiring and paint. Tongues of flame licked up the sides of the fuselage. There were terrible bullet holes everywhere. Rudi clambered over the wing and up to the shattered cockpit. Acrid smoke and heat washed up over his legs, and his boot soles scraped over bright diamonds of chipped glass on the wing. He looked into the cockpit at what was left of Hans. And then up at the sky. Everything fell away.

Major Theo Heinrich stood by Rudi's bed in the base hospital, studying the ashen face. Rudi was unconscious but they had taken care of him quickly, cutting the clothing away from his leg and shoulder wounds and giving him a unit of blood. There was desperate activity all around, the sounds of the medics working, whispering, cursing. And the wounded groaning and cursing. The stench of warm raw blood and of burned flesh and scorched fabric and urine and alcohol and ether made Theo light-headed, nauseated. Even in his leather flight jacket he was chilled by the evaporation of his sweat-soaked clothing. Occasionally he pulled at a near-empty bottle of schnapps while he watched Rudi's face for some change.

He paid little conscious attention to the distant shelling that shook the flimsy wooden hospital building. He shivered, in mild shock. One of the medics had given him a cloth soaked in some bitter stinging solution to wipe the half-dozen cuts on his face, and had bound the gash in his lower arm.

There was a lot of noise outside, still distant. He now realized that the perimeter of the field might be under attack by ground troops. He listened for light weapons fire, but heard none. He had resolved to stay with Rudi and, he reasoned, he could lend little help to the fighting with a wounded arm. Nonetheless, he looked around for a weapon. Scraps of clothing, boots, tattered flying pants, even helmets and oxygen gear – all from the wounded – littered the floor. A medic came over, mechanically checked Rudi's pulse, covered him with a blanket and moved away to the next bed. Again the ground trembled. A metallic tinkling of chrome and glass floated in the ward.

Four beds away Theo saw the P-51 pilot. They had brought him in just after Rudi, thirty minutes ago now. Half-drunk, Theo walked over and looked down at the wounded American. He seemed unconscious, though his eyes were slightly open and fixed. He was breathing but no one was tending him. Good, Theo thought, perhaps he will die on his own.

The American looked very young and his face was full and healthy-looking even under the pallor of shock. His brown leather flying jacket was still zipped tight, the sheepskin collar scorched and spattered with darkened blood. There was a bad gash across the left ear and his neatly-cut brown hair was matted with more blood. Like all of them, he too smelled terribly of sweat and smoke and fuel. The American's gloved hand twitched. Theo then noticed the bloodied holes in the shoulder and upper arm. And he read the name patch: Lowen.

Theo walked back to Rudi. He was a little dazed and he found an empty wooden medical supply crate and pulled it up to Rudi's bed and sat down. There was some color in Rudi's face now. Theo drank some more and wished again he could find a weapon somewhere. He was very tired and he hurt everywhere with every movement. Blood had seeped into his arm bandage which had grown heavy and wet. He decided to sit still for a while. The shelling had receded, he noticed.

Now what? he thought. Every aircraft in the *Jagdgeschwader* is junk. Are we really losing, could it be? The goddamned Americans. How could they do it? Thousands of them, just like that overfed bastard Lowen, in clean uniform, probably no more than six hours out of a warm dry bed, a rich breakfast with real coffee in his belly, a little hangover from English ale. Bastard. And flying those murderous P-51s, more of the endless tide of American aircraft, so many that they no longer bothered with camouflage paint. Just fly them brand new, shiny aluminum bright, 500 miles from England to escort the B-17s and still have enough fuel to beat up targets of opportunity on the way back. That's what you are; a target of opportunity. You and Rudi and young Hans, his bloody brains all over the cockpit. Now all of Germany is a target of opportunity. Relentless, the Americans. Blowing everything to hell. Homes. Schools. Farms. Everything. And killing. The children. Mothers. Wives. Fathers. Grandfathers. Grandmothers. Everyone.

Theo half-dozed, listening to the frantic movement in the

10

ward around him. Flashes of the air battle flickered in his mind's vision like a projector gone amok. Planes everywhere, fireballs and wide flat trails of smoke from falling planes, the bitter cold, the adrenaline pumping wildly as you kicked and stamped and pulled and pushed at the controls . . . shooting, fleeing, diving, turning, attacking . . . he was so weary. And the bombers . . . most got through, he knew. Before the P-51s, not so many B-17s got through. There was a chance then.

But not now. Where did so many airplanes come from? Two years ago no one had ever heard of a P-51 or a B-17. Theo shook his head and stared coldly at the two medics working on Lowen. *Let him die. He tried to execute us. Let him die.*

Rudi's eyes opened, fluttered. Theo sat up, leaned over, and took out a cigarette. Rudi turned his head and focused his blue eyes on Theo. He looked confused, almost in panic.

Theo leaned closer. 'Rudi?'

Expressionless, Rudi stared at him for a moment, then looked around sleepily. The floor quivered beneath them and the windows rattled from explosions now not so distant. Light mortars, Theo thought to himself. Not good. He watched Rudi, waiting for him to speak.

'Theo,' he whispered with great effort.

'It is all right now,' Theo said. 'All over. Here.' He held the bottle up to Rudi's lips.

Rudi tasted, grimaced. 'Water,' he rasped.

Theo looked around, spotting a canteen in a heap of discarded gear beneath the next bed. He lifted it up, unscrewed the cap, and put it to Rudi's lips, watching him swallow weakly. 'Smoke?' Theo held up the cigarette.

Rudi stared at the cigarette, then shook his head. 'How bad—?'

'Not bad, not bad.' Theo tried to make his voice soothing. Gunfire rattled somewhere. He was so tired, dizzy, and his arm was throbbing.

'What's all the noise?' Rudi said slowly.

Theo shrugged. 'I guess it is the war.'

Rudi was staring again, as if he saw nothing. Theo began searching through his pockets for a match. He gave up, staring at the bent cigarette as if it were a puzzle. There was light automatic weapons fire outside, not far away. The medics worked on.

11

'The American . . .' Rudi said, as if he were patiently explaining something very simple, 'in the Mustang . . . got Hans. Blew his head off.'

'Yes.' Theo nodded. 'Well, now we have the American. Right here, so . . .' he sighed, not able to think of more to say.

There was a disturbance at the end of the ward. Several men at one time were pushing through the door and crouching. They were wearing strange rounded brownish-olive helmets and dirt-brown jackets. And they held automatic weapons. Even from that distance Theo recognized the muzzle of a Thompson .45, but he was too exhausted to do anything but watch.

The first American was a sergeant and his face was very dirty and his hands were very dirty and his uniform was very dirty. Behind him crouched other dirty American soldiers. They all looked as if they had been rolling around in the mud. The sergeant stood up first, slowly, keeping the machine gun pointed out with the muzzle weaving back and forth like a snake searching for prey. His eyes moved with it. He stepped forward. In the beds, those wounded who were conscious looked on, stupefied. Rudi had seen nothing yet.

Theo watched the sergeant coming closer, until their eyes met. The American stopped, then cautiously walked closer, his eyes seeking Theo's hands; one around the bottle, the other still holding the cigarette.

Theo looked down the barrel of the machine gun, feeling – to his surprise – very little fear. He was in fact greatly relieved. Better the Americans than Ivan, he thought. Perhaps they would all live now. Sorry, Rudi, we did not get the American bastard sooner. We did all we could. You did all you could. Hans did all he could. Honorably.

Theo looked up at the sergeant, who lifted his chin slightly and spoke. 'Stand up, Kraut.'

'Perhaps you could give me a light, Sergeant,' Theo said in English, rising slowly.

BOOK I

A GATHERING OF EAGLES

CHAPTER ONE

During the weeks prior to his vacation, Rudi had carefully prepared all matters under his jurisdiction for the eventuality that he would not return.

Such attention to detail was true not only to his nature but to the nature of his profession as well. All current projects had been reviewed and placed in a series of files, along with orderly notes which would permit his associates to carry them forward well beyond the two weeks he was expected to be absent.

All items on his personal list, including insurance policies, will and documents of ownership, had been placed in sealed envelopes with the appropriate instructions. There were also six personal letters, sealed, addressed and stamped. All this material had been delivered in one package to his attorney. There were now but two tasks remaining; to pick up the cartons of high-intensity navigation lights which had arrived the day before, and to pick up the boots which had taken several weeks longer than expected.

Before coming to work that morning, Rudi had closed up the house and stowed his luggage in the trunk of the car. There had been a couple of hours of last-minute paperwork, mostly signatures, and now he paused to consider the empty desk top, the drawers cleaned of all personal items and papers. There were photographs on the wall that would remain, as would a dozen or so books. It was perhaps a touch melodramatic, he felt, this tidying up in case of no return, but he also felt responsible for doing it. He then turned the pages of his desk calendar ahead two weeks to 8 May 1976 ... thirty-one years since VE Day.

He planned to return. He liked Sunwest Aviation. He liked the office and the old gray metal desk and he liked the people he worked with and he liked what he had been doing for a living for the past eighteen years. His professional life and his personal life had become so pleasantly welded after all these years that he frequently looked back and reminded himself that he was indeed a fortunate man. In all that time since Germany the only event that had torn loose the fabric of his life was losing Linda. He remembered feeling then much as he did now, that the funeral was the end of one phase and the beginning of another. There would be a new experience and he would go forward.

Abruptly he stood, collected his coat and briefcase, and left the office. He spoke brief good-byes to several of his staff and wended his way through the corridors down to Receiving. The cartons of lights were waiting, tied together neatly, with check-out pass in order, just like the hundreds of other times he had carried out boxes of aluminum and plastic pieces. He backed the silver BMW CS1 coupé up to the loading platform and placed the cartons in the trunk, leaving it open as he drove to the gate. He surrendered the pass slip, chatted with the security guard – who gave the cartons no inspection before closing the trunk – and then drove in the glaring midday heat toward West Hollywood.

Rudi always liked the small custom shoe store where the eight pairs of boots were waiting, each pair in a fine gray cardboard box with the shoemaker's name imprinted in gold ink on the cover. He examined each boot carefully, checking the sizes against his order slip. The boots were perfectly crafted in soft black high-gloss leather, beautifully done with what he believed to be Old World care. He paid the bill with traveler's checks and helped the clerk carry the boxes to the car, leaving him with a generous tip.

Standing beside the BMW, he removed his coat and slipped it over a hanger in the back. He then removed his silk tie, loosened his collar, and got into the car. There he checked the seat position, adjusting it for more recline, and then the rearview mirrors on each door. Removing his sunglasses, he cleaned them slowly, put them back on, and reached for the interior rearview mirror. In adjusting the mirror he caught a glimpse of his own face and he turned the mirror to look at himself. Behind

16

the sunglasses his blue eyes were hidden but he knew they were clear and sharp. It was not a bad face and it did not look like fifty-six. Except for the fine crow's-feet, the mouth lines and the dozens of tiny near-invisible scars from glass wounds in the war, the tanned face was acceptably strong, and there was not an excessive amount of gray in his close-cut reddish hair. He was not displeased with the way he looked. He fastened his seat belt, then carefully pulled on calfskin driving gloves, snugging each finger tight, and closed the Velcro tabs over the wrists. He started the engine.

Intently he threaded the BMW through traffic down to the Santa Monica Freeway. The dash clock read 1.20 so he would be well ahead of Friday afternoon rush-hour traffic. Smoothly he accelerated onto the freeway eastbound, the car darting out into the traffic flow. He permitted himself a small smile. Now, finally, it was beginning.

He was pleased. Everything was in order. He felt very good, very healthy. He was trim and lean and his reflexes, he knew, were quite adequate. Even the car felt especially good and healthy. He loved the sleek design, the flawless silver paint, the leather bucket seats, the stark black interior and aircraft-like dash layout. He could feel the parts of the car — suspension, steering, tires — working in concert, propelling him forward through the buffeting of crosswinds and the draft of eighteen-wheelers.

Clear through to Riverside County he was kept busy with the driving, maneuvering through hordes of vehicles bound for desert weekends; campers towing dune buggies, dusty pick-ups with yellow dirt bikes tied in the back, Cadillacs and Mercedes bound for Palm Springs, all escaping the blanket of heavy heat and brown smog. Rudi tolerated the sprawl of Los Angeles, hating it secretly but willing to endure it for the pleasure of his work and the weekends in Phoenix with Marta and Eric. He could not count the times he had made this trip and always he loved it. Two hours out, very soon now, the countryside would change to desert. No more rolling sand hills covered with sand-colored condominiums, no more taco stands and service stations. The traffic would thin away at Indio, long before the Arizona state line, and by the first hint of sunset he would be in the true desert.

At Blythe, just a few miles from the border, he stopped and

17

filled the gas tank, removed the black vinyl covers from the auxiliary driving lights, and arranged the Beethoven cassettes in order: a half-dozen piano sonatas, the Emperor concerto and, for sunset, the Pastorale. And then two other symphonies for after dark. Following a quick inspection of the tires, he was prepared for the several hundred miles remaining.

Flying through the early evening, Rudi settled himself in the bucket seat and leaned back into the headrest. The BMW nearly drove itself, growing lighter and even more tractable at speed. It was a long and lonely haul now, but beautiful with the magnificent spectacle of sunset and the black ribbon of macadam unreeling before the flight of the silver coupé. The solitude and majesty of this part of the trip always gave him the best time to think.

He found it distinctly curious that the last seven years of his life had brought him to this particular moment, rushing at 89 m.p.h. into the great American desert.

He stopped at the border for the agriculture check, declaring to the uniformed officer that he carried no fruit, no flowers, no vegetables. Oddly, the moment's contact with uniformed authority reminded him that he was also crossing the line between lawful and unlawful. As he accelerated away, he felt he had finally passed the point of no return.

If there was a beginning, it would have been when he bought the first Messerschmitt 109 eight years before, sight unseen, from a collector in New York. How hopeless it had seemed when he opened the crates. The wings and fuselage still had battle damage and the rudder was gone. The prop was missing, as was the canopy, and the tires were flat and rotted. He wrote to Theo for help in finding the pieces he needed. Theo found them quickly.

With Eric's help, Rudi began reconstruction of the 109 in rented hangar space at Phoenix Skyharbor International. His brother-in-law was intrigued with the great 12-cylinder Daimler-Benz engine and quickly brought it to life. The plane was structurally sound and well preserved and, since it was the later G model, the best of the 109s, Rudi knew it would be easy to sell as a restored warbird. And before it was halfway completed, a tractor-trailer came to the hangar with a gift from Theo – another Me-109G in much better looking crates. With the papers for Rudi to sign there was a note from Theo: *Build*

18

this one for me and we will fly together once more.

As both planes took shape, they consumed all his leisure time. All his weekends were spent in Phoenix, and all his energies and talents were brought to bear on the challenge of improving the 109, correcting its original weaknesses, and updating the systems. It was at this point that Sunwest sent Rudi to England on a consulting project with the RAF and he took a weekend to visit Theo in Bremen. On the last night they had gone out for an elaborate dinner. Even now Rudi had no trouble in recalling the grand carpeted hall with much crystal and many waiters, where they ordered yet another bottle of wine and more coffee, sitting at the cleared table as the restaurant grew empty and quiet. They had had a great deal to drink, so much that they both seemed to have reached a plateau where they were no longer drunk, where they could think and speak clearly. They talked about the war and they talked about flying and they talked about women and they talked about getting old and they talked about the new Messerschmitts.

'I have been thinking about this for a year now,' Theo said, gazing at the ceiling and swirling the wine around in his glass goblet. 'Now imagine, just imagine if we had a Staffel, eight planes.'

'Eight?'

'Yes. All flying together. Can you imagine that?'

Yes, Rudi could imagine. He could even hear the engines.

'And imagine,' Theo continued, 'that we find six other 109 pilots and organize the Staffel as a military unit. Everything just like the war.'

Rudi leaned back in the wide gilt chair and took up his coffee in both hands. He looked closely at Theo, conscious of his wealth and position, of his fine dark gray suit and fine sharp mind.

'It is a wonderful idea, yes?'

'It is a wonderful idea,' Rudi agreed, 'but—'

'But, but, *but*!' Theo nearly came up out of his chair. 'No buts!' He grinned suddenly. 'I have thought this over for almost a year, my friend.'

Rudi was able to imagine Theo sitting at the head of a corporate board table as easily as he sat at this one. He could think of nothing to say.

'Would you build six more planes?'

'It could be done.' Rudi stared at Theo.

'Of course,' Theo nodded. 'I will continue to finance everything. I can find six more.'

'Six more G models?'

'Of course. I find them and I ship them. You build them and you own them.'

'I see,' Rudi said simply. He took up his pipe again and slowly began to pack in tiny bits of tobacco, using the time to think about the fact that he was quickly being drawn into a most unusual deal.

'Also.' Theo reached for the wine bottle in the silver bucket, patted it dry with the white towel and poured both glasses half-full. 'Also, I will find the other six pilots. What do you think?'

'It could be done.'

'Of course it can be done. It will be done. What do you think eight restored Gustavs would be worth in America? A hundred thousand dollars apiece, perhaps?'

'More. Perhaps twice that.'

'Enough, yes? The planes will be yours if you put this all together, organize it. You will do it?'

Rudi smiled faintly. 'I will give it some serious thought.'

'Some serious thought.' Theo smiled back and began tapping two of his fingers on his wine goblet.

Rudi then realized that Theo was expecting a reply, expecting him to be giving it serious thought now, while he waited. The two men stared at each other, smiles just slightly faded and frozen.

'I have given it some serious thought,' said Rudi. 'Yes.'

'There is one more thing,' said Theo quickly.

'Yes?' Rudi knew instantly that the 'one more thing' would be even more unusual; it was the manner of deal-makers.

'The Staffel will fly combat missions.'

'Combat missions.' Rudi wanted to laugh.

'Of course. Is it not logical?'

'Logical to fly combat missions in the United States?'

'Of course, of course! We do not have to declare a war. We only have to fly and shoot.'

'Theo, it is illegal to fly armed aircraft.'

'*Ach*!' Theo threw up his hands. 'I do not care about legal; I care about logical! Don't you see?'

'I'm afraid I do not see.' Rudi began rubbing his temples.

'Rudi, my friend.' Theo was now speaking in a tone of voice clearly born of experience at patiently leading lesser-minded men to greater visions. 'It is merely the logical extension of all that we are doing. All of it; the planes, the men, everything authentic. The missions must follow. It is then the complete experience. *Wenn schon, denn schon.* If it is to be done at all, then do it properly. Fighter pilots fly fighter planes and fighter planes fight.'

Rudi watched Theo straighten and lift his chin, as if he had finished a lecture and was now prepared for questions.

'Fight who?' asked Rudi, staring.

'I don't care who,' Theo briskly replied. 'I don't care how. You figure it out. You plan it. We should have two – no, three – mission plans, just like the war. It is very simple.'

It turned out to be more simple than Rudi had expected. Theo sent more 109s and all the spare parts they requested, and Rudi and Eric simply kept building 109s until there were eight. It took almost four years.

The mission plans were not so simple. Rudi began this part of the project with mixed feelings, all of which opposed each other and none of which were comfortable. The objective was to recreate as authentically as possible the experience of combat flying. What could fighter planes fight if there were no fighter planes to fight with? If there was to be gunnery, at what would they shoot? Round and round. Until he decided, finally, that he had agreed only to create the planes, not to fly them.

In time, Rudi devised the first two mission plans. One was feasible, one was fantasy, both were brilliant. Theo would love them. But he had no idea whatsoever for the third plan until he ran across an article in the *Times*, a photo story about the Confederate Air Force – a group of Texas pilots who restored and flew Second World War combat planes – appearing at an airshow near Los Angeles. There was a photograph of the CAF Deputy Commander, climbing down from his Mustang. The CO was a veteran of the European theatre, decorated and retired, and his name was Roger Lowen. On that quiet Sunday morning Rudi found the nucleus for his third mission plan.

Now, one year later, Rudi reached out to touch the briefcase behind the passenger seat as he drove into the desert. All three mission plans were under his hand, accurate in every detail, typed neatly, in black binders. Finished, they gave him the most unusual sensation that the entire project was then complete, whole. Perhaps Theo was right, for the sense of completeness came – to Rudi's surprise – not from the planes being finished but from the three black binders. He had kept his part of the agreement, all of it, and the mission plans had become a logical extension of the Staffel project, even though they would never be used. There was nothing more to do. Except fly.

The planes, his planes. How perfect they were, waiting in the desert, hidden in those clapped-out tinder boxes that once were hangars. Such lovely brutal lines, such splendid scoops and bulges, such a hard elegance to the long narrow fuselage, the bluntly squared wings and the oddly splayed and spindly landing struts. An evil airplane, a pure fighting airplane, for seven years the reigning demon of the skies over Europe. Until the Mustangs came. And now it faced extinction, like the majestic black condors of the American West. This greatest of warbirds, once in numbers exceeding 36,000, was nearly gone from the face of the earth.

Dusk when it came was spectacular, splashing a flood of orange and golden light across the hazy stretches of gray sand and over the salmon-pink and russet mesas. Rudi cruised with the tach at 3200 r.p.m., an easy ninety-plus in fifth.

The operation would be under way in less than twenty-four hours, with Theo's arrival. There was nothing more he could do, nothing he had not thought out carefully. And yet, with the action so close, it had suddenly assumed more urgent dimensions. They were about to operate fully armed aircraft – in violation of God-knew-what laws – that were not FAA registered. He was about to assume second-in-command of a paramilitary group of Luftwaffe veterans, five of whom he had never seen. And sooner or later, he would have to deal with Marta when she discovered that both he and her husband had been less than entirely truthful about what was going on.

The two Cibie driving lights under the bumper of the BMW threw out sweeping cones of glaring white light 200 yards into the desert darkness. He lowered the window a few inches and turned off the air-conditioning. He breathed deeply from the rush of still-warm air, dry in his nostrils with the tar-oil fragrance of hot blacktop. The reflective green road sign flashed past: Phoenix 250 miles.

'Since we are not accustomed to wearing swimming suits, we shall have to change our habits when your pilot friends arrive.' Marta smiled at her brother as he eased himself into the bubbling Jacuzzi across from her.

'Perhaps they would like the custom after all.' Rudi winced as the hot water ringed his thighs and tingled up around his naked torso.

'With me the only woman, I'm sure they would. Perhaps I would too.'

Rudi dipped his head under water, then leaned back. The swirling water was truly soothing. Whatever subtle aches had crept into his muscles during the eight-hour drive began to fade. Above them the desert sky was strewn with the glittering dust of countless bright stars gleaming in the pure clear air. The underwater lights glowed up through the bubbles and tinted the under-surfaces of his sister's angular face like a Degas painting of a cafe singer. Marta was a small woman with shining white teeth and a permanent caramel tan from long and regular hours by her backyard pool. Her dark blond hair was pulled into a haphazard pile on her head.

'You had a good trip?' She spoke to the night sky, her head resting on the pad of a folded towel.

'Easy, yes. I'm not the least bit tired.'

'Because you are excited, yes?'

'I suppose . . . yes.'

He did feel very good. He was glad that he and Marta were alone.

'Well,' said Marta, 'this water will put you to sleep soon.'

'It is wonderful. Where is Eric tonight?'

'He stayed late at the shop, then I know he went drinking with the boys. His last day before vacation, so he'll roll in about two-thirty.' She gave particular emphasis to 'the boys' in a gently mocking manner, much like a high-school girl. 'He's very excited about this, you know.'

'Good.' Rudi opened his eyes, searching the stars. 'And how are things with Eric at the shop?'

'Fine. The money is good and they're very busy. It's remarkable how many people can afford to buy a BMW. He has a good assistant manager and can be away and not worry.'

'He is talented. Quite good with engines. It's a special skill.'

'Here,' Marta said, rising up from the water. 'You must put

this under your head.' Through half-closed eyes Rudi watched her reach out for his towel, fold it into a small pad, and place it under the back of his head. 'There. Isn't that better?'

'Much.' Rudi closed his eyes again. The image of her body so close had startled him. For all the good and usual reasons he enjoyed seeing Marta nude, as he often did in the Jacuzzi and pool, and the fact that she was his sister created a comfortable barrier that kept him at ease. Unexpectedly, seeing her body this time reminded him of Linda. Memories stirred in him and he pushed them away.

'And I will pour you some cold wine,' she said. 'I must be the good hostess, starting now.'

Rudi kept his eyes closed, listening to the gurgle of wine as she poured. He waited until she had settled back into the water before opening his eyes.

'Are you all right about this, our Staffel?' he asked.

'Yes . . .' She left the word hanging, drawing out the *s*, playing with the bodice of little bubbles that foamed around her breasts. 'Yes, I am all right.'

'It is very good of you to have us all here. Is Eric all right about it?'

'Oh, he's fine. I am the only one with worries.'

'There is some risk, but—'

'Well, I do not want to go to jail. I want to get rich with my real estate. I don't like the idea of risk.'

'If we are disciplined and lucky we will all be back to our routines in two weeks.'

'Drink to that.' She sighed. They touched glasses.

'Is the money enough, for everything?'

'Please, Rudi, it is enough. Don't worry. All the menus are worked out and most of the wine and food is already here. It's all under control. And I will enjoy being hostess to your flying club. All those mennnn.'

'I am sure they will find you charming.'

Marta took a long sip from her wine. 'I am glad they are not younger men so Eric will not be jealous.'

'Is he being jealous these days?'

Marta shrugged. There was something in the gesture, and he caught a certain sober note in her voice.

'Rudi, I want a promise from you, about Eric.'

'What is it?'

'I don't want to lose him.' She stared into the water as if remembering something. 'Once he mentioned – a couple of weeks ago, I think – that he would like to fly with you and the rest of your crazies. Don't let him do that.'

'I won't. It's a promise. And there are only eight planes.'

'And don't let him get hurt,' she added, looking up at him. 'You'll be fooling with guns, bullets and bombs and gasoline, and I don't want to think of any accidents.'

'Eric can take care of himself. And, there are no bombs.'

'That doesn't matter and you know it. There are accidents.' Her voice hardened. It was the first time he could recall Marta ever being curt with him.

'Our procedure will be even more strict than the military. We will be very careful, I promise.'

Marta was absently scooping handfuls of hot water over each of her glistening brown shoulders. 'When will I see your planes with the new paint?'

'Whenever you wish.'

'Are they painted the same as they were in the war?'

'Exactly.'

'Eric said they have swastikas painted on them.'

Rudi thought for a moment before he answered. He could sense that Marta was working on something. 'Of course. On the tails.'

'Do they bother you, the swastikas?'

Again Rudi thought over his reply. 'No.'

'It might bother other people, don't you think?'

'It will not bother any of us. The planes are restored in every detail. The swastikas are part of that detail.'

'Must they be?'

'Marta, the war is long over.'

'For many people, Rudi, swastikas will never be over.'

'And for many people the white star on a blue circle will never be forgotten either. I am one of those people. Aren't you?'

'I was too young. I was . . . frightened more than anything. I do not remember hating Americans, only hearing that I should hate the Russians. I never saw Russians, and the Americans I saw were very nice.'

'The Americans I saw were not always so nice.'

'No . . . well, it does not matter now. I love this country. It is my country now and I like it.'

'As you said, it does not matter now.'

'What do you feel now, Rudi, for Germany? Or against Americans?'

Rudi poured another glass of wine, thinking.

'I hated the Americans then. Or perhaps it is more accurate to say that I feared them. Mostly I remember being stunned by the endless numbers of their bombers and fighters. No matter how many we shot out of the sky there would be even more the very next day.

'Now I feel nothing against America. I understand the war now, much better than I did then. But,' he paused, 'I don't have any overwhelming – yes, that is the word – any overwhelming loyalty to Germany. Now I am loyal to myself. I have been fortunate. I have had a good life here. I am an American.'

Marta sipped at her wine. The cold surface of the glass had turned white with condensation. 'But,' she said, 'Theo is not. The others are not.'

'It won't matter. We are sharing a moment of the past. This isn't a war.'

Marta was quiet for a few moments. Rudi could almost hear her thinking. What did she want? He waited for the next question, knowing there would be more.

'The planes. They all have guns?'

'Yes, they all have guns.'

'And that makes them illegal to fly?'

'Yes.'

'Do they have bombs?'

'No bombs, I told you. Just guns.'

'What are you going to shoot?'

'Whatever targets we can find in the desert. Rocks. We are not going to shoot at people. Is that what you are afraid of?'

'I am afraid of accidents.'

'That's silly. Do you think—'

'It's not silly! Eight pilots flying around with loaded guns is not silly. It frightens me, Rudi.'

'Marta, we are not going to shoot at people.'

'Why do I find that so difficult to accept?'

'Believe it,' he said patiently. 'Just believe it.'

She watched him over the rim of her glass.

'As I have told you,' he went on, 'we are going to conduct a two-week flying exercise within a military discipline, with every detail as authentic as it was during the war. Part of that detail is aerial gunnery, shooting.'

Marta continued to stare at him as if searching for something hidden. For now, he decided, she had accepted his answer. With her eyes still on him, she raised her hands and loosened the tangle of her moisture-darkened hair. The movement raised her breasts above the water. Rudi settled his head back on the towel-pad and closed his eyes.

'I would think,' Marta said in a voice now calm and measured, 'that in order to get involved in this, your Staffel, a man would have to be somewhat . . . unusual, different.'

'Yes.' Rudi was relieved that she had turned a corner.

'I will be curious to meet them.'

'Three tomorrow. Four Sunday.'

'How shall I be, for these unusual men? Shall I be gracious and charming? Beautiful? Shall I also be . . . alluring?'

'Of course,' Rudi opened his eyes. 'All of those things.' She was still fooling with her hair. She held pins in her teeth and her breasts were still exposed, shining wet. She took the pins from her teeth and smiled at him, but only with her mouth. Her eyes, green and shining too, did not smile at all.

'Well, it will be fun,' she said, sliding back down into the foam. 'I will enjoy it. And I will do it well.'

CHAPTER TWO

Watching television was not Roger Lowen's idea of the best way to spend a Friday evening, but there had been a rerun of *High Noon*, the first in many months. He'd always liked that film, always liked Gary Cooper, and he watched it every time it ran. And this particular time, like every other, he came away restless and disturbed. Damned film did that. He never knew why.

Good ol' Coop, cool as ice, the aging lawman trying to hang up his guns and get married. Then the black-hats come after revenge and he has to load up his six-shooters just one more time. All alone, nobody willing to back him, except an old guy with one eye looking for some excuse for being. And a kid, shining with hero-worship, who doesn't know any better.

Not his new wife either. Grace is packing her bags and bugging out pronto, until the Mexican woman – Coop's ol' faithful flame – straightens her out; stand by your man. Great stuff. And doesn't pale Grace pick up a hefty .44 and blow the black-hat away, right between the shoulder blades? Sure ... maybe back then, Lowen mused, but not any more. These days they'd be on the first train out, you bet, while you got your balls shot off.

It seemed like a very old movie now, the dialogue so clipped and simple, a fairy tale. Everything so clear-cut. Nothing confusing, not at all like real life where nothing was clear-cut. Nothing.

When the film ended Lowen watched the Late News, then got up and snapped off the TV and went to the kitchen. He opened a cold can of beer and filled his pipe and went out onto the patio.

The air was warm and humid and the plastic-covered cushion of the patio couch was damp. He could smell the fishy Gulf eight miles to the east. He liked the night, the vast sparkling Texas sky. In fact he liked the patio furniture and the patio and the house and even Brownsville, for all its faults. And he liked his friends and he loved his wife and he loved fishing and he loved his three-year-old Corvette and, most of all, he loved the Confederate Air Force.

He was alone in the house. Jean was out with friends, bowling or bridge, he forgot which. She was quite independent and he had found it a new but likeable experience to live with a woman who came and went as she pleased. His first wife had come and gone as she pleased too, until finally she went and didn't come back, for a week, whereupon she confessed that she was hopelessly bored with her life and had found someone who had promised to change it. While there was still time.

The divorce was clean and quick and he had not lost a great amount of money. In time he recovered financially, but never fully recovered the other things he had lost. It had shaken something deep. After a time he recognized that what was shaken was his sense of loyalty, of what loyalty was supposed to be. He had been betrayed, that was it.

There was also an unexpected compassion for her, as if it were not entirely her fault for catching this late-in-life wanderlust, nor was he honestly able to blame whoever it was that enticed her away. No, he blamed Everything That Was Going On, everything being – in combination – what was on the TV and in the papers and magazines. She had merely been a victim of trends.

In this vein, Roger Lowen had become bitterly disturbed over the quality of life in the entire country. Things had changed, as anyone with half a brain could clearly see. There used to be certain truths. Honor was honorable. Dishonesty was dishonest. Immorality was immoral. He could make a long list. Who was changing these things? Where did it begin, this idea of calling what was black not black, but white? Did it take no more than *saying* something was white, when it was black, to make it white?

Where it began, when he had first recognized this confused rage, was in Vietnam – the real beginning of this calling something different to what it really was. Fools, they wouldn't even call it a war. And as one familiar with war, he was appalled by the carnage, by the double-talk, by the suppression of truth and, finally, by the inexcusable indifference to the veterans of combat. In war, as in other contests, one won or lost. We lost and called it something else. Lost also in the fall of Saigon – the 'bugging out' – was Roger Lowen's faith in the political, military and moral credibility of his country.

What was lost was honor. It was the beginning of a contagion that infected all that he held to be stable and decent, the beginning of an altogether new era of duplicity. With that great bloodbath of disregard for human life there had seemed to follow a great wave of disregard for honor as well. No person now seemed beyond corruption, not in all the land.

So he was disappointed with his first wife in the same way he was disappointed in his country: both had fallen victim to some terrible deterioration.

The Confederate Air Force had become the most pleasant tonic for Lowen's bitterness. It was a fine fraternity of honorable men, and the paramilitary structure of the CAF was the perfect system of order for a group of men who restored, maintained and flew the fighting planes of the Second World War. There was honor and pride in this order and if there was an element of militarism it was only in the recollection and preservation of a time, of an orderly war in which – then – everything had been clear-cut. Black was called black. White was called white. Good was good. Evil was evil. There had been no question in the minds of those who had fought, never. And no one was evasive about patriotism or duty.

Lowen remembered the war well, though VE Day had come just after his twenty-sixth birthday. The experience of aerial combat was still vivid, surpassed only by the remembrance of the passions of war; the clear fire of conviction that the United States and its Allies were destined by divine right to battle the greatest evil in all history, and the clear strength of justification for using any method to achieve victory and to restore the ravaged human condition in Europe.

How well he remembered being intensely proud of his country, his Stars & Stripes, his uniform, his Air Force, his P-51 Mustang, and his destiny. How well he remembered being willing to give anything, including his life, to be among the avenging angels of death to an enemy that murdered women and children.

He had fought well for twenty-two months and 189 missions and had had the good fortune to be rescued by advancing infantry within hours of crashing near a German airbase. He was decorated, he had recovered from his wounds, and he was returned home, proud and eager for his share of time in the best country of all.

For almost two decades it had been the best, until the day J.F.K. was shot. In Texas yet. Godamighty. It was the first time since the war that he had said aloud: How could this happen? In this time, in his state, in his country?

In time he had fashioned an answer to his question. However abstract, it was none the less an answer. It – anything – could happen. Anything. And this answer, obtuse though it was, was made to serve. Roger Lowen lived with it, knowing nothing better. But it was a poor answer because it disregarded his understanding of what was good and what was evil. He only knew what used to be good and what used to be evil. So he stuck with that.

Lowen was not particularly well educated, and if asked to define paranoia he might have managed, but he knew well enough that the times, more than ever, required him to cover his own ass, and he did this with vigilance. He drew careful lines around the pleasures of his life and guarded them and coveted them and took pride in being skilled at them. There were always intruders and intrusions and he dealt with them directly and forcefully. He knew that there wasn't much of life left, really, and he wanted to keep whole what he had ... and to enjoy everything to the end.

He loved Jean and treasured her, most of all because she too had clear-cut perceptions about being a woman and a wife.

And he loved flying. He loved it because it was an experience that had not changed in thirty years, because it was demanding and unforgiving, beautiful and exhilarating. He was a prudent pilot, a good pilot. He could have flown a lighter, safer and more comfortable aircraft, but the brutish Mustang was his badge of honor; he was, after all, a proud member of that select and slowly shrinking fraternity of Second World War fighter pilots. And though he had never told anyone, the truth was that being a combat pilot had been the most exciting part of his life. The CAF preserved perfectly that pride and time.

On this Friday midnight Roger Lowen was temporarily in

harmony with his world. His woman would come home soon and they would sleep in the comfort of their bond. And over the weekend he would be at Rebel Field with the others, crawling over the Mustangs, preparing them for an airshow the following weekend in California.

The streetlight cast a cool blue band of dim light across the wall of a darkened second-floor apartment bedroom in south Phoenix. The light passed over the bed but did not fall upon the man or the woman who lay side by side. The woman was alternately lifting her legs, exercising. As each leg was raised, straight and tense, toes pointed, it entered the band of light and then was gone.

James Webb watched with contented fascination. They were outstanding legs, with each muscle clearly delineated when flexed. They were very tanned, these legs, and they had quickly caught his eyes when he had seen her at the bar in the Buena Vista. Pamela, her name was Pamela.

She was a splendid score for a Friday night, the first in three weeks, and he felt very lucky.

Webb did not see himself as an especially attractive man. He felt cursed with mediocrity, a man of medium age, medium height, medium looks and medium means. To counter this, he kept trim, stayed tanned, dressed well and hunted tenaciously, doggedly pushing for a score. Most often he landed women of medium looks and medium skills. Not this time, however. Nothing was medium about Pamela. She had just done things to him that few other women had ever done, and done them better. And now she was showing off her splendid legs and counting, in tiny grunts, as each lovely limb scissored up into the light.

'Sixty,' Pamela gasped, dropping one leg rather heavily.

'Sixty each?'

'Sixty each. Twice a day,' she panted. 'Keeps belly flat, legs in shape. My legs are the best part of me.'

'Close.'

'How are you?' she asked, turning to him.

'Fine. And you?'

'Wonderful.' She stretched, hard, with a long breath, then grasped his hand and held it, as if they were good friends. He had forgotten her last name. Two years divorced, Webb had deliberately neglected to cultivate the knack for remembering women's names, either first or last. With one eye peeking over the pillow where his face was half-hidden, he studied the mounds and curves and shadows of her body. Oh man. She seemed, even in the half-light, to radiate invisible extra energy, as if in their lovemaking she had drawn from his, like a transfusion.

'You make love with a certain . . . um . . . intensity,' she said. 'Why is that?'

'I didn't know that I did.'

'What are you intense about?'

'You,' he replied.

'What else?'

'I don't know.'

'Is nothing in your life intense? Is it all perfect?'

'Of course it's not perfect.'

'What is the most intense part of your life?'

Webb decided to be patient. It was possible that she cared a little, so why not do word games? So he thought about his answer for a few moments.

'I guess I am intense about my . . . work, my job.' He had almost said 'career' but it seemed like such a jerky word, like the recruiting posters. There was no gamble in talking about the Air Force since Pamela was not one of the anti-military types.

'Isn't everyone?' She sighed. 'Well, I can see how it would be tense to fly airplanes all day.'

'I don't fly airplanes. I'm not a pilot.' He decided not to add 'because of my eyes', as he often did, at least to men. One did not reveal one's weaknesses so quickly to a new woman. 'Although, I have a civilian license and I fly as a hobby.'

'Oh, I thought you were a jet pilot.'

'No.'

'Then what do you do in the Air Force that makes you intense?'

'Investigative work. It's something like police work. Stolen goods, pilfered cargo, accident investigation, things like that. It's very dull, actually.'

'So you are . . . restless?'

'Williams isn't exactly the sort of duty base for moving up the ladder. I feel like I'm stuck here.'

'Why did you come here, then?'

'You go where they send you. No choice.'

Pamela rolled on her side toward him, her head of tangled dark-curled hair supported by one hand, her elbow jammed into her pillow. 'You like airplanes a lot, huh? All the pictures . . . things in the living room.'

'Yeah, old warplanes. A hobby.'

'Every guy has a hang-up for machines. I used to go with a racing driver from Tucson. I quit seeing him because he was always working nights on his goddamned cars. He always had black goop under his fingernails, but I liked him. He was crazy.'

Webb wondered if racing drivers could race if they wore glasses.

'I like men who go fast,' she said abruptly. 'Airplanes, cars, motorcycles. Do you have an airplane?'

'Too expensive. I'd want one of those Second World War fighters, warbirds.'

'Second World War,' she said, thinking. 'Germany, Japan.'

'Yeah, and British and American.'

'Which do you like best, which airplanes?'

'German, I guess.'

'Why German?'

'I guess because they were unique. Somehow they were more warlike, those planes. The Luftwaffe had a . . . a history. Blue Max, Richthofen, Red Baron, all that.'

'They wore tall black boots.'

'Yeah, and very spiffy uniforms. They had style. They were very professional, very dedicated.'

'But they lost. Why did they lose?'

'Bad decisions. Hitler didn't listen to good advice. When we came into the war we just built more planes, bombed them out.'

'I see,' Pamela said, stirring and rising from the bed. The streetlight caught the upper half of her body from the side, shadowing the soft channel of her spine. 'I have to go to the bathroom. Will you wait for me?'

'I'll wait for you,' he promised, watching her.

When she returned, she paced around the room. So much energy, Webb thought, and half of it belonged to me. He wanted to sleep, but got up and pulled on a pair of white gym shorts. Pamela was wearing his yellow terrycloth robe, the perfect color for her tan.

In the kitchen they made coffee and sliced up cold fruit. With

34

her coffee mug in one hand, Pamela prowled about the living room while Webb sprawled on the couch. It was a comfortably furnished room with many framed prints and pictures arranged with care across the textured white walls. The pictures were of airplanes and there were models of the same airplanes on the desk and on the bookshelves, where there were books on airplanes. She looked at everything, turning on yet another lamp when she couldn't see well enough.

'What are these signatures here?' She had stopped at a framed print. He came up beside her.

'That's a Spitfire and the pilot is a British ace named Tuck. These are Messerschmitt 109s and one of the pilots is a German ace named Galland. That's Galland's actual signature and that's Tuck's actual signature. This other signature is the artist's, Frank Wootton. This number here indicates that this print is the eighty-fifth of the series.'

'These are really their signatures?'

'For real. I sent away for this print. A hundred and fifty bucks.'

'That's a pretty plane – the Spitfire?'

'Yes.'

'And those are ugly planes, the German ones. What are they again?'

'Messerschmitt 109. That's my favorite plane.'

'And this?' She pointed to a model on the bookshelf below.

'Mustang P-51. It's my favorite plane, too. They are still flying, these planes. All over. I'm going to fly in one.'

'You're going to fly it?'

'No, ride in it. There's an airfield over in California where they give you a ride in a P-51. Would you like to go with me?'

'No way I'm getting into anything like that.'

'You don't have to ride; just come along and watch. They're having an airshow up there next weekend. All the airplane freaks who own these fighters come to this show and fly around, shooting blanks and having mock dogfights. Let's go, make a weekend of it.'

'A weekend? What do we do for a whole weekend?'

'Look at the planes, watch the show, take photographs.'

'For two days?'

'Sure. We'll get a motel, have a good time. You'll love it.'

Pamela reached up and pulled his face down to hers and kissed him lightly. It seemed to Webb the kiss was more maternal than passionate.

'Thank you for asking,' she said softly. 'You won't be offended if I don't go, will you? I'm just not into old airplanes, not for a whole weekend, you know? Another place, another weekend, OK?'

'Yeah ... well.' He watched her, puzzled. Without her make-up she looked a little tired, and her eyes seemed ... distant, as if she was really somewhere else. He had noticed this before, when they were drinking. Sometimes she was there, sometimes she was not.

'I'm sorry,' she said without sounding sorry, wrapping the robe more closely around her neck as if she were cold.

'I thought you liked airplanes.'

'I didn't say I liked airplanes. I said I liked pilots.' Her voice now seemed as remote as her eyes.

'Somehow that doesn't seem to make a lot of sense.'

'Who says anything has to make sense?'

'Hey, easy ... I just thought you'd like to go.'

'No.' She looked around nervously. 'Do you have a cigarette?'

'There, on the table.'

She snatched up the pack, picked one out. 'I was married to a pilot, at Luke.' She paused to light the cigarette. 'He was on a training flight and they went down over in California, in the desert.'

'I'm really sorry,' Webb said after a moment.

'It was a long time ago. Two years now.' She looked at the cigarette in her hand. 'I just haven't gotten around to leaving yet. Isn't that strange?'

'I don't know ... but I don't think so. I think we do pretty much what we want to do.'

CHAPTER THREE

Rudi was early for Theo's flight. He checked the video screen for the gate number, then went to the lounge area and found a solitary seat next to the huge glass windows where he lit up his pipe and looked out over the acres of airport concrete. Saturday was a busy day. Within his view six of the great passenger jets moved back and forth, deceivingly massive and slow as they lumbered into or away from their berths. Ground support vehicles scurried under the shadows of giant wings.

In recent months Rudi had found himself dwelling upon Theo's — what was the term, status? position? station? Yes, 'station in life' was the phrase. Theo's station was very different. Theo had power, lots of power, not only in the corporate world of West Germany but in the whole of Europe. One did not reach the top without certain singular characteristics. One had them or one didn't. He himself didn't, Peter Schilling didn't, and it was unlikely that the five German pilots would either, since Theo would surely pick men who would not be difficult to lead.

Most certainly, a captain of industry achieved command in the corporate battlefield through essentially the same set of instincts as any captain of war. It would all fit. And, he reasoned, it would support Theo's ability — and his right — to command, aside from his backing of the Staffel. Yes, he would be comfortable serving under Theo in a military structure. Yes, it was just the right arrangement. They would be a good team.

Theo was easy to spot when he appeared in the crowd of arriving passengers flowing through the doorway. He was tall and distinctive — the distinction, Rudi noted, of power and wealth: his tanned straight-nosed face, thin silver hair, his tailored clothing. Even the way he moved, boldly and subtly aloof, set Theo apart. And when his eyes found Rudi, over the heads of the crowd, his smile revealed wealthy white teeth as well.

'Ah, Rudi!' Theo raised his hand as if in benediction. 'It is so good to see you at last! You look well, so healthy!' They grasped each other at upper arms.

'And you, my friend. Welcome, welcome!'

'Four years, yes?' Theo grinned.

'Yes. And a little more.'

'You look four years younger.'

'Thank you. I hope you are right. Did you enjoy the flight?'

'Marvelous! I have never seen this part of the world. Marvelous! Endless mountains and desert, *endless*! And the air, absolutely crystal clear. From twenty-six thousand feet I could see pebbles!'

'I am glad you are here, finally,' Rudi said, guiding Theo through the crowd. 'Marta is waiting outside. You must be prepared for the heat.'

'Ah, my friend, I am prepared for anything. And how is your lovely sister? And her husband – I have forgotten, I am sorry, his name?'

'Eric, Eric Malzahn. They are looking forward to everything.'

'It is most generous of them to have us, most generous. And are you looking forward to all of this as well?'

Theo turned and reached up to grip Rudi's shoulder, as if he expected a most crucial reply.

'Yes. For a long time. And you?'

'Of course, of course. I cannot wait to see the planes.'

'So I thought. Well, it will not be long.'

'Ha,' Theo laughed. 'Since I have waited six years to see what you have done with all the junk I have sent you, I believe I can wait a few hours more.'

Down the escalator and along to Baggage Claim they talked of Germany, of international economy, and of the electronics industry – all in brief scraps. Rudi listened closely, genuinely interested in understanding more of Theo than ever before. It seemed necessary now.

'Your room, Theo. I hope you find it comfortable.' Marta led Theo into the small bedroom with yellow walls and white curtains. There was a bureau and a small desk with a lamp and chair. Rudi followed them and placed Theo's bag on the bed.

'Thank you. It is fine, fine. Am I alone?'

'Rudi felt that the Commanding Officer is entitled to be alone,' she replied. 'Now, if you will excuse me.'

Theo turned to Rudi as Marta left the room. 'The others?'

'There are two bedrooms, with three beds each. And I do very well on a fold-out couch in the den. Here.' Rudi reached into the closet. 'Your uniforms: two dress, two flying suits.'

'Ah.' Theo walked over and reached for the gray uniform jacket. 'I would like to try them on now.'

'Perhaps when we return from the airfield, Theo. It will be dark in three hours.'

'Very nicely done.' Theo was examining the soft gray fabric. 'Where did you have them made?'

'In Hollywood, of course.' Rudi grinned. 'They are accustomed to making up orders of authentic German uniforms. Each button is correct, as you will see. And the boots are there, in that box.'

Theo was proceeding to change; first the gray breeches and then a long-sleeved white cotton dress shirt. 'How much daylight did you say we have?' He buttoned the shirt without looking down. 'Three hours?'

'At best.'

'And the travel time to the field?'

'Forty minutes or so.'

'Your uniform?' Theo sat down on the bed and took one boot from the box, turning it over in his hands. 'Ah, these are very fine. Well done.' He tugged on the boot, looked up. 'Your uniform?' he said again.

Rudi was confused. 'Yes, I have it.'

'Perhaps you would be good enough to put it on?' Theo grunted as he pulled on the second boot. 'We should always be in uniform when we are at the field, either dress uniform or flying suits. Don't you agree?'

For a moment Rudi weighed the question. Theo was wasting no time. 'Yes,' he said finally, feeling as if he had somehow made a tiny error. 'I'll change.'

'The other two pilots; what time do they arrive?'

'Schilling at eight-thirty. Osterhoudt at nine forty-five. Marta will pick them up.'

'Excellent.' Theo stood, tucking in the white cotton shirt.

'Perhaps you would see that they change into uniform and are then brought directly to the field as promptly as possible?'

'Yes, of course.' Rudi stood at the door, watching Theo slip on his jacket. The fit was very good and the boots were very shiny.

Theo looked up. 'Is there something else?'

'Theo?'

'Yes?'

'The clock is ticking now, isn't it?'

'Yes, Oberstleutnant,' came the reply, with a quick smile.

'Tell me about the field.' Theo buckled on his seat belt as Rudi shifted the Jeep into second gear out of the driveway. 'How far did you say?'

'About thirty-five miles on a good road. Six miles on no road. I have a ten-year lease under an assumed name. It was long abandoned, in poor shape.'

'Is it marked on flying maps?'

'Until two years ago. Now the maps don't show it.'

Theo had to talk loudly over the noise of the engine and the rushing wind. 'And what are the facilities? Water? Power?'

'There is power from our own generator. We have storage tanks for both water and fuel, and trailers to refill them.'

Rudi began to sweat simply from the effort of conversation. The goddamned uniform. Theo's was still buttoned tight, he noticed.

'The runway; how long, how wide?'

'More than sufficient. It's adobe, hard clay. Even if we run off the edge, the sand is firm enough.'

'Can you not see the runway from the air?'

'Nearly impossible. Sand on the surface, everything the same color. We have constructed camouflage, you would call them movable bushes. We place them on the runway when we are not flying.'

'Security?'

'Wire fence with electronic alarm system, surrounds the entire property. Just a few wires; it keeps nothing out, but the alarm sounds if anything disturbs it.'

'If they were looking for this field, how easily could they find it?'

'It would be very difficult from the air, as you will see. Eric

40

and I have flown over it many times, looking for ways to improve the camouflage.'

'And from the ground?'

'You will see very soon. Six miles of sand trail that will rearrange your kidneys.'

Theo was quiet for a while. Before them the empty blacktop road stretched like an arrow into the bleak desert. Dusk was coming sooner than Rudi had guessed. He glanced at Theo, who seemed to be enjoying the stark scenery. Distant ridges were turning rich purple under the vast yellowing sky, but the heat was still intense. By now Theo would be regretting his idea of wearing the uniform.

When they came to the turn-off there seemed to be no road at all. Rudi changed down. The Jeep nosed off the highway and ground forward in low gear.

'Hang on tight,' he warned. 'It's a rough ride from here on.'

After miles of tedious jolting, Rudi stopped suddenly. White dust swirled around the vehicle. 'There.' He pointed ahead. 'See that drop-off in the wash? A trap. Instead of going on, we turn like this.' He cranked the wheel over and drove along the wash for twenty yards before easing down into the pebble-strewn stream bed and crossing over.

'Yes.' Theo was holding onto the dash. 'Well done.'

Several miles later the desert floor began to incline upward. Rudi stopped at a flimsy wire gate between two metal stakes and got out to release the lock and alarm. They pulled through, and he got out again to close the gate and reset the alarm.

They drove up the incline for a quarter of a mile along a barren brown-rock ridge, then crested the top and rolled steeply downward in second gear. A great expanse of desert spread before them, the sand turning pale pink-gray in the dusk. At the bottom of the road ahead were two wooden hangars very close together. Even so close, they blended artfully, except for their shadows. Camouflage netting covered parts of the buildings, blurring their shape. No runway was apparent.

'Remarkable!' Theo exclaimed, peering forward.

Rudi parked against one hangar, under the net cover, and they stepped out. The desert's silence rose up and covered them like a veil.

With Theo following, Rudi went to a small door at the side of the hangar and unlocked it. They stepped inside. Rudi flicked a light switch. They stood in a small low-ceilinged room, about twenty by twenty, with bare white beaverboard walls. So intense was the contained heat of the room that it seemed as if they were immersed in hot water. A small window, covered with translucent plastic, held an air-conditioning unit. Rudi threw another wall switch and the air-conditioner came to life with a rattle. There were a dozen folding chairs arranged in three loose rows and a battered desk in front, much like a classroom. The wall behind the desk held a large blackboard with what appeared to be map rolls mounted above it.

'Briefing room,' Rudi said.

'Ah yes.' Theo nodded, tugging at the top buttons of his jacket. 'Is there water?'

'In the hangar. We even have a small refrigerator. Perhaps you would care for a cold beer, Oberst?'

'A beer? Yes.' Theo looked around, plainly pleased.

Rudi opened a second door, into near darkness, and Theo followed. Rudi threw another switch and the interior of the hangar lit up before them. Two light blue 109s disguised with bolt-on wheel fairings, phony nose cones and rounded rudders were parked wingtip to wingtip. Rudi brought over two bottles of beer, handing one to Theo.

Theo downed half the bottle in quick gulps, his eyes sweeping the dim interior of the old hangar, the barren walls patched with plywood, the workbenches, drums of oil, crates covered with plastic sheeting.

'– In this blue paint,' Rudi said, 'our practice flights will not attract attention. There are two more down at the airport hangar.'

'The other four?'

'In the other hangar. All the ammunition is there, too. This hangar is for maintenance. We have extra lighting, fans, workbenches, storage, parts.'

'I see. Remarkable.' Theo drained his beer.

'Another?' Rudi smiled. 'We have plenty.'

'Please.' Theo wiped his mouth with a handkerchief.

'Then we will see the other Gustavs.'

Rudi brought out two more bottles, snapped them both open and handed one to Theo. 'This way. Outside again.' They re-entered the briefing room and stepped outside.

'Truly formidable heat,' said Theo. 'How can you work there?'

'All the assembly and engine work was done in the airport hangar where we had more equipment; a hoist, engine stands, electricity. And good ventilation and fans. Then each plane was flown out here. The heat is not so bad after a while; you become accustomed to it.'

They walked along the wall of the closed hangar doors to the next hangar. Of similar size and design, it seemed older and even more sun-bleached and weather-beaten. Scales of what appeared to have been white paint covered much of the building and small hills of drifted sand lay against the sides.

Rudi unlocked the two sliding doors and pushed one wide enough for them to gain entrance. It was nearly dark inside and a wave of heat rolled out, bringing familiar scents of oil and fuel. Rudi paused, then resumed pushing the door wider and wider. Evening light flooded in and revealed four Messerschmitts. They were not at all like the others. Theo stared for a few seconds.

'So,' he said quietly. 'So.'

All four 109s were painted with full battle markings: flat sky-blue on the undersurfaces of the wings and halfway up the fuselage, while the top wing surfaces, top half of the fuselages and tail sections were covered in flat mottled brown and tan. The blunt noses pointed upward like great metal sharks, the air scoops underneath like half-opened mouths; yellow spinners tapered to black cannon ports. Triple black prop blades, tipped in the same bright yellow, grew like great sword blades from the spinners. Bold black-and-white crosses stood out starkly on the flanks and wings. Each cockpit was covered by a plastic sheet.

'So,' Theo whispered, shaking his head. 'So.'

Even to Rudi these four planes were disturbingly different from the other four. Not waxed, the colors were dull and flat textured. They were brutal-looking, not so much carefully constructed machines as inanimate creatures, like dragons born of the very desert wastes that surrounded them, their colors the blue of the sky and the tan and russet of sand and rock. Curious, Rudi thought, how malevolent they looked now, how different.

Theo moved finally, still staring at the planes, and stepped forward, as if he were hypnotized. The slick soles of his new boots scraped on the gritty floor. He went to the closest aircraft and reached up to touch the port exhaust and the large rectangular scoop above it.

'Tropical air filter,' he said, nodding in recognition.

Theo then placed his hand on the leading edge of the starboard wing and walked the length of it, fingers trailing, until he had gone completely around the wing to the fuselage. He stopped, then moved along the fuselage, his fingertips skimming the long flat flank, across the insignia, up the spine and all the way back to the tail fin. He stared fixedly at the black swastika on the fin, then traced one finger up the trailing edge of the rudder and pushed it gently.

'So.' Theo spoke, more to himself than to Rudi.

After a few moments he walked around the tail and back down the other side of the plane, out of Rudi's sight. Rudi stepped under the nose in time to see Theo climb – rather nimbly, he thought – up on the wing root to stand by the cockpit. Folding back the plastic sheet covering the open cockpit, Theo appeared to study the interior. For a moment, Rudi experienced a curious flashback, seeing Theo by the cockpit as if he were about to leap in and roar away to do battle. Outside, Rudi heard the faint scratching roar of a jet climbing over the desert.

Theo stepped down gingerly. Rudi watched his face as he came around the wing and stopped, his eyes still fixed on the plane. He reached up, startling Rudi, grasping him by both shoulders.

'Rudi,' he whispered, 'they are marvelous, do you hear? They are marvelous! I cannot believe my eyes!'

Theo snapped his arms back and pivoted where he stood, facing the planes. 'Now tell me about them. All of it. Again!'

He paced about back and forth along the wing as Rudi recited the list. Impatiently, Theo punctuated each item with '*Yes!*' His hand darted out to each part of the craft as Rudi's list went on. '*Yes! Yes!*' And again he climbed with surprising agility up to the cockpit, lowering himself in.

Rudi climbed up after him, pointing out each detail, Theo touching each of the instruments as Rudi ticked them off. New ventilation here. *Yes!* New VFR radio. *Yes!* New altimeter. *Yes!* New pressure gauges. *Yes!* New seat. *Yes!* And on to the end.

'Now,' Theo said again, pulling himself up and out, then stepping down, nearly leaping from the wing. 'They are ready to fly?'

'They are all ready to fly. At this moment.'

'You are to be highly commended,' Theo whispered, looking

around at all four aircraft. 'Highly commended indeed.'

They turned out the light and closed the hangar doors. It was deep dusk now; a violet haze lay on the horizon, and the far mesas seemed to float like ghost ships in a sea of low fog. The silence had become a presence. Theo stopped, looking away, then back at the hangar, then at Rudi.

'I have never seen such a . . . such an incredibly desolate place. It is perfect. Perfect.'

They returned to the briefing room and opened two more bottles of beer. Theo pulled a folding chair to the desk and sat down, motioning for Rudi to take a chair in the front row. They sat for a moment facing each other, Theo with hands folded, Rudi with his beer in one hand, unlit pipe in the other. For a moment Rudi felt as if he were in school, as if he should sit straight, shoulders back.

'Now, Oberstleutnant,' Theo said quietly. 'The time?'

Rudi looked at his watch. 'Eight-twenty.'

'When do the pilots arrive?'

'Schilling should be on the ground about now. Osterhoudt at nine forty-five. Tomorrow in the afternoon, Beissemann and Kesler; early evening, Weinert and Rendel. They are each flying different airlines, all from different points. Marta will meet each of them.'

'This Schilling, a good man?'

'Yes, I believe so. He's a racing driver on the weekends he isn't flying.'

'What is his profession?'

'Selling cars. Age fifty-one, and I believe he has a birthday next week. He has been flying for a long time, except for two years after a divorce. He has time on twin-engined craft and is part owner of a Cessna Cardinal. He's in fine physical condition.'

'You talked to him about the war?'

'Yes. As you suggested.'

'His feelings?'

'Like you and me, he does not think of it, not often, he says.' Rudi thought a moment. 'I was struck by his . . . his sense of the immediate, as if what happened yesterday, or ten or thirty years ago, meant nothing. Day to day, that sort of attitude. It took him very little time to agree to come.'

'Will he shoot?'

45

'Yes, he will shoot.'

Theo thought this over, for a minute or so, reaching up once to scratch at his ear. It was getting dark now and Rudi was painfully hungry. He pulled out his pipe and pouch and began to stuff tobacco into the bowl.

'Security.' Theo spoke suddenly. 'All the pilots returned their letters promptly?'

'Yes, every one.'

'Our vehicles; what are they?'

'The van, the Jeep, a beater truck—'

'Beater?'

'Beat-up. Old. Dirty,' Rudi explained. 'But it runs perfectly. And there is Marta's sedan if we should need it, and my car. The van will hold us all for travel back and forth.'

'And supplies?'

'Plenty of oil. Plenty of fuel. Sufficient spare parts, barring any unexpected events.'

'Duty roster?'

'All worked out for the first week. We rotate everyone on maintenance with Eric and me. And rotate on kitchen help; Marta cannot do it all alone.'

'Yes, of course,' Theo smiled. 'Always the KP! Did you rotate me as well, Oberstleutnant?'

'Not yet. However—'

'I will volunteer. And on maintenance as well.'

Theo stood up, smoothed his already smooth silver hair, then tugged at his jacket collar. Rudi studied his every move, trying to forget his hunger by puffing slowly on the pipe. His own collar was uncomfortable but it didn't seem to matter. In fact, he felt more in control and even more prepared in the uniform.

'Ah yes.' Theo turned. 'I nearly forgot. Ammunition.'

'Eighteen hundred rounds cannon remain from testing and sighting-in. About eighty thousand rounds machine gun. Eric and I used only what was necessary. There's a fairly high rate of dead rounds and there is a lot of tracer.'

Theo came back to the table and sat down and folded his hands again. His gray eyes pierced Rudi's pipe smoke.

'And finally,' said Theo almost jovially, his eyes squinting, 'we come to the last detail, yes?'

'The mission plans, all three, are complete, Oberst,' Rudi said quickly, taking a tiny delight in snatching a little drama away

46

from a man who was, he felt sure, going to bring more than a little drama to all concerned.

'I have no doubts that they are as meticulously prepared as each of those marvelous Gustavs.' Theo waved his hand to acknowledge the airplanes waiting on the other side of the door.

CHAPTER FOUR

In a comfortable aisle seat on a Continental 747 bound for Phoenix, Peter Schilling reflected that this 'flying vacation', as Rudi Felbeck had presented it, was such a crazy caper that the two thousand dollar price tag seemed suspiciously modest. Felbeck could have hit him up for five grand and somehow he would have scraped it together. So here he was, cruising at twenty-eight thousand and getting wrecked on Finnish vodka, and it still seemed right. Even the stewardess, a tanned slender woman with lovely ankles, was as good an omen as he needed. She smiled a great deal and kept the little clear bottles coming. Vacation.

He recalled being initially intimidated by Rudi's buttoned-down intensity, those blue eyes behind tinted California eyeglasses. But he was sincere, and so – what? religious, yes – about the Staffel. Rudi had given such a splendidly dramatic presentation, following a letter and two phone calls, when he came to Milwaukee to meet with Schilling.

They dined at Milwaukee's best German restaurant. Schilling found it amusingly melodramatic, like a spy movie, that two ex-Luftwaffe pilots should meet in this clinking bustling temple to their former culture. Unlike Rudi, Schilling's tastes had long ago fastened on American food, yet the tart wines and platters of steaming cabbage, even the blond-braided waitresses with mounded chests and Teutonic calves, quickly became comfortably appropriate. For a moment he was sad for Germany, for what his country had once meant to him so long ago. The history, the music, the little towns, the forests. Then the nightmare of the war and then the Russians and then the ship and then New York and then Milwaukee. All was past and lost. There was only now. And he was glad that this stranger Rudi, another survivor from the fractured past, another countryman, had appeared, for whatever reason. Schilling was not accustomed to being tracked down and sought out for any special expertise. He was flattered and he clearly felt a fateful and genuine aura about this dinner meeting.

'You understand,' Rudi was saying, 'that I have a proposal. You may find it somewhat . . . unusual.'

Schilling continued spreading a slice of black bread with a wedge of iced sweet butter.

'To begin with, you are one of the few men who could meet our requirements. There are qualifications, necessary qualifications, and you have them.'

'I've passed the semi-finals and these are the finals.'

'Exactly.' Rudi looked at him closely. 'Did you enjoy the Luftwaffe, the flying?'

'Enjoy?' Schilling looked off thirty years away. 'Yes. Yes, parts of it. Not when somebody was trying to kill me. Not the ending of it. Not defeat. There were times . . . moments.'

Schilling hesitated, looked up as if something enlightening might have been found on the ceiling, then cleared his throat. 'You must understand. I'm not used to being asked about my experience in the war. I would like to know what it is you want me to do, or buy, or whatever.'

'Fair enough.' Rudi spread the napkin on his lap and took knife and fork to the veal dish being placed before him. Schilling waited, watching Rudi saw into the meat.

'We are putting together a special group of 109 pilots,' Rudi said finally, without looking up from his plate. 'You are invited to join this special reunion, for a two-week flying vacation.'

Schilling unfolded his own napkin, placing it on his lap, then reached up and scratched lightly under his chin: it was a habit that he fell into when confronted with a situation that required more comprehension than was ordinarily within his reach. 'A reunion,' he echoed, looking up once again at the ceiling of dark wood beams where smoke formed in a white haze. Downstairs in the main dining room he heard the fragile metal music of a zither.

'Yes,' Rudi replied. 'Like I said, a rather unique group. Actually, only the Commanding Officer and I know each other, but we all flew 109s. It is a small group. We can only invite six, for a total of eight. No more.'

'Why only eight?'

'Because we have only eight Gustavs.'

'You have eight Gustavs?' Somehow Schilling immediately believed this.

'Eight. Yes.' Rudi scooped up a forkful of red cabbage. 'Perfectly restored. They are quite sound. Like brand new. Better, in fact. To continue, our thinking was to organize as a Staffel. Everything is to be exactly as it was in the war. Or nearly everything.' He smiled. 'Perfectly restored aircraft. Proper uniforms. Military. And lots of flying.' Rudi drained his wine glass and held it out for more as Schilling poured. 'Of course, when we are off-duty we will enjoy ourselves. Everything is provided. Good food, good wine, all comforts. Our quarters will be in a private home, with a pool. Two weeks.'

'Why the military—' Schilling searched for the word, waving his hand in a small circle as if he might pull the right term from the air.

'Organization? Discipline?'

'Yes.'

'First, because it is more authentic. Everything is to be correct, an experiment in reviving the esprit, the essence of our experience as fighter pilots. Without the war, of course.

'And second, because the order and discipline of a military structure will provide the best system of maintenance and safety. Without a system, without order, can you imagine how difficult it would be to organize a schedule, maintain the aircraft?'

Schilling again scratched at his chin.

'Well, what do you think?'

'It appeals to me.'

'How much does it appeal to you, Mr Schilling?'

'Very much.'

'The price is two thousand dollars, plus air fare. Does it still appeal to you?'

'Yes.'

'Actually, it is a very small amount. It will be used for our pleasure; food, wine, tailored uniforms, other expenses.'

'I understand,' Schilling said.

Rudi sat back as the waitress cleared the table and brought coffee. Schilling toyed with his cigarette.

'Intriguing,' he said finally, looking up. 'Who commands?'

'My friend Theo Heinrich, who is financing the operation. I will serve as Executive Officer.' Rudi brought out his pipe and pouch. 'You see, it was Theo's idea, this Staffel, to build the planes, do everything in perfect detail, to duplicate our experience. Every element possible except the bad weather, the flak . . .' Rudi trailed off, glanced up at Schilling.

Schilling was studying the amber wine as he swirled it slowly around in the glass. He had gone back in time, recalling terrible frigid mornings in Hungary, Romania, Russia . . . Mud frozen rock-hard . . . The wretchedly balky engines . . . Scrambling into the tiny dark cockpit . . . The bitter defense over the homeland . . . Bombers endlessly filling the sky, blowing apart, sliding over and down . . . The smells of engines and burned metal and flak . . . The boredom and the horror, the fear and the relief, the dry weight of tension lying above the stomach. What fool would want to relive any of that? He looked up at Rudi.

'It would be . . . curious to do it again,' he said finally. 'Without the war. Without the fear.'

'Yes,' Rudi agreed. 'It is an interesting experiment. Not quite as exciting, though, without the risk . . . the test of combat.' Rudi held a match to the bowl of his pipe, puffing it slowly. 'Risk does make it a special experience. You drive racing cars, don't you? So you know about that.'

'It is too bad there can't be some of that risk again. It would be more . . .'

'Authentic.'

'Yes.'

'Well,' said Rudi casually, 'we have given that some thought, as a matter of fact. Some sort of simulated combat . . . You see, the guns are restored as well. To be completely authentic, we thought that we should include gunnery exercises.'

'Live ammunition?'

'Yes, as I said; authentic.'

Schilling thought this over for a moment. 'Good.'

'But, you see, there is a problem; flying armed aircraft is illegal. There really is no way around that. A real problem.'

'A problem,' Schilling repeated. 'The problem, if I understand it, is that you want to find enough pilots who are crazy enough to fly armed 109s, so what you want to know is whether I'm crazy enough. Is that close?'

'Exactly.'

'Well, I'm crazy enough.' Schilling smiled to himself, at his own words.

'Odd, yes,' Schilling replied. Indeed, he thought.

Now he leaned back in the plush cushioned seat and gazed out over a cotton plain of clouds. They would be close to Arizona. He reached into his jacket pocket and unfolded a sheet of paper. He would read it one more time.

3 March 1976

To: Schilling, Peter M.
From: Executive Officer 76 Staffel
Subject: Travel Orders

1. You have been accepted as an officer of 76 Staffel with the appointed rank of Major effective for the duration of operations commencing 24 April through 6 May 1976 in Phoenix, Arizona. The following constitutes orders for travel and for security relating to this operation.

2. As agreed, all aspects of this operation are to be kept in absolute secrecy and all directives concerning security are to be followed to the letter.

3. You will immediately make one-way flight reservations to arrive Phoenix Skyharbor International airport on the afternoon or evening of 22 April. Reservations will be made under fictitious name and paid for by cash only. No telephone number or address to be given to reservation clerk. Upon securing this reservation, write in your flight number, airline and arrival time in the space provided at the end of this letter and return promptly by mail.

4. One piece of checked luggage of any size, plus carry-on luggage, is permitted. Since airline regulations require identification of checked luggage use the same fictitious name as reservation. Be careful to avoid any items in luggage that carry your name or initials. Check carefully for tags, monograms, papers, books, etc. No weapons of any kind are to be carried.

5. Upon arrival collect luggage and go to taxi zone where you will be met by a tan-coloured Dodge van license 466-ZTF. Allow 30 minutes waiting time.

52

6. The telephone number (602) 628-5549 is for use only in the event of unforeseen delay in arrival of van. Commit number to memory and do not write it down. If it is necessary to call, use only pay telephone.

7. As you are aware, there is always risk involved in any flying operation. Carry any medical insurance cards on your person for presentation upon arrival. It would be advisable to arrange your personal affairs to accommodate the remote possibility of sickness or injury during this operation.

8. The return address on this letter is for any correspondence; commit it to memory. It is not to be written down or given to anyone. There will be no way for anyone to contact you in Phoenix but you will have the opportunity to telephone if the need arises.

9. Quarters for the duration of this operation will be in a private home with all amenities: food, liquor, flying suits, dress uniforms and boots. Limit personal items to essentials; remember that temperatures are extremely high. Attached find a suggested list. Please fill in spaces provided for measurements from your tailor so that we may fit uniforms properly. You may wish to bring your service decorations.

10. The schedule for the operation will consist primarily of flight time five days a week. There will be sufficient recreation time allotted. Dress uniform will be the order for all dinners. Military courtesy and discipline will be the order except when off-duty.

11. As agreed, you will contribute the balance of $1500 US currency toward expenses. This amount in cash will be paid upon reporting to the Commanding Officer immediately upon arrival. Additional cash should also be carried for return flight ticket.

12. It is emphasized that these instructions are designed for the security of all officers of 76 Staffel. Any cause whatsoever for discipline during this operation will be considered grave and will merit punitive measures as determined by the Commanding Officer. Your signature on this document indicates that you, as an officer of 76 Staffel, understand and accept all orders and regulations accordingly.

Rudi Felbeck
Oberstleutnant 76 Staffel

Schilling had made a copy of the letter before signing it and mailing it back as instructed. He had read the copy dozens of times, always smiling at the mention of 'his tailor'. None the less, he had gone to a tailor to get the required measurements.

Closing his eyes, he silently recited the telephone number once more, then he got up and went to the tiny lavatory in the back of the plane and tore up the letter, flushing the pieces down the toilet. He returned to his seat, ordered another double vodka, and then set the hands of his watch to Mountain Standard time.

He got off the plane drunk. It was very pleasant being drunk and having the cheerful freedom of vacation. Seeing other travelers carrying brightly colored shoulder bags reminded him that vacations were purely for fun. Fun was lots of sun, lots to drink, and women. And, with luck, fast machines of some sort. Well, he thought, this time everything but the women. For a moment he had the giddy recognition that this vacation was unique, an exclusive adult experience, like the movie he had seen where the Old West was authentically recreated in every detail, including astonishingly lifelike robots, robot gunslingers who could shoot (and be shot) and robot saloon girls who could screw (and be screwed). He wondered if Rudi had made some provision – under the heading of 'all amenities' – for women.

At Baggage Claim Schilling found no baggage to claim. Carefully he inspected every piece of luggage that slid down the metal chute, but his was not among them. His watch told him that the flight had been late and that the thirty minutes was going quickly. Worse yet, he was too loaded to remember the phone number. Finally his bag came tumbling down, and he snatched it up and headed for the exit doors. As he stepped through he was shocked at the heat – it was, as he had heard, exactly like stepping into a sauna.

The van was waiting. When he opened the passenger door, Schilling saw that the driver was – very unexpectedly – a tanned handsome woman, wearing wide round sunglasses.

'Hello,' he managed without slurring, staring at her for a moment longer than he intended.

'You are Peter Schilling?' She smiled as she extended her hand. 'Major Peter Schilling?'

'Yes.' He took her hand briefly as he climbed in, shoving his bag between the seats into the back and shucking off his shoulder bag. The effort made him dizzy.

'I'm Marta, Rudi's sister.'

'A pleasure. Rudi told me about you.'

He slammed the door and removed his nylon jacket, stealing a glance at her squarish face and wide smile and blond-brown mane of strawlike hair. Another glance for her lean body and brown legs. She wore a sleeveless white blouse and knee-length khaki shorts and worn running shoes with blue-and-white stripes. Looking at her made his throat dry.

'Welcome to Phoenix,' Marta said. 'Did you have a good flight?'

'Yes, thank you. Is it always this warm here? Christ.'

'You'll get used to it. Here, I'll turn the air-con up a bit.'

She reached for the dash switch, looking over her passenger directly and boldly. He was a very different-looking man, younger than she expected, with careless thick gray-white hair and a hawklike face. His expression seemed somewhere between amused and arrogant.

'Thank you,' Schilling acknowledged, 'but don't turn it up higher than . . . usual. I've never been here. Arizona.'

'Well, I'm sure you will find it quite different.'

I think, Schilling thought, that I will find nearly everything quite different. Starting with you.

'You are from Munich, is it?' Marta pulled into traffic.

'Milwaukee.'

'Of course. You have no accent. It's the other pilot, Osterhoudt, who is from Munich.'

'How many of the others have arrived?'

'Rudi came Friday, then yesterday Theo. And one yet this evening, Osterhoudt, in about an hour or so.'

Schilling found his cigarettes and took one out and stuck it between his lips. Now the goddamned lighter. Too much vodka. He started through his pockets once again, beginning to feel clumsy.

'Would you mind not smoking, please? I really can't stand it, closed up in here,' Marta said, looking straight ahead. 'It's already eight-thirty. You were late.'

'The plane was late . . . Mrs—? I don't recall your last name.' Schilling put the cigarettes in his shirt pocket.

'Malzahn. Marta Felbeck-Malzahn.' She smiled again. 'But

please call me Marta. I don't like *Missus*. Now . . .' she paused to concentrate on her driving, glancing at her thin gold wristwatch. 'Eight-thirty. It's later than I expected. I think we will wait instead.'

'Wait?'

'For Osterhoudt. It doesn't make sense to drive you out to the house and then come back for him. Would you like to have a drink while we wait?'

'Coffee. No drink.'

'Very well,' she said, turning off into the airport parking lot.

They locked the van and began walking across the pavement. Reeling from both the vodka and the heat, Schilling inhaled deeply. The terminal seemed a mile away. The sky had turned an incredible orange-yellow. He glanced at Marta striding purposefully just a step ahead of him. He didn't like being led and he caught up, just a little bit . . . agitated, yes. This goddamned smart-ass woman. She wasn't glamorous, not exactly sexy, in beat-up running shoes and those ludicrous socks with the little blue puff-balls above the heels. Not exactly sexy with no make-up, either, though the tan was nice. And her legs weren't even quite long enough and her chest – he glanced over – wasn't anything special. No big goddamned deal. She wasn't very tall either, scuffing along with loose hair tangling in the blast-furnace breeze. Screw her, she doesn't like smoking.

He glanced at her again. Christ, but she was queerly magnetic. Ridiculous that she should have that particular combination of whatever it took to set him off. He remembered that love was always a fucking ambush; quiet one moment and there they were the next. When you sober up a little, he thought, you'll cut out this crap. And by then she would do or say something unacceptably stupid. Sooner or later they always did. From the corner of his eye he saw her looking up at him.

'How are you making it? Standing the heat?' As if she expected him to fall down at any moment.

'It's all right. I was in the Foreign Legion. This is nothing.'

She laughed, to his delight, and stuffed both hands in the pockets of her khaki shorts. 'You may smoke now. I just don't like it in the car, all closed up.'

In the blessed coolness of the terminal coffee shop they went through a cafeteria line and found a table. Schilling had orange juice and coffee, Marta selected tea and yogurt. She pulled off her sunglasses, put them in her purse. 'We have just under an hour,' she said, pouring the hot water from a little stainless steel pot. 'Do you know Osterhoudt?'

'I don't know anyone except your brother.'

'Rudi asked me not to talk about the Staffel, so I won't. I'm supposed to take you and Herr Osterhoudt back to the house, where you are to change into uniform. Then Eric is to take you directly to the field.'

'Eric?'

'My husband.'

'Is he a pilot?'

'He helped Rudi build the planes and he flies them very well, but he isn't a Staffel pilot. He's a good mechanic. He volunteered to help, with "maintenance" Rudi calls it.'

'I see.'

'He was in Vietnam, in helicopters.'

'What does he do for a living?'

'Service manager for BMW.'

'Good cars. Very quick.'

He sat cautiously in the contoured plastic chair, bracing both elbows on the table. His head was swimming. He studied Marta's face. It was not a model's face and it was, thankfully, not a young and pampered face. There were tiny lines at each eye and delicate smile lines from the side of each nostril to the edge of the wide Scandinavian mouth. The nose, thin and abrupt, was slightly crooked. All the parts were there, the large gray-green eyes and generous alabaster teeth, the wide angular jawline. Yet they were not precisely arranged, something subtle was slightly off, perhaps the distance between the eyes, perhaps the minutely off-center nose, so that the composite of her face was not completely beautiful. To Schilling, however, she was stunning.

'I've lost my goddamned sunglasses,' she said suddenly.

'In you bag,' he said, blowing the *r*.

'Ah yes. In me bag.' She grinned. 'Are you married, Major?'

'Not any more.'

'Children?'

'No.' He could not keep from staring at her. 'You?'

'No.'

Schilling took a deep breath. He was not feeling well at all.

'What is it that you do for a living?' she asked.

'This and that.'

'I'm in real estate. Phoenix is a good place to be in real estate.' She returned his gaze over her steaming cup of tea, held in both hands. 'Are you staring at me?'

'You're attractive.'

'Thank you. And you're loaded.'

'Thank you.'

'Rudi said you race cars.'

'When I'm sober.'

She watched him with a patient half-smile. 'I was born in Cologne. Where are you from?'

'Dresden.'

'Have you been back since the war?'

'There was nothing to go back to.'

'I had forgotten. You are the only American, besides my brother, in the Staffel, yes?'

'The only German-American,' he corrected. 'Then there is you. Aren't you in the Staffel?'

'I am the cook . . . and the hostess,' she said as she spooned lemon yogurt into her mouth. 'I will make you eat your carrots.' She looked at her watch impatiently.

'You will all eat your carrots.'

In the dark Schilling was confused, thirsty, still slightly drunk. The Jeep ground to a stop. Stuffed in the back, he could taste the dust. He stretched his leg, mindful of the new boots, to get out. In the front, Eric Malzahn and Franz Osterhoudt were stepping down.

At the house, both Schilling and Osterhoudt had been prodded quickly into uniform and then driven through the night for what seemed like a hundred miles, most of it over the most gut-wrenching desert Schilling could have imagined, to what was apparently the flying field. In the starlight he could make out a large hangar, with no lights except for a small window. And then a second hangar.

'Major Schilling,' Eric called, 'please come with me. Major Osterhoudt, would you wait for just a few minutes?'

A door opened and in the light from inside Schilling recognized Rudi, who came out to shake his hand. 'Welcome.' Rudi took his arm. 'Come in.'

Schilling blinked in the light of the barren little room, stared at the stern silver-haired man in plain gray dress uniform seated behind a small wooden desk.

Rudi straightened, stood with heels together. 'Our Commanding Officer, Oberst Theo Heinrich,' he announced. 'Oberst, this is Major Peter Schilling.'

Schilling squinted at Theo. 'Oberst,' he acknowledged.

Theo stood up, almost at attention. He was taller than he looked while seated. Schilling reacted slowly, but also came to attention, locking eyes with Theo. No one spoke. No one moved.

'A salute, Major, would be appreciated,' Theo finally said.

'Sorry, Oberst.' Schilling snapped his arm up. It took but a moment to retrieve from memory the proper military phrase for reporting to an officer. *'Melde gehorsamst.'*

Theo returned the salute and looked him over. Schilling stared straight ahead, at attention.

'Major Schilling, as of this moment you are an officer of this unit under my command. Military courtesy is in effect during this operation except for time off-duty. Is that clear?'

'Yes sir.'

'You may stand at ease, Major.'

Schilling relaxed slightly, his eyes sweeping quickly around the room. Except for chairs there was absolutely nothing but the desk and the blackboard behind Theo. Like a tiny schoolroom.

'You were instructed to bring the balance of the cash payment,' Theo said. 'Did you?'

'Yes, sir.' Schilling withdrew an envelope from his jacket pocket, took one step forward to place it on the desk, and then stepped back. Theo continued to look at him. Fierce-looking sonofabitch, Schilling thought, keeping a pleasant expression.

'At your earliest convenience, Major,' Theo said, 'you will collect any personal belongings that have any identification – wallet, papers, medical insurance cards – and turn them over to Oberstleutnant Felbeck. They will be kept in a safe place. Tomorrow will be good enough.'

'Yes, sir.'

'Your flying schedule will begin at 0700 hours tomorrow morning,' Theo said briskly. 'I have reviewed your record, Major, and I am proud to have you as an officer of this unit. That is all.'

They exchanged salutes, but Schilling remained fixed where he stood; he had forgotten how to do an about-face. Was it the left or the right foot that lifted?

'Is there something else, Major?' Theo asked.

Schilling lifted his right foot, testing. Yes, the right! 'Only,' he said quickly, 'that I am pleased to be here.' He turned a perfect about-face and strode to the door.

'Please send in Major Osterhoudt,' Rudi called after him.

CHAPTER FIVE

For the first time in thirty-one years Schilling sat in the cockpit of a flight-ready 109 with the engine turning over. It was a peculiar feeling, the sort of feeling that had a funny name he couldn't remember this early windless Sunday morning. He peered to one side of the cage-like windscreen and the high nose obstructing his forward vision. Across the concrete apron he saw dozens of private aircraft already moving to the taxi area. They seemed very small and fragile, so many white geese waddling out to play in the shadow of this predator. Odd to be sitting among them in this rumbling monster, disguised, at the Phoenix airport.

Eric had started the other 109 for Rudi, who would accompany Theo, Schilling and Osterhoudt separately on brief familiarization flights. Schilling had forgotten how cramped the 109 was, like the cockpit of a Formula car. His shoulders barely cleared the sides and his knees were high, close to his hand on the stick. He remembered the 109s of the war being dank inside, usually odorous, but this one was hot and dry and light in clean gray paint. It smelled richly of oil and metal and fuel and enamel and fiberglass, as if new. The thinly cushioned racing-car seat held him comfortable and secure, tight against his hips and lower back. The instrument panel above his hands was a clean flat black, neatly laid out. Though all the instruments were in a familiar location they were different in design and color: black-faced with red, white or green symbols. Very sanitary. He scanned the dials, watching the temperatures edging up. No trick at all to running up this baby in this kind of heat. Not like those bitter frozen dawns of the Eastern Front.

Rudi clambered up to the cockpit and leaned in close.

'Are you all checked out OK?' he yelled over the noise.

'All OK,' he yelled back.

Rudi glanced over the dials. 'Trim set one-third flaps?'

'One-third.'

'It's not so different from the old Gustavs.'

Schilling nodded.

'Do you have any questions?'

Schilling shook his head.

'All right.' Rudi hesitated. 'Remember that this hot air isn't as easy to bite into, so be sure to crank it up and take your time getting off the ground. We've got plenty of runway. Use it.'

Schilling nodded once.

'Keep your eye on me. Are you all set?'

'All set.' Schilling touched a gloved forefinger to his brow.

Rudi patted him on the shoulder and was gone. Schilling checked his harness, tugged his gloves tight, and adjusted the nose-bridge of his sunglasses. Once again he pushed the receiver headset more snugly over his ears. His new flying suit fitted as well as the new uniform. Of similar cut and color to wartime Luftwaffe issue, the lightweight tan fabric was tailored like a jumpsuit with zippered arm pockets, chest pocket, left leg pocket, and a right thigh map pocket with plastic window. The ankles and wrists had Velcro closures, as did the mandarin collar. Very neat.

He glanced down at the typed information – cockpit checklist, instrument settings and procedures – on the white paper under plastic on his thigh. None of it was all that different or new. Rudi's thirty-minute briefing had been thorough. His eyes scanned the dials again, noticing the rapid increase in oil temp. He wondered what weight oil the massive twelve-banger would need in this heat. He loved the sound of it rumbling before his feet and he fed a little fuel into it, like revving a car. Power, sweet power! Impatiently he glanced over to where Rudi was idling twenty yards away in the other 109. How strange it looked in light blue with the funny wheel fairings and pointed nose.

Rudi nodded, lifted a hand, then his voice came over the headset, requesting clearance from the tower for both planes. Schilling boosted the throttle a notch. The plane began to shake as the prop spun into a transparent blur. Rudi motioned him forward. Schilling released the brake and began to roll.

***

They were back to the house well before the high heat of noon. Theo and Rudi went directly inside. Schilling and Osterhoudt stood in the driveway looking around. Eric lowered the van windows an inch, then came over to the two pilots.

'Remarkable country,' Osterhoudt said to Eric, sweeping his hand to take in the arid landscape around them. 'Peter and I were in the dark last night when you abducted us, remember?'

'Just following orders, Major.'

'Schilling glanced at Eric – he was becoming interested in this man who had Marta – then he looked over the house: white stucco with orange-tiled roof, set back some fifty yards from the dusty road like a small fortress surrounded by bone-dry, rock-strewn moonscape. Most of what was visible of the house was the eight-foot wall, glaring white in the raw sunlight, with gray-green vines crawling along the top and creeping down the stucco sides. The only other visible dwelling was half a mile down the road.

'Nice place,' Schilling said. 'You could hold off the Indians for weeks.'

Osterhoudt turned. 'Are there Indians?'

'Some,' said Eric, straight-faced, 'but they're friendly.'

'I see.' Osterhoudt returned his attention to the desert. 'Such space, I have never seen such space. And such color!'

And such heat thought Schilling.

'Cold beer inside.' Eric was looking at Schilling. 'Major?'

Schilling watched Eric as they entered the house. Though he was the same height as the slight Osterhoudt, Eric was tough-looking, broad-shouldered. There was no trace of humor in his soft-spoken, slow-moving manner, nor in his dark eyes and rounded unlined face. A wide mustache hid his upper lip and his hair was thick and glossy black. He reminded Schilling of a civilized bandit. Surely he was much younger than Marta. They made, Schilling decided, an unlikely couple.

Inside they found a cold luncheon spread on the bare darkwood dining table: sliced meats, cheeses, bread, cucumbers, scallions, tomatoes and fruit. Bright yellow napkins and earthenware plates rested in neat stacks beside a large wooden bowl of fruit. Eric pulled cold cans of beer from the refrigerator and frosted steins from the freezer.

Theo and Rudi, both in dress uniform, came in from the patio carrying wooden trays. Osterhoudt and Schilling moved to stand, but Theo waved them back in place. 'Do not get up, gentlemen, please. You are off-duty now. The Oberstleutnant and I are going out to the field, which you will see more clearly tomorrow. Two of the other pilots are arriving soon. Frau Malzahn has gone to meet them.'

Rudi glanced at his watch. 'We must leave soon. Eric, you'll bring Major Beissemann and Major Kesler directly to the field, in uniform?'

'Got it.'

'Now is there anything you need?' Rudi addressed Schilling and Osterhoudt.

Osterhoudt stood up. 'If I could make a request, Herr Oberstleutnant?'

'What can I do for you, Franz?'

'As you are aware, I am a musician. Next month I am scheduled to participate in a concert performance. I need to practice daily, when I am off-duty, of course. It would not interfere.'

'Yes, of course.'

'Since I could not bring my instrument, the viola, perhaps in a city of this size one could be rented?'

'I'm sure it can be arranged. Marta will take care of it easily. Do you need to go with her to select the one you want?'

'I would prefer to, yes.'

'Consider it done. Tomorrow afternoon, when we all return.'

'Thank you, sir.' Osterhoudt sat down.

'Now ... enjoy yourselves.' Rudi buttoned his collar. 'Cocktails at eight, followed by dinner. Perhaps one of you might volunteer to assist Marta with dinner preparations. We will rotate everyone to KP beginning tomorrow.' He turned to Theo. 'Oberst, shall we go?'

Schilling watched the two men turn and leave, their boots tapping slickly on the tile floor. How perfect they looked, he thought, and how strange the uniforms are with no insignia.

Schilling and Osterhoudt stood languidly shoulder-deep in the blue pool, cans of beer close at hand on the tiled rim.

'Well, Peter, what do you think of this, this reunion?'

'So far so good.'

'Strange to be military again. Or is it paramilitary, in English?'

'All the same,' Schilling replied. 'Strange to fly the Gustav again.'

'Yes, I thought they were remarkable. Very clean, beautiful.'

'Still not easy to put down.'

'Did you notice the sight in place, the gun and cannon triggers?'

Schilling nodded.

'Heinrich said there would be gunnery. What do you suppose we'll shoot at?'

Schilling had been thinking about that, too. 'Lot of desert out there. Probably we'll shoot up a hell of a lot of rocks.' He grinned. 'Maybe some Indians.'

Osterhoudt laughed, his lined face crinkling at the eyes and mouth. He was a likeable man, delicate and self-composed. The whiteness of his hair, combed forward and neatly trimmed, was matched by the same whiteness of his brows. To Schilling he seemed wise, refined.

Schilling popped open another beer.

'How do you like living in America, Peter?'

'I like it,' Schilling answered thoughtfully. 'I don't know much else. I went into the service at eighteen, was shot down over the Channel in forty-four, a POW until forty-six. I came over in forty-eight.'

'Ah, the Channel. Twice I got my feet wet, twice in one month. Forty. Well, no danger of that during this tour, eh Peter? I am from Leipzig. When the war ended we were based near Augsberg. Couldn't even fly; no petrol. We had twenty aircraft and more ammunition than we could ever use. The Americans just came down the road and through the gate and everybody took to the woods. I walked to Munich and have stayed there ever since. The Americans never found out I was Luftwaffe.'

'How did Theo find you?'

'Ah, he did not find me. He found a friend of mine, another pilot. Introductions were arranged.'

From inside the house they heard voices and they had a glimpse of the new pilots, both carrying briefcases, as Marta led them through the dining area to their rooms. The taller of the two was a big man in a light suit, with thick hair and a deep tan. The other one looked like a bookkeeper: slender, balding, with odd glasses. Minutes later Eric was hustling them, in uniform, back out the door for the trip to the desert field.

'Well, Peter, it is time for a nap.' Osterhoudt boosted himself out of the pool and began to towel himself dry. Behind him the glass doors opened and Marta came out. She wore sunglasses, a white polo shirt with wide cranberry stripes, khaki shorts and no shoes. She carried a very large glass of iced tea.

'Frau Malzahn.' Osterhoudt smiled, pulled on his robe.

'Hello, Franz.' She looked at Schilling – 'Major – ' and took a chair in the shade of the table umbrella.

Osterhoudt wrapped the towel about his neck. 'Perhaps you would permit me to assist you in preparing dinner, Frau Malzahn.'

'Franz, you must get on a first-name basis with the cook. I would be delighted to have your help. We can drink all the cooking sherry. Or maybe something better. Do you cook?'

'As a hobby.'

'Me too,' she laughed.

'What time shall I report?'

'Seven would be fine. Eric will do steaks on the grill.'

'Good. Then you will excuse me until then.'

Schilling watched Osterhoudt leave. From the edge of the pool he smiled stiffly up at Marta, unable to determine if she noticed from behind the sunglasses. 'Fine place you have here,' he said lightly.

'Thank you, Major.' She took a long swallow of the tea. 'Are you enjoying your vacation so far?'

'So far.'

'I understand the flying went well this morning.'

'We have all done it before. The kites were fine.'

'Kites?'

'Planes.'

'Yes. My brother is a perfectionist. He likes detail. Sometimes it prevents him from seeing . . . other things.'

She drank more tea, somewhat nervously, Schilling thought. He could easily see her feet; they were just a little bit long, but narrow and brown, and the nails were enameled peach.

She removed her sunglasses and crossed her legs. Schilling watched. They were good legs.

'When do you think I'll be on a first-name basis with the cook?' he asked.

'Whenever you wish.'

'I mean when will you stop calling me Major?'

'Rudi advised us, Eric and me, to use rank unless otherwise –' Her hands fluttered up to substitute for a reason – 'unless otherwise. Besides, I prefer to use rank since we are all being so military.' She stood up. 'Now if you will excuse me, Major, I have a few things to do – meat to thaw, champagne to cool, that sort of thing. Our first dinner, you know.'

'Will there be carrots?'

She glanced at him as she turned. 'Mind the sun, Major. You'll burn.'

Schilling swam, slightly drunk and alone. The water was soothing and warm, so soft that he seemed oiled as each leisurely stroke pulled his body through the water. He lost count of the laps, and when he was tired he floated a while, basking in the heat. The pool made him feel wealthy, though he knew he never would be. Something about living in the United States made you feel as if you had to be wealthy. It was like a disease. Stupid thinking. Drinking was the best cure for useless stupid thinking like that. It always worked. For a while.

He decided to oil up and tan on a deck chair. His forehead was burning, he realized, and he covered it with a towel and lay on his back and thought about the women he didn't have, one in particular, and about the women he once had, one in particular.

After a while, he heard people in the house and soon Eric brought out the two new pilots, now in swim trunks. Schilling stood up for Eric's introductions.

'Beissemann, Gustav.' The larger man had a firm generous grip, a chest like a wrestler, and a slight bemused smile.

'And this is Walther Kesler.' Kesler's hand was as narrow and cool as his overall appearance. Not at all like a bookkeeper, Schilling decided. Kesler's eyes were concealed by opaque reflective-silver sunglasses.

'Herr Schilling, a pleasure.' He spoke flatly, bending forward from the waist, his mouth half smile, half grimace. Schilling was sure that he would have heard Kesler's heels click had he been wearing shoes.

The pilots swam, splashed, and drank in the pool for the next hour. For a short while Kesler had done laps alone and, as he churned by – now without his mirror sunglasses, his thin hair plastered back over a high skull – Schilling was startled by his eyes; even in the water they seemed without lustre, and were of the most unusual gray-purple.

Beissemann, instantly the most popular, was a handsome

smooth man. It was his thick blow-dried hair, so dark on top with patches of gray over both ears, that made him seem much like a genial buffalo. Schilling already thought of him as Major Bison, so similar was his name, and he found himself tempted to smile whenever he looked at him. Major Bison flew for Lufthansa and seemed to have a highly developed taste for old wine and young stewardesses. With a beer in each hand he gave a short speech, christening the group Felbeck's Flying Circus, and challenging all of them with a hundred-dollar bet as to which pilot would find a woman first in this Godforsaken desert.

Well, thought Schilling, the party was under way.

With the arrival, very late in the afternoon, of the last two pilots – Horst Weinert and Anton Rendel – all were now present, neatly uniformed and animated in conversation as they collected by the pool in the early dusk. Theo moved among them, pausing to chat. The poolside table held a silver bowl of ice, numerous bottles and a platter of hors d'oeuvres.

The sky was changing rapidly, a vast canopy of rouge and powder-blue sweeping overhead to the luminous flame-orange band delineating the western horizon. About to set, the perfect fiery disc of the sun balanced for a moment on the dark peak of a distant mountain and cooled to the color of simmering embers, its last rays gilding the edge of a single errant ribbon of indigo cloud. The pilots turned to watch, arrested with glasses in hand, their faces glowing golden in the dying light. As Theo looked, the images of his pilots, soft gray cloth and glossy ebony boots, were painted in perfectly reversed reflection upon the mirrored surface of the aqua pool. He searched his memory for so similar a scene . . . yes, a print in the dining room of Irmela's apartment in Bremen, by the artist . . . Parrish, yes Parrish.

Theo hovered from pool to kitchen to dining room, noting every detail. All was in fine order and on schedule. The dining table was particularly pleasing, set with shining crystal and gleaming silver, ringed with white luminescent china against a tangerine tablecloth.

He was also pleased that he might have underestimated the ability of the pilots to readjust to the 109s after so long a time. Schilling and Osterhoudt had appeared to be completely comfortable at the controls that morning. So, he smiled, even before we sit down to the first meal, four of our eight pilots are checked out on preliminary flight. Not bad. Not bad at all.

'Gentlemen, if I may have your attention.' Rudi spoke from the end of the table. All the pilots were seated while Franz poured champagne. Glowing candles touched the crystal with reflecting flashes of gold. Rudi inhaled, resolved at all costs to appear sober. He could not recall so pleasant an event since his wedding. The others waited.

'On this unique occasion . . . as your Executive Officer I welcome you. Oberst Heinrich and I have looked forward to this moment for many years. This Staffel was an idea that seemed at first impossible . . . and now we find it a reality.' Rudi paused, looked to Theo.

'Since a long speech before dinner is even more cruel than a long speech after dinner, I will make no speech at all.' There was light laughter and applause.

'There are several small matters, however, the first of which is an announcement. One of your comrades has volunteered for permanent KP, every day. Obviously a man of good taste, he has most likely fallen in love with the cook. And he is Major Franz Osterhoudt.'

Franz stood briefly to laughing cheers and enthusiastic applause, bowed, nodded to Marta, and sat down.

'And about the cook.' Rudi reached for his champagne. 'How fortunate we are to have so charming and lovely a woman . . . to relieve the boredom of looking at each other, and to keep us from malnutrition. I give you our hostess Marta Felbeck-Malzahn.'

As one the Staffel were on their feet, smiles turned toward Marta, glasses raised and emptied. With grace Marta acknowledged each pilot, her smile a gift to every one as they took their seats. Rudi remained standing as Franz refilled each goblet.

'During most of nineteen forty-two at Abbeville . . . I had the best *Wart* – mechanic – I ever knew, a man who loved airplanes, especially the engines. Mine always ran perfectly. Though my life depended on it, I never worried. I will never forget him. There is another man like that, and we have the good fortune to have him with us. I give you our host Eric Malzahn.'

Again the Staffel stood with glasses raised. Eric held up his

69

own glass while the others drank, then tossed it down as quickly. All sat.

'And finally,' Rudi concluded, 'there is a gift at each place. You may open them now.'

He sat down. Theo leaned forward, whispered his approval. Each of the small silver-wrapped packages contained an identical black chronograph watch. The pilots immediately strapped them on. Franz began refills while Marta served cups of vegetable soup. Viennese waltzes played at low volume on the stereo.

Theo sat alone at the head of the table. Of all the chairs Theo's was the only high-back, a heavy dark Mexican piece of carved complexity, crude metal rivets, padded armrests and wine-colored upholstery. To his left was Rudi, Kesler to his right. So, he thought, we are all together. Finally. The image of his Staffel reflected in the aqua-blue pool in the soft pastel of sunset remained in his mind as vividly as a photograph. They were good men, not a beer-belly in the lot, good men who loved flying. Common men. And as good common men they would be malleable. They would respond, in war as in business, for war and business were of course the same. They would respond to praise, respond to recognition, respond to reward. And they would perform, perform again, perform almost any act if precisely motivated.

There we have them: aeronautical engineer, car salesman, airline pilot, classical musician, insurance broker, university instructor and building contractor. It would not be too difficult. He now felt very much in control, drinking a silent toast to . . . command. Such a fine-edged game. He would play it superbly. It was control and it was discipline and it was the planning of objectives and it was the achievement of objectives. At all costs.

And how radiant Frau Malzahn is looking, her skin glowing, those sun-browned breasts swollen in the grasp of her bodice. Definitely an asset, even though she is somewhat forward, like a man. So clearly is she savoring her exclusive role, this soft pigeon preening among aging eagles. At that moment Marta laughed aloud in conversation with Beissemann.

Theo then rested his attention upon Schilling. Of Rudi's pilot he knew the least, and he studied this lean and solemn Schilling lounging back relaxed, introspectively removed, one hand holding both cigarette and champagne. Somewhat arrogant-looking, Theo mused, noticing then that Schilling's attention was directed not inward but outward, directly at Marta. Theo watched. He had seen the look before. Ah, already we have an eagle hunting the pigeon.

As if he had been called aloud, Schilling turned and met Theo's eyes, and raised his glass. Theo returned the gesture. Schilling was drunk and hungry and having a good time and the glass he raised to Theo was his fifth. Quick of the Herr General to catch me gawking at our hostess, he thought. He'll write that down in his little book. He drank, as did Theo, and turned away. He ached from the swimming and his forehead was sunburned, but oh he was in fine spirits. Fine spirits sitting in this soft gray, very nicely tailored uniform with not a single badge or insignia or emblem. Fine spirits in these fine high boots. And not a little surprised that 'Felbeck's Flying Circus' was so far everything it was promised to be.

And more. Marta. In the candlelight she shone. Burnished gold-straw hair, gold rings at each ear, a simple gold bracelet. Some sort of shiny beige-white dress held by thin shoulder straps. Beissemann made her laugh. Schilling knew he could not make her laugh. He wondered if Eric made her laugh.

Eric's charcoal-broiled steaks were well received, as were the fat foil-wrapped baked potatoes, chilled salad and serving bowls of fresh peas and cold cucumbers in cream. Osterhoudt watchfully made the rounds, a white towel the badge of his new position, pouring Burgundy into fresh goblets, and waving his hand in time to the waltzes from the stereo.

After the dessert – chilled green grapes and vanilla ice cream with hot fudge sauce – coffee, cognac and cigars were passed around. Then Rudi stood, signaled to Eric to turn off the stereo, and tapped his fork lightly on his water glass.

Schilling settled back and began to unwrap a cigar, pleasantly, drunkenly receptive to whatever speech Rudi was about to make.

Rudi began by telling them how he and Theo had been ambushed by the Mustang on their own runway in 1944, and how their flak caught the Mustang and how they and the Mustang pilot were in the field hospital when the Americans overran the base. Schilling liked that story. Then Rudi described the restoration of the 109s, noting that Theo paid all the bills – Schilling especially liked that part – and then Theo's idea of recreating a Staffel, every detail as authentic as possible. Rudi continued with security: no one to leave the house alone, no one to carry any identification, no phone calls without permission. He then passed out typed sheets with regulations and a preliminary duty schedule.

Schilling reached for the cognac bottle and his eyes caught Marta's. She was smiling. He nodded, looked back to his bottle, pulled the cork, and poured. The sight of her did good strange things to him, those butterscotch breasts popping out of the top of her gown. God give me one chance to run my tongue down that valley and beyond. There was a pause; Rudi held for complete attention, silence, then spoke. 'I present to you our Commanding Officer, Oberst Theodor Heinrich.'

Theo was on his feet before Rudi sat down and he spoke – 'Thank you, Oberstleutnant' – before anyone could decide to applaud. He raised his left forearm, pushed back his sleeve, and looked at the new black watch. 'Now – ' he grinned at all of them – 'you see, no one will have an excuse for being late during the next two weeks.'

Then he leaned forward until his fingertips touched the table. The room became quiet. Theo raised his chin slightly, and even Rudi was startled by the change in Theo's face, the fierceness in the gray eyes, the tiny twitch of muscles a parenthesis to a slight pursing of the thin mouth. Even his jaws and teeth seemed locked tight. Theo stood still, rigid, eyes still piercing, sweeping each face. It seemed intolerably long before he spoke.

'*Ich . . . bin . . . der . . . behlshabende . . . Offizier . . . dieser . . . Staffel.*'

In the exact same firm cadence he repeated in English, 'I . . . am . . . the . . . Commanding . . . Officer . . . of . . . this . . . unit.' Each syllable lay heavy in the smoky candlelight, weighted. At the end of the declaration he paused yet again. There was no person present who doubted what they had just been told.

Marvelous, Rudi thought, as startled as any of the others. And now Theo remained silent for so long a time that Rudi began to wonder if that was all he was going to say.

'I have little to say to you at this time,' Theo continued in English. 'Soon enough you will hear plenty from me.' He paused again, eyes still sweeping, piercing. 'I too wish to welcome you. Our most gracious Executive Officer, Oberstleutnant Felbeck, has devoted years of preparation for this occasion.

You will be stunned . . . to see the aircraft awaiting us. Now, on the eve of this great adventure, I promise that you will not be disappointed.'

Rudi glanced quickly around the table. Every eye was riveted upon Theo, who now drew back and stood ramrod straight.

'Once again,' Theo said reaching for his wine, 'we will have a toast.' All stood quickly, silently, glasses raised. 'To 76 Staffel . . . the last unit of the Luftwaffe.' Theo drank quickly, his glass empty before anyone's. All drank, then sat down again – except Theo, who placed his goblet carefully on the table without looking down.

'I have been fortunate in my life,' he said, his voice now reflective. 'I have worked hard and I have been rewarded. Rewards are always good, good for the soul. All of us, as veterans, as *eagles* of the Luftwaffe, deserved reward . . . reward for bravery, for patriotism . . . but we were *deprived* of that reward, *deprived* of recognition, deprived . . . by defeat.' He paused, looking intently at each pilot in turn. 'It is my reward,' he went on, 'to command this unit. It is my reward to fly with each of you. And this unit is now your reward; to be the best and the last.'

Here again he paused and looked down for several seconds. Rudi found himself suddenly engulfed in a vast flashback of the war, a mad replay compressed into seconds, of the agony and hope and loss and death and beauty and pride and final futility.

Theo raised his eyes and continued calmly: 'Because I have personally been so fortunate since the war . . . I wish to share my rewards with men, with eagles, who were denied theirs.' From his tunic he brought out an index card and what appeared to be a thin black leather billfold. He held both objects in one hand, card on top. He glanced at it, then looked up. 'Major Schilling, step forward.'

From the far end of the table, Schilling was so startled that it took him a moment to rise, careful to set aside his cigarette, and walk to the head of the table where he stood at relaxed attention before Theo.

'Peter Schilling,' Theo said without looking at him. 'Four years, nine months' service. Rank of Oberstleutnant. JG Three *Udet*, France. JG Three, Russia. Four hundred and fifty-nine missions. Nineteen kills. Iron Cross First Class. Major Schilling, I salute you!'

They exchanged military salutes and shook hands as Schilling accepted the leather case without expression. When he was seated, Theo pulled out another wallet and consulted his card. 'Major Osterhoudt, step forward.'

Franz came along slowly, his face pale and serene, looking much like a priest with his white Caesar-cut hair.

'Franz Osterhoudt. Five years, six months' service. Rank of Hauptmann. JG Fifty-one *Molders*, France. JG Twenty-seven, North Africa. Six hundred and thirty-three missions. Twenty-nine kills. Iron Cross First Class. Major Osterhoudt, I salute you!'

Franz saluted, smiled at Theo as they shook hands, looked at his gift, and retreated.

'Major Beissemann, step forward.'

Beissemann lifted his bulk easily from his chair, laid his napkin aside and, still smiling, came forward.

'Gustav Beissemann. Four years, eleven months' service. Rank of Hauptmann. JG Fifty-four *Grunherz*, Holland and the Eastern Front, Leningrad. Eight hundred and forty-two missions. Thirty-one kills. German Cross. Major Beissemann, I salute you!'

Beissemann saluted promptly, solemnly accepted his gift, glancing once at all the others at the table, then stepped back.

'Major Kesler, step forward.'

The click of Kesler's heels was audible as he snapped to attention and saluted, eyes burning in the candlelight, mouth tight.

'Walther Kesler. Six years, eight months' service. Rank of Major. JG Two *Richthofen*, Western Front. SKG Two-ten, Eastern Front. Twelve hundred and sixteen missions. Fifty-eight kills – ' here Theo looked first at the other pilots then back at Kesler – 'Knight's Cross,' he finished. 'Major Kesler, I salute you!'

Even to Marta, already mesmerized by Theo's recitation of the figures preceding the term 'kills' for each man, it was evident that Kesler's achievements had a special effect on the others; in the candlelight a current of subtly perceptible electricity circled the table. Kesler snapped a return salute, shook hands impassively and turned a perfect about-face.

'Major Weinert, step forward.'

Slender and scholarly, Weinert glided forward like an athlete.

'Horst Weinert. Five years, six months' service. Rank of Hauptmann. JG Twenty-seven, North Africa and JG Fifty-three, France. Nine hundred and seventy-six missions. Thirty-six kills. German Cross. Major Weinert, I salute you!'

Weinert saluted nervously, breaking into a crooked smile as he shook hands and accepted his gift with a slight bowing gesture.

'Major Rendel, step forward.'

Rendel moved rapidly for his blocky, rugged size. His wiry gray hair shone like pewter and his shaggy brows knitted in what seemed to be grateful confusion.

'Anton Rendel. Six years, five months' service. Rank of Major. KG Seventy-seven, Norway. KG Fifty-two, Eastern Front. Eleven hundred and twenty-one missions. Forty-three kills. Knight's Cross. Major Rendel, I salute you!'

Once again the air was charged with the magic of the words 'Knight's Cross'. Marta glanced over at Schilling. He was leaning forward, arms on the table, hands folded together, his attention entirely on the ceremony. How much more the killer he looks, she thought, than the man who now saluted Theo.

'Leutnant Malzahn, step forward.' Theo's voice had changed neither pitch nor pace and he caught Eric in the act of sipping coffee. He paused, the others waiting silently, then rose to his feet and came forward.

'Eric Malzahn. Two years, three months' service, United States Army. Rank of Chief Warrant Officer. First Air Cavalry Division, Air Mobile and Medevac. One hundred and six missions. Vietnam. A different time, a different place, a different war ... perhaps even less rewarding than ours. Leutnant Malzahn, I salute you.'

With relief, Rudi noted that Theo paused long enough for Eric to present the American salute and that he returned it in kind. Eric shook hands hesitantly, took his gift, and returned to his seat. Marta, Rudi noted, had followed the presentation with intense curiosity, her hands at the table's edge.

'Oberstleutnant Felbeck, step forward.'

Rudi stood, taking three measured steps around the corner of the table to face Theo at attention. To his surprise, he felt a curious surge of respect for Theo. And a very real sense of obedience for his authority.

'Rudolph Felbeck. Six years, two months' service. Rank of

Hauptmann. JG Twenty-six *Schlageter*, Western Front. Seven hundred and ninety-eight missions. Twenty-eight kills. Iron Cross First Class. Oberstleutnant Felbeck, I salute you!'

Rudi saluted, shook hands, and returned to his chair. The others shifted and moved, the tension of formality was relieved.

'And now,' Theo concluded, 'if we could resume playing the waltzes again, let us enjoy ourselves.'

Only when Schilling retired, and remembered the black leather wallet in his tunic pocket, did he take a look at it. Embossed on the grained calfskin surface was the tiny silver heraldic eagle of the Luftwaffe. Inside he found ten hundred-dollar bills in fresh US currency. They were real. He lay awake for a while, wondering what they were all going to shoot at.

CHAPTER SIX

'Captain Webb reporting, sir.' Webb saluted briskly, returning his hand to his side so that his curled forefinger was in perfect alignment with the seam of his right trouser leg.

'At ease, Captain.' Colonel E. B. Butler, Commanding Officer of Williams Air Force Base, returned the salute without looking up. He slid a file folder to the center of his immaculately barren desk, then leaned back in his chair, folding his hands together with both thumbs pointing upward. For a moment or two he looked over the young officer with the perfect creases, modish-trimmed hair, gold-rimmed sunglasses and smooth tanned face.

'Captain, I have your request for transfer here. You're not very specific about your reasons for such a request. What are they?'

'I believe I'd do better somewhere else, sir.'

'Somewhere a little more . . . exciting.'

Webb knew his Commanding Officer well enough to know that the question was not a question, but an aside. So he gave no answer.

'I would think this duty would be pretty good for a single man.'

'Yes sir, but I think I'd have a better opportunity to move up if I were somewhere else.'

'Move up? You've got some time in here, good time. You've got a good record, Captain. Not much to do here, I realize that. There's always a . . . a slump, after a war. Things quieten down. Everybody relaxes for a while. Then they get restless and they want to move around. Some of them do crazy things: complain

. . . drink . . . carry on . . . get divorced . . . get out of shape. Crazy things.' He paused, as if waiting for Webb to continue instead. Webb said nothing.

'However,' Butler went on, 'it never stays quiet for long. There's always a bunch of assholes, usually the gooks or the camel drivers, cooking up trouble in one place or another, Captain, and before the ashes cool off over in Vietnam there'll be another action. There's always been war, always will be. We'll wake up one of these mornings and the newspapers will be full of it. And then it'll start all over again. Never fails.'

'Yes sir.'

'If you move out, then I've got to find myself another OSI officer, haven't I?'

'Yes sir.'

'One as good as you, of course. Now would that be easy?'

'No sir,' answered Webb mechanically.

Colonel Butler again looked Webb over, then got up from his chair and walked to the window. He looked out over the field, and the runway where several white T-38s were taxiing out, the whine of their jets building faintly in pitch.

'Captain, to tell the truth I could think of several bases where I'd rather serve, myself. One of the things I've learned in the Air Force is that an officer should perform in an outstanding manner regardless of his assignment. Always be ready. Sooner or later, something comes up. The pay-off. You're a career officer, aren't you?'

'Yes sir.'

'I appreciate your . . . ambition, your eagerness. If this particular point in time seems dull, you can bet it will get busy sooner or later. Just hang in.' Butler turned away from the window. 'Is there anything else, Captain?'

'Yes sir.' Webb shifted on his feet. 'Could I request some time off next Friday? I'm going over to a field in California for an airshow, a fly-in. For the weekend. The Confederate Air Force is coming up.'

'If I remember, you're a photographer of sorts, right?'

'Just a hobby, sir.'

'Well, Captain, take a lot of pictures. Especially of the B-25s if there are any. You'll need Friday afternoon and Monday morning, will that do?'

'Yes sir. Thank you.'
'That's all then, Captain. You're dismissed.'

Webb stepped outside into the glaring midmorning sun. Damn, it was hot already . . . heat bouncing off everything like an open oven. Even the blacktop of the base parking area radiated reflected heat like a bed of coals. He opened both doors of the gleaming blue Datsun 260Z to let the heat escape. He was irritated, nervous. The request for transfer might have been a poor move. In the career game every move counted for – or against – promotion, and now he wasn't sure whether the interview with Butler would help or hinder him. But it was done now, a step taken. He was not comfortable with the colonel's reaction, but there was nothing to do but deal with whatever came next. Webb thought about Butler's request for shots of the B-25. Sure, why not? Bring back some nice slides and score a few points.

He headed north toward Phoenix and his health club. The air-con cut in and he settled into the bucket seat, cruising at an easy sixty-five. The car felt good. He loved the sleek design, the shining waxed Air Force blue paint, the stark black interior and aircraft-like dash layout.

Webb worked out every day, sometimes in the evenings, sometimes at noon. Though he did not especially enjoy it, he worked hard to stay in shape, to look Air Force, like the recruiting commercials. It was necessary. So he kept his stomach flat and his hair trimmed and his uniforms crisp and his shoes mirror-shined. And his aviator-style gold-rimmed prescription sunglasses were the most expensive.

Not to worry, he reminded himself. Just do everything right, like you have been. Hang in. Maybe Butler was right about that. Hang in for the long haul. He clicked a new Pink Floyd tape into the cassette player and cranked up the volume.

> I don't need no arms around me.
> I don't need no drugs to calm me.
> I have seen the writing on the wall.
> Don't think I need anything at all.
> All in all it's just another brick in the wall.
> All in all it's just another brick in the wall.

Webb was not so enchanted with the Air Force, not like he was at the beginning. Above all, he had expected glamour. Now it seemed no different from working for a big company. All the rules, all the games, seemed no different for a career officer than for a young executive. You always had to watch out, and trust no one. He realized he was not exactly synchronized with the Air Force; in step, yes, but not in sympathy. He'd been lucky to escape a Vietnam assignment, but the war had filtered grimly back to him. Dark stories from other officers, about dope coming in with KIAs, about the metal coffins streaming back endlessly into California airbases, about falsified casualty reports and pay-offs and black-market fortunes. Too many stories. They left him with an undigestible distrust of people like Butler, of the entire military complex.

No, it wasn't what he thought it would be. Quite sincerely he had wanted to make a contribution to his country, to serve. Quite sincerely he had wanted to guard and preserve what he knew was good, right. He was baffled by what had happened to this vision, by the dissolution of this once clear image. Something had changed. Webb had grown up with admiration and respect for the military, and now it seemed gone out of fashion. Likewise he had cared, really cared, for his country, the United States of America. Where were those feelings of honor, of nobility, he had expected to feel? Hell, it took courage just to wear a uniform in public now. It was in fact a very real risk. Vietnam had done that, goddamnit. Among all the other dreadful consequences, it had turned the military into something evil, something ominous and inhuman.

Hell, it was just a company, a huge conglomerate, wasn't it? And the product was war. A company with a few guys at the top who made decisions about wars and a whole bunch of guys at the bottom who fought them and then a huge bunch of guys in the middle. Webb knew very well where he was in the chain; he was in the middle. Just another brick in the wall.

Even worse than finding out that the Air Force wasn't what he expected was the discovery that it wasn't even what it once had been. He felt he had been misled.

He was not prepared to be disappointed in jet airplanes. True, they were sleek, marvelously advanced, so blindingly fast and deadly. Yet complex and impersonal, certainly unromantic. And he found modern air combat tactics equally complex and impersonal, a realm of electronic wizardry in which robots were pitted against one another in hypothetical encounters at such mind-boggling speeds that missiles were fired by electronic triggers at radar-detected targets far beyond the limits of human vision. One of those suckers up your tail-pipe and you never knew what hit you. Or where it came from. Just *whoosh*, *bang* and gone. Star Wars! Planes that could nearly circle the planet. Planes that could take off straight up from where they sat. Planes that could carry enough explosive to evaporate a city. Planes that cost so goddamn many millions of dollars you quit counting. Planes that flew so fast their own noise couldn't keep up. Planes that went all the way up to the boundary of space Wow.

Damn, they made him nervous, those planes, made him nervous just to think of controlling them. He wanted a joint And more Pink Floyd.

Mother do you think they'll drop the bomb.
Mother do you think they'll like this song.
Mother do you think they'll try to break my balls.
Mother should I build a wall.
Mother should I run for President.
Mother should I trust the government.
Mother will they put me in the firing line.
Ooooah is it just a waste of time.

There you are: Captain James Webb, United States Air Force, an expert on the past, carried on the apocalyptic wave of the future, dragging the useless baggage of a passion for history.

How different it had all become.

In the first air combat of the First World War one pilot fired a pistol at another, an improvement over throwing rocks and bricks, which had also happened. Then there were shotguns and rifles and, finally, a machine gun mounted on the nose and synchronized to fire between revolutions of the wooden prop – an innovative convenience which became a fatal inconvenience if the synchronization was upset. And on the morning of 5 October 1914, when a French flyer shot down a German, the plane became a weapon.

All those brave fools who launched themselves skyward in those fragile wood and fabric crates must have had a uniquely crazy stripe of daring, blind courage. What did it take to sputter off into the blue, into their own private war among the clouds, with no parachutes, no radios, no armor? Hardly more than model planes, these winged soapbox racers wired together and painted brilliant crimson, blue, green and sand, bearing emblems of their respective flags and units, slashes and bars, numbers and letters, and the symbols of ancient tribes, of heraldry: arrows and lightning bolts, panthers and dragons, hawks and hornets.

And these new warriors soon devised their own personal symbols: tailored uniforms, scarves of bright colors, polished boots, leather gloves. And esprit. None of the shit-slop muck of the trenches for these daring volunteers, these gentlemen often titled, these privileged daredevils. What an achievement it was merely to get airborne, to navigate by hand-held compass above the green and mud patchwork of Europe, to drop a little bomb now and then, to fight and kill each other. It seemed miraculous that they could cause each other harm. If they died of bullet wounds or became a torch falling with, or without, their stricken craft, it was simply unfortunate, as all war is unfortunate. But they did not murder each other. Certain mutual rules of conduct, an unwritten code, developed. There was pride in skill and there was respect for courage. Bravery in the fight well fought was often acknowledged by a wave, by returning to opposite corners for another match another day.

With the Second World War, one pair of wings replaced two, yet the esprit remained; the code, chivalry, honor and the heraldry of the elite. One man, one machine, against another.

Now these planes, those that survived, were called warbirds. Some rested in museums, some were carefully preserved and restored, and some still flew.

And whatever grim chivalry once existed in mortal combat above the clouds, whatever romance remained in the symbols of eagles and naked women painted on fuselages, whatever primeval pride had evolved to the victory tally marks on rudders, whatever charming heritage had persisted from the titled nobility of Europe, and whatever indulgence in male vanity could be traced to shining boots and scarlet scarves . . . had faded, nearly gone away. This gave Webb the second most depressing sense of loss in his life.

* * *

'We will fly in the standard *Schwarm*, two *Rotte* each. Red Schwarm will be led by Oberst Heinrich and I will lead Blue Schwarm,' Rudi began, standing behind the little desk, facing Theo and the other six pilots and Eric, all sitting in folding chairs. They wore fresh tan flying suits and they perspired in the little briefing room, though the air-conditioner rattled bravely against the morning heat that seeped in.

'For security purposes, we will address each other over the radio transmitters by rank and the number of our aircraft,' Rudi continued. 'We'll practice, beginning now, at all times while on duty. So, Red Schwarm will be Oberst One, Kesler will be Major Five, Beissemann Major Six, and Rendel Major Eight.

'Blue Schwarm will be Oberstleutnant Two, Blue Leader. Schilling Major Three, Osterhoudt Major Four, and Weinert Major Seven. Clear?'

Rudi turned to the chalkboard behind him. 'Our schedule this week will consist of three subjects. The first is Maintenance—' he chalked the word on the board— 'including orientation of all new details on the craft.

'The second, Navigation—' he chalked the word on the board— 'will include map reading and learning the two special routes selected for approaching the field. We'll call them A and B routes.

'The third, Flying—' he chalked the word on the board— 'will be practice. The Gustav was designed for rough fields, as you know, but takeoff and landing have always been its worst problems and the new craft are not all that different. A ground-loop will be a write-off, so stay alert. We'll fly four planes in practice this week. Questions?'

Rendel lifted his hand. 'Are we flying armed?'

'Not for a couple of days, Major, until we get sorted out a little. Now if there are no other questions we'll move out to the hangar.'

They formed in a group in front of the closest 109. Rudi rested his hand on the nose cowling. He smiled.

'Come closer . . .' He spoke seductively. 'Touch it . . . look at it . . . This is an old lover, this plane, yes? I want you to recall everything about her. Remember, remember everything.'

The pilots moved forward and laid hands upon the warm metal wings, closing around Rudi.

'Do not be deceived by her make-up, this powder-blue. She

is still the same, only much better . . . much better.' He reached up and gripped one black propeller blade. 'All engines are the DB 605As, rebuilt with state-of-the-art improvements. All plumbing and electrics are new. Every engine has been run in and flown. We're getting an easy 1800 horsepower, without boost, and airspeeds well over 450 kilometers per hour.

'There are numerous changes. The props are larger, wider, redesigned, and made of fiberglass. The struts are new, much lighter and stronger. Lightweight alloy wheels. Special new tires. The fin is larger, as is the rudder, originally made of wood. Ours are not wood.'

As he spoke, Rudi had completed a circle of the plane, the others trailing. Schilling noticed that Rudi's hand had not once left the surfaces of the 109. Now Rudi was once more at the nose section. He reached up and touched the long squarish scoop above the port exhaust bank.

'Tropical sand filter, with improved new filter material, from motorcycles they ride in the desert. Below—' he pointed to the large bomb-like belly tank— 'auxiliary fuel tank. Though the tank is designed to be jettisoned, we'll fly with it at all times, just to confuse observers about our range.

'Within both the airframe and wing assemblies we've made numerous changes, primarily new materials to lighten and strengthen the aircraft. Control overall is noticeably improved; the sum of small changes.

'Armament is as before: twenty-millimeter nose cannon with standard load of sixty rounds. Machine guns, engine-mounted, seven-point-nine millimeter with standard load of a thousand rounds each.

'The cockpit has so many changes I'll let Eric go through it with each of you in turn. You'll find a much improved ventilation system, all new instruments, new radio-transmitter and padded fiberglass seat designed for racing cars. Plus, the Galland hood, as you see if you look closely, is retractable, on rails, for open cockpit flying.'

The men responded with applause. Rudi smiled; the new canopy had been one of the most difficult projects of all.

'I know that you will agree that we must pay close attention to becoming thoroughly reacquainted with these Gustavs. We cannot afford an accident. Safety must always be first. Questions?'

* * *

In the early dusk of their first full day of flying, the pilots of 76 Staffel were gratefully submerged in the pool and Jacuzzi. Theo stretched, lethargic in the heat. His thighs and neck ached. Perhaps there would be time for a nap before cocktails. He was glad to see Rudi come outside in his swim suit, carrying a drink in one hand, towel in the other.

'Pull up a chair,' he said expansively.

Rudi wrapped the towel around his neck and winced as he settled into the chair. 'God, I ache all over. How are you?'

'Excellent,' Theo lied. 'It was a good day.

'Not bad,' Rudi agreed. 'What do you think?'

'I think perhaps we overestimated how long it would take to get used to the Gustavs.' Theo reached for more water and ice. 'We are going too slowly for them. We must accelerate the schedule, until we are pushing ourselves. Do you agree?'

'Perhaps.'

'Tomorrow, we will load ammunition. All tracers. Perhaps some low-level practice. To keep them awake, yes?'

'I thought maybe later in the week . . .'

'Our boys should get their money's worth. Impatient.'

'Who is impatient, Theo?'

'I am impatient, so they must be impatient, Oberstleutnant! These are fighter pilots! This is a combat unit!'

'Combat unit,' echoed Rudi.

'Yes, combat unit. Tomorrow we double the flying time. Each sortie on full fuel load.'

'Theo, this is a vacation for these people. Not a combat unit.'

'No?' Theo turned, his expression suddenly fierce, impatient. 'Then what would you call what we have here, Oberstleutnant? Perhaps a tea party?'

Rudi weighed his answer, disturbed by Theo's vehemence. With an effort he remained calm.

'I do not want to risk these men, the planes, until it becomes absolutely necessary. It is only the second day, Theo.'

'Will another day make a difference?'

'It will reduce our chances of trouble.'

'It will reduce our proficiency, Oberstleutnant.'

Rudi remained silent.

'We will load and fire tomorrow. You will take your *Schwarm* up first to find target areas.' Theo seemed calm now.

'I have target areas. I will show you coordinates. Eric and I used them.'

'Excellent. You worry too much, my friend. The more practice we have, the less chance we have for making mistakes. You can see that, yes?'

'Yes.' Rudi spoke with concealed reluctance.

'And one more thing, Oberstleutnant.'

'Oberst?'

'*Wenn schon, denn schon.*'

Rudi sipped at his iced tea, considering Theo's point of view. Yes, if it was worth doing, then do it right. Yes, proficiency was critical. Theo was right. What difference would another day or two make?

'Ah, they are all good boys, yes?' Theo smiled benevolently, watching the pilots.

'Very good.'

'They are enthusiastic. They have all asked me about the combat missions.'

'All?'

'Of course!' Theo exclaimed. 'That is why they are here.'

Rudi could think of nothing to say.

'What have you decided about our Colonel Lowen?' Theo asked then.

Rudi shifted gears, alert now to Theo's quick-change act. 'He is a long way from here.'

'Eleven hundred and eighty-two miles, as I remember,' Theo said, staring at Beissemann and Weinert in the pool. 'Well, tomorrow we will decide.' He paused. 'Why do you suppose Beissemann is wearing his cap in the pool?'

Rudi looked at Beissemann. 'To keep the sun off.'

'He is already tanned. Where did he get it, that hat?'

'He and Eric went out and bought caps for everyone. The sun.'

'But Beissemann's cap is different. What are the words on it?'

Rudi smiled. 'It says "Space Cadet".'

'Space Cadet?' Theo sat up, glaring toward Beissemann. 'What does that mean, Space Cadet?'

'It's all right, Theo. Major Bison is good for all of us. We could use two of him.'

'He looks like a juvenile delinquent in that hat.'

He did indeed, Rudi noticed. Like one of the Dead End kids with the cap down to his eyebrows, the bill turned up. He remembered that Eric had mentioned that Major Beissemann had demanded to be taken to a novelty shop where he had purchased the cap, a rubber monkey mask, and a large bag of mysterious items. 'It's all right, Theo. You don't think Lufthansa would permit juvenile delinquents to fly 747s, do you?'

Beissemann was getting pleasantly loaded. Peering casually from beneath the cap stuffed over his eyebrows, he did not miss Theo's glaring attention from across the pool, or Rudi's various expressions as the two men talked beyond earshot.

Just as Schilling's narrow face was permanently set in what seemed to be an expression of ill-concealed contempt, Beissemann's natural expression seemed to be that of ill-concealed amusement. He knew it was easy to assume that this expression indicated a glowing good humor, since people liked and trusted him easily at first meeting. In fact he was not at all outgoing; his face only lied that he was. There were times when he stood at a mirror contemplating this peculiar twist of nature and wishing that he could untwist it. The matter of appearing to be amused was not, however, a total lie; his view of the world was indeed one of contemptuous amusement. All about him fools ran the world in a most murderous and haphazard manner. Disasters were merely the cruelest of jokes.

From this point of view, Beissemann looked upon the Staffel as neither bizarre nor foolhardy, nor even risky. He found it clever. He was enjoying it immensely, and though he believed that both Rudi and Theo were most likely somewhat mad, he admired them immensely, convinced that anyone who could have dreamed all this up was surely more genius than criminal. Furthermore, the 109s were indeed impressive.

And finally, somewhat to his own surprise, Beissemann was admittedly touched by Theo's rationale, by the appeal of the pride and the esprit de corps of his experience in the Luftwaffe. Beissemann loved his country. He had been loyal then, and was now, and he was proud of his service as a fighter pilot.

He was also enjoying his vacation. His interest in the availability of women was second only to his growing curiosity about what Theo and Rudi were cooking up. It certainly had marvelous potential.

'Hey, Major Three!' he called to Schilling.

'Major Six.' Schilling came curving around like a porpoise, drifting over.

'Here,' Beissemann offered, 'have a beer.' He retrieved a cold can from the styrofoam cooler on the pool edge. Schilling accepted, wiping water from his face.

'Now,' said Beissemann conspiratorially, 'what do you think the Herr General is planning for us, over there with the Oberstleutnant?'

'Dinner menu?'

'Ha. Maybe.' Beissemann laughed. 'Osterhoudt says that our charming hostess has forgotten her German cooking. But, I don't care.'

'I don't care either.' Schilling popped the tab off his beer.

'Neither of them—' he nodded toward Rudi and Theo— 'drink enough. They should drink more. Like you and me.'

Schilling laughed. 'Nice hat, Major Six.'

'What do you think they're going to do for the fireworks?'

'Don't know.'

'If you look in the hangar by the back wall, under those plastic sheets, you'll find enough ammunition to start the war all over again.'

'Good.'

'Now, you're an American, Major Three; what would you like to shoot up with a Gustav?'

Schilling raised his chin and scratched around his neck and jaw, thinking. 'The IRS . . . Standard Oil . . .' Schilling had a pleasant fantasy of what he could do to an oil storage facility with a 109 loaded with high-explosive cannon shells.

Beissemann laughed. 'Well, they're out of our range. How about the Goodyear blimp? That's in our range.'

'Doubt if we could hit it.'

They both found this unusually funny.

'Now, Major Three . . . do you think the Herr General and the Oberstleutnant might be a bit crazy?'

'We are all crazy.'

'Well, I'll tell you what I think. Felbeck and the Herr General have gone to a hell of a lot of trouble here to fight the war over again. The only thing missing is somebody to have the war with. Now if you organized a Staffel right down to the boot soles, what would you pick to shoot at?'

Schilling shrugged. 'Airplanes.'

'Of course. Now . . . where are there airplanes around here?'

'Everywhere.'

'And there's Air Force everywhere, too. There are two bases within twenty minutes' flying time.'

'That's not it.'

'Of course not,' Beissemann agreed, 'but that's how you have to think. It wouldn't be civilian aircraft, and it isn't going to be Air Force because they'd plaster our ass. So what's left?'

'There isn't anything left.'

'Yes there is . . . but I'll be damned if I can figure it out.'

'Because,' Schilling explained, 'you're not crazy enough.'

Seventy-six Staffel's first fully operational flight was Blue Schwarm. Rudi led his pilots line astern through A and B routes, both very low level. They swept around towering mesas, skimmed across the pink desert floor, and banked through rock-strewn valleys between great salmon-colored cliffs. Then they leveled out at 10,000 feet, formed in echelon of two elements of two, and practiced combat flying. The 109s snarled in the crystal sky, swooping like pale blue swallows set free, their pilots straining with competitive pleasure, maneuvering smoothly in concert. Then Blue Schwarm spiraled down to 3000 feet and leveled out to begin their first run of gunnery practice.

In the hangars, the other pilots heard the distant growl of Blue Schwarm returning and they came outside to watch the landings, shielding their eyes and searching. A cluster of four cross-shapes appeared to the northwest, then opened up, one plane dropping down for approach.

Eric watched. It was the first time he had seen four of them in the air at once and the first time he understood how menacing and powerful they could be. The first craft settled nose up nicely, and rolled along the strip. Dust swept behind the 109 as it taxied closer. That would be Rudi leading. The next 109 was lining up now.

Eric squinted. This would be Schilling. The 109 was coming in a little high, but level and – Eric blinked; *no landing gear down!* He leaped forward and ran, pumping furiously out across the strip, ripping at his shirt front. Down the center of the runway, shirt off now, he ran toward the 109 looming closer in head-on silhouette, its flaps down like a great mechanical bird alighting . . . without claws extended. Thrashing his shirt in the air, Eric screamed in frustration.

The 109 was at 100 feet and dropping, no more than two city

blocks away ... seventy feet ... Eric whipped the shirt maniacally ... fifty feet .... When the nose came up the pilot would never see him .... The nose came up. He could hear the engine revs dropping. He thought of the propeller and prepared – the engine roared to life! Twin puffs of sooty smoke billowed out of the stacks. Eric dived for the ground, eyes closed.

The 109 howled overhead, blasting him with prop wash as the plane clawed for purchase in the hot thin air. Its shadow flicked over him as he rolled in the dust, blown sand stinging like needles on his back and arms.

He struggled up, nearly deafened, squinting through the dust. He could smell the hot oil-carbon exhaust vapor. He watched the 109 skating desperately down the runway ten feet off the surface. On his knees, he mouthed *no no no, up up up*. His breath heaving, eyes glued to the silhouette of Schilling's 109, Eric prayed, *Get him up, God, get him up*! Yes ... Schilling gained a yard, two ... lifted ... a little more, now. Eric got to his feet, watching the 109 lifting away. He began walking back, checking to see that the next 109 on approach was coming in wheels down.

Eight minutes later and last in, Schilling made a perfect landing. Taxiing up, he shut down all switches and released his harness. The other pilots stood in a tight group by the hangar, Rudi out in front. *Fuck*, thought Schilling. On the ground, still wobbly, he braced to walk forward. It was not easy. As some deference to discipline he decided to leave his suit zipped and his gloves on. When he drew close to Rudi he removed his cap and tucked it under his left armpit. He stopped, at attention.

Rudi took off his sunglasses with his left hand. His blue eyes bored into Schilling's. The ticking of hot metal from the aircraft was the only audible sound. Thankful that he was slightly taller than the Oberstleutnant, Schilling picked a spot on Rudi's hairline upon which to fix his eyes. Just like a goddamned cadet, he thought.

'Did your indicator lights malfunction, Major Three?'

'Sir, I honestly cannot recall,' Schilling replied. This was true. He was still shaking inside at the thought of his prop whacking Eric into chunks of meat. And he had been too busy with the second landing attempt to recall the first. Had he forgotten? Had the goddamned lights failed? Christ ...

'Perhaps a little too much to drink last night?' Rudi was asking.

'I don't believe so, Oberstleutnant.' Within his peripheral vision he saw Eric standing among the others, coated with dust like an aborigine.

'If you break one of my aircraft, Major Three . . .' Rudi's voice, dry and cold, broke off and let the warning hang.

'I will be extremely careful, Oberstleutnant.'

'You will also find something red – a cloth or ribbon – and tie it to your landing gear lever before you go up again. Understood?'

'Understood, sir.'

Rudi turned to Theo. The Commander looked a moment longer at Schilling, then turned and addressed the others. 'Proceed immediately with aircraft inspection, refueling and rearming. Red Schwarm will go up as soon as the Oberstleutnant approves each craft . . . and I trust that all of us will remember to lower our landing gear.'

'Dismissed,' Rudi said quietly to Schilling. They exchanged salutes.

Schilling caught up with Eric and Beissemann in the hangar.

'Nice landings, Major Three.' Beissemann grinned. 'I liked the first one best.'

Schilling turned to Eric. 'I owe you one, Leutnant.'

'No sweat,' Eric replied.

'I'm not sure about the indicator lights.'

'No sweat, Major Three. We'll check it out.'

Drink in hand, Schilling drifted into the kitchen where Marta and Franz were preparing dinner. Outside, the other pilots of 76 Staffel splashed about in the pool. He watched Marta chopping bright green peppers on a wooden cutting board. She had a clear drink on ice that Schilling guessed to be a martini.

'Frau Malzahn?'

'Hello, Major. Did you have a good time today?'

A good time, he thought. As if we had been playing in a sandbox. 'I need to ask if you might have some . . . ribbon. Red. Or maybe a rag, some red cloth?'

She looked up. 'Red? For what?'

'The Oberstleutnant has requested that I find a ribbon . . .

91

red. Or cloth. A small strip will do.'

Marta scooped the pepper chunks onto a plate and then dumped them into a stainless steel bowl half-full of chopped onions. Behind her Franz was up to his wrists in flour and thin cuts of veal; he glanced at Schilling and looked up at the ceiling.

'How odd.' She frowned. 'Why would Rudi do that?'

'It's for the aircraft. A safety measure.'

'Oh, I see. Well, then you'll need eight of them?'

'No, just one.' Schilling was sure that Osterhoudt smiled, eyes heavenward.

'Only one aircraft needs a . . . safety major, Measure?' She giggled. 'A safety measure, Major?'

'The sherry?' Schilling nodded toward her drink.

'Yes, the sherry,' she replied, lifting the glass and watching him over the rim as she drank. Osterhoudt started to slap the veal cutlets around with a most disturbing sound, like the slapping of flesh.

'Well, Major Measure, orders are orders. We will see what we can find.' She wiped her hands on her apron and walked past him, trailing a wonderful scent of salt-sour perspiration mixed with whatever perfume she wore and a trace of what some women smell like.

'Come with me,' she said. 'Franz will do better without me.'

Schilling followed, through the living room to the open bedroom door, where he stopped.

'I don't have ribbon, but—' She stooped at a large dark Spanish dresser and pulled open a drawer. 'Just maybe,' she said absently. 'What do I have red?'

Schilling glanced around the bedroom as Marta dug through the clothing. He decided not to look in the drawer.

She held up one nylon stocking. 'Not red, too bad,' she said as if to herself. 'Here.' She pulled out a small red scarf. 'Would this do?'

She watched him intently. In her other hand she still held the stocking. Damn her, Schilling thought, looking at neither the scarf nor the stocking, but at her. She waited. Schilling heard Beissemann laughing outside the open glass doors of the bedroom that led to the pool.

'Yes,' he said finally. 'It will do fine.'

They continued to stare at each other.

'Take it, Major; I can do without it.'

Don't reach, Schilling thought.

'The indicator lights failed,' he said. 'There were spent cartridges, empty shells from practice . . . jammed in the wheel housing, in the wiring.'

'Yes, I know.' She was holding the scarf out closer. 'I'm glad that you are all right, glad you both are all right.'

Now it was OK to reach. Schilling took the scarf without looking away from her and put it in his shirt pocket and buttoned the flap over it.

'Thank you,' he said.

'You are entirely welcome, Major.' Still looking at him, she let the stocking fall. It drifted softly down and landed, hanging from the drawer edge.

'Dinner,' she said. 'After you, Major.'

Marta awakened to music. It reached her faintly, subconsciously at first. Perhaps someone had left the stereo on in the den, or a radio? No, it was too real, with the crystalline presence of an actual instrument . . . Franz practicing.

Entranced, she lifted away the sheet, careful not to disturb Eric as she got up and moved to the glass door and slid it open. Her bare feet touched first the cool metal doorsill, then gritty still-warm concrete as she moved toward the pool. The early light was cerulean, dream-like, as if she were seeing through a blue lens filter.

Franz was seated on one of the poolside chairs by the far wall, his left hand curled high around the neck of the viola, his white head bent forward. His right hand wielded the bow lightly by fingertip. He wore the tan flying suit and his feet were bare.

Marta breathed the sweet perfume of flowers and the faint chlorine scent of pool water. The air was of that perfect temperature where clothing of any kind seems pointless. And as it was that time of early dawn when she often swam naked, she gave no thought to the gossamer transparency of her yellow gown.

As she came around the pool, she was astonished at the magnetism of Franz's music, astonished that such sound could come from a single musical instrument. Never had she heard anything quite like it. The notes changed and merged as a rivulet of flowing water − soft to strong, light to weighted, narrow to wide − spilling down the scale, sliding into the darkness of an elegy. Magic.

When she drew close, she could see that Franz played with

his eyes closed, oblivious. She eased herself onto a chaise longue, hardly daring to breathe, her eyes fixed on the rippling tendons of Franz's bow hand as he played. Now he seemed to repeat a passage. Then again, yet it was different, a different key, the same haunting and sinuous melody, a solitary liquid silver thread gently winding round itself, changing strength as it changed key. It opened her somewhere within, opened her as helplessly as the parting, the surrender, of lovemaking. Still repeating, the melody faded with each duplicated passage, sawing softly until it trailed off into silence.

Franz held the bow in place for a moment, then lowered it, slowly opening his eyes to hers. In those eyes she saw the distance of years; they widened, changed, came back from wherever he had been . . . to focus, finally, upon her. Only the reflex of a smile, a shadow there and gone, touched his lips. He did not speak.

'Again?' Marta whispered.

Franz lifted the bow, paused, then resumed playing, repeating it all. This time the music touched her even more deeply. It made her heart hurt, resurrected feelings with no name, mournful and distant, as sharp and dully shining as a new knife.

Then the visions came. The dead of Cologne, the waxen gray of vacant faces, the stacks of corpses in the carts. She thought of her father, his face flickering clear and then gone – gone in ashes under the bombs, gray dust. All those who had died she thought of as children, flushed and vibrant, scrambling free on grass slopes under a spring sky. Gone, all gone. All of them gone, uncounted. Motionless, mesmerized, she listened, sensing that somewhere beneath that swelling surface of precision and beauty something fearful loomed suspended, a lethal and inevitable Godless terror, waiting.

Then as quickly as she had descended, she was lifted once again by the single silver thread of sound that now dissolved at the end of Franz's bow.

He sat back, carefully lowering the viola against one arm, his hand draped tenderly over the rich wood. It struck Marta that the deep orange-brown grain shone exactly like the polished wooden stocks of Eric's rifles.

'*Guten Morgen*, Frau Malzahn,' said Franz softly.

'*Guten Morgen*, Herr Osterhoudt,' she whispered.

Tears suddenly filled her eyes and spilled out, streaming

down her cheeks. Helplessly she shrugged. Salt drops tapped on her breasts, slid between, began to evaporate in the dormant heat.

With tilted head Franz watched her.

'What was . . . that?' she said finally.

'Berlioz,' he answered, setting the viola aside. 'Profound . . . lovely . . . wonderful . . .'

'Wonderful, yes. Oh, I am . . .' Again she shrugged, giving up the search for words.

'I hope I did not disturb you.'

'Oh, it disturbed me very much.' She smiled, eyes shining wet, and brushed both hands over her cheeks. 'But not in the way you mean. Dear God, Franz . . . it was beautiful.'

'It is only my part,' he explained. 'What you heard was the first and second movement, just the solo part. It is the recording we bought yesterday, Berlioz's Second Symphony, known as "Harold in Italy".'

'Is what you played on that record?'

'Of course, plus all of the other instruments.'

'I cannot believe . . . that you played that, Franz.'

He smiled. There seemed a blush to his face that quickly faded; he looked, for a moment, gravely wan and tired. 'Thank you, gracious lady. But it is not so good as Herr Zukerman, on the recording. Perhaps in the next two weeks . . .'

'No, no,' she said, not knowing why. She clasped both hands at opposite elbows as if chilled, rocking slowly, looking away as if she were alone.

Franz watched her for a moment.

'Frau Malzahn, do you know Beethoven . . . Bach . . . Brahms?'

Marta shook her head, still staring away.

'They are the giants, the masters, of the world's greatest music. All German. And there is Schubert, Schumann, Wagner, Strauss, Bruckner, Mahler . . . all German. Did you know that?'

Again she shook her head slowly.

'Have you ever been to a concert?'

Again she shook her head. Tears came.

Franz seemed to think about something for a while, staring with Marta at the silent pool. The whirring whisper of a hummingbird could barely be heard among the flowers that covered the wall above them.

'A woman of your age,' Franz said finally, 'should know music.'

This time Marta nodded twice, unable to speak.

'It is not too late, not at all. There is enough time . . . enough music, for all your life.'

Dumbly she nodded again, weeping silently.

'I wouldn't want you to miss that.' Franz paused, kneading slowly at his neck and throat. Then he looked over at Marta. 'I would be honored,' he said, 'to show you the way.'

'Please,' she whispered.

'Well.' He spoke brightly now. 'No concerts, ever . . . Well, Frau Malzahn, I wish you could come to mine, but . . .'

Marta looked up. 'May I listen, now, every morning?'

'Yes, of course.'

She stood up. An errant breeze penetrated her pale gown. 'I won't bother you, Franz, I promise. Please continue now.'

Franz lifted the viola, replaced the chin-pad, and took up his bow.

'I won't talk,' Marta said quietly, looking over the pool. 'I'll just swim.'

Turning her back to him she stood at the edge of the pool. She hesitated a moment. No, she thought, it is fine. We are merely trading, his beauty for some of mine. Crossing her arms over her breasts she lifted the gown up and off; it floated over a chair and settled. Soundlessly she entered the water, warm blue oil. Franz began to play. Marta swam.

CHAPTER SEVEN

Leading the pilots of Red Schwarm on their second and last flight of the day, Theo set on a level course at reduced speed. His flying suit was damp and the harness belts dug into his shoulder and his lower back ached. He longed for a cigarette and a cold drink.

He pulled off his headset and scratched vigorously at his scalp, then smoothed his silver hair and replaced the headset. He scanned the instrument faces automatically; all was in order. Looking out to his right he watched Kesler's 109 cruising alongside slightly below. Expressionless in his mirrored sunglasses, Kesler lifted a gloved hand in informal salute. Nodding in return, Theo also watched Rendel and Weinert behind and below Kesler in perfect formation.

All four 109s were now transformed in appearance: a light coat of flat tan-pink enamel had been sprayed over the upper wing surfaces and most of each fuselage. Large white single numbers – five, six, seven, eight – had been painted just behind each cockpit. From each set of exhaust ports a dark oily streak of exhaust residue stained the sides of each aircraft just over the wing roots, and the twin cowling troughs of the engine-mounted machine guns were soot-darkened from muzzle blast. A thin smile passed over Theo's face. The 109s were beginning to look like combat planes.

He had worked them hard today, flying through both A and B routes four times, and three times leading them down for rock-hopping gunnery practice, their tracers like Fourth of July fireworks caroming off canyon walls and slabs of sandstone. Then they had climbed and split into pairs, each pair attacking the other. It was all rote for these boys, Theo could see; they turned with each other in near-perfect precision, always working to get inside the turn, rolling and diving and climbing. They were all having a very good time.

Theo glanced at the compass face and checked their bearings. Twenty minutes' fuel and they still had ammunition. Above them the late afternoon sky was half blue, turning to soft rose on the eastern horizon. Below, the intricate textures of the desert topography began to take shape as the sun slid lower and raised shadow. The massive rock formations, shallow canyons and flat-topped mesas were turning violet on the shadow side and copper to the sun side.

Theo waggled his wings and began to drop. No good staying this high; just that day they had spotted three civilian aircraft and a flight of four Air Force jets. They leveled off and skimmed along a low range of jagged mountains.

Then under his port wing Theo spotted an object. He dipped the wing, looked again, then spoke into the R/T. 'This is Oberst Leader. Keep formation, throttle back, and circle. Form on Major Five. I'm going down for a look. We may have a target.'

Theo dropped to port, wheeled around and descended. What he had seen was a box-like object standing dark and solitary on the sand floor of a long narrow valley between two mesas. At 600 feet he flew along the mesa tops, banking slightly. With the sun behind him he could see perfectly now. As the shape grew larger he throttled back for a good look. It was a van, battered and bleached, with one door hanging open and the wheels half-buried in the sand. An excellent target. Enough shooting of rocks, he thought.

'This is Oberst Leader. I'm coming up. Form on me, line astern. We have a target, an abandoned vehicle. We'll have the sun behind us, so you won't have any trouble seeing it. Hold your fire until you have target square in your sights. I want accuracy. I want precision. Acknowledge, Five.'

'Five here.' Kesler's voice was a little excited.

At 2000 feet Theo turned and throttled on for the run. Glancing back he saw flashes of gold glinting off the wind-screens of the three planes coming up fast behind. Good boys.

'Gun sights on . . . arm guns.' Theo's voice was calm. 'Keep your distance, now . . . here we go.'

✳✳✳

'A long day,' Rudi said to Theo. The two men sat in the Jacuzzi, goblets of cool Riesling close at hand. 'Did your practice go well?'

'Excellent, excellent. I am pleased. The flying and the gunnery are perfect. And your boys?'

'Frankly, they're better than me. All three of them.'

'We had an excellent target this afternoon.' Theo's eyes were closed, head back on a folded towel. 'An abandoned vehicle.'

Rudi became alert. 'What kind of vehicle?'

'A van. It was a derelict. In a valley about fifteen minutes northwest.'

'How do you know it was a derelict?'

'Ah, it was a wreck; door hanging open, wheels buried, as if it had been there for years. And it was far away from any road. I went down alone, right on top of it, to be sure.'

Rudi picked up his wine glass and sipped. It was his second and it went well with the deep heat of the swirling water. The sun was nearly down and dinner would be later than usual. He was thinking about the van. 'Out there,' he said finally, 'you never know. All kinds of people run around in the desert in all kinds of beat-up vehicles.'

Theo smiled. 'I remember; they are called "beaters", yes?'

'We should not shoot up anything like that again. It might give us away.'

'It was a good target, Rudi, a *real* target.'

'We will have real targets soon enough. Now we have a van sitting in the desert full of bullet holes.'

'Lots of bullet holes.' Theo smiled again, eyes still closed. He remembered how perfect a target the van was. They came screaming down the valley at thirty feet and the dark van was so clear in the sights in contrast to the pale sand. He remembered the flashes and sparks flying off the wreck, sparkling bright in the blue shadow of the mesa. He also remembered – and now it nagged him – that the van blew up under Weinert's fire. He had seen it as he banked away; an orange and black fireball glowing in the valley. He remembered being astonished. How could there have been petrol in it? Well, he decided, no point in telling Rudi about that. He opened his eyes and sat up.

'Don't be angry, Rudi.' He picked up the towel and wiped his face. 'It was too fine a target to resist, so much better than shooting at rocks.'

'Well, it's done. Let's hope it was a derelict.' Rudi poured both glasses full. 'One more before dinner?'

'Yes, thank you. And what is the gift tonight?'

'Binoculars.'

'And tomorrow night?'

'Scarves.'

'Yes . . . scarves.' Theo paused, looking upward. 'Such a marvelous sky. Such colors. We must have a unit insignia designed and painted on. I think an eagle and the sun. An orange sun. I have made a simple sketch. Could we have the Leutnant make the stencil?'

'He will paint the other four while we are flying tomorrow.'

'Very good.' Theo turned to Rudi. 'We are prepared now, don't you think?'

'Yes.' It was true, he thought.

'We will train hard tomorrow . . . tomorrow is Major Schilling's birthday party, yes? And then stand down Friday for service and painting. Agreed?'

'Agreed.'

'And tonight,' Theo said, rising from the steaming water, 'we will discuss the mission plans.'

After dinner Rudi and Theo carried coffee and cognac into the den. Theo placed the black binder on his lap, then took out his cigarettes, lighting one slowly as he opened the binder.

It was just getting dark. Franz had retired early as usual, and Eric was preparing to take Beissemann and Schilling to a film. There was laughter in the kitchen where the others were cleaning up from dinner. Rudi took a sip of cognac and began filling his pipe, choosing among the brown strands of tobacco and placing them in the pipe bowl with deliberate care.

'I have made a few notes, Oberstleutnant,' Theo announced quietly.

No doubt, Rudi thought, the first note will be *Wenn schon, denn schon*.

'We'll go over the first two missions,' Theo said, 'beginning with the airshow.'

Rudi held a match over his pipe.

'The term "fly-by".' Theo rubbed at his chin and jaw. 'What does it mean again?'

'To provide an aerial demonstration . . . by flying low to the ground for the benefit of spectators.'

'Ah yes, exactly. You see this airshow as a fly-by . . . where we perform, fire tracers, do some aerobatics, yes?'

'Basically. The show is exclusively Second World War aircraft. We'll certainly be the main attraction.'

'I am sure of that.' Theo smiled. 'You have been to this airshow?'

'Last year, yes.'

'And the display aircraft were parked in the taxi area as you marked on the map?'

'Yes.'

'We will attack these aircraft.' Theo sipped his cognac, watching Rudi.

'It is an option,' Rudi said

'Oberstleutnant.' Theo spoke almost in a whisper. 'It is what we will *do*.'

Rudi stuck his pipe back in his mouth, sucked and puffed. He was not exactly surprised. In the writing of the plan, he had intentionally made no mention of firing on anything but the runway, though it was implicit that the display aircraft would be irresistible targets. He also remembered feeling relieved of responsibility. It would be Theo's, as now it was.

'We must be absolutely certain that no spectators are hurt,' he said finally, puffing out smoke.

'Of course,' Theo agreed. 'It is a perfect plan. I congratulate you once again.'

Rudi nodded from behind his smokescreen.

'You are sure of the range, the fuel?'

'Positive,' Rudi replied. 'If we are careful. Eric and I flew the route last month.'

'I agree that you should lead this mission. It makes sense. And I will lead the second, yes?'

'Agreed.'

'And now . . .' Theo leaned back and folded his hands over the black binder in his lap, 'about our friend Colonel Lowen. He will fly to the airshow, you are certain?'

'I am sure the Confederate Air Force will be there. As for Lowen, I don't know, but it's likely. As I indicated, the chance of intercepting him is remote. But possible.'

Theo smiled. 'Wouldn't that be a fine scene?' He opened the binder suddenly, searching with a finger down one of the pages.

'Yes.' He looked up. 'Well, we have his telephone number. Well done.' He handed the open binder to Rudi and gestured toward the telephone. 'Perhaps we can determine if the Colonel will attend the show . . . and perhaps we could arrange to meet him. In the air.'

'He won't be armed, Theo.'

'I know he won't be armed,' said Theo patiently, 'but I think it would be more . . . impressive if we met him in the air, yes? We will need to convince him that we are—' he paused.

'—real,' Rudi finished.

'Yes, exactly.'

Rudi glanced at the telephone, thinking: how simple.

'Now,' Theo said, 'if you would give the Colonel a call. Your English is perfect, mine is not so.'

'I'm not sure . . . exactly how.'

'Be a newspaper reporter. He will be accustomed to that.'

'Yes . . . yes.' Rudi hesitated, then picked up the binder, located the number, and dialed. There was a pause, a faint clicking, then the ringing once, twice, and a male's voice. 'Hello.'

'I am calling long distance for Mr Roger Lowen.'

'Yes. Speaking.'

Rudi felt a tickling urge to laugh, as if he were making a prank call. Could that voice be the man who put the scars on his arm and leg, the man who chopped Hans into that grisly mess?

'Colonel, my name is Becker, writing for the *Los Angeles Times*. I'm doing a piece on the airshow at Chino field this weekend and I was wondering if you would give me some information on the Confederate Air Force?'

'Be glad to, Mr—?'

'Becker, Richard Becker. I understand you'll be flying to Chino with a group of warbirds. Can you tell me what types of aircraft will be there?' Rudi took a pen.

'Well, I'm flying with five P-51s. Are you familiar with Second World War aircraft, Mr Becker?'

'Quite familiar, actually.'

'Then you know the P-51.'

'Yes. We're thinking about getting some aerial photographs around Phoenix if we can schedule a camera plane when you pass through. Could we arrange to meet you?'

'Could do. Hang on a moment . . . Yes, let's see . . . We'll refuel in El Paso at about 0630 hours. That should put us over Phoenix at about 0715, just south of town. We usually follow US Ten right on over.'

'Altitude? Airspeed?'

'Fourteen thousand all the way. And we'll be loafing along about two-fifty. It's a nice drive, good scenery.'

'We'll look for you just southwest of Phoenix. Would that be all right?'

'Fine,' replied Lowen. 'We'll try to make it right on 0715.'

'Excellent. At 0715. We'll watch for you, Colonel, and we'll plan to go on over to Chino with you. Perhaps we can have dinner and a short interview.'

'Sounds good, Mr Becker. Just look for five Mustangs.'

'We'll be looking, Colonel. Thank you and goodnight.'

Rudi replaced the receiver. His palms were damp.

'Well done, Mr Becker.' Theo gave a small chuckle, his face beaming. 'Well done, indeed. And now the second mission.' He reached for the binder.

Rudi scrambled mentally to switch from the conversation with Lowen to the second mission. After a good belt of cognac, he picked up his pipe again and relighted it.

'A brilliant plan . . . a perfect plan,' Theo said.

'Quite different from the first.'

'Not at all different, Oberstleutnant!' Theo spoke sternly, as if surprised. 'Not different at all.'

Startled, Rudi looked up at Theo; his eyes seemed to glint now, no longer in good humor.

'No different at all. Quicker. More precise. But no different! One pass, in and out, then gone! Except . . . as before, you left out one detail.'

'Yes,' Rudi said, knowing with real dread what Theo would say.

'We fire, Oberstleutnant. We fire on the parked aircraft, just as we did the first mission.'

'Fire?'

'Yes, of course; fire! Why do you seem surprised? Does it make you feel better if I say the words you have neglected to write? Of course we fire! It is what you planned, whether you wrote it or not, and it is a perfect plan. It is early on the Sunday morning, with no one around. We are too low for radar, there is no anti-aircraft defense, we make one pass and twenty or thirty minutes later we are home!'

'Jesus Christ, Theo . . .'

'I lead this mission, Oberstleutnant.' Theo bit off each word as he spoke, teeth flashing. 'Do you think there is any difference in one plane or another?'

'Yes, there is a difference! The aircraft at Chino are civilian aircraft. Not Air Force.'

'Are you saying – ' Theo's voice turned calm – 'that you will not fire?'

'I am saying that we should not fire.'

'I see.' Theo took up his cognac, swirling it slowly as he looked back at Rudi. '*Es geht um die Wurst.*'

'Why? Why does everything depend on it?'

'*Wenn schon, denn schon*, Rudi.'

'*Ein tolles Unternehmen*,' Rudi said after a moment.

'Dear friend Rudi,' Theo whispered, leaning forward. 'Of *course* it is a mad undertaking. The entire *operation* is a mad undertaking. Have you ever doubted that?'

Motionless, Rudi stared back at Theo.

'Mad?' Theo continued. 'Mad? It is brilliant, so brilliant that it *seems* mad! Can you not see how one could be confused? . . . how one could not, at first, see the distinction between the two?'

Rudi made no answer. Could it be, he thought, that we are truly mad? Both of us, all of us? Is it madness that inspires Theo? And could he somehow make each of us mad as well? And why, he wondered, am I not afraid?

'All of what we do on these missions,' Theo said, still in a whisper, 'is the final chapter for the Luftwaffe, Oberstleutnant. It must be fitting. It will be fitting. Now . . .' Theo leaned back and took a cigarette from the red-and-gold box. 'You think about it.'

'The others . . . may also be reluctant.'

'We will see, yes? That is my responsibility as Commander. Do you agree?'

Rudi was watching the cigarette smoke rise up from Theo's hand in a soft thin white line that curled and drifted away. He was conscious of the quiet house now. For the first time it occurred to him that he might lose one of his beautiful airplanes.

'Make way! The torte!' Osterhoudt exclaimed, rising from his chair.

Schilling turned to see Marta, followed by Theo and Rudi,

bearing a great white cake on a silver platter. Her face was aglow with the light of dozens of tiny candles. The cake was stunning, a beautiful creation of baked meringue, whipped cream, fresh strawberries, and chips of bittersweet chocolate, with tiny candy violets dotted around the sides. The candles flickered, dripping wax in water-like drops. The other pilots gathered to the table, champagne in hand.

'Quickly, Major, a wish,' Marta said, stepping back.

Schilling contemplated the field of fragile candles, half of them melted. Then Marta and the others were singing to him. Ludicrous. Dutifully he smiled, then reached for a champagne bottle, put his thumb over the top, shook it once, and sprayed the mist over the cake, instantly extinguishing every candle. There was laughter and applause. Marta was holding out a silver cake knife.

'It is your honor to cut, Major.'

'Such a fine cake. You would do better, I think.'

'As you wish.' Marta slid the blade surely into the ornate sculpture of meringue, cutting a huge wedge.

'You see,' said Osterhoudt, 'Frau Malzahn with some practice has mastered the *spanische Windtorte*.'

'Nonsense,' said Marta seriously. 'Franz held my hand all the way. I wasted two dozen eggs at least.'

'No fool, this Major Four,' Beissemann remarked. 'He is always in the kitchen because he is holding hands with the cook. And getting loaded.'

'Always the loading,' Osterhoudt agreed. 'In the morning I load the machine guns and in the evening I load the dishwasher, yes?'

Schilling found this drunkenly funny and he reached impulsively to Osterhoudt's shoulder and squeezed the muscles of his neck, then clapped him across the shoulder blades.

'Major.' Theo stepped forward, hand outstretched. 'To your health!'

'Oberst.' They shook hands and touched glasses and drank.

'Now.' Theo turned to the others. 'On such an occasion we must have the waltz. Our good Oberstleutnant has arranged for an orchestra to play so that we all may dance. Clear away!'

From the den Rudi called, 'The orchestra is assembled and ready!' They heard first a terrible scratching noise, then a muffled curse, and then the first bars of a Strauss waltz, vibrant and happy. The pilots applauded loudly.

'It is customary for you to have the first dance, Major Three,' Beissemann reminded him. 'If you can stand up.'

There was more applause. Impossible, Schilling thought. I have not taken a waltz step in twenty years. Marta waited.

'It is my choice,' said Schilling, 'to have the last. The honor should go to our Commanding Officer.'

There was applause from every pilot as they turned to Theo and to Marta, her hands clasped over her bodice, head tipped demurely. Theo stepped forward, bowed formally, and took Marta's hand. Without hesitation they swept out and across the tiled floor to more applause.

Schilling followed their steps enviously, eyes on Theo's shining boots and Marta's slender feet, counting silently to himself as he watched them glide and whirl, smiling at each other. They seemed for a moment to be oblivious of place and time.

When Marta had danced with every pilot, she came to the table for a glass of water. Rudi reset the record, this time with no accidents. Schilling was ready, and tipsy, for his turn.

'Major?' Marta smiled expectantly, setting down the glass, her face glistening from exertion.

Half-drunk, Schilling was dazzled. Now that he was about to hold her, she seemed a different creature in the careful art of her make-up; bewitching, powerful and completely self-assured. He found no revelations in the opalescent depths of those gray-green eyes with lids dusted aquamarine over spidery black lashes, no promise in the wet, orange-peach, flattened-heart shape of her mouth so perfectly painted.

Her hand darted to his shoulder, long crimson fingernails flashing by his neck. Gold shone from filigree earrings and from her hair, parted center and bound tight in a sweep over each ear to form a braided bun at the top. Taking her hand in his, he reached up and placed his other hand at her waist, breathing in first her damp scent of sweat and perfume – reminded instantly of the scarf in his pocket – and then the warm cognac of her breath. Had this not happened before? he thought suddenly. Yes. Self-conscious in new gray uniform with the collar starched stiff . . . Aneka . . . The loud and crowded hall dimly hazed with smoke around them . . . Wasn't it Christmas? Yes, of 1939. The windows frosted and the air heavy and moist, scented by apple and holly, spice and fir . . . Aneka . . . Gold-braided hair in a bun. Perfume and the priceless moisture of her mouth. Yes. He had counted the steps then, too, and was half-drunk then, too. So long ago.

Schilling stepped off. There was applause. They danced.

Crazy, thought Schilling. What now? He was jammed between Beissemann and Weinert in the dark, jostled mercilessly as the van lurched over the desert road. Far from sober, the other pilots hooted at Eric's driving as he whipped the wheel back and forth, bouncing in his seat. The van's headlights struggled through the dust kicked up by Rudi and Theo in the Jeep ahead. A strange birthday, Schilling decided; dancing and drinking champagne one moment, and then herded out to the field the next. The goddamned Herr General had surely lost his mind.

When they staggered out of the van beside the hangars it was bright enough by starlight for the pilots to follow Theo to the second hangar. They grew quiet with expectation; no one had yet seen inside this other hangar and it was now clear that some new event was about to take place.

With Rudi and Eric helping, Theo slid the great door aside and stepped into the dark. A single overhead lamp came on, casting a circular pool of dim light on the floor. A wave of heat escaped from the interior, carrying odors of oil and paint.

Glancing down, Theo positioned himself in the center of the circle of light, hands clasped behind his back, his hair illuminated like burnished silver, his boots gleaming. The others gathered closer, as if in formation. All was still. Theo, face downward in shadow, waited a full minute before lifting his chin. The overhead light sculpted his forehead and cheekbones and nose as he spoke.

'I have gathered us here . . . to commend you for your performance in training.' He delivered the words firmly. 'I am honored . . . to command the finest, the last, Staffel of 109 pilots.

'We have shared a wonderful experience this week. It has been a great pleasure, this sharpening of our skills . . . in concert with each other. It is a reawakening! It is a rejuvenation! . . . to once again feel the pleasure of precision, the pride of being a fighter pilot of this unit . . . unique in all the world.

'We are now a team, and we bear the heritage of our country.

We have survived ... and now three decades after the Americans bombed our cities, our homes, our people ... we fly across their country.

'Three decades. I ask each of you to look back three decades ... for all of us are close to the end. Now we can look back and see what we have made of our lives ... look back and recall the dreams come true ... the dreams abandoned.

'And we can look back to what we once were: eagles of the Reich. We gave all in support of the Fatherland. We did not fail! We did our best. And none were better. None! It is that common bond which binds us here together. Each one of us had to have that spark still glowing ... that pride.'

Theo paused and tipped his head forward into shadow again. The black silence of the desert lay wrapped like a great warm blanket around the pool of light.

'And so,' Theo said quickly as he looked up again, 'I ask you to consider where you now stand. I ask you if that spark has once again been fanned alive! If once again, from the ashes of the war, there has risen – like the Phoenix – a select group of eagles reborn: 76 Staffel. *Graue Adler*. Gray Eagles.

'As if by some magic, some warp in time, we have – each one of us – been *destined* to stand here at this moment in the land of our former enemy, *destined* to fly again, *destined* to revive that esprit of the greatest fighter pilots of all time, *destined* to add ... a final chapter to the history of the Luftwaffe, a history that the entire world thinks has been written, has ended. *It has not ended!*'

Theo paused. No more than six feet away, Rudi sensed that he and all the others were willingly, gradually, coming under Theo's spell. Riveted by the drama of Theo's voice, by the contrasts of light and dark, by the very uniforms they wore, no one dared to move. Theo's eyes seemed to glow under the shadow of his brow. Sweat beaded the tanned forehead and his very physical body seemed at the verge of bursting out of the immaculate uniform.

'You must *believe*,' Theo continued, his voice urgent, 'as I do, that such destiny has brought us together here. You must *believe* that some deeper force beyond our comprehension has inspired this Staffel ... Gray Eagles ... true Luftwaffe pilots.'

Theo spread both arms from his side, one hand touching the wooden upright of the doorway. Eerily a dull light materialized above in the hangar and as it grew stronger around them, the four airplanes took shape in the gloom. Though no word was spoken, the electricity of near-supernatural surprise flowed through each pilot as they recognized, for the first time in thirty-one years, battle-ready 109s. The hangar lights cast a soft glow over the perfect mottled camouflage paint of each airplane, prop-blades like swords, great black-and-white Balkan cross insignia on the fuselage flanks. And painted below, the bright new eagle/sun heraldry.

'There is no such thing as coincidence.' Theo's words had energy now, momentum. 'We transcend coincidence! We transcend history! And now we can transcend our own dreams, our own mortality! We stand at the brink, at this moment. Think back, just a week ago! What did you see when you looked down the path ahead, to the end?

'Now look again at what is ahead. Is it not quite different? Is it not illuminated with the light of destiny?

'We have been given this opportunity. Think carefully . . . of that path you looked down ahead. To go home to what you were then, to go home to the rest of your lives . . . solitude . . . memories.

'We can, from this moment, become part of history! We can take this ultimate step . . . to join such men as Galland, Moelders, Marseille, Rudel, Hartmann.'

Theo paused, his eyes searching the face of each man. 'I do not believe there is one among you who can ignore destiny. I do not believe there is one among you who does not feel transformed, who does not feel prepared, for this step forward into history. And I do not believe there is one among you who will hesitate.' He waited a moment as if daring the faint of heart to step forward.

'That—' Theo pointed to the airplanes without looking at them— 'is my craft. Number One. That is Oberstleutnant Felbeck's, Number Two, with twenty-eight kill markings painted on the rudder. Number Three is Major Schilling's craft, with nineteen kill markings. And Number Four is Major Osterhoudt's craft, with twenty-nine kill markings. Tomorrow we will stand down from flying and complete the painting of the other four aircraft. And then we will have a briefing for our first mission . . . Saturday morning.'

With no more than a moment's pause to let the announcement of the mission settle, Theo went on, 'You see . . . we have kept the promise we made to each of you, Oberstleutnant Felbeck and I. *Now will you follow?*' Theo's voice grew strong, as sharp and hard as blade steel. 'Will you step forward and join together? Gray Eagles! *Graue Adler!*' Theo's arm lifted, his hand outstretched. 'And let me hear, together, *Graue Adler.*'

Nearly as one the chorus rose, filling the cavern of the hangar, echoing out over the darkened desert.

'*Graue Adler! Graue Adler!*'

Hesitant at first, Rudi's voice joined with the others as they converged on Theo and came together clasping hands. He was both sweating and chilled from Theo's performance, and though he knew that it no longer mattered, he also knew that he had been – indeed they all had been – seduced by some primitive lust more entrancing and overwhelming than that of any woman who ever lived. Corks popped. Glasses appeared. One of the men, bearish Rendel, thrust an icy green bottle of foaming champagne into one of Rudi's hands and then grasped and shook the other as in a vise of flesh. Rendel's eyes met his, just a glance, but they shone with such liquid passion that Rudi knew, clearly, that there was no longer any question. 76 Staffel would fly the three missions.

They were back at the house not long after midnight. Schilling weaved out to the pool in the dark and staggered into a chair, vodka bottle in one hand, glass in the other. The vodka was such a loving friend, always there to soothe what hurt. He smiled, setting the bottle down on the concrete and fumbling in his tunic for a cigarette. He liked the uniform, especially now, the gray softness of the fabric, the tailored closeness across his chest and stomach and thighs and seat. And he loved the boots tight around his calves, glossy and black. Yes, he liked this uniform; it made him feel . . . secure.

Fifty-two years old . . . and all of it had been pleasant and temporary. The women had been pleasant and temporary and the apartments had been pleasant and temporary and the cars had been pleasant and temporary and the jobs had been pleasant and temporary. Christ, over half a bloody century.

He sat up straight, sucking in his gut and flexing his shoulders. Drunk or not, you're OK, he thought. Nothing hurts very often and everything works and the reflexes are good. Not much left. Theo was right. The end wasn't too far off. It could be Goodnight Nurse next week or next month or next year. Sometimes you just dropped where you were, sometimes you never knew what hit you, and sometimes, best of all, you could go out right in the saddle. That would be the way. He shrugged and drank.

'Well,' he said aloud, 'you haven't done much with it but you haven't made a mess of it, either.'

The cars and the planes were always good, but the women were the best part of it. He missed them all, every woman who had ever loved him, even for an hour. It was the real fountain of youth, making love. It gave him life, it *was* life, the best of life. Was there nothing else? Fifty-two and the answer was no.

Sondra died in the crash. They were getting him out and there were beautiful sparks from the torches and it was taking a long time and there were glass chips everywhere like glittering snow everywhere: the dash, his lap, her lap. They'd given him a shot while he was still in the seat and before he drifted off he could see the tortured junk of the other car locked to his and he remembered hoping peacefully that the driver was dead too.

Grace went away when she lost her son in Nam, went to Malaga. She couldn't live in the States any more. He went to see her once. She lived in a very small house near the sea and the wind blew sand under the door. Her body was so much younger than her years and she was tanned and healthy-looking and then she died of cancer and it was a year before he found out.

Laura the lovely librarian disappeared, too, in San Francisco. No woman he knew had legs like hers. For hours he would embrace her around the thighs or calves and even sleep holding them. He had never done that again.

It turned out that the first and the last were the best and the worst, though. He wondered what Aneka would have been like now. Such golden hair; it would shine, glow, in the sun. He'd heard that she was lost in the bombings, that there was nothing left for a dozen blocks where she lived.

And the last was Ellen. It all seemed fine and then she just quit, like that. No alimony, no reason, nothing. Just good-bye and don't come after me. He was drunk for so long.

Now he drank some more. He liked the Staffel. He was having a good time, a very good time. One of the best. He liked them all, especially Franz and Major Bison ... and Rudi and even Theo. All of them.

111

Marta was different. He knew most of the time how to get women to love him a little without loving them back very much. Keep it pleasant and temporary. Until you ran into someone like Marta. Someone like Marta was dangerous. You couldn't just stop in the middle and stay there. There was nothing to stop you and you slid all the way down and if she didn't go with you then you were trapped on the bottom alone. He moved his hand to his tunic pocket and touched the red scarf.

A shadow, a step, at his side. Schilling looked up, hoping it was Major Bison, but it was the good bandit Leutnant Malzahn, his face ghostly green in the pool reflection.

'Major Three. Happy birthday.'

Schilling nodded. The gyroscope in his head malfunctioned and the pool and the house and Eric tipped crazily to the right.

'Mind if I sit?' Eric asked.

'Make yourself at home, Leutnant.'

'Not sure I can hit the seat with my ass.' Eric tumbled into the next chair.

'Owe you one.' Schilling paused, looking over at his host. 'There were no spent cartridges in the wheel . . . housing. Were there?'

'Nah.'

'Indicator lights were working. Right?'

'Yeah.'

'Well . . .' Schilling smiled without humor. 'Buy you a drink?'

'Got one, thanks.' Eric raised a glass, ice tinkling.

'Party was good,' said Schilling thickly. 'Thanks for party.'

'Marta's idea. Thank her, and Major Osterhoudt. They made that cake; what do you call it?'

'*Spanische Windtorte.*'

'What?'

'In English, Spanish Wind Cake,' Schilling replied.

Eric was quiet. He seemed to be thinking about something because he stayed absolutely still.

'So,' he said finally, 'how does it feel to be fifty-two?'

'Not much different.'

'Not much different than what?'

'Than forty-two.'

'But different?'

Schilling turned to Eric. 'Not much different.'

Eric hesitated. 'Didn't mean to be personal.'

Schilling recognized in Eric's voice the sort of regretful sincerity that made some drunks endurable. He decided to muster some sincerity for this husband of Marta. After all, he reminded himself, the good Leutnant did save your ass.

'I'm not . . . too far from forty,' Eric went on, 'and I've been thinking about it.' He paused. 'I thought only women thought about that.'

'Everyone thinks about that.'

'Anyway, I was just curious.'

'About what?'

'About the difference.'

'Well, Leutnant.' Schilling stopped to light a cigarette. 'The biggest difference is . . . that it's not so easy to go four rounds in one night.'

Eric stared at him for a moment, then grinned, then laughed. They both laughed, the helpless laughter of being hopelessly drunk. Schilling knew that Eric would decide it had to be funny, would laugh and let it pass without asking the real question.

'I don't understand them.' Eric was suddenly serious again.

'I don't understand them either,' Schilling admitted. He hoped that Eric wasn't going to say anything about Marta. 'You worried about going four rounds at fifty, Leutnant? Or at forty?'

Eric laughed, uncomfortably it seemed. 'Nah.'

'Good. No worry about it. They just get better.'

'They get better.' Eric repeated the three words as if they composed some canon of great value.

'If you're good to them,' Schilling added. 'And if you learn how to keep them. I never learned how to keep them. But I know that going four rounds has nothing to do with it.' He again glanced at Eric, amused at the blank expression across the dark tanned face. The thick black mustache seemed just a little too big.

'Come on, Leutnant,' Schilling said, slurring his words. 'Nobody goes four rounds, for crissake! Forget four rounds. Just concentrate on . . . one real good round.'

'One good round.'

'They don't want Superman. They just want someone . . . to care. A whole lot.'

'Care a whole lot.' Eric didn't sound convinced.

Schilling took a drink and leaned back in the chair and looked up at the stars. It seemed as if he could see forever. It was a picture of infinity, those stars, and it made him feel small and old. Stupid thinking again. From the corner of his eye he saw Eric take out a thin cigarette and tediously light it with a wooden match. Eric took a long drag from the joint and held it in.

'Four hundred and fifty-nine missions,' Eric said, 'and nineteen kills.'

It took a moment for Schilling to recognize that Eric was talking about him. 'What about it?'

'What was that like?'

Schilling thought about it for a minute before putting an answer together. 'Hazardous. Hard work.'

'It must take something . . . different.'

'It was a long time ago.'

'Could you do it again?'

'If I had to. I had to then.'

'I'm not sure I could do that.'

'You could if you had to. You know how that is . . . Nam.'

'I never faced anybody. I shot at everything that moved, from the chopper. It wasn't much of a contest.'

Eric's memory now dredged up terrible things, terrible sounds, especially the sound of the choppers, that muted whickering clattering drone of giant olive bugs, like incendiary hornets banging out rounds. And terrible sights, that chopper hit on the pad, just as it was landing. Incoming round dead center. Just *whoom*! and that mother was totally alight with everyone inside, everyone gone, they thought . . . until when it seemed half consumed and some of the guys started coming out. Jesus, you couldn't believe it. No way to forget. Just carried the grunts in whole, loaded up with rounds and hot to get some. And carried them out in pieces, in body bags, a torso here, a booted leg there. Meat wagon. *Help me*, they said if they still had jaws. *Help me*, they said if they weren't drowning in their own blood. *Help me*, their eyes said if they couldn't talk. Fucked-up mess that whole scene was. Don't mean nothin'.

'Well, I can't imagine going up against a P-51,' Eric said then.

'You don't have a lot of time to think about it.'

'Did it . . . sometimes happen that you didn't want to shoot? Like buck fever?'

'Sometimes, but it doesn't last long.'

'It goes away?' Eric took another hit.

'No, you die.'

'Like that?'

'Like that.'

'Like . . . like the fastest gun. Like a duel.'

'Something like that.'

'Hey Major,' Eric said after a moment. 'You want a hit of this? It's good.'

'Got this.' Schilling lifted his glass. And am I drunk, he thought. What the hell time was it? Stand down tomorrow, a break. Then the mission – he glanced at his new watch – about thirty hours away.

'Hey Major,' Eric said again. 'I'd like to fix you up. If you want to, I mean. Birthday present.'

'Fix me up?'

'Yeah. A lady. I know some good places.'

'A lady. Very thoughtful of you, Leutnant.'

'Tomorrow night, for sure. A birthday present.'

Schilling stood up. It took great care and patience to get out of the chair. 'Tomorrow night . . . and goodnight, Leutnant.'

'Tomorrow night. Just you and me.'

'I'll bring my cane.' Schilling went reeling toward the house.

In the little room he had a great deal of difficulty getting both boots off and finding each button. He was short of breath. So much food, champagne. He never expected this kind of birthday, strangers who sang to him, toasted him, made a silly white cake, beautiful cake, with candles. A goddamned Staffel in the goddamned Arizona desert. He liked them all very much.

He stared at Osterhoudt sleeping, breathing so shallow. Good man. He seemed oddly pale beneath the tan, seemed so far away.

CHAPTER EIGHT

Both Schilling and Osterhoudt were surprised to be awakened by Rudi before dawn.

'We must put an hour on the other planes, the new ones,' he explained, 'before it is too light and there is air traffic. There is coffee in the kitchen. Hurry now.'

Schilling dressed quickly, thankful that his hangover was merely awful and not monumental. After a cold washcloth and two Alka-Seltzer and coffee, he crawled into the van in complete darkness with Osterhoudt, Rudi, and Theo. Eric drove.

During the ride he lowered a window and breathed in. Now wide awake, he felt for the first time a low-voltage charge of excitement. The night before, after Theo's speech in the hangar, he had walked up to Number Three and touched the flat paint that smelled fresh and volatile, and had counted the nineteen vertical black kill-marking bars on the rudder. His Gustav. Now he would be flying it. He glanced at his watch, the phosphorescent dots of each hand glowing in the dark. In twenty-four hours all eight planes would be flying together for the first time.

First light was breaking as they reached the field and rolled out the four 109s. Each plane started up easily. Eric scrambled from cockpit to cockpit as the pilots buckled in, checking each set of instrument readings. Then with Rudi leading, the four planes taxied out into the dawn and lifted off.

'The mission tomorrow,' Rudi announced to the assembled pilots, 'is a strafing attack on an airfield in California, 302 miles due west.'

Sensing how heavily each of his words had fallen in the space of the tiny briefing room, Rudi waited, watching for reaction. The pilots shifted in their chairs, glancing at each other. All of them were hot and dirty and weary: the day had been spent on final servicing and painting and now all eight 109s waited, fueled and armed, immaculately prepared.

'Weather,' Rudi went on, 'is perfect ... according to last night's TV weather girl. There are no fronts between here and target. Flying time is one hour forty minutes with full fuel load and a cruising speed of 200 miles per hour at 12,000 feet.'

He turned and pulled down a rolled map sketch beside the blackboard. 'The airfield is about five miles south of the town of Chino and is surrounded by grassland and dairy farms. This drawing – ' Rudi took up a pointer stick and touched the tip to the board – 'shows the main runway here, northeast to southwest; length 2000 yards, width 50 yards, and crossed here by a smaller runway about half that length, east to west. These lines indicate taxi areas in front of the control tower, here. In this area will be our target; probably several dozen aircraft that will be familiar to you, including Mustangs.

'Once or twice a year this airfield is the site of airshows featuring World War Two aircraft, where owners and pilots gather and perform flying demonstrations for the public. These planes – our targets – are displayed here.'

He set the pointer down and took up a piece of chalk. 'We should be over target at 0930 hours. The airshow will be open and most of the planes should be in place. Hopefully the crowds will not be too large yet. Our procedure over target will be as follows: First, we'll come in over the field at about 200 feet on the first pass.' He chalked the numeral 1 on the board, followed by the words SLOW-OBSERVATION. 'I will notify the tower to clear the display area of all spectators while we look everything over.

'The second pass – ' he chalked the numeral 2 on the board – 'will be the only practice run we'll make, right down the runway. Our circle will be clockwise, north of the field. At the northeast end of the runway there's a road bordered by high trees. We'll come in right on top of those trees and drop down on the deck. This is a fast run to get the feel of it, so concentrate. Oh, and the flak should be very light.'

With the pilots laughing behind him, Rudi chalked the words

PRACTICE-FAST on the board.

'Again we circle around for the third pass, which will be exactly the same except—' he chalked the numeral 3 on the board— 'this time we'll open fire ... using the runway as a target. Machine guns only; don't waste cannon rounds. Just make another high-speed run like before, and shoot up the center of the runway. It's big enough so we all should be able to hit it.' Laughter again rippled through the room as Rudi chalked the words PRACTICE-FAST-MG on the board, then the numeral 4.

'On our fourth pass we come in exactly like before, but this time we angle to the right of the strip, on line with the target aircraft which are about 200 metres to the right.' He produced a red marker pen and quickly made a dozen X marks. 'By this time, the tower should have the display area clear of spectators and ground personnel. If not, then I will decide what we will do.' He wrote ATTACK-CANNON/MG on the board.

'We will fire only on the parked aircraft in this area. We must be especially careful not to endanger a life. We must be especially careful not to fire on any emergency vehicle, or ambulance, or fire truck, if they happen to be in the target area. And we must be especially careful not to hit each other. Keep your distance.'

Rudi paused, secretly feeling much like a schoolteacher. For a moment that came and went, he found it preposterous, unbelievable, that he was briefing a Staffel of 109 pilots for a strafing mission.

'We will make two attack passes. We have plenty of ammunition so keep on the buttons. Walk your fire into the targets and be careful not to overshoot. We don't want any stray rounds, which is why we'll pull up after target and begin the turn to go around again. After the second pass, we make the same turn and head home.' He wrote the numeral 5, then ATTACK-HOME on the board.

'You'll be given maps, marked with all necessary information, for the return leg. We'll split up after the last pass, fly very fast and very low on parallel courses leading back to the A and B routes when we approach Phoenix. And we will repeat this briefing in the morning before takeoff.

'In the meantime, study your maps and routes. Even numbers

118

take A route, odd numbers take B route.' Rudi paused. 'Now; questions?'

'Oberstleutnant?' Kesler's hand went up. 'What about air traffic in the target zone?'

'I will instruct air control to clear all traffic, but keep an eye out.'

'Oberstleutnant?' Rendel this time. 'What procedure do you advise if we are intercepted?'

'By jets?'

'By Air Force,' Beissemann called out.

Rudi set the pointer on the desk and picked up his pipe and struck a match to it. 'Presuming that Chino air control was quick enough to call for help – which I doubt – it would take at least twenty minutes, probably thirty, for jets to get there. The chances of this happening are, I feel, next to none. On our return trip we go flat out for the first thirty minutes, which will put us almost 200 miles east. Plus we'll be split up and miles apart, on different routes.'

'But,' Beissemann persisted, 'what if we have the Air Force on our tail, just by bad luck?'

'Well, Major Six, I'd suggest prayer.' Even Beissemann had to laugh at this. 'Just remember,' Rudi went on, 'they can't fly as slow as we can. If you get the Air Force on you . . . do what they tell you. Get your wheels down quick so they don't fire on you, land and then run like hell. You're on your own. Next question?'

'Radio procedure,' Theo reminded him.

'Radio procedure will be absolute silence the entire mission, unless it is necessary to speak. Use only German, never English. Also, a word about fuel and range. The Leutnant and I have flown to Chino and back, with the belly tanks, simulating our mission tomorrow, including the attack passes. We're right on the edge of our range so watch your fuel coming back. Slow down if you have to. We'll take off on internal fuel, switch over to auxiliary when we form up. If you run short and have to set down, camouflage the plane as best you can and get to a telephone. Anything else?'

It was quiet for a moment, then Theo rose and stepped forward to the little desk.

'Oberstleutnant Two will lead and command this mission. I will lead the next mission. We cannot tolerate any accident, any

loss of life. If we should accidentally machine gun a spectator
. . . we will all be hunted – to a man – as killers.

'After that, our biggest risk is each other. Concentrate on
what you are doing. Be aware of the man ahead of you.

'And finally, there is a most unusual possibility about this
mission. By coincidence, the Oberstleutnant has located the
American P-51 pilot who attacked us in Germany in 1944 . . .
and he is expected to attend this airshow, flying a Mustang. It is
possible, since we know his altitude and route, that we may
intercept him on the way to target. If this should happen, the
Oberstleutnant will make the necessary decisions and we will
follow his orders.'

In the silence of the room the only sound was yet another jet
scratching across the sky. Theo moved his gray eyes to every
pilot individually.

'I know,' he said finally, 'that each of you will perform
flawlessly.'

Eric shut off the ignition and rested both hands on the top of the
steering wheel, not looking at Schilling beside him. It was just
dark and they sat in the crowded parking lot of a Spanish-styled
building with a red neon sign over the arched doorway.
Customers, young and well-dressed, filed in, laughing and
calling to each other.

'Buena Vista,' Schilling read the neon sign.

'A good place,' Eric said. 'You can't miss. Lots of ladies. And
they're all ages.'

'You're not joining me?'

'I have somewhere else to go. Alone.' Eric reached in his
pocket and handed over a small scrap of yellow paper. 'Call this
number at exactly one-thirty. If you've got a live one, then call
from her place. I'll arrange to pick you up.'

Schilling reached for the door handle.

'It's early,' Eric said, still looking straight ahead, 'so if you
don't see what you like right away, be patient.' It was clear that
Eric was in no hurry to leave. Schilling watched him fingering a
thin little cigarette. A match flared, and Eric inhaled.

'Want a hit?' He held it out to Schilling.

'I'm flying tomorrow.'

'Some of this and you can fly tonight.' Eric insisted, laughing.

In the pink semi-darkness of the neon sign Schilling caught

Eric's calm gaze. He felt that Eric was studying him.

'By now,' Eric said, 'I imagine you're ready for a little R&R. With nobody to look at except Marta.'

'Well, she's good to look at,' Schilling said lightly. Be careful now, he thought.

'She seems to like you.'

'And Osterhoudt and Beissemann,' Schilling reminded him.

'Not in the same way.'

'I hadn't noticed.'

'No?'

'No.'

Eric appeared to think about this, taking another hit off the joint and staring over the wheel. 'Well,' he said absently, 'she is difficult to read sometimes. I don't know what she wants.'

'Ask her.' Schilling decided to keep it moving.

'It wouldn't be what she really meant.'

'It's a problem.'

Schilling watched a particularly exotic-looking woman enter the Buena Vista alone, long legged and tall. Through the open car window he could hear her high heels clicking on the tile pavement.

'You tight about the mission tomorrow?' Eric asked.

Schilling looked over at him. 'No.' He smiled thinly. 'Right now I'm tight about the mission tonight.'

'Yeah.' Eric grinned. 'Well, good luck, Major. Call me.'

'One-thirty,' Schilling promised, opening the door.

Without watching Eric pull away, he entered the arched doorway of the Buena Vista, pausing at the tiled vestibule beside the green spiked fans of a potted desert plant. Patrons three-deep at the bar and every table taken. Candlelight flickering from crimson cut-glass cups. Tanned arms and faces. Babble of laughter and clinking of glassware over recorded guitar music. Silk blouses and gold gleaming dully from wrists and fingers. Gardenia and coconut scents of mixed perfumes and suntan oils. Women everywhere, sleek and polished.

In a narrow hallway he found the telephone in use by a stocky man in a beige suit. Schilling leaned on the cigarette machine and waited. The man on the telephone, plainly drunk, was hunched over, receiver in both hands, pleading tediously with a woman to join him. He ignored Schilling.

After a few minutes Schilling lit a cigarette and stood a step closer. There was a touch on his arm and he turned to see the exotic-looking woman with the long legs and clicking heels.

'Are you waiting for the phone?' Her hair tumbled over her shoulders in mahogany waves.

'It may be a long wait,' he answered loud enough for the drunk to hear.

'I'm Pamela.' She held out a slender brown hand.

'Pamela. My name is Peter.'

'Do you have a dime, Peter? The bar is too crowded to get change.'

Fishing in his pocket, Schilling glanced down the front of her blouse, open braless cleavage, her tanned chest a V-shape above half-moon swells of white. Major Bison would whimper at this one, he thought. He dropped a dime in her palm.

'I won't be long,' he said. 'Just going to call a taxi.'

'So early? I haven't seen you here before. I mean, I would remember if I had.' She smiled. Her teeth seemed to glow.

'I think I'd remember you, too.'

'What do you do, Peter? For a living?'

'I'm a pilot, this week.'

The drunk on the telephone was making promises of dinner. He belched loudly.

'Oh, a pilot.' She held up a cigarette, waiting for a light. 'Are you in the Air Force?'

'In a manner of speaking.' Schilling lit her cigarette and then turned to the drunk. 'Hurry up.'

'Fuck off,' the drunk said thickly without looking up at him.

Schilling snatched the receiver out of his hands, hung it up, and then grabbed him by both shoulders and pushed him up against the wall and leaned in so close they were almost touching noses.

'You have bad manners,' said Schilling. 'This lady wants to make a phone call and so do I.' Face to face with the drunk, Schilling was startled at his youth, the smooth unlined face and flushed cheeks. Not twenty-five, he guessed. And smelling of too much fancy cologne.

'See you outside, Dad.'

'Fine.' Schilling pushed him aside. 'Right after I make my call.'

The drunk weaved away, straightening his jacket. From a sticker on the telephone Schilling found a taxi number and dialed it. As it rang he looked over at Pamela leaning against the wall, arms folded. One breast seemed to be pushing the other half-way out of the flaxen yellow blouse. She watched him, toying with a gold chain at her neck. Wet lips, perfect mascara, a face so smooth and perfect. Not twenty-five either, he thought as he ordered the cab. Christ, they're all so young.

'I'm sorry you have to leave,' she said as he hung up.

'Maybe I'll be back.' He walked away, pushing through the crowd in the vestibule, and stepped outside into the heated air. No drunk waited.

Schilling got out of the cab at the end of the driveway and watched it drive off. A dog barked forlornly in the silence of the desert night. He stood in the darkness and gazed for a few minutes at the stars scattered endlessly overhead. The house seemed empty, a small fortress in flat gray starlight. He knew that Franz slept soundly, and that all the other pilots were gone: Theo, Rudi, and Kesler to a concert; Rendel, Weinert, and Major Bison to a film.

Scaling the wall was far more difficult than he had expected. After three attempts, he dropped over the other side into a narrow space by the front door and then stepped gingerly over an assortment of clay planters, feeling rather foolish about crawling around in the dark like a burglar. He came to the back corner of the house by the master bedroom.

He took a moment to straighten his clothing and wipe the clay dust and grit from his hands. Only one corner of the house obscured his view of the pool.

He moved forward and peered around the corner and saw Marta easing naked into the Jacuzzi twenty feet away, her back to him. He felt immensely silly, inexcusably childish. Marta was waist-deep now and she leaned back against the tiled rim and scooped water over her torso with cupped hands. Schilling decided to step out, hoping to time his words at the moment she looked up.

'*Gnädige Frau*,' he said quietly, using the formal greeting of respect. Gracious lady.

Visibly startled, Marta twitched and raised her arms over her chest.

'Jesus *Christ*!' she flared. 'What the fuck are you doing, materializing like that?'

123

'Didn't mean to frighten you.' Nice work, he thought, thankful she could not know how foolish he felt.

'Not at all, Major. Just mild cardiac arrest. Do you have a key? How did you get in, by parachute?'

'Over the wall.'

'Over the wall?' She watched as he walked over and sat down cross-legged on the concrete. 'You were watching me then?'

'Only for a moment. I just got here.'

'Your timing was pretty good, Major.'

'Perfect.'

'Meaning you got to see my tits. Lucky break, huh?'

Schilling was not prepared for that and he wasn't sure how angry she was yet so he said nothing. Marta continued to glare at him, her hands still over her chest, watching him take a pull from her bottle of white wine.

'Well Major,' she said curtly, 'I suppose I should be . . . indignant or something. Outraged . . . angry . . . Order you out.' She paused. 'But—'

'But?'

'But here you are, so to hell with all that.' She sighed, shifting her hands so that each of them rested on opposite shoulders. 'Where is Eric?'

Schilling shrugged, then brought out a fresh pack of cigarettes and searched in the dim light for the tiny gold tape around the top of the pack. Finding it, he pulled it around all four sides, discarded the cellophane top in the ashtray, and then lifted the foil flaps, tapped out a cigarette and put it in his mouth; all without looking at her. It all took what seemed a very long time.

'I see,' she said finally. 'Major, if you don't talk to me then we cannot get on with . . . with what is happening here.'

'What is happening here,' he repeated, careful not to make it a question.

'Yes, what is happening here. Where's Eric?'

'He left me off, a bar, and went somewhere else.'

'And you took a taxi?'

Schilling nodded once.

'Why?'

'I wanted to see you. Alone.'

'Well, you're doing pretty good so far.'

'So far.'

'Now what?'

Schilling was not prepared, again, and he glanced back and forth between the gray-green eyes and his cigarette.

'I mean,' said Marta, 'this is the scene where Burt Lancaster visits Deborah Kerr alone in the house and makes his big move, isn't it?'

Artfully, he hoped, Schilling concealed his loss for words by watching her silently.

'As I recall,' she continued, 'Burt said "I want you" or something like that. To get the idea across.'

'I would like to have thought of something more original.'

Marta was holding a curious smile, her face damp from perspiration. Her arms remained crossed, hands on shoulders. Schilling found her pose amusing since much of each breast was exposed beneath each elbow.

'What do you want, Major?'

'You.'

'Well, now we know where we are. Are you drunk, Major?'

'Not at all.'

'I think you drink too much.'

'Not enough, I was thinking.'

'You should try this instead,' she suggested, revealing a damp joint in one hand, keeping it close to her shoulder. 'If I wasn't half ripped, I'd probably be more ... delicate about this. Did you really crawl over the wall, *lurk* in the shadows, just to get a look at me?' She smiled to herself. 'How quaint.'

Instead of answering he took another drink of wine from the bottle.

'Well—' she spoke more to herself than to him— 'I want to smoke some more of this.' She eased down into the water, holding the joint by two fingers above the surface. She reached for the matches, then stopped when the movement began to lift her breasts out of the water. Exasperated, she glanced over at him, shrugged and rose up suddenly, now standing waist deep, and then leaned over to scoop up the matches. Touching the flame to the roach she took a deep drag and then tamped it out carefully in the ashtray. Holding her breath, chest expanded, she lifted her chin and closed her eyes. Seconds passed before she breathed out. Still without looking at him, as if he had vanished and she were alone, she finished off a little wine in her glass, set the goblet down carefully on the concrete, took hold of the chrome handrail and came up the submerged steps, shining wet and giving off water vapor like steam, to stand above him, feet slightly apart, about a yard away, facing him.

Still seated cross-legged, Schilling looked up. Once again subordinate, he thought. His eyes, now at the same level as the shadowed texture where her slightly-parted thighs joined, watched scores of fragile bubbles vanish as they rode the rivulets of water that streamed over and around her breasts and down across the single dimple of her flat brown stomach, snaking quickly, racing around and down her thighs and legs. Great God, he breathed silently to himself, such power simple flesh could have.

'Is this what you crawled over the wall for, Major?'

'Close enough.' His heart was working.

She reached for the white towel over the chair and began drying her arms, still watching him.

'I'm not doing this to tease you.' Her voice had become less aloof, even apologetic. 'I am flattered by your . . . interest in me. It has not escaped my notice, as you may have thought.'

She continued to dry herself above him, now drawing the towel around her shoulder blades and working it down her back. 'It's just that I don't know what to . . . do with it. I find you attractive as well. I don't expect that has escaped your notice either. I mean, things are crazy around here, don't you see? I've got a crazy husband and a crazy brother and a house full of crazy pilots.'

She finished drying her legs and she draped the towel back over the chair and pulled on a gray sweatshirt. A large picture of Mickey Mouse covered the front of the baggy garment. She yanked up both sleeves to the elbows, still naked from the waist down, still talking. 'I can't have you and Eric at each other's throats . . . and that's what's going to happen. That's all I need. I just don't want to deal with that.'

Schilling watched her pull on a pair of tattered denim cut-offs.

'When you came back here,' she said, zipping up the fly, 'what did you expect me to do?'

Schilling shrugged.

'Were you so sure Eric wouldn't come back?'

'Yes.'

'Where did he leave you?'

'A place called the Buena Vista.'

'Oh yes, a good place for lucky shots. You should have stayed.'

'I don't think so.'

'Where did he go then?'

'I don't know. It was not my concern.'

'Perhaps you would show me the number he gave you?'

'Perhaps not.'

'Yes.' She sighed. 'I guess it wouldn't be the thing to do. Loyalty. Just a little secret between the boys.'

'I honestly don't know where he went.'

'Well, where would you guess, Major? Wouldn't you guess he was *shtupping* some little *Schatzi*? A little extra action, yes?'

'I don't know. It is not my concern.'

'Bullshit. You knew he had something lined up and it would be perfectly safe to come back here.'

Schilling remained silent. The pulsing of his heart had returned to normal. Now he grew uncomfortable, drawn into the web of some hidden marital feud as a witness whose testimony might well be used as a minor weapon in yet another skirmish in the war that never ended. He marveled at the transformation in Marta's voice, from silk to steel in six or so sentences. He began to understand what it was that Eric couldn't understand. There was a fury rising beneath the surface of this woman.

'You and I are not going to get any closer, Major,' she said. 'No action with Frau Felbeck-Malzahn tonight. I'm sorry to disappoint you.'

'This may be close enough,' he said evenly. 'I don't think I'm enjoying this any more.'

She smiled unexpectedly and then gestured to the chair beside her own. 'Come up here, Major. Just sit in this chair, will you? And talk to me for a while and then get the hell out.' Once again her voice had softened. 'One strip-tease is all I can handle tonight,' she added, lighting up the joint again.

Schilling got to his feet and took the chair next to her. It was quiet for a short while as they stared at the glowing blue pool at their feet, much, Schilling thought, like a married couple sitting on their porch to watch the sun go down.

'I shouldn't have fooled around with that stocking the other day. I'm sorry,' she said with what seemed to him genuine regret. 'Did you tie the scarf to your airplane?'

'No. It was not necessary.'

'Where is it then?'

'In my pocket. My uniform.'

'Does it smell like me?'

'Don't know.'

'Are you going to carry it . . . into battle? Or whatever it is you're going to do tomorrow morning?'

'Don't know.'

'Did you carry someone's scarf in the war?'

'Yes.'

'What was her name?'

'Aneka.'

'Did you love her?'

Schilling did not answer.

After a moment Marta leaned her head back on the chair. 'Please don't fool with me, Major. I can't handle it.'

'I'll try not to.' Screw this, he thought.

'If you want to do something for me, don't let anything happen to Eric. Or my brother. I'm afraid. What is it that you are going to do tomorrow morning?'

'Flying to an airshow.'

'What will you do there?'

'Show off. That's what airshows are.'

'I'm sure you'll be a big hit.'

'I suspect you're right about that.'

She turned her head to look at him, then stood up.

'Excuse me, please. I'll be right back. Can I get you something?'

'A beer.'

When she returned he was standing by the pool.

'I called a taxi.' She was holding the beer out to him. 'If you hurry back to the Buena Vista you'll probably still get laid.'

'One strip-tease a night is all I can handle, too,' he said without humor, lifting the tab from the icy wet can. She was standing close.

'I'm sure you could handle more—' her voice came even softer than before— 'but not with cold hands.'

He looked at her. Those gray-green eyes. He fixed on them with his own as they came up to him. He put his mouth over hers, holding the beer can away. Her one hand slid up over his

128

shoulder and around his neck, fingers touching his ear and then weaving into his hair.

When they drew apart he said, 'Cancel the taxi.'

'Not a chance,' she whispered.

He looked down.

'No cold hand, OK? Just the warm one.'

He moved his hand up under the baggy sweatshirt along the ripple of her ribcage and spread his fingers wide and put his mouth back to hers. After several minutes she drew back rather suddenly, pushing at his chest with her fingertips.

'Wait outside now, please? And be careful tomorrow. I'm coming out to the field in the morning to see you all off. And to take some pictures; orders from the Commanding Officer. Goodnight, Major,' she said, stepping back and folding her arms over Mickey Mouse.

BOOK II

ATTACK

CHAPTER NINE

At 0505 hours stars faded, dissolved. Cloudless, the sky lightened from black to blue-violet to slate and then lavender. Dewless and desolate in the growing light, the desert took form in the soundlessness of a vacuum, the vista of an empty planet where any sound however slight might carry forever in the dry crystal air. No life stirred yet among the wiry skeletal bushes that dotted the sweeps of pink sand, or among the drifts of shattered rocks stretching away to hazy mesas silhouetted at the coral-tinted horizon. No breath of breeze touched the wind sock above the hangars.

At 0555 hours there were the sounds of footsteps shuffling in the sand, then the metallic creak of machines moving, being pushed. Hushed whispers. Then the precise lidded click of a camera shutter; once, twice. More muted words. Boot soles scraping on metal skin.

At 0615 hours, suddenly, there came a metallic whirring, a quick whining and tearing cough from the intricate steel throat of a 12-cylinder inverted-V Daimler-Benz 605A aircraft engine. In lightning sequence all twelve cylinders detonated in violent ripping blasts. Blue flame belched out like dragon's breath from each of the twelve exhaust ports in two banks of six, low and behind the 109's nose, followed by sooty clouds of soft carbon. A great crack of backfire lashed out over the engine's fury and the black three-bladed propeller stirred, turned, and spun clockwise whirring into a shadowed circle that sliced into the dawn air and then seemed to reverse direction as the engine gathered power.

Another engine whined, coughed, caught. Now twenty-four

cylinders fired in perfect ear-splitting time. Then another engine, and another, until all eight were joined; ninety-six fuel-injected cylinders howling in roaring unison, building in layers of shattering sound that overwhelmed the dawn, rolled like waves of thunder across the sand, and sent small creatures scrabbling out of shelter among vibrating rock.

Pilots settled in the seats, fastened the hardware of their belts, adjusted headsets, caps and sunglasses, tightened thin black gloves tautly over and between each finger, sorted maps and papers and slipped those selected into the plastic window map pockets on their right thighs. They studied the instrument faces on their panels, scanning from top left to bottom right, watching red needles quiver and shift: coolant temperature . . . induction temperature . . . oil pressure . . . oil temperature . . . manifold pressure . . . fuel pressure.

Gloved fingers sought out toggle switches in sequence, lifted fuel mixture knobs, pushed at throttle handles, adjusted airscrew pitch controls. Looking out of open canopies, eyes scanning control surfaces, they tested flaps, slats, ailerons, rudders, elevators; each part jerking, lifting, moving spasmodically, as if awakening.

When the temperatures and pressures were correct, the pilots applied more throttle and adjusted fuel mix and pitch, feeding the engines and pushing them up another octave. The aircraft quivered on their spindly struts under contained power, pulling as if on invisible leashes. First one then another lurched forward hesitantly, noses pointed skyward as if testing the thin air, whirling props scything in dark circles, exhaust ports breathing blue fire as the engines were changed in pitch, howling higher. The eight 109s jerked and rolled into a ragged line.

Hands clamped over pained ears, Marta was awe-struck by the thundering exodus of the lumbering craft. In their dull mottled warpaint they loomed larger and far more menacing than they had been singly. Now they were truly evil, monstrous prehistoric mechanical predators, their tails and wings flexing lifelike, as if resurrected from desert pits. Even their colors were dull and reptilian, pale blue of the sky, tan-pink of the sanded wastes, mottled russet of sun-baked rock. And all breathing blue fire and translucent soot. A chill of fear rippled through her. They were death machines.

'*Ruuudiiii*,' she screamed, her voice lost even to her own ears in the maelstrom of dust and rumbling engines. '*There is nothing beautiful about them!*'

All eight engines climbed another octave, deafening. The 109s had jockeyed into position now, wingtip to wingtip, and she could see down the line of them, her brother closest, Schilling next, and she was glad, fleetingly, that they were side by side. In this nearly perfect alignment the pilots of 76 Staffel seemed oblivious to all but their aircraft and each other, removed from Marta, removed from the past and the future, together now in full strength for the first time.

Wind blasted the front of Marta's body, pressing her damp blouse to her chest, yanking her windbreaker back, abrasive against her bare thighs and shins, whipping her tangled hair, stinging her eyes. Shielding her face, protecting her camera, she cowered alone in the storm of propwash. Then the storm moved away, following the planes as they turned, rolling forward, and began to taxi out to the runway.

Now she saw Eric standing out by the strip in a haze of blowing sand dust. His dark form startled her. He seemed taller and thinner, even sinister, his eyes covered by goggles, his arms raised outward Christ-like, gloved hands poised as if he were conducting this terrifying chorus. *Dear God, are they mad? Could it be, all of them? Eric too?* He raised one arm and pointed one gloved finger skyward. From each of the open cockpits she saw arms raised, black gloved fingers pointed skyward. The engines climbed another octave. Eric lowered his arm and all the pilots did the same. Every plane quivered now, tails flexing, straining to be let loose. Keeping one hand raised palm up, Eric swept the other forward and the first 109 – Rudi's – lunged ahead. Marta covered her ears again. The ground trembled. Eric signalled the second 109 away; Schilling rolled forward, following Rudi as he powered down the strip. Again Eric's hand swept forward, releasing Osterhoudt next. And again and again until the last of the eight – Theo – jounced howling down the strip and rose into the dawn sky, shrinking with the others into tiny cross-like shapes, their great thunder fading. In the distance a final beam of sunlight bounced a flash of glare off a canopy. Then they were gone.

Eric still stood by the runway a hundred feet away, his back to her. The silence settled, so intense that for a moment Marta thought she had gone deaf. She cleared her throat and spat. Eric stood as if transfixed, gloved hands hanging at his sides. She walked out to him and came to his side but still he did not move. She touched his shoulder. He turned, eyes distant behind the dark-rimmed goggles, and looked at her as if she were not there. Then he turned and started off toward the hangars, pushing the goggles up over his forehead. She had to take longer steps to keep up with him and in the hot silence their footsteps were the only sound.

Impatient as she was, she sensed the familiar self-isolation that came with his occasional dark moods. This time his indifference seemed charged with a kind of tense energy. She glanced over at him with compassionate curiosity, as if he might give her a signal, a sign, for the opportunity to reach out and connect, but he seemed impervious. And there was a taste of fear in her mouth, dry and lifeless as blown sand, that robbed her patience and overcame compassion.

'Where are they going?' she asked finally. She expected no answer and got none.

'What are they going to do?' she tried again. And again no answer.

They had reached the dim cavern of the first hangar, stepping from fresh morning light into shadow. She pulled off her sunglasses. Once her eyes adjusted, she searched out a clean rag to clean the camera. She had taken only two shots of the Staffel but the image through the view-finder remained hauntingly imprinted in her memory, as sharp as if she were still seeing it. Hastily assembled without ceremony, nervous and moody, the nine men clustered next to one of the airplanes, the new orange scarves bright at their throats, their tan flying suits blending with the flat paint, their expressions remote. Only Theo and Beissemann seemed pleased, almost smiling, while Franz alone looked peaceful. She especially recalled Schilling's placid stare and petulant lip, as solemn as Kesler's intensity behind those weird mirrored sunglasses. She could not recall – though she tried – the expressions of either Rendel or Weinert. Or of Eric. Or of Rudi.

But she did recall realizing, in the mere seconds it took to frame the Staffel and click off two shots, that four of these nine men had seen her without clothes.

She watched Eric pushing a peculiar little machine-thing on fat doughnut wheels, with a black cord looped over the handle.

The heat was coming into the hangar now and she felt gritty and coated. Her back tickled with sweat under her blouse. She glanced at her watch. It did not seem possible that only ten minutes ago she had watched Rudi and the others lifting off. Now in the heavy heated silence it was as if she and Eric had been abandoned. She walked over to where he was standing at a workbench arranging some tools.

'When will they be back?' she asked.

Eric looked at his watch. 'Three, three-and-a-half hours.'

Marta pulled her camera strap over her head and placed it on the workbench and then took off her nylon windbreaker. 'Those marks on the tails, those bars; what are they for?'

'Kill markings,' he answered without looking at her.

'Kill markings?'

'Each bar means the pilot destroyed one enemy airplane.'

'Each bar means one man killed, then?'

'Not necessarily. Just one aircraft destroyed.'

'I see. Like badges. Or stripes on a sleeve. Was it just our side that did that, painted on kill markings?'

Eric looked over at her and grinned slyly. 'Which side do you mean?'

'Our side,' she said stoutly. 'The German side.'

'No.' He grinned again. 'Our side did it, too. All fighter pilots do it. Since the First World War. And the Second and in Korea and Nam and they do it today.'

'I see. And was a bomber worth just one mark?'

'One plane, one bar,' he answered patiently.

'How many men in a bomber?'

'Depends. The B-17 had ten or twelve, I think.'

'So one bar could mean ten men killed?'

'Or ten bars could mean ten planes destroyed and no men killed.' Eric looked over at her again. 'Franz told me he had a friend, another pilot, who was shot down twelve times, which meant he was responsible for twelve kill markings on British and American planes.' He continued to watch her. 'Why are you so obsessed with this . . . killing stuff?'

'I could have sworn it was the other way around.'

'You're getting so fucking uptight. Why is that?'

'I'm frightened.'

'Of what?'

'Of this.' She waved her hand to take in the dim hangar, the

137

workbenches, the drums and cartons and crates.

Eric turned back to the workbench. He seemed not to have heard her. His forehead was perspiring and his shirt was dark with sweat.

'Doesn't it frighten you?' she asked.

'No.'

'Turns you on, yes?'

Eric looked up again, his eyes bright. 'Didn't you like it really? All that noise. All that power. It takes a lot of balls to do what they're doing.'

'That's everything, balls, isn't it?'

'Come on, didn't you like it?'

Marta was confused. The intensity of his questions, the expression on his face was doing something new and fearful to her. It made her breathe a little harder. Too late she realized that her silence was an answer in itself.

'Didn't you?' Eric pressed.

'It frightens me.'

'But isn't that what you liked? All that thunder and power. You liked it. Say it.'

'It's insane. Those are war planes!'

'It's real, Marta. Real.'

'What kind of guns are they?'

'Machine guns. Cannon.'

'Machine guns. Cannon,' she repeated. 'How many?'

'Two machine guns, one cannon each plane.'

'Are they loaded?'

'They're loaded.'

'How many bullets in each plane?'

'Two thousand machine gun. Sixty cannon rounds.'

'Two thousand times eight,' she whispered ... 'sixteen thousand, plus sixty times eight ... four hundred eighty. Sixteen thousand four hundred and eighty.' She looked at him. 'Show me.'

'Show you what?'

'Show me the bullets.'

Their eyes joined. Eric seemed to be deciding whether or not he was going to grant her some special privilege. 'Over there.' He pointed to the corner of the hangar. 'Under those plastic sheets.'

Marta went over to the stacks of small wooden crates and

pulled back the translucent plastic cover. Eric had followed her and now he was close behind her as she stared at several opened boxes. She reached into one of them and held up a heavy blunt-nosed metal cylinder about six inches long. 'What is this?'

'Cannon shell, twenty millimeter. And for crissake don't drop it. Put it down.'

She did, carefully, then reached into another box. 'And these?'

'Machine gun, seven-point-nine millimeter. Don't drop those either.'

She held a fistful, perhaps six. They were oddly greasy and much heavier than she had expected, with sharp brass-colored pointed tips, and they were slightly slimmer, though longer, than a lipstick tube. They felt peculiar and alien. She had never touched a bullet before. 'What do you do with them? How do you put them in a gun?'

'First you load them in belts,' he explained, watching her, 'and then the belts go in canisters, containers, in the plane. And then the belts feed into the guns.'

'I see.'

'Like this,' Eric said, reaching down into another box and pulling out a loaded machine gun belt. The movement startled her. The belt of bullets crawled up in his gloved hands like a metallic serpent, clicking ominously as it uncoiled, growing longer as it was pulled out. Marta took a step backward, watching the belt draped from the wooden box to Eric's hands, swaying of its own weight. She placed the bullets in the crate and wiped her hands on her denim cut-offs.

'Put that . . . thing back in the box, will you please?'

'What's the matter; don't you like it? Official genuine Luftwaffe ammunition, like Rudi and your Major Schilling and all the others used in the war . . . On your side,' he added, grinning.

'My side my ass.' She stared at him. The belt shifted in his hands, clicking again. 'What makes you all crazy to shoot things? This macho-shoot-bang-kill stuff. Where does it come from? There's a connection somewhere, I know there is, between screwing around with guns and screwing something else.'

'May be.'

'It turns you on more than this, doesn't it?' She raised her hand to her breast and lifted it once. 'Not so exciting anymore, not with all the guns to play with. Not so exciting as somebody else either, yes?'

Eric moved very quickly. The belt of bullets seemed to leap from his hand, one end swinging clicking around her, and he easily caught the loose end with his free hand. Marta jerked backward but was caught, encircled. The bullets were heavy around her waist and the pointed tips pressed into the sweating flesh of her lower back when she tried to pull away. She pushed against his chest.

'I've got sort of a theory,' Eric said close to her face, breathing the words. He drew the belt a little tighter, somehow got one gloved hand free, and ripped her blouse apart down the front. One white button popped up high over his shoulder. With two quick movements he pulled the fabric down over her shoulders.

'Oh my! Is this rape, Mr Macho?' she snapped, wincing as the bullet tips bit into her back.

'I've got sort of a theory,' he said again, 'and it's not about rape.'

She swung on him, but she was too close to connect, able to move only so far with her blouse binding both arms at the elbows. Instead, her wrist smacked the side of his face. Her movements caused the bullets to bite again but she clenched her teeth and did not cry out. Eric's rough gloved paw seemed so large. Four leather claws slipped down her sweat-slicked chest, one hooked over the center clasp of her bra. She froze, breathing heavily, her heart beating its way up her throat.

'Don't,' she warned, not yet afraid. 'The bullets ... are hurting me.'

'You like the bullets,' he whispered.

'Wrong.'

'And you love the planes and you love the guns.'

'Wrong. *You* love it.'

'Yeah, I do.' He smiled. 'Each cannon is so long it goes clear through the engine. And the breech goes into the cockpit, almost between the pilot's legs. Did you know that?'

'Hot stuff,' she said squirming.

'And the shells. Nice shape, don't you think?'

Silently she glared at him, furious that she couldn't control her breathing.

'One of those shells would fit into you very nicely.' His gloved finger tugged a little at the clasp. 'They have a lubricating preservative, but if you were wet enough . . . How would you like that?'

'How would I like it, Mr Macho?' Now she was a little afraid, but she knew it was possible not to show it.

'I like the bullets. I like the guns. I like the way they're put together and they way they work and the weight of them and the smell of them and the power of them . . . you're right. Don't you think I could do what they're doing, what your Major Schilling is doing? Is that what turns you on?'

'Not my Major Schilling.'

'I understand.' He spoke soothingly. 'I understand about Schilling, because he climbs into that airplane and because he did it so many times before and because he killed other men. That turns you on, huh? That's what guns are all about, see? What war is all about. The ultimate contest. Winners live, losers die. The ultimate reality. I know you don't want it to be that way and I don't want it to be that way, but that's the way it is. That's the way men are made and that's the way women are made. Hard and soft. Strong and weak. We are the warriors, with the guns.'

'That's bullshit, too,' she said, breathing in sharply.

'No, it's just the way things . . . are.'

'Stop it.'

'You wet, Marta?' He pulled the belt a little tighter.

She bared her teeth.

'It's all right if you are,' he continued. 'That's what I'm saying. That's the way it is. Am I right?'

'Let me go.'

'You getting it on with Schilling yet?'

'What do you care?'

Eric drew the belt closer and she arched her back to avoid the pain. Then he yanked his hand down and she felt the bra come apart at the center clasp and one shoulder strap all at once.

'Are you?' He was lifting the remaining strap over her shoulder. With her back arched, her breasts were lifted higher, exposed, cooled by the air. For a moment she was proud of them.

'*Are you?*'

'Eat your heart out,' she said, trying to control her breathing. 'How do you like it the other way around for a change?'

'Let's see if you're wet, Marta.'

'Don't touch me, you prick.' Desperate now, she thought of crying. For a second Eric unexpectedly loosened the belt and – before she could react – he pulled it higher so that it bound her ribcage, placing the spiked row of bullet tips just under both breasts and under both shoulder blades.

'Damn you,' she moaned, trapped tight now.

'I just want to see if I'm right.'

His gloved hand was clutching the belt where it crossed at her side. His other glove skimmed over damp skin, belly to hip bone. Three rough fingers crawled the hollow of her hip and hooked over the top of her denim cut-offs.

'Don't. Don't. Don't.' Her words strained through clenched teeth.

'Take them off. Or I tear them off.'

She stared at him, lips pursed, hoping her eyes revealed nothing. I'll call your bluff, lover, she thought; Godzilla couldn't tear off Levi shorts. Not with one hand.

'It's your choice.' He tightened his grip.

'Go ahead,' she breathed, her eyes half closed.

He moved his hand. She hit him so hard across the cheek that tiny drops of sweat flew off his face. She heard her blouse tear apart at the back. She snapped up one knee but to her surprise Eric was quicker. By reflex he straight-armed her with the hand holding the belt, keeping his other hand clamped over her cut-offs, and propelled her nearly off her feet backwards crashing into the wooden crates. The motion of Eric's arms pulled more of the belt out of the box and it dragged across the floor – twisting, clicking – from the fist that held her. The sound made her flesh crawl.

Unable to arch her back to escape the wicked picket fence beneath both breasts, she had no choice but to protect them with her hands. As if nailed against a wall by Eric's piston fists, she was helpless. Like a butterfly pinned.

'Now.' Eric's voice was hard, his cheeks red. 'Take them off.' A bright bead of scarlet hung at the corner of his mouth.

Her eyes seemed dry and heavy-lidded and she struggled to keep them open. She knew then she was lost. There was nothing more she could do. She lifted her breasts and Eric let out the belt enough and she let her hands fall away and her eyes drift closed. She reached down, pushed away the gloved fist, and unfastened and unzipped. The cut-offs brushed down her legs.

'I won't hurt you,' he whispered. 'I would never hurt you.'

'I don't want anything . . . to happen,' she said helplessly, eyes still closed.

His hand moving, rough gloved fingers back in the hip hollow, hooking into the nylon waistband and tugging the silk-like fabric down.

'I don't want anyone else to die,' she said. 'So many died,' now in a whisper, as if she was repeating something she had read. 'They're all . . . gone.' She began to feel weak. Her knees trembled as Eric worked the elastic lower and let it drop away. There was an extraordinary cooling sensation.

'Step out,' Eric ordered.

She did, keeping her eyes shut. To keep her balance she grasped the shoulders of his damp shirt, feeling child-like as she lifted one leg and then the other free. Her eyes snapped open, blinking. Eric. She could smell him, feel him. He was wonderful, strong and whole and alive. He raised his free hand then and clamped white teeth over the fingertips of the soiled glove and pulled his hand free and let the glove fall from his mouth.

'Don't die!' she cried out, grabbing in panic at his shirt with one hand, the other fist in his hair, shaking him nearly off balance. Free of the glove his fingers traced over her collarbone, skating on the film of sweat down over one nipple and over the web of bullets and over her belly and lightly across her bush and then under.

She clutched at him, eyes wide and fixed, and her mouth opened with a faint intake of breath. His hand came away and slid back up over her body.

'You see . . . I am right,' he said, pushing the fingers into her mouth.

'Jeeee*sus!*' exclaimed one of the Mustang pilots over the R/T at the moment 76 Staffel flashed across high in front of Lowen's flight, in pairs, from right to left in a half-roll so that every Mustang pilot clearly saw all eight 109s, their tan-brown mottled paint and bold black crosses and gleaming canopies. Images gone in a blink.

'Gawd!' said another Mustang pilot as the five P-51s lifted and bucked in 76 Staffel's turbulent wake.

'Beeee*autiful!*' said a third Mustang pilot. 'Roger, did you *see* those sumbitches? Messerschmitts, they looked like.'

'This is Leader,' Lowen cut in sharply. '*Can it*!' He spoke reflexively, seconds later than the three pilots, seconds during which he had been paralyzed by fright, a heart-stopping fright that jerked him up in his seat.

The passing of the 109s had a devastating effect on Lowen. The eight craft had come appallingly close and were traveling appallingly fast and were inordinately precise in attack formation. There was the split-second reaction to impending collision, replaced a split-second later by rage at the aggressiveness of so terribly close a pass, replaced a split-second later by the shock of recognition, a vision of doom that resurrected long-dormant nightmares and pierced him through. He felt as if his heart might fail him. Nothing he could recall had ever frightened him so.

For a moment the warning *Break right*! had leaped up his throat but the 109s were gone. He had stopped the chatter of his own pilots instinctively, to take control, and now what he needed to control was his own disbelief. He followed the 109s at nine o'clock, watching them curve around, perfectly aligned, in a turn that would bring them behind his flight. In the classic attack maneuver.

'Hey Leader,' called one of his pilots. 'They want to play.'

'Knock it off.' Lowen barked. 'Tighten up on me now and stay straight and level!'

Lowen glanced around at the other four P-51s. Easy now, he thought. He watched the 109s a mile off, still banked in the turn. They were all Messerschmitt 109s, no question. Remarkable, they looked brand-new.

Lowen's panic was dissolving into embarrassment. He hoped his terror had not been transmitted over the R/T and he was satisfied that his order to stay tight and steady was correct. Only one other pilot, Fitzgerald, would know the cold fear of being jumped by enemy fighters, taken completely by surprise. Now Lowen became furious at being surprised, furious at the outrageous risk taken by the 109s in coming so close. Crazy bastards. He looked back, not without admiration for the perfect attack positions taken up by the Messerschmitts now leveled off and coming right up their tails. Godamighty.

Steady now, he thought. His heart still raced.

'This is Rebel Leader, to, ah, Messerschmitt flight. Do you

read?' Lowen kept his voice as calm and lazy as he could, having decided that, of course, the 109s were making for Chino. He also decided not to get indignant about being frightened. The 109 pilots could be forgiven for being a bit frisky, the bastards, in such beautifully restored aircraft. He could see the lead pair closing in his mirror. With a slight chill he recognized the blunt snouts, scoop mouth below, and twin oil coolers under each wing.

'This is Rebel Leader to Messerschmitt flight,' he repeated into the R/T. 'Do you read? Over.'

'We read you, Colonel,' came a clear voice over the headset – in perfect English, Lowen noted with relief. 'This is 76 Staffel Leader.'

'Good morning, Seven-six,' Lowen said casually. You rat bastard, he thought. 'Beautiful ships you boys have. Absolutely beautiful. Are you headed for Chino?'

'Affirmative, Colonel,' came the reply.

Lowen looked back. All eight 109s were spread out behind his flight in four pairs at about 200 feet. 'You gave us quite a wake-up, Seven-six.'

'Watch for the Hun in the sun; isn't that what they told you, Colonel?' replied the 109 leader in a voice curiously familiar, a voice that touched another needle of panic somewhere down deep with 'isn't that what they told you.' Lowen was not yet calmed. To his knowledge there were but three 109s – one of which was in the CAF hangar – in flying condition in the United States. Eight of them, anywhere, he would have heard about. He could only tie them, with tenuous logic, to the airshow.

'Where are you from, Seven-six?' Lowen asked.

'Germany, Colonel Lowen,' came the reply. 'We are from Germany.'

Partly as a release from tension, he was tempted to laugh. The pilot had called him by name; a new question. Lowen found himself with no answer at all. Now he feared that something had gone haywire in his mind something had short-circuited and shifted him into some weird psychological time warp. He checked his oxygen apparatus, breathed deeply. *Easy now, those bastards are just screwing with you. Relax.* As some confirmation of reality, he scanned his instrument panel then glanced at his watch – 0755 hours – and then looked carefully at the reality of the other four P-51s in tight and steady echelon to starboard, clear and shining. He saw Anderson looking at him. Then he turned in his seat to confirm the eight Messerschmitts; yes, they were no mirage, a hundred yards behind. He could see the nose-cannon ports and the cowling troughs for the machine guns. They were all G Models.

'Ahh . . . Seven-six, you know my name,' Lowen called. 'Have we met?'

'A long time ago, Colonel,' came the response. 'April forty-four, an airfield in Germany. Do you read?'

Lowen paused, confused, thinking. 'Affirmative, Seven-six.'

'There were three of us then,' said the 109 pilot, 'on approach, our wheels down. We are pleased to see you again, Colonel. Do you read?'

'Loud and clear, Seven-six.' *Steady now*, he thought. 'Seven-six, my sense of humor is not working too good today. Now you boys back off. How about it?'

'Do you remember Germany, Colonel?' came the response.

'I remember,' replied Lowen. 'Now get off my tail, Seven-six. This is no—' Something struck his plane, a quick hail of stone-like rattles. The Mustang twitched and the vibrations pulsed up through his seat and up through his hand on the stick. Tiny red streaks like fireflies whizzed past his canopy and a pattern of dark spots zipped across the aluminum surface of his port wing. Chips of glinting metal flew up and away.

'Leader to Rebels,' he called. 'Hold formation.' He stared at the dozen or so torn holes in his wing. Bastards are really *armed*. Could this be?

'Now Colonel,' the voice came calmly in Lowen's ear. 'You see we are armed.'

'We are not armed,' Lowen said. 'Repeat, not armed.'

'I realize that, Colonel. Now you will be sure to keep your flight in formation. We are all prepared to fire if you move out of line. Advise your pilots, Colonel. Now.'

'Leader to Rebels,' Lowen called. 'Now listen up. Those holes in my wing are real. I don't know what's going on, but we will hold formation. No one breaks, no one talks, unless necessary. I want each of you to acknowledge. Anderson, acknowledge.'

'Anderson, Leader. I read you.'

'Can you see my damage?'

'Sir?'

'Damage. Can you see where I've been hit?'

'Uh, yes sir. Under-surface port wing, light damage . . . flaps . . . holes across landing gear . . . several in belly scoop. Over.'

'Okay,' Lowen said. 'Gardner, acknowledge.'

'Gardner here, Leader.'

'Meredith, acknowledge.'

'Meredith here, Colonel.'

'Fitzgerald, acknowledge.' Lowen looked back and down at the only other combat veteran. He desperately wanted to talk with Fitz, decided to try it. Screw the Krauts. Or whoever the hell they were.

'Fitzgerald here, Roger. You okay?'

'So far,' Lowen responded, relieved just to hear Fitzgerald's level voice. 'Fitz, what do you think we have here?'

After a pause the answer came back, 'Twilight Zone.'

'This is Seven-six, Colonel. Acknowledge.'

'Rebel Leader here, Seven-six.'

'Colonel, you will reduce airspeed to one-eight-zero and open up your formation. Do it now. Over.'

'Open up, Rebels,' Lowen ordered. 'Back off to one-eight-zero.'

'Thank you, Colonel. I estimate our time to Chino at about forty-five minutes. Do you agree?'

'I'd have to recalculate at one-eight-zero,' Lowen answered, 'but that's close enough.'

'You navigate, Colonel, and we'll follow. You can relax a while. And think about Germany. Transmit only when necessary.'

With relief Lowen noticed that the 109s had backed off considerably, above and behind his flight. He first studied each single instrument face closely, looking for signs of trouble. All was in order. He looked at his watch 0818 hours — then again at each of his P-51s stacked in wide echelon to his right.

Think about Germany? Godamighty. Lowen loosened his flight suit at the collar. His mouth was dry and he was sweating a lot. The sun had really heated up the cockpit under the plexiglass canopy. He drew out his red thermos and took a long drink of orange juice; the juice and the red plastic cylinder were reality, he thought, recalling Jean filling it the night before.

Then he remembered the camera plane out of Phoenix. Shame they missed us, he thought. What a picture this would make. With a handkerchief he wiped his forehead and eyebrows, adjusted his sunglasses. So many questions. Who would know about those three Me-109s in Germany? Who would arm a 109 and shoot holes in his damned wing?

'Seven-six Staffel Leader, this is Rebel Leader.'

'Go ahead, Colonel.'

'We need to vary our speed now and then to keep from loading up.'

'Do what is necessary, Colonel. I will leave it to you. Over.'

Slightly below, some hundred feet from Rudi's starboard side, Schilling was being highly entertained by the little drama around him, particularly by Rudi's audacity and control. It was Kesler who had spotted the five silver specks just west of Phoenix at 0725 hours, but Rudi who had decided to follow them for a while before setting up the attack pass. Schilling grinned again. Lowen must have shit himself when Rudi opened up on him. In fact it had startled Schilling not a little, the tracers suddenly spewing out only sixty-odd feet away, the spent shells dropping away like tiny bombs under Rudi's blue belly. Schilling was fascinated by the P-51s so close and below, by their polished aluminum surfaces, bright blood scarlet and butter yellow trim paint, great white stars on blue circles, sleek symmetry and blade-like wings and elevators. So clean and shining bold, deadly as a chrome Magnum. He had faced P-51s only twice in combat and they had savaged his flight. Formidable bastards. Lowen must be crawling out of his skin by now. He wished he could raise Major Six on the R/T for a couple of laughs; Bison was probably hysterical.

Schilling shifted in the seat, loosening the collar of his flying suit. It was hot now in the cramped cockpit. He scanned his dials automatically and longed for a cigarette.

His hand touched the soft bulge of the scarf in his zippered chest pocket. Visions of Marta came then. Rising shining wet and naked from the bubbling green-lit water. That eternally lovely S-curve of her breasts hanging as she reached, the splendid swaying of them together as she toweled her back, watching him, and then pulled Mickey Mouse down to hide them. In his hand there was still the sensation of cupping that soft loose weight and he imagined he could still taste the herbal smoky flavour of marijuana and the pale grape of the Riesling in her mouth. And how strange her kiss was: intimate yet removed, willing yet reluctant.

At 0853 hours and 10,000 feet, the thirteen warbirds crossed the state line into California.

CHAPTER TEN

Webb was having a fine time. One of the first in the gate, he had shot a complete roll of 35mm slide film in the first forty minutes. The light was good and he wanted to get all the static shots before the sun burned off the haze and before the crowd got too heavy. He now had photos of the Planes of Fame Museum fighters; the slender graceful Spitfire, the ponderous B-17 in fresh olive paint, the sleek mottled blue-green Me-262 jet, the immaculately restored P-51B in sand and green with British markings and, especially, the Museum's rare Me-109G with black-and-white spiral-painted nose spinner. By standing close to the 109 he could peer into the narrow dusty cockpit. Untouched by restoration, its Galland canopy secured by padlock, the cockpit was a fascinating remnant of history. He could see the black plywood instrument panel, dials frozen by time, wiring haphazardly taped, even hand-painted German gothic lettering by some of the instrument faces. The stick, tarnished dark, was topped by a red gun button with a metal flip-shield. Unpadded, the narrow metal seat seemed too small for any pilot. He imagined for a moment this very aircraft rolling out across the fields of France to launch a counterattack against the waves of B-17s bound for Berlin. Doubtless the pilot's fingerprints still remained somewhere inside.

He crouched under the wing of the 109 in the shade to reload his Minolta, carefully inserting the film and aligning the sprocket teeth. From his shoulder bag he took a lens tissue to the 50mm lens and then the viewfinder. Inside the bag was a new 50/300mm zoom lens, a special purchase for the flying shots. Then he smoothed suntan gel over his face and arms.

After adjusting his blue cap, he stood up and went in search of a B-25 for the Colonel.

Spectators streamed around him as he moved among the aircraft on display. A long line had already formed at the beer tent and the aroma of sizzling hamburgers blended with the petroleum smells of oil and fuel and hot blacktop. Dozens of vendor booths offered T-shirts, airplane posters, books, patches, and sun hats. He made a mental note to return to the book vendor later in the day. Helicopters clattered overhead carrying spectators up for a bird's-eye view and the P/A system played a rousing march from *Victory At Sea*.

He soon found a B-25, two in fact, parked side by side. By the nose wheel of the first B-25 sat the owner-pilot, a lanky man in rumpled jeans, WWII officer's cap, and leather flight jacket. Reflective aviator glasses covered his eyes but his head moved slowly left to right, tracking a leggy teenager in short-shorts passing by. Webb walked around the B-25, stooping under the wing and touching the warm aluminum skin. The bomb bay doors were open and he ducked under the fuselage and stood up in the dim rectangular cavern, barely five feet across. The bomb racks were gone and the metal-ribbed interior was painted flat zinc-chromate green. The bay took up the entire midsection of fuselage, leaving no passageway from front to back.

By tapping the fuselage wall he noted that between the ribs, identical to a balsa model plane, there was nothing but aluminum skin. He shook his head. How many thousands of men had gone to battle with nothing but this flimsy metal membrane between them and death?

Returning to the front of the bomber, he looked through the plexiglass 'greenhouse' at the tiny tin seat for the nose gunner, and at the back of the instrument panel mazed with wires. So narrow, so spartan. How could three, four men be jammed so tight and still fly hours of combat? He pictured a youthful Butler huddled in the nose of this twin-engined relic, dodging flak over the Mediterranean like Art Garfunkel and crew in the movie *Catch-22*.

Webb circled the B-25, took a dozen photos. Now the CO had his shots; assignment completed. He nodded again to the mirror-eyed pilot slouched in the aluminum lawn chair and then headed toward the aircraft parked out near the strip.

Webb's watch read 0835 hours and already there were picnics

being spread. He could smell fried chicken and newly-mown hay and suntan oil, and even the manure from the surrounding dairy farms. Coolers were opened, beer cans popped and hissed, shirts and shoes came off.

Webb moved through the crowd, fresh in his white knit shirt and pressed khakis. He felt a trace of pride in his own cool image, neat and crisp: Air Force, even on holiday. With Pamela at his side all would have been perfect.

The twenty-eight warbirds scheduled to perform in the afternoon were lined up in two neat rows on the taxi strip. Webb picked out a dozen Mustangs, several blue-black gullwing Corsairs, a bare-metal P-40 with shark mouth painted on, a beautiful blue Hellcat, and a matching blue Avenger torpedo bomber. A little industrial truck was slowly towing a delicate dark-green Zero out to the display, followed by an Army ambulance and a gleaming red crash truck. He unsnapped the camera cover, switched the battery indicator to ON, and moved toward the parked Mustangs.

How he loved the P-51s, great silvery birds, the Corvette of fighter planes, sleek noses bright scarlet and pure yellow, great paddle-prop black blades with yellow tips, low-slung belly scoops and narrow tapered waists, sharp square-tipped wings. The Mustang was distinctly American even now; bold, shiny, big, colorful, and loud.

For a moment Webb debated whether to fit the zoom in case more warbirds came in. It was still early and the runway was only a few hundred feet from where he stood. He looked through the viewfinder at the empty strip, a band of concrete in a field of green, soft in the gray haze. No, he decided to shoot out the roll on the parked planes first, then fit the zoom. Happily he focused on the closest P-51. These airplanes were the only thing Webb cared for as much as women.

'Colonel Lowen, this is Seven-six Leader.'

'Go ahead, Seven-six,' Lowen replied. His plane bobbed in new turbulence at 7000 feet.

'What is your ETA Chino?'

'Fifteen minutes or so.'

'You may begin descent whenever you decide, Colonel. Now listen carefully: you will raise the tower and tell them you have an emergency and that they must clear the field immediately of all ground personnel and spectators. Give them any reason you wish, but you are responsible for persuading them to clear the field immediately. Do you understand?'

'Loud and clear, Seven-six.'

'You will lead your flight straight in and you will land together. Is that clear?'

'Very clear, Seven-six.'

'At the end of the runway you will pull off on the grass to your left. The other four will pull off on the grass to the right. All of you will then get as far away from your aircraft as fast as you can. Any questions?'

'No questions, Seven-six,' Lowen answered. Sonofabitch, he new what that meant.

'Clear with your pilots individually, Colonel, then proceed.'

'Any questions, Anderson?' Lowen called over the R/T.

'Negative, Leader,' came the reply.

'Gardner?'

'Negative, Leader.'

'Meredith?'

'Negative, Leader.'

'Fitzgerald?'

'Negative, Leader.'

'Here we go then. Descend on me.' Lowen pushed at the stick and scanned his dials. His oil temp had shifted toward the red. Everything else – no, hydraulic pressure down. He cursed under his breath, looked back once more at the eight 109s, and then turned his attention to the descent.

Below, he could see the entire San Bernardino-Riverside-Los Angeles basin in a massive brown haze of smog. He studied the desert, following US 10 and picking out Palm Springs. Riverside would be dead ahead in that brown crap. Now at 6000 feet. The turbulence increased as they descended into warmer air. The four Mustangs in echelon off his starboard wing lifted and dropped like silver boats in the swells of a gentle sea. He saw Anderson looking at him and he raised a gloved hand reassuringly. Rechecking his dials, he saw the oil temp now against the red, hydraulic pressure steady but low, altitude 5000 feet and dropping.

'Chino Tower, this is Mustang 45545 calling Chino Tower.' Lowen pressed the headset closer, searching in the faintly crackling silence.

'Mustang, this is Chino Tower.' The flat casual voice from air control was clear over the R/T. 'Go ahead.'

'Chino, this is Mustang Leader with five P-51s twenty-five miles north-northeast descending at 4000 feet. Our flight is scheduled in for airshow. Request immediate landing clearance. Over.'

'Mustang Leader, we have unlimited ceiling . . . but heavy ground fog with limited visibility at about one mile. We have . . . three aircraft holding outside our zone waiting for clearance. Circle northeast at 2000 feet until we can clear you in. Over.'

Wonderful, Lowen thought; a traffic jam in a ground fog with eight crazy Krauts on our ass. This is gonna wake up the FAA boys straightaway. He cleared his throat. 'Chino, this is Mustang Leader Colonel Roger Lowen, Confederate Air Force. We have an emergency, repeat emergency. Must have immediate landing clearance for all five aircraft. Do you copy? Over.'

'Read you, Colonel,' the voice came back quickly. 'Come ahead. Do you need emergency vehicles?'

'Affirmative, Chino. We have a hazard to all ground personnel and airshow spectators. Field must be cleared, repeat must be cleared, immediately. Alert all available emergency vehicles. Advise clearing airspace your zone, repeat clear airspace immediately. Do you read? Over.'

'Ahh . . . we read you, Colonel. Can you describe emergency?'

'Listen up real close, Chino.' Lowen took a deep breath, glancing behind to reassure himself that the eight 109s above and behind him were real. 'We have been attacked and fired upon by eight armed aircraft, repeat armed aircraft. They are following and they have ordered the field cleared. I believe they are going to attack. Do you copy? Over.'

'Attack?' repeated the air controller, his voice an octave higher. Lowen tried to imagine the man's expression.

'Affirmative, Chino; attack. They have fired on us. This is for real, Chino.'

'Ahh . . . Colonel . . . can you identify, ah, attacking aircraft?'

'Eight piston-engined Messerschmitt 109s, Second World War vintage with German paint and markings. No ID numbers. They have fired on my flight and I have damage. Over.'

'Do you have fire or injury?' Now the air controller seemed very alert.

'Negative, Chino. Can you pick us up on radar?'

'Ahh. . .' the voice paused, then came back hesitantly.

'Affirmative, Colonel. We show . . . thirteen craft.'

'You got it, Chino. Now get your act together, buddy, because these bastards could be on you in five minutes. Are you clearing spectators?'

'Ahh . . . affirmative.'

'Chino, we are on approach at 3000 feet. We are landing all together. Are we cleared?'

'Affirmative, Colonel. Good luck to you.'

Steering by familiar landmarks, Lowen strained to see through the haze below. Visibility was about five miles, he guessed, much better from above. He knew he was on line.

'Okay, Rebels,' he said calmly over the R/T. 'We're going in. Make it smooth. Forget the bandits now and let's get down in one piece. Who's on tail back there; Fitzgerald?'

'Fitzgerald here,' came the reply.

'What are the bandits doing?'

'Backing off a bit now. Behind and high, about 600 feet, forming in pairs line astern.'

Godamighty, Lowen thought. It's gonna hit the fan for sure.

'All right . . . Gear down.'

Hydraulics whined, landing gear indicator light blinked on green . . . airscrew pitch control . . . airspeed . . . temp – *Damn*, it was well in the red now. A glance backward showed the other four Mustangs lining up perfectly. There, the strip was in sight now, a long tan concrete band surrounded by brilliant green, off to the left, past the tiny flashing white fog beacon.

'This is Staffel Leader,' Rudi said in German over the R/T. 'Form on me, in *Rotte*, astern.' To his right he saw Schilling moving up tight below his wing. He was sweating now and his mouth was dry. The ground fog lay thinly over the grasslands below. Spikes of trees stood ghost-like above the white veil of haze . . . Like France then . . . Scattered rectangular shapes, flat-roofed sheds, yes, hay sheds. He could make out patchwork fields . . . spidery thin fences . . . roads . . . and cows; there were black-and-white cows everywhere he looked. He could even smell hay and manure. Like Holland then.

'This is Staffel Leader.' Rudi kept his voice steady. 'We will make first pass slowly for observation. Follow me.'

He glanced over the dials. Altitude 1800 feet and dropping. The Mustangs were tight in line, down to about 300 feet.

Reflections from the sun marked them clearly. He strained to see ahead of them, looking for the strip, cursing the ground fog. Was it an illusion that the canopy was fogging up with condensation?

'This is Staffel Leader. Open canopies for observation.' He slid back his own canopy. Surprisingly cool air swirled around him. He could see ground shadows skipping along under Lowen's Mustangs now. Ahead of them he saw the strip. And a pinpoint of rythmic white light: fog beacon.

Lowen throttled back. He was lined up perfectly, trying to concentrate on his approach without thinking of the twelve fighters behind him, four of which could inadvertently ram into him and eight of which could shoot him to pieces.

The P-51 slowed and began to settle. *Concentrate now* ... Road full of traffic and line of trees ahead, strip beyond. Airspeed 150 ... 140 ... For a terrible second a chilling flashback of the airfield in Germany came to him; the fog and the gray mist ... the three Me-109s ahead, smoking, battered, wheels down ... the savage elation as he lashed into them with the 50s ... *Please* ... hunched down in the seat, shoulders taut, imagining himself in the sight of one of the 109s behind him. *Not like this, please* ... Airspeed 110 ... 100 ... Strip coming up ... huge white block numerals Two and One ... scores of black tire marks zipping under the wings ... The Mustang touched down, tires chirping once.

'Beginning pass,' Rudi announced. Vision was improving, he noticed gratefully, as they lost altitude. And the Mustangs were on the strip. From the rear they looked as if they were going to pile into each other. To the right he saw the display aircraft and the white shaft of the control tower topped by a black structure of steel and glass. Right on the money, now. More stick ... 200 feet ... 150 feet ... Line of trees coming up.

Rudi and Schilling crossed the tree line sixty feet apart at 150 miles an hour. The strip popped in view, huge block numerals Two and One, hundreds of black tire smudges. They went into a half-roll and held it as they thundered down the runway, scanning the display area. Rudi took careful note: perhaps two dozen planes, a good distance from the crowds on the grass ... Spectators around the planes; were they moving away? And not

156

moving very fast. Some of them were waving! Damn! Red crash trucks. Some fool putting along on a little motorcycle. Why wasn't the field being cleared? He was reaching the end of the strip and could see the Mustangs rolling to a stop, Lowen's on the left in the grass and the other four on the right. Rudi began to climb and bank. He had seen children, lots of children.

The five P-51s came down so tightly together that spectators scrambled up from the grass in awe, sure they were being treated to a demonstration not yet announced. Webb, listening with only half an ear to the P/A system trying to cajole the crowd away from the display area, was sure that he was witnessing some sort of mild emergency and he moved forward, sighting his camera. It was then that the great thundering growl of engine reached him. He stopped in astonishment as four pairs of what appeared to be – yes, Messerschmitt 109s – came over banked to starboard so that their identically perfect camouflage paint and bold black-and-white crosses were clearly brilliantly visible only several hundred feet away. The combined chorus of eight Daimler-Benz engines, even at one-third power, sent a tremor across the ground, a massive resonance that traveled through Webb's body and rippled gooseflesh across his back.

Cheers and applause broke out among the crowd. Cameras clicked around him as he fumbled at the lens focus. Spectacular! Eight 109s! He was sure of it; those high squarish tails, blunt snouts and narrow canopies. And all identical, even to the sequential white numbers behind the cockpits. Beautiful! Webb caught the last pair in his camera as they passed and banked away. Surely they would come around again, and this time he would be ready.

He then realized that the P/A announcer was warning spectators to clear away immediately. Confused, he looked out at the Mustangs. The pilots were scrambling out. He wondered why.

Climbing out of the pass, Schilling tucked in behind Rudi to circle the field and set up for the next pass. As they swung north over the field, Schilling remembered odd details: the spinning props of the P-51s clustered on the grass, a canopy sliding open, the spectators shambling away, an olive-drab Army ambulance with huge red cross, the display aircraft in two neat rows. He grinned. The folks down there were about to get an airshow.

'This is Staffel Leader—' Rudi's voice in German over the R/T. 'Close canopies. Arm guns. Gunsight switches on. This pass we fire on runway. Machine guns only. Open up . . . keep your distance . . . mind your belly tanks.'

Schilling pulled his canopy forward, slamming it into place and closing out the turbulence. His gloved hand darted out to throw switches. Red lights winked on.

It came on now, the feeling. It was the feeling of the pace lap in a racing car and it was the feeling of thirty-some years ago over Europe, that tightening of the stomach, the tautness of the muscles in his thighs and arms, the absolute concentration so fiercely intense, nerves drawn like a bowstring. His eyes riveted on Rudi's 109, now a mile ahead. His own plane grew light under his control, as if the machine was drawing its nervous energy as much from its pilot as from the howling engine. Then Rudi's plane lifted just a bit, and began to nose down. Schilling was wired in now, tracking. It was like a roller coaster lifting, lifting. The engine revs climbed, power coursed through the airframe, the seat. The adrenaline charge kicked in then, like overdrive. Following Rudi's trajectory perfectly, Schilling crested the top of the invisible curve. His stomach lifted, as the plane dropped. Rudi was really on it now, dropping faster and Schilling could feel the jostling of his wake. Marta, he thought. As if he had thrown a switch, Schilling disconnected his concentration from Rudi's 109 and locked onto the runway, a thin line in the haze about two miles ahead.

'*Kameraden*!' Theo's voice over the R/T. '*Die Zeit ist gekommen*!'

You got it, Herr General, the time has come all right, thought Schilling, watching the tiny band of concrete hover in the sight, closing his gloved thumb lightly over the button on the stick as he nosed down. Here we go . . . tree line coming . . . gone . . . Runway, *squeeze*! Banging clatter shook the plane, smoke whipping back, smell of bitter-sulfur cordite, runway zipping underneath, tiny orange dots shooting out.

In seconds Schilling was at the end of the strip, streaking over the parked P-51s, over the heads of the pilots running across the grass. He had a euphoric urge to wave to them.

The first 109 came so fast that Webb missed it; a tan rocket streaking no more than twenty feet off the runway, gone before he could get the camera on it, the howl of the engine trailing a second or two behind. He was stunned by its speed.

Now the second 109 popped up over the trees, dropped low, came rocketing down the runway. Fast, too fast. He cursed as he failed to pan quick enough. He had a glimpse through the viewfinder; sunlight flashing off the cockpit, dull fuselage surface, black Balkan crosses on the flank, white numeral Three, thin black swastika clearly on the fin. And firing blanks! Smoke whipping back, tiny flashes over the nose! Wonderful!

He crouched, ready this time. He caught the third 109 over the trees and started banging off shots, panning well, tripping the shutter as fast as it would go, elated that he was catching the muzzle blast of the guns. In less than a minute the remaining five 109s had passed, their piercing guttural exhaust notes ringing in his ears. He had never heard such a furious sound before. He loved it. God, they were splendid planes, so ugly and beautiful! Outstanding! He watched the last of them melt into the haze.

Webb checked his frame counter – eleven shots left – and crouched by the tail of a Corsair, waiting, his eye on the distant line of poplars.

'This is Staffel Leader,' Rudi said calmly in German over the R/T. 'This pass our targets are the four Mustangs to right of the strip, repeat four Mustangs only. Steady and smooth, now. And keep your distance.'

Rudi was north of the strip on the third go-around. He had made the second pass without firing in order to see if the display area was being cleared. And it was; the spectators were running now and the two rows of display planes sat alone. And the Mustang pilots were all clear of their planes. Good, good. Now his gloved fingers threw switches. Red lights blinked on: sight . . . guns armed. Sweat itched behind his ears. Rudi was high, very high now. And there was the taste, that marvelous metal taste, the taste of invincibility, however false and fleeting. Oh, he knew the true taste. His senses floated in sublime pride. The plane, his plane, howled over the haze, light to his touch. Steady now. He began to turn.

'Oberstleutnant Leader—' a new voice rasped oddly over the R/T. 'This is Major Four . . . leaving formation.'

Osterhoudt. What the hell? 'I read you, Major Four,' Rudi

replied. 'Circle at 2000. Do you read?' Rudi was in the turn now, setting up for the run. Franz sounded queer. And he did not answer.

'Oberstleutnant Leader, this is Oberst One.' Theo's voice now. 'I'll pick up Major Four after last pass. Good hunting!'

Good Theo, Rudi thought, flipping up his gun-button shield. The strip coming into the sight now ... trees coming up ... thumb on the button, forefinger on the trigger.

In Webb's viewfinder the 109 slashed leaves off the top of the poplar as it burst into sight, dipped, and came howling down the runway at an altitude of ten feet. Fire flashed out of the nose and the cowling, and the banging clatter of gunfire came over the demonic scream of the engine as it went by. Webb's mouth opened. Geysers of concrete dust spewed up in a stitching line that ran off the runway and kicked up clots of dirt across the grass and then reached the Mustangs. Pieces of shining metal danced and chipped off the P-51s and all four aircraft seemed to shake like wet dogs. One of the sleek bubble canopies erupted in a burst of sparkling fragments.

Oh man, it's real, Webb thought. *No, no, it's a stunt.* Hands shaking, he turned the camera back to the treeline, feeling a chill rippling along his forearms. The next 109 came as fast and low as the first, nose flashing, pouring fire into the P-51s, one of which collapsed on one wing.

The third 109 seemed so low it would crash, spewing out distinct lines of tiny white and orange fireballs that arrowed ahead directly into one of the P-51s which shuddered, spraying pieces in every direction, and exploded violently in a huge boiling globe of orange flame. Webb stopped shooting. The sharp deep boom of the explosion washed over him.

Mesmerized, he watched the fourth 109 clear the trees, drop, and make the run. White globs, like golf balls, were streaming out of the nose and all of them were hitting the Mustangs. He panned and caught the fifth 109 as it flew through the huge rising billow of black smoke. He got off three frames and ran out of film. Another P-51 blew up. Pieces of aluminum, more orange flame, an aileron sailing up, turning over in the air. The sixth 109 now, guns chattering. Smoke thick and black, flame boiling, covered the wreckage. The seventh 109 flashing by, guns winking, through the smoke.

'Jesus,' Webb whispered to himself, still transfixed, crouching by the tail of the Corsair. He wondered if there was something he should do. Wasn't there another 109 due? He could hear the crackling pyre of the P-51s in the silence. He stared, scanned the sky, the treeline. Nothing. He heard the 109s in the distance. There was something peculiar . . . yes, yes: he was alone on the display strip. Among the twenty-odd warbirds there was no one but him . . .

No, there was someone, someone running toward him. A man in a yellow raincoat – how strange, he thought – waving, yelling, running down the line of aircraft, toward him. Webb looked up at the runway, the line of poplars; another 109 appeared, banking a little. But this time head-on. Then he understood.

Please God, there must be some mistake. Little fire flashes all over the nose of the 109. Webb bolted, ran. Then there was the sound of hail, deadly hail all around him, snapping cracking hissing whining smacking. Metal whizzed in the air like hornets. Running hard, eyes riveted on the 109 as it silently grew larger, he could see white dots spilling out toward him and banging into the parked aircraft. Pieces flying up, chips of concrete dancing struck him stinging. Then over his head the Messerschmitt a silent monster fifteen feet above, rocket-shark gaping scoop mouth, bright blue belly and teardrop tank. There and gone. Spent shells sprinkled clinking on the concrete. Then the roar of its engine slammed at his eardrums. Webb dived onto the grass and rolled.

Shaking in panic, Webb scrambled crabbing across the grass. Someone else running, a man in brown running low. Webb heard a scream, a terrible sound, and he turned. Fifty feet back under the wing of the Corsair the fireman in the yellow raincoat writhed on the pavement. Webb got to his knees, shedding camera and shoulder bag. The running figure, a P-51 pilot, reached the fireman. Webb scrambled to his feet, knowing he had an instant – no more – to run one way or the other. He ran toward the two men, charging low across the grass.

Looking up he saw another 109 clear the trees. He reached the two men. The fireman, eyes wild, clutched at his leg. A small geyser of blood came up between his fingers and spurted bright and shining crimson across the yellow slicker.

'*Drag him!*' yelled the pilot, grabbing at the fireman's arm. '*Drag him!*'

161

Webb grabbed the other arm, hooking his hand under the armpit, and together they scrambled toward the grass. The hail came again, smacking, cracking, banging into the aircraft, whining over their heads. Webb prayed as they struggled, dragging the fireman, fifty feet, sixty . . . a great dry *boom* came up behind them and a shock wave of heat and pressure pushed against his back. The three men fell. Flaming pieces of debris rained down around them.

'Belt, belt, *belt*!' the pilot was yelling at Webb. 'Your *belt*!'

Webb rolled in the grass, clawing his belt loose. His hands were slippery, wet. Blood. He whipped the belt off and the pilot began wrapping it around the fireman's thigh. *So much blood.* Webb felt his gorge rise, filling his throat. His hands were red — why?

'His arm!' Webb croaked. 'He's hit in the arm, too!'

'Fix it!' the pilot snapped.

Webb blinked at the pilot. The scream of the passing 109 blasted their ears. Webb twitched in panic. The pilot had such a kind face, fatherly and tanned, with gray wavy hair.

'*Fix it*!' the pilot yelled in his face, struggling with the belt. 'Handkerchief! Anything!'

Webb snapped to, struggled at the fireman's shoulder, yanking the yellow slicker back. God, more blood. Handkerchief, Webb told himself. He tied it high around the soaked sleeve, with fingers stiff as sticks.

The pilot finished tightening the belt. 'Let's go!' he yelled, crouching on his knees.

Webb grabbed the fireman's wet arm and staggered up, terrified, glancing backward. The hail came again. Pieces flying off the Corsair. Orange flame and black smoke rising down the line of planes. The three men lumbered across the grass. Webb thought his chest would explode. His mouth filled and he swallowed, stumbled and fell. Another 109 screamed by. God, would they ever stop?

'Here,' gasped the pilot. 'Stay here. Lie flat.'

Webb had no breath to speak. He stuck his face in the grass. Every muscle in his body felt spastic, rubbery. The grass smelled wonderfully green and fresh. All he wanted in the world was to stay alive.

'You all right?' the pilot said to the fireman.

Flat on his back, pale and wild-eyed, the fireman nodded once, looking at the sky.

'There we go.' The pilot pointed.

Webb looked up to see a box-like Army ambulance bouncing across the field toward them. The olive-drab vehicle slewed to a stop and the doors burst open. Three medics in fatigues and polished black combat boots, one of them a woman, sprawled onto the grass.

'Just him!' The pilot pointed to the fireman.

One of the medics pulled open the rear doors of the truck, yanked out a stretcher, brought it over. Together Webb and the pilot helped roll the fireman onto the stretcher and then load it. Another explosion behind them. Debris pattered over the truck. The woman medic, crouched between Webb and the pilot, looked at each of them, her eyes wide and blue, her expression a question mark.

'I'm all right,' the pilot said.

The girl turned to Webb. She was pretty and thin and in control and she seemed too young and frail to be there.

'Me too,' Webb said to her, then turned and threw up. The ambulance roared off across the grass. Webb was on his knees drooling.

'They won't bother us,' the pilot said calmly. 'They just want the planes. Here comes another.'

Webb fell down in terror, glancing up. Another 109 streaked through the wall of smoke, guns winking. He could hear the bullets snapping and whining off the pavement and the cannon shells banging into the burning planes. The Corsair blew up violently, caving in and drawing one gullwing back, sending debris pinwheeling up out of the orange flash. Behind it, another plane blew. Webb hugged the ground. Flaming junk sailed and scattered in all directions. An aircraft wheel, blown free of its strut, scooted and bounced crazily down the row of flaming hulks. A wave of heat smelling thickly of burning rubber and paint reached them. Webb gagged.

'They gotta be out of fireworks any minute now,' said the pilot.

'Sure,' Webb replied, digging in with his fingers as another 109 whispered through the wall of smoke with cannon blazing, guns sparking. Webb could hear the terrible hail sound as it passed and he could see the pilot and the big number One on the fuselage and the bomb-like belly tank. The plane lifted away, followed by its own howling sound.

Webb and the pilot waited a full minute, watching the planes burn fiercely. A double explosion tripped off down the line and more oily smoke rolled out. The pilot stood up tentatively, eyes down-field. Webb decided that the pilot was more brave than crazy and he stood up, too, still shaking.

'Godamighty,' the pilot said to himself.

Webb looked up at him.

'I think they're gone,' said the pilot after a moment, his head cocked.

All Webb could hear was the sound of the aircraft burning and the sirens wailing closer. The pilot started walking. Webb caught up, wiping his hands on his pants. His clothes were a mess. At a hundred feet they stopped, staring at the inferno. As solid as a wall, the wave of heat reached them and the smell of burning rubber seemed to cover Webb with an oily film. He gagged again, retched. Occasional hissing and popping and crackling accentuated the furnace-like roaring.

Beyond the transparent shimmering curtains of heat, the blackened structural skeletons of the warbirds writhed and parted and settled in the wind-whipped pools of burning fuel like the remains of great dying beasts. Fire trucks rolled up then, lights flashing, men leaping off in silver coats, dragging out hose lines.

'Show's over now.' The pilot turned and held out his hand. 'I'm Roger Lowen, Air Force, retired. Confederate Air Force now.'

Webb shook Lowen's hand. 'Webb, James Webb. Captain, Air Force. You were flying one of those P-51s?'

'Yeah. The one they didn't get.' He pointed toward the flaming pyre of the four Mustangs out by the runway, through the flat rolling now-thin veil of smoke to the far side of the strip, where a single P-51 sat whole and shining in the sun.

As Theo climbed out of his final pass he watched the rest of the Staffel fade away homeward in the hazy air. His early elation was now darkly tempered by Osterhoudt's strange departure so early from the attack. Climbing and turning, he searched the sky for the tiny speck of the circling 109.

'Major Four, this is Oberst One. Do you read?' There was no answer. Methodically, Theo took one quadrant of sky and searched it thoroughly. Then he scanned another, his eyes sweeping in parallel lines.

'Major Four, this is Oberst One. Do you read?' he repeated.

Then a dot, yes, to the left, ten o'clock. He locked his eyes on the plane and steered to port. As he drew closer he glanced at the fuel indicator, then his watch. Three minutes, four now.

'Major Four, this is Oberst One.'

He eased off the throttle, reminding himself to be careful with the fuel. There was no margin. As he drew close to the 109 he realized that it was flying oddly, the nose a little low. It seemed to be drifting. Now he could see the rudder, bent just slightly . . . strange . . . Franz was banked right, but flying left, counter-clockwise, against his circle. A chill of premonition stirred inside Theo as he reached up and jerked the canopy backward. Cool turbulence washed over his sweat-soaked flying suit. He fixed his eyes on the cockpit of Number Four as he lined up to come alongside.

'Major Four, acknowledge.' Franz's plane was not moving fast. Theo backed off on the throttle, closing now at 100 metres.

'*Major Four, acknowledge*,' Theo repeated. There was no answer. He glanced at his watch. Five minutes. He was above Franz and behind, closing at fifty meters. He eased the stick forward and leveled off and came up along Franz's tail at about ten meters. He could get quite close because he knew, now, that Franz would not suddenly move into him. Franz was gone, his head resting against the canopy, sunglasses askew. His mouth was open and there was an unmistakable whiteness to his face.

'Can you hear me, Major Four?'

Silence crackled in his headset. He glanced at his watch. Six minutes now. He glanced up at the fuel gauge. There was no time, just moments.

'Can you hear me, Major Four?'

Just you and Franz now, he thought. All alone in the sky over America. He remembered getting drunk with Franz over dinner in Munich. Now just you and me Franz – No, he corrected, just you, Theo. Franz would go down eventually, into the crowd or a house or a church that was full. It was the way such things happened. Time for another decision, Commander. All your life you have made decisions. He looked down. Nothing below but empty grass fields. Now.

As if it were something separate from his arm or body or will, his gloved hand moved up and flicked the gun-arming switches. The red lights came on staring at him, devil's eyes now.

'Can you hear me, Major Four?' he called again.

He dropped away from Franz and then he pulled back on the stick and climbed up behind the 109 with the numeral Four so white, unmarked by the flames and smoke of the attack. Seven minutes. Decisions all your life. Combat all your life. Usually winning, seldom losing, long after money was enough. No different than war. He knew what other men said about him.

'Can you hear me, Major Four?' Theo said quietly this time.

He pressured the rudder a little, watching Number Four leaning lazily in its slow circle. He lifted the nose a little, letting Franz drift into the sight, filling it. He is sleeping now. Between the number and the cross . . . With his thumb he flicked up the hinged gun-button shield and curled his forefinger around the cannon trigger. Get closer, he thought. Get very close and be very careful just the same. God forgive me, I do not know another way. He squeezed his fingers together.

CHAPTER ELEVEN

Theo taxied up to the hangars, noting that the other six aircraft had already been rolled inside. He shut down all switches and slid back the canopy and unbuckled his harness, pausing a moment in relief before lifting himself up to climb out. Every muscle in his body ached, and he was drained from the tension of the return flight, almost two hours skimming over the empty desert with his fuel gauge needle crawling toward the red.

With the engine shut off, the welcome silence washed soothingly over his senses and the hot breeze cooled his damp flying suit. As he climbed down, Rudi came up and handed him a wet towel and a plastic container of ice and water.

'Everyone is back?' he asked Rudi.

'Except Franz.'

The other pilots began pushing Theo's 109 toward the hangar. Theo drank half of the ice water and then poured it with the ice into the towel and held the towel against his neck as he walked.

'When my plane is inside,' he said without looking at Rudi, 'close the door and bring the others inside please, Oberstleutnant.'

As they reached the briefing room door Kesler brought Theo a bottle of beer and another container of ice water. Theo went alone into the room and set them on the little desk, then unzipped his flying suit and drank the water. He could hear himself swallow in the quiet of the little room, even with the air-conditioner going. Then he sat down and lit a cigarette and held up the bottle, icy cold in his hand. It was Beck's and he took a long draught of it and it tasted marvelous. When he set the bottle down, the bubbles hurried to the surface and made the foam cool green through the bright emerald glass. He stared at the red-and-white-and-black label, reading the words BRAUEREI BECK & CO and BREMEN GERMANY before taking another pull. Bremen seemed very far away.

The others filed in silently. They all carried Beck's bottles and they sat down in the folding chairs, except for Marta and Rudi who stood against the back wall. Theo wiped his face again with the towel and put it back around his neck and smoothed back his wet silver hair. Rudi reached over and switched off the rattling air-conditioner and the room was quiet.

Theo looked up, his eyes resting for a moment on each face in turn.

'Major Osterhoudt,' he said carefully, 'will not return.' He paused, glancing downward at the green bottle and then taking a drag from the cigarette. 'After the third pass, as you probably heard over the radio transmitter, he requested to leave formation. You also heard the Oberstleutnant tell him to circle and wait at ... 2000 feet. After our last pass over the field, I caught up to him, to Major Osterhoudt ...'

Theo paused again, as if remembering, then continued deliberately, as if testifying in court. 'He was flying in a wide turn, a circle, and he had apparently failed, physically ... holding the aircraft in this ... circle. Many times I attempted to raise him on the radio, without success. I flew at his wingtip for ... three, four minutes. I could see him clearly. He never moved. His head was resting against the canopy, as if he had fallen asleep, and his mouth was open. I am sure he was dead. Or paralyzed; the same, yes?'

Theo looked up at the others, seeing Marta raise her hand to her mouth.

'There was no time,' he continued, 'no petrol. There was a decision to be made. He would have gone down – perhaps into the spectators, a home, a church. When I had no more time and when I was certain that there was no more choice ... I came up very close. I had some cannon rounds left and I put them into the fuel tank and it exploded instantly. It was quick.'

Theo looked at the pilots. All of them were staring at him blank-faced. Marta had covered her mouth with both hands and Theo found himself wishing she were not there. At her side, Rudi reached over and touched her arm. Theo realized that they all expected him to say more. It was very hot now.

'It was not an easy . . . choice to make.' His voice had no modulation. 'If there is any man here who would have done otherwise . . .' Theo studied each pilot, leaving the sentence unfinished, hanging in the charged silence.

'It was the right decision, Theo,' Kesler said quietly.

The others moved then, as if awakened, shifting in their seats, some nodding absently, staring down or away.

Schilling lit a cigarette, the words branding themselves in his mind, tightening in his stomach. Franz, the hollow disbelief of a friend lost. Now it was very much like the war. He could feel the shock in the room and he felt for Marta and all the others, especially Rudi and especially Theo. Schilling had learned long ago that the glory – such as it was and in whatever form it took – of being the leader of anything always carried a higher price than the value of the glory. When it went bad, the leader always caught it and now he was watching Theo paying up. The Herr General looked much older today, wet and rumpled at the little desk, but yet he sat straight, and Schilling admired him.

Eventually, and it seemed an eternity to Schilling, Theo stood up and brushed back his silver hair with one hand, his gray eyes alive again.

'This is most unfortunate . . . this accident,' Theo spoke firmly now, 'the loss of a pilot, a friend. We must not permit this misfortune to unnerve us. It must be accepted . . . endured. We go on living and eating and laughing and drinking and talking to one another. Pilots are sometimes lost . . . it is that way. We must go on.' Theo stood even taller and straighter, as if he had tapped some new source of strength.

'We must service the aircraft immediately and then we will go back and have our brunch with fine champagne. The mission was a success. You are to be congratulated. The Oberstleutnant and I will make arrangements for Franz . . . a service. Now we must get on with . . . what we have to do. If—' he added, — 'there are no questions.' Theo waited.

'Herr Heinrich, a question.' Marta's taut voice came like a block of clear ice in the hot little room. 'Will you paint another kill marking on the tail of your airplane?'

No one moved in the room and the silence seemed to freeze everything. Theo continued to stare at Marta as if she had not spoken at all, eye-to-eye across the heads of the pilots. He could see she was sweating and he found himself perplexed that she should be wearing the windbreaker in the murderous heat. Her gray-green eyes seemed cat-like in the glistening tan of her face.

'Frau Malzahn,' Theo's voice was patient, 'victory tabs are painted on an aircraft to indicate that an enemy aircraft was destroyed.' He paused, seeing her lips purse, quiver, and he knew it was her only try. She wouldn't fight. Not yet. It was the first time he recognized that Marta might become a problem.

'It was unfortunate. I know you were close to Franz . . . and we were close to him as well, yes?' He looked around at the other pilots as if they might silently concur. 'We all feel as you do.'

Marta continued to stare at him as she moved, stepping sideways, feeling along the wall with her hand until she reached the open door to the hangar and slipped through it.

'We must service the aircraft,' Theo went on, 'fuel and ammunition. The Oberstleutnant will supervise the inspection of each one. Fuel internal tanks only; leave the belly tanks empty. We will brief for our next mission later, when we are rested. You are dismissed now.'

As the pilots cleared the briefing room, Theo sat back down at the desk. For a moment he recalled with agonizing clarity the explosion of Franz's plane as the cannon shells crashed into the fuselage, the sudden billowing orange fireball, the wing ripping off, the nose section falling quickly streaming white smoke from oil and glycol, the prop still spinning as if nothing had happened.

He looked up. Weinert still sat in his chair, looking at him. Rendel stood by the doorway to the hangar, also looking at him. Both men were wet, haggard.

'Yes?' Theo said, sitting up straighter and breathing in. The two men looked at each other, then back to Theo.

'Theo,' Rendel began, moving forward.

'Oberst,' Theo corrected him. 'What is it, Major?'

Rendel again looked at Weinert, then back to Theo. 'Oberst,' he said, 'I have decided . . . I wish to request that I be permitted to leave.'

Theo stood up, then looked over at Weinert. 'Major Seven?'

'Yes, Oberst. It is also my decision to leave.'

'I see,' Theo said. 'Please sit down, won't you, Major?'

He walked over to the door and out into the hangar and returned quickly with three wet bottles of beer and gave one to

170

each of the two men, then he sat on the edge of the little desk while lighting a cigarette. He had closed the door to the hangar when he had returned, and switched the air-conditioner back on. It rattled and wheezed bravely in the closed room. The three men looked at each other calmly without saying anything. Theo was proud of them because they didn't look away or act embarrassed; he had chosen them well.

'I will help with the servicing of the aircraft,' Rendel said.

'Yes, and I will also,' Weinert said quickly.

Theo drank some of the beer and then wiped his mouth with the towel at his neck. He could not afford to lose two men now. But he knew they were weary and dehydrated and in shock over Franz. Because of his own fatigue he could not think of a way to deal with them then, but he felt that there was still a chance to keep them.

'We will miss you,' Theo said finally, standing up, 'but it was our agreement. When we return to the house I will have Frau Malzahn make the arrangements. You are dismissed.'

The two men stood wearily and moved toward the door. Theo followed them and looked out into the hangar. The engine cowlings were up on all three craft and the men were loading ammunition. He called Rudi over. 'Are there any serious problems?'

'Nothing serious. Oil leak in Six, coolant leaks in Five and Eight.' Rudi wiped his face. 'The heat is the real problem.'

'Have each man strip down as much as possible,' Theo ordered. 'No more beer. Have each one drink water, as much as possible, and have them pour it over their heads. Perhaps we could rotate them into the briefing room with the air-conditioner.'

'I will see to it,' Rudi said. 'We have also put on the fans.'

'How is your sister?'

'Upset, you understand?'

'Yes, of course. You will put her in the room first?'

Rudi wiped his hands and then walked across the hangar to where Marta was sitting in a folding aluminum chair by a workbench. She was sleepy-looking and red-eyed and her hair was plastered damply over her forehead. The nylon of her windbreaker was stuck wetly to her chest and arms; he could see the form of her nipples.

She looked up. 'I do not feel well, Rudi. How long will it be?'

171

'Not long. Here, you must drink more.' He went over to the ice chest and brought back a large cup of ice water. 'Stand up.'

Marta struggled to her feet, swaying. Rudi took her by the upper arms. She was clammy through the nylon. He wiped her face with his towel. 'Take off this jacket, for God's sake.'

'Can't,' she said tiredly. 'I ripped my blouse apart. It's gone.'

Rudi looked around, wondering how she could have done that, then went over to the workbench and came back with a pair of shears. 'Hold your arms up,' he ordered. Carefully he cut the sleeves off the windbreaker at the shoulders, then two slits halfway up the sides.

'Now, keep drinking. And wet yourself down thoroughly.'

'Your hostess is not so beautiful now.' She smiled. 'Not so beautiful for all our brave pilots.'

'Thoroughly,' he repeated. 'Or I will pour it over you myself. Then go in the briefing room. I'll be there in a minute.'

Rudi went around to each of the men, ordering them to drink water, wet themselves down, and take turns cooling off. He took two cans of iced tea to the briefing room. It was markedly cooler inside and he found Marta sitting at the desk, wet and dripping.

'How are you doing?' he asked, sitting down heavily in a chair.

'Much better,' she answered listlessly, 'I look like a drowned rat.'

'You look fine.' He glanced at his watch. 'We are rotating everyone in here every fifteen minutes. We will be through soon. I don't think Theo is very well.'

'I can't imagine why.'

'He is doing what must be done.'

'Is this what is done? Service the aircraft and then have a champagne brunch?'

'Yes, that is what is done.'

Marta sniffed loudly, staring down at the can of iced tea in her hand.

'Back off a little,' Rudi said. 'Do you think it is easy for him, for any of us?'

'What will be done? About Franz?'

'I don't know yet. A service of some sort.'

'What about Franz, Rudi? What is he now, chunks of charred meat out in a field over in California?'

'They ... there are personnel, fire crews, the FAA, authorities. We will get in touch with them. It will be taken care of. We will see to it. Please, try not to be disturbed.'

'Disturbed? Disturbed?' her voice rose bitterly. 'Do you think I am blind? Look at your beautiful airplanes out there. They look like you fought the war! Disturbed? I am sitting at a Luftwaffe base in America in nineteen seventy-six and I should not be disturbed? What in God's name did you all do this morning . . . besides lose Franz?' Her face began to come apart and her eyes filled.

'Marta—'

'Theo will get you all killed!'

'Theo, Theo, Theo!' Rudi exclaimed, leaping to his feet. 'Do you think we are all puppets, that Theo pulls the strings and we dance? He is a good commander, better than I could be, better than anyone else here could be! How do you think he feels about Franz? It was an *accident* that Franz died in the plane, Marta. Theo was right; he might have gone down in the crowd. There were children in that crowd. Dozens, hundreds of children. I *saw* them. I flew over the field and I saw them!'

'Who else died, Rudi?'

'Franz was the only . . . casualty.'

'Casualty, that is the word, yes?'

'Yes, yes, yes. Theo did not kill him. He could have died in bed, he could have fallen over at the dinner table, but he happened to die in the plane. From the stress, the excitement. And . . . he died doing something he wanted to do, Marta. It was his time to die.'

'And whose time will it be next?' she whispered.

'We know what we are doing and we know why. If you do not understand it then you must at least give us the room to do it. All of these men were carefully chosen. They want to be here. If it is not to their liking, then they are free to leave.' Rudi sat down again, wiping at his face with the towel. 'You must . . . bear up under this. It was bad luck. It was . . . cruel, what you did to Theo. Though we all understand.'

'Rudi?'

'Yes?'

'If it had been you and Franz, instead of Theo, would you have done the same?'

He rubbed the back of his neck slowly and closed his eyes and sighed. 'I saw the children. We flew a slow observation pass over the airfield and I looked very carefully. It was my responsibility to do this because I was leading the mission.' He opened his eyes, then looked up at her. 'I would have done what Theo did.'

Marta watched him impassively for a few seconds. Then she looked at her watch and then back to her brother. 'The champagne should be on ice for at least an hour before lunch. Can I go soon?'

'Yes, you have been wonderful.'

'It was my agreement.'

'Do not worry.'

'Yes, I will worry. For you, for Eric, for all the others.'

'Perhaps,' Rudi said, standing up, 'you might think of saying something, eventually, to Theo.'

'He is going to get all of you killed.'

'If so, then it will be because it is our agreement.'

After he had walked Marta to the Jeep, Rudi went over to the second hangar where the other four planes were being fueled and armed. He found Eric and Major Bison loading cannon shells in his own plane. The engine cowling was up and it looked like the hood of a Model-T Ford the way it was hinged down the center and raised on both sides.

Eric looked up. 'Any problems with this one, Rudi?'

'Nothing. It ran like a watch.'

'Well, you got glycol and oil all over the place,' Eric said. 'But not a lot. I've tightened all the lines. Where the hell did all the oil come from?'

'Smoke,' Rudi said, looking over the engine.

'Smoke?'

'From the ones burning,' Major Bison said. 'We flew through the smoke.'

'And the dents?' Eric asked.

'Debris,' said Rudi. 'From the explosions.'

'Jesus,' Eric muttered, looking back and forth between the two men. 'Other than . . . Franz, how did it go?'

'Other than Franz,' Rudi said, 'it went exactly as planned.'

Eric looked over at Rudi. 'Did Lowen show up?'

Major Bison laughed. 'The Oberstleutnant flew up his tail and shot a few holes in his wing. It was very entertaining. We followed them – there were five P-51s – to the airshow and we shot up four of them on the ground. We left one; Lowen's.'

'Jesus,' Eric said again, looking at Rudi for confirmation. 'Yeah?'

Rudi wiped his face with the towel.

'Well,' Eric said to him, 'they're gonna come looking for us after all that, aren't they?'

'Unless we have bad luck, it will take them a long time to find out where we are,' Rudi answered. 'If we are lucky, we will all be gone by then.'

Eric closed the cowling and stepped down the ladder stand. Major Bison gathered several empty ammo crates and took them away. Eric was watching his brother-in-law closely.

'Rudi,' he said, his expression studied and urgent, 'I want to tell you something about fighter pilots, just in case you find yourself with one in your rearview mirror. I've been around those guys in Nam and I know a few from Luke, so this is straight.' Eric hesitated for the proper effect.

'I'm listening,' Rudi said.

'Rudi, those guys don't fuck around. They're like tough cops. They've been primed and pumped and programmed and they're flying around in multi-million dollar arsenals, just itching to shoot something. They got no war, and that's all they're designed for, see? So if you tangle with them, man, remember; they're lookin' for a fight.'

Rudi smiled thinly. 'I have seen such pilots before.'

'Not,' Eric replied, 'when they could fly three times faster than you.'

From a distance the Mustang appeared perfect – unlike the other four, their blackened skeletons and engine blocks strewn across an area of burnt grass and gray ash two hundred feet in diameter. When they came around the tail Lowen reached down and touched the bullet holes that stitched across the aluminum surface parallel to the wing root fairing.

'Guess they didn't miss this one after all,' Webb said.

Lowen stooped down, peering under the shadow of the wing. Webb stooped too, seeing the light coming through the bullet holes.

'Sonsabitches,' Lowen ran his hand down the shaft of the landing strut, then held it up, rubbing his fingers together. 'Hydraulic . . .' He then scooted further underneath, touching a half-dozen ragged-edged holes in the belly scoop. Dark fluid was seeping into the grass below. He crawled out and stood up.

Webb decided to keep quiet. He wanted to lean on the wing

too, but decided he shouldn't. 'Sir,' he said finally, 'do you think it's okay if I smoke?'

Lowen glanced down the wing at him. 'Better not. Something might blow up.'

Webb nodded and turned away. Lowen continued to watch him, disappointed that his humor had passed Webb by. He turned back, staring across the field, not seeing the fire trucks still parked, lights flashing, by the steaming ruins of the destroyed planes. The Mustang was out of commission for a while, no doubt of that.

'Bastards mean business.'

'Sir?' Webb moved closer.

'You don't have to call me "sir", Captain.'

'You don't have to call me "captain" then, sir.'

Lowen looked at him, tempted to smile. Gold sunglasses, perfect haircut, even tan, but otherwise the captain was a mess, his white shirt and khaki pants a gray pastiche of blood, vomit and smoke residue.

'What do you do in the Air Force, Captain?'

'OSI, at Williams.'

'You did well, helping with the fireman. Good job.'

'It was my fault he got hit. He was coming after me.

'What the hell were you doing out there, anyway?'

'Shooting pictures.' Webb patted the camera bag.

Lowen grunted, then returned to thinking about the German pilots. At least one of them spoke perfect English, as well as German. And was their pass over Phoenix planned? How would they know to intercept him? The answer seemed within reach, as if it were a puzzle. Yes, the reporter from the *LA Times*. Now he connected the voice over the R/T. Of course . . . what was his name? Becker, yes. So it was planned.

Lowen reached up and ran his hand along the curved aluminum nose of the P-51. Then why hadn't they shot him to pieces in the air – perfect retribution – as he was coming in? They had destroyed the other four Mustangs, had left his for a reason. He felt a small knot of growing dread. And of surprised recognition: They were gunning for him. They wanted a fair fight, not murder. Could it be?

Stripped to their shorts, Schilling and Beissemann sat in the little bedroom, waiting their turns in the shower. There were three beds, each against a wall. The empty one had belonged to Franz. The viola stood in one corner in a black case.

'Well, Major Three,' Beissemann said.

'Well, Major Five,' returned Schilling automatically.

Beissemann looked around the room. 'Let's get it over with.'

Schilling reached down under the empty bed and pulled out a worn brown leather suitcase and put it on the bed and opened it and sorted quickly through the contents, separating the clothing from everything else. Beissemann took Franz's civilian clothing from the closet and folded it neatly in the suitcase and closed it. Left on the bed was a shaving kit, a glass vial of tiny white tablets, a small stack of sheet music, writing materials, several paperback books and a leather photo folder. Schilling opened the folder and a sealed envelope fell out; the words 'Oberst Heinrich' were handwritten on the front. He put the envelope aside and looked at the two photographs. The one on the right was brownish black-and-white, obviously taken some years ago, of a slender woman of about forty. She was seated on a stone bench in a small garden where dappled sunlight came through the trees. She wore a dark stylish dress with pleats from below the hips, dark stockings, and black patent-leather shoes. Her features were pale and fine, her hair probably dark blond, parted center and pulled back, and she looked at the camera with a mischievous expression as if she was about to wink. Somehow Schilling was sure Franz had taken the photo.

The other photograph, in color, was of a young woman, ample-chested and very pretty, with dark hair in the frizzed style currently popular. She was smiling with perfect teeth and she wore a shawl of earth colors over a blue turtleneck. The photo was taken in a yard and there were pine trees thick and dark behind her.

'Wife and daughter.' Schilling held the folder up for Beissemann to see. 'Wife died years ago.'

'Yeah.' Beissemann glanced at the pictures.

Schilling slid the photo of the daughter out of the plastic window. Underneath it was a smaller photo of the same woman with children all around her: five. On the back of the portrait photo was a note in green ink:

Dear Dad,
         Here is the photo I promised and here is my new

177

address, since you might misplace it, where you can always find it.

Love, M

Schilling made a mental note to point out the address to Theo if he was going to write a letter. He put the photo back in the leather folder and closed it. For a moment he thought about someone going through the photos he had in his own wallet. No children, no wife pictures. Stupid thinking, he reminded himself. He put the folder in the paper bag Rudi had provided, then added the writing materials, books, and music. He read the label on the medicine vial: nitroglycerine. He dropped the vial in the bag, then held up the envelope for Beissemann to see. 'What do you think of that?'

'I don't think anything of it,' Beissemann said tiredly. 'During the war I had to do this sort of thing all the time, for years. Hurry up.'

Schilling took the suitcase and the bag to Theo, as he had been instructed. When he came back, Beissemann had two fresh beers for them.

'The Herr General said there will be a service for Franz just before dinner,' Schilling told him. 'We are to pass the word.'

'Our hostess really got on the Herr General this morning, didn't she?'

'She liked Franz.' Schilling was truly sorry for her.

'We should get her some flowers, from all of us. Maybe we send some to the daughter, too.'

Schilling nodded. It was a good idea. They were quiet for a while. He heard the shower going and hoped there would be hot water.

'Well, Major Three,' said Beissemann finally, 'what do you think the authorities will do?'

'Not sure.' Schilling was thinking. 'But, I think the party is just beginning.'

'*Nehm ich an*,' Beissemann agreed. 'Do you remember our talk in the pool last Sunday, about targets? We only fueled up internal tanks today, yes?'

Schilling looked at him, waiting.

'That gives us the range, one way, of a maximum of two hundred miles. I looked at a map and there is nothing within two hundred miles. Nothing. There is Flagstaff to the north and

Tucson to the south and that is all. East and west, sand and rock. And that Colonel is from Texas, so it isn't him.' Beissemann grinned and added, 'There is someone who is pissed.'

'He'll be next,' Schilling said. 'I've got that much figured out. Next week we'll fly to Texas. Want to take that bet?'

By agreement among the Staffel pilots their lunch was postponed a couple of hours. After showers, Weinert and Rendel dressed hurriedly and put their suitcases in the hallway by the front door and went out to the pool and shook hands with each of the others and then left with Eric for the airport.

Marta spoke to no one, busying herself with preparations for lunch, declining even Rudi's assistance. The flowers came, white roses, and she put them on the dining room table, still in the box, where Franz had sat.

Rudi and Theo decided to have the lunch served by the pool and they joined the others, now just Kesler and Schilling and Major Bison. The sudden absence of three pilots, and Eric, was heavy among them all. Rudi kept looking at his watch, calculating Eric's progress and hoping that he would drive fast. Major Bison managed finally to make them all laugh and Rudi wished there was some kind of medal that could be awarded to him.

Theo stood in uniform at one end of the pool under the twilight sky. To his right, Rudi and Eric stood along the side of the pool, while across from them Schilling and Beissemann and Kesler gathered at equal distance from each other. They were all clean and shaved and rested and still a little drunk, and Schilling was again feeling a particular comfort in the snug fit of the uniform and the high glossy boots. Somehow it gave him – and he assumed the others – a little more strength for a funeral service. He saw Marta appear at the glass door across the patio and silently slide it open. She wore a white sleeveless sundress with a lacy-white shawl over the shoulders and her feet were bare. In her arms she held the white roses wrapped in green paper, cradling them like a child, and she leaned against the aluminum door jamb as if she was waiting for someone. Schilling wished it were him.

When the pilots were still, Theo waited a full minute or two or

179

three – to Schilling it could have been one or five – and then withdrew a folded paper from his uniform pocket and opened it. Schilling glanced back at Marta and was startled to see someone behind her, in uniform. It was Rendel, and he walked out on the patio and came up alongside Eric and took his place, staring straight ahead.

Theo was looking at the paper, holding it some distance from his eyes, and when he looked up to speak he saw Rendel and stopped only a moment before he spoke, his voice even and firm: 'Major Schilling collected Franz's personal belongings, where he found this letter . . . which I will read to you. "Dear Oberst Heinrich. This letter will be found in the event of some misfortune. I write it with the knowledge that I am not as physically fit as I had told you. There is the possibility that my recent heart trouble will again occur. If this should happen, I pray that it does not endanger anyone else. Forgive my untruth, but I could not resist the opportunity to join you. Good luck to all. Franz Osterhoudt."'

Theo folded the letter and put it back in his pocket and then looked up, first at Rendel again, and then the others. 'In the absence of a chaplain, it is normally the responsibility of the commanding officer to conduct the ceremoney, the service, for those who have fallen. In this instance,' Theo paused, 'Oberstleutnant Felbeck has requested the . . . responsibility, the honor.'

He stepped backward and Rudi walked around the corner of the pool and they exchanged places. Rudi looked around at all of the pilots and then over to Marta, who had not moved.

'This pool,' Rudi said clearly, 'is a good place to do this for Franz. I did not know it, but he practiced here early every morning before anyone was awake.'

From the corner of his eye Eric caught the tiny dark form of a hummingbird darting hovering silently among the flowers that cascaded over the back wall. He marveled at its agile flight, the invisible blur of tiny wings as it dipped at the blossoms. Little sonofabitch could out-maneuver any airplane ever built, for its size. Overhead a jet scratched against the sky and he resisted the temptation to look up at it.

'We gather here,' Rudi continued, 'as is the custom of men, to pay respect . . . to the passing of another man, our friend and comrade. It is also the custom to remark upon what sort of man he was ... perhaps to recognize, to be inspired by, his contribution to ... the good of other men, of mankind.

'Franz Osterhoudt was a classical musician, and I am sure that his music contributed greatly to the common good. Greatly. We knew him as a pilot who served his country honorably and well, a pilot who loved flying, a pilot who had the spirit ... to join us in this endeavor. He died in the pursuit of that spirit, and it is hoped that he went quickly, easily. In our mourning we can remember that he died doing something he wanted very much to do. He will be missed ... Franz, wherever you are, we salute you.'

Oddly, Eric thought, since there was no cue, every pilot came to attention, including himself, and saluted in perfect unison. When their hands dropped, Rudi turned and went toward the house and the others followed.

Marta had slipped to the far side of the pool where she sat in a chaise longue with the white roses heaped in her lap. Eric stopped at the doorway and looked over at her but she did not look up. She had not spoken to him, or anyone, all day. Now she was so clean and brown and beautiful in the white dress and shawl and with the white flowers. Marta pulled one of the rosebuds loose and separated the petals with one hand and then tossed the soft glowing-white chips onto the blue water. Eric turned and went inside.

Anton Rendel was the immediate center of attention as they gathered at the table, shaking his hand in welcome. When it was Eric's turn he looked closely at Rendel's craggy face, curious that he had decided to return, and managed it with such drama, such timing. It turned out that he had called from the airport, that Marta had answered, and that he had asked her to pick him up without telling the others. Eric imagined that Rudi and Theo were very pleased, and Schilling and Kesler and Major Bison, too. And he himself, to his surprise, was very pleased.

As they were seated, sipping at water and fooling with the business of uncorking wine and pouring the glasses and passing them, there came a gradual silence, as if no one knew what to say. Rendel had been the first to receive wine and he had placed it on the table, holding the glass by the stem and turning it slowly without tasting it, looking at it as if he was reading a crystal ball. Perhaps sensing some unexpected drama, Marta came from the kitchen to find the pilots staring at Rendel, who still seemed

181

oblivious to them. She quietly sat down in her place.

After a moment Rendel looked up. He still appeared remote, but in his bearing, the delicate manner in which his large brown hands held the fragile wine goblet, and the perfect neatness of his uniform, there seemed to be a new and stronger presence. It was fascinating to Eric how Rendel had suddenly become larger merely by leaving and returning.

Now he spoke without looking up, 'Horst Weinert and I went to the airport. There were many people, travelers, and we each of us got a ticket on the different airlines at the different times. We had three, four . . . hours to wait. So we had time to talk. We talked about the Staffel. Weinert felt that the Staffel was a wonderful . . . idea, a wonderful achievement. So much like the war. So much not like the war. He felt it was wonderfully real, like the war, so wonderfully real that we were going to get killed.' Rendel seemed to smile a little, it was hard to tell, and he raised his eyes – craftily, it seemed to Eric – and looked around the table. 'I think he is correct,' Rendel added, then returned his attention to the wine goblet revolving slowly in his paw-like hand.

'While we were waiting, Horst and I, there across from us was an old man. He was not well. He was tended by two women. I do not know how old he was, not terribly old, not much older than me, but he was not capable to do anything for himself in the wheelchair and he trembled a lot.' Here Rendel suddenly lifted his hand, palm down, and held it rock-steady for a long moment, looking at it. 'And,' he went on, lowering his hand, 'he drooled now and then. And I think he had . . . those tubes. I decided to come back then.

'Being a pilot in the war . . . was the best, and the worst, experience of my life. The Oberst, the Oberstleutnant, and the Leutnant here . . . have given me the chance to have that experience, without the bad part. So I stay now.'

He raised the glass and looked at Theo and Rudi, and then down the table at Eric. At that moment, Eric had the notion that he would have followed Rendel into battle in Hell itself. And if Rendel was willing to follow Theo, as apparently he and Rudi were . . . then he would do it too. No sweat. Gung ho.

'So,' Rendel said, 'I salute the three of you . . . for a remarkable idea . . . and the brilliant execution of it. I salute you all as well, too.' He put down the glass. 'Weinert and I decided

that the final mission would be to challenge the American pilot.'
He turned to Theo. 'Is that so, Oberst?'

Theo stared placidly at Rendel as if he had not spoken, and
gave no reply.

'Very well.' Rendel smiled. 'Well . . . you are going to need
me. The Mustang is a very tough airplane. And I am the best
fighter pilot in this Staffel.'

Eric glanced from Rendel to Theo, sure that beneath Theo's
calm wrinkled mask there was a smile imprisoned.

But it was Major Bison who broke the silence, bursting out
with a merry vehemence across the table; 'Rendel, you stupid
cabbage-head, tomorrow you will be trembling and drooling and
peeing in your knickers when you see where we are going on the
second mission!'

As laughter exploded around the table Major Bison stood and
tossed down his wine. '*I* am the best fighter pilot in this Staffel
and already I am trembling and drooling!' He grabbed up the
bottle and drank from it. The others applauded uproariously.

'I missed the briefing?' Rendel asked. 'Where are we going?'

Bison began to laugh too, wine leaking from his mouth. 'I
don't *know*,' he howled, nearly falling down. 'Only the Herr
General and the Oberstleutnant know!' The laughter of the
others welled over him, rampant and contagious. 'And maybe
they don't know,' Bison went on hysterically, 'but since *I* don't
know, that's why I'm trembling and drooling!'

'First on KPNX news across the nation tonight, a bizarre twist
and spectacular fireworks at an airshow for warplanes in
California. After this message.' The image of a polished blond
newswoman vanished from the TV screen, replaced by a
soft-drink commercial.

Eric glanced at Marta who stood back by the doorway to the
den.

After an automobile commercial and a toilet bowl cleaner
commercial there appeared a picture of crowds milling about
parked airplanes and, at the bottom of the screen, the words
FILM COURTESY KHOF SAN BERNANDINO in tiny white block
letters. Then a male announcer's voice-over: 'Chino airfield
near Riverside, California is the site of annual airshows where
owners of restored World War Two fighter planes display
their aircraft and perform flying demonstrations and mock air

battles. At this morning's opening of the Chino airshow, over four thousand spectators witnessed a real aerial attack by eight vintage German fighter planes in authentic World War Two battle colors.'

The film switched to a long shot of the Mustangs landing and then a closer shot of the four P-51s taking hits, throwing debris and then exploding. The cameraman had tried to catch the 109s in flight but there were merely flashing torpedo-shapes streaking across jumpy film footage.

'Then the attacking planes circled the field and began strafing a line of parked display aircraft,' the announcer continued.

Eric gaped at the screen. The cameraman was a little quicker now and he had caught the 109s with surprising clarity as they swept over the parked planes, noses flashing fire, only thirty feet off the ground. He saw one, two, four of them exploding, huge billowing orange flames and rolling black smoke. Another 109 zipped across the screen, the big white numeral Three clear on the fuselage – Schilling, Eric thought automatically. Jesus, it was like a war movie, like combat footage from Nam.

'The value of the twenty-six aircraft destroyed was estimated by Chino officials to exceed four million dollars and the aircraft owners claimed even more.' Now the screen showed firemen with hoses, spraying the burning wreckage. 'Miraculously there were no fatalities or injuries among spectators, but emergency crewmen sustained numerous injuries from minor burns and flying debris while fighting stubborn blazes for over an hour. The only seriously injured was a Chino fireman who was wounded by machine gun fire and remains in fair condition.'

'*Verdammt*!' muttered Theo suddenly behind Eric.

The film cut to a close-up of the burning hulk of what Eric recognized as an F4U Corsair under the spray of foam nozzles. 'Following the attack, an even more bizarre incident took place two miles west of the airfield where one of the attacking planes crashed in a field, setting off a large grass fire. There were eyewitness reports that the plane was destroyed in mid-air by one of the other attacking planes. The pilot did not survive.'

The picture showed fireman dragging hose lines through deep yellow grass where small fires burned, then a close-up of the 109's tail section upside down in the smoldering black ash, the swastika and kill markings barely visible in the smoke and glare.

'FAA officials had no information on the destroyed aircraft, or the identity of the pilot. Airshow officials identified the attacking aircraft as rare and authentic World War Two German Messerschmitts, but claimed no knowledge of any such aircraft flying in the United States or of the identity of the eight pilots. Within thirty minutes of the attack, a flight of Air Force jets arrived from March Air Force Base near Riverside to conduct a wide-search operation, but the seven mystery fighters were never sighted.'

Rudi leaned forward and turned down the volume as the news film switched to a different story, then sat back in his chair, pipe clenched in his teeth. He looked around at the others as he puffed contemplatively. It was Major Bison who spoke first.

'Well, Major Three,' he said to Schilling, 'you looked absolutely dashing on the telly there. Wonderful profile.'

'Well, Major Five,' Schilling replied, 'it's great to be a star.'

The others laughed, except for Marta, who continued to watch and listen. Eric studied her for a moment, remembering her in the hangar, slick with sweat, teeth bared. She was beautiful then, beautiful now. And she was watching Schilling, Schilling the brave star . . . and Beissemann the brave comedian . . . Rendel the brave volunteer . . . Rudi the brave brother . . . Kesler the brave knight with the cross . . . and Theo the brave commander. She is watching, Marta the brave hostess, and she misses Franz the brave musician. Jesus, they *are* brave . . . and now by God the Herr General is flying them all into the history books, making all of them heroes. On television yet. He was simply doing it, right here and now doing it. All of them . . . except you, Eric the brave . . . rapist? . . . the brave mechanic? She's not looking at you, she's looking at them. And especially she's looking at Schilling. He looked at Schilling. Schilling looked like a German fighter pilot should look, like they looked in the movies, stern and lean and light-haired and square-jawed. And he had gotten into one of those 109s this morning and blew those mother planes apart and been on TV and there he sat, whole and cool. Guts. All of them.

After drinking with the other pilots awhile Eric came to bed very drunk to find Marta already asleep. He turned on the bathroom light after he had closed the door and he steadied himself against the wall with one hand while he urinated, thinking about the TV images of the flashing 109s and the burning wreckage. He brushed his teeth, watching himself red-eyed in the mirror. He had good teeth. He shook the brush out and put it in the rack and then peeled off his shirt and looked at himself. You are brave too, he thought. He had crawled into the Huey every time, never hesitating, with the ammo boxes banging on the steel floor, loading up, swaying, lifting, empty shells clinking underfoot everywhere, M-60 yammering clattering, firing and being fired at, red and white embers sailing up silently curving arcing banging. He was brave. All that wet red meat and dribbling red syrup on the floors sticky on the empties and he still hung with it, just stayed stoned and hung in. Hung in right to the end. Honorable discharge. He was brave. Hell, it was brave just to *go*, not to mention *fight*, brave just to not freak out when you were sure but absolutely sure you were jammed up the asshole of the Real World and would never get out whole.

But no woman had ever looked at him for being brave there. Not even Marta. It never seemed to be anything to her, not admirable, not anything except – what was it? – unfortunate.

He leaned on the sink to keep his balance, swaying, looking around the bathroom as if in a dream, Jesus, what a mess it was. Stuff hanging everywhere, mostly hers . . . nice stuff, stuff he never minded, really: T-shirts . . . blouses . . . panties – messed up a pair today, he thought . . . stockings . . . pantyhose. He lifted a stocking off the shower curtain rail where it was hung to dry and he put it to his face and closed his eyes. Brown wispy oddly-coarse fabric, such a strange texture, so sexless without the leg and foot to fit it. His mouth, lip, still hurt where she had struck him but he had, he knew, not hurt her really except for the bullet tips and there was no blood. He wanted the stocking to smell like her but it only smelled like soap. All he wanted, above everything, was for her to look at him the way she looked at Schilling.

He opened his eyes and then he folded the stocking neatly and stuffed it in his pocket and then turned off the light.

CHAPTER TWELVE

In black pre-dawn darkness Eric sat at the wheel of the van with the engine running as the pilots climbed aboard. Nervously alert, he could feel a small band of tension above his stomach as if some obscure muscle had seized and knotted. He was unusually aware of the other men as they settled in their seats.

Images of the TV news film repeated themselves in his mind's eye. Jesus, they were putting out *boocoo* rounds, pieces of crap flying every which fucking way. For the first time he was beginning to understand why they had embraced Theo's command, why they were willing to do what they were doing. Gambling on history.

It was remarkable also that they could be so old, and yet so quick, so sharp. He remembered Rendel holding out his hand, steady as a statue, over the dinner table. And the day that Schilling, working with him on an engine, had dropped a ratchet from shoulder height and caught it before it fell past his waist, without even blinking, returning to his work as if nothing had happened. Damned sharp dudes, still.

All of them aces several times. In what were to him ancient times, they had flown years, not months but years, of relentless aerial combat against the Russians, the British, the Americans, flying against the best – Spits, Mustangs, Thunderbolts. And the Forts. Bet your ass it took some kind of brass bowling balls to go up against a B-17. That sucker packed a dozen fifties and he knew damn well what it took to fly into a shitstorm of .50 caliber armor-piercing.

There was no way not to respect them all, even that

goddamned Schilling. It was crazy what they were doing. Rendel was right; it was crazy-brilliant. And it looked now as if the Herr General was right. So far.

He glanced at Theo by his side, the tanned placid face staring straight ahead in the green glow of the dash lights. There was the scent of expensive aftershave; he found it odd but exactly right that Theo would put on aftershave to fly a mission. It reminded him of that Colonel in Nam who had walked through formation one hellish rainy week, talking up the troops. Every grunt on the line smelled so bad they couldn't stand each other – wet mold rot, gun oil, kerosene smoke and BO – but that Colonel smelled like pine trees and leather. It seemed all right somehow, just like the Herr General seemed all right. Nobody doubted their guts no matter what they smelled like; they'd been where it smelled different.

Well, he was a good pilot, he reassured himself. Not nearly as good as these dudes, but he could fly the 109. He had followed Rudi every which way, had kept right up, smoothly, on dives and rolls and turns and gunnery runs when they were testing up north. Hell, yes, he could shoot and he could keep up.

'Our mission this morning will be an exercise in low-level high-speed attack . . . and careful navigation. You will see why we have practiced the A and B routes so carefully.' Rudi picked up a piece of chalk. At the top of the board he marked a small circle, then tapped out a dotted line to the bottom of the board where he marked an X. 'Our target,' he spoke matter-of-factly, 'is Williams Air Force Base, a flight-training facility located fifty-two miles south-southwest. Our objective, again, will be to fire on parked aircraft.'

Say what? Eric nearly spoke aloud. Seated behind the other pilots, he caught only Schilling and Major Bison exchanging glances. Major Bison seemed amused. The others contined to watch Rudi as he chalked more dotted lines on the blackboard, forming an inverted triangle with the target X at the point and the original vertical dotted line – the flight path – bisecting the triangle into two halves. He then marked an A at the top-left corner and a B at the top-right corner.

'Takeoff will be at 0530 hours.' Rudi glanced at his watch. 'We will form up line astern at 1000 feet, open up to one-mile intervals and fly directly to target on one heading. The entire

188

route is over low mountains and we'll stay down close all the way.' He traced his finger from the circle down the dotted line to the X. 'We make one pass over target and split off alternately left and right . . . and return, either north or northeast, on straight line courses to the A or B routes back to the field.' With the chalk he followed the two sides of the triangle to the corners, then back to the circle. 'Very simple. Very quick. Flight time to target will be about twenty minutes, the return route about forty-five minutes. A little more than one hour.

'Flight order will be Oberst Leader' – he chalked the numeral 1 on the board – 'Major Five Kesler, Major Eight Rendel, Major Six Beissemann, Major Three Schilling, and I will bring up the rear. After the attack pass, Oberst Leader will turn left for the first return leg to A route and, following, Major Five will turn right to B route and so on alternately.' Rudi turned to the pilots. 'Are there questions on the route?'

Eric stared dumbly at the chalk diagram. *We're going to hit Willie?* No way, he thought. No way this could be true. Like whacking a hornet's nest with a two-by-four. Rudi was bananas. Theo was bananas. They were all *dinky dau*. His mouth was dry and his stomach seemed turned to stone. This was not at all what he had expected.

'Radio procedure,' Rudi went on, 'is the same as before, German only. The Oberst will call brief orders on approach to target and give a countdown. Your route sheet has all the figures and a map sketch in case you have a problem.

'About five minutes before target we'll pass over a low mountain range and come down to about 100 feet on approach. The land is wide and flat and visibility will be excellent. We'll stay at a hundred feet until we reach the boundary of the airbase, marked by a highway. Once we cross the highway we are past the telephone lines and can drop down to about thirty feet. You'll see the runways.'

On the other half of the blackboard he drew two diagonal lines and above them a semi-circle like a large letter C, then a small square to the left of the C.

'The target aircraft are parked between this area, the flight line, and the tower.' He touched the square with the chalk. 'The aircraft are parked together in lines of about ten or twelve each in this area between the buildings and the tower.' Rudi made dozens of little crosses around the outside curve of the C. 'The tower is painted red-and-white. You'll see it early. The planes are to the right of the tower, so just guide in on the tower. There are so many aircraft you'll have no trouble finding targets. We have only one pass, so open up early and walk your fire right through ... and then get out.' He paused and put down the chalk. 'Any questions on target?'

In the interval of silence Eric was dumbfounded that no one spoke. He looked around, then down at the route sheets in his hand where the triangle sketch was reproduced with little numerical markings. He would soon pass them around.

'It is Sunday,' Rudi went on. 'There is no flight training on Sundays and the field will be deserted. All aircraft on the flight line are trainers, painted white. Very easy to see. You may see fighters but these are also for training purposes. There are no armed aircraft, and there is no anti-aircraft defense.'

Eric knew all of these facts to be true, as did any civilian pilot in the Phoenix area. He also knew that civilian air traffic could, and often did, blunder into Willie's airspace and still have the right-of-way over military aircraft, strange as it seemed.

'Question, Oberstleutnant.' Schilling raised his hand. 'Is there no radar operating on Sunday?'

'When no flying is scheduled the tower and radar are closed down.'

'Oberstleutnant?' Beissemann spoke next.

'Following the attack, would they call for armed fighters from another base?'

Bet your ass, Eric thought.

'It's possible,' came Rudi's reply. 'There is an operational fighter base, Luke, just twenty miles west of Phoenix.'

Bet your ass they're operational, Eric thought.

'However,' Rudi continued, 'I don't think base personnel will react that fast. We have a very strong advantage of surprise. Even if they called immediately for fighters from Luke I don't think they could get over to Williams in less than twenty minutes ... and in twenty minutes we'll be long gone. Since I am last in attack order' – Rudi paused, smiled without humor – 'I'll let you know if I'm right.'

A murmur of laughter rippled among the pilots.

Eric checked his watch. 0513 hours. His stomach knotted tighter. Rudi motioned for him to pass out the route sheets and he distributed them to each pilot, keeping one for himself. He was now certain that he was the only sane man in the room. Or was it that he was the only non-brave man in the room? Was this no different than Nam, where bravery was a form of temporary madness? He looked around at the others, all fresh and clean and outwardly calm, very organized and military-looking in their tan flying suits and careful orange scarves. Gray eagles to the bloody teeth, in fifteen minutes they were calmly going to crawl into the 109s and just zip down the road and shoot up Willie, just like Chino yesterday, just like that. Oh Jesus. The Herr General was right. One way or the other the Staffel was going into the history books all right.

'If we are intercepted,' Rudi was saying, 'the procedure is the same as before. If jets show up and signal you to land, do it. Then get away. They can't land, remember. We have an excellent – better than excellent – chance of returning undetected. Our camouflage is very effective and no fighter radar can pick us up at low altitudes. Be careful, be calm. Keep at least a mile apart going in and remember to stay at a hundred feet – there are telephone lines – until you cross the highway boundary. Guide on the tower, targets to the right. Questions?'

Rudi turned to Theo, who stood up and glanced over each of the pilots. Without looking down he drew his gloves from his pocket and began to pull them on. 'This is a quick and simple mission,' he said briskly. '*Es geht um die Wurst*; everything depends upon it. It has been carefully planned. As before, our biggest risk is to each other, yes? Keep your distance, mind your belly tanks ... *Ich baue auf dich* ...' He paused, snugging the gloves over his fingers and closing them at the wrists ... 'and, good hunting.'

The pilots stood, pulling on caps and gloves and slipping the route sheets into their plastic thigh pockets. Eric folded a route sheet into his pocket and pulled on his heavy work gloves. Rudi came over to him.

'Leave the hangar doors open, Leutnant. When we come back we'll get the planes under cover immediately. We're running late so you need not wave us off.'

'We should fire up all seven,' Eric suggested, 'in case one doesn't run right.'

'Good,' Rudi agreed. 'Let's go.'

'Rudi?'

Eric looked into calm blue eyes, an expression devoid of

emotion. Madness? 'Watch your ass, huh?' Eric said. 'Remember what I told you.'

In minutes all seven aircraft were rolled out and started up and turning over. There was trouble with Number Three, Schilling's, and the others looked on impatiently from their cockpits as Eric checked it out, leaning over the cockpit at Schilling's shoulder, scanning the dials. *Keep busy*, he thought. The ground trembled with the thunder of the engines, even at low revs. Eric could feel the vibrations in tingling waves through his feet as he stood on Schilling's wing.

'Looks OK!' Schilling shouted over the engine as he stuffed cotton plugs in both ears.

'You want Seven, just in case?' Eric yelled back.

Schilling shook his head vehemently, pulling his gloves tight.

Eric leaned in and yelled, 'Watch your ass, Major Three!'

Schilling nodded. Eric leaped down from the wing and the 109 jerked forward. The others were taxiing out now, slowly, letting the engines get smooth, flexing flaps and elevators. The noise was deafening. Propwash blew dust around Eric as he watched, adjusting his motorcycle goggles. *Keep moving*, he thought. He felt very weird and light. He watched Number Two, the last plane – Rudi – turn and move away, rudder waving back and forth. With Rudi's propwash whipping at him, he went over to Number Seven where it idled empty. He pulled the wheel chocks away.

'Keep moving,' he said aloud, alone. He went around to the port side of the plane and stuck his right foot in the fuselage step aperture with the little hinged flap and hoisted himself up into the cockpit. *Just keep moving. One hour, that's all.* He settled into the seat and scanned the instrument faces. Smooth as silk. He looked up. The others were out on the strip now and Theo was lifting off, retracting his wheels the instant the plane left the ground. Beyond the strip, the first rays of dawn crawled across the tips of distant mountains like orange-gold lava.

Eric boosted the throttle a little, watching the needles move on the panel, then pulled out the route sheet and unfolded it and smoothed it out and slipped it into the plastic thigh pocket. He checked the instruments again. Lookin' good. He thought it was funny how his stomach hurt and his mouth was dry, like Nam. *Shoulda brought a Coors, man.* He looked out on the strip. Schilling was lifting off and Rudi was rolling. *One freakin' hour, man, one freakin' hour of brave.* He thought about Marta and about the way she looked at Schilling and the way they waltzed together. He pulled off the work gloves and threw them over the side. *Keep moving.* He drew the belts over his shoulder and buckled in, then took out the thin black calfskin gloves and tugged them on, snugging each finger tight. It was the first time he had worn them and they smelled good. He released the brake, pushing on throttle. The engine rose in pitch. Number Seven jerked forward. He leaned out, watching pale blue flame spitting from the exhaust ports, feeling the airframe tremble with contained power.

He got off smoothly and went up to 500 feet and started a slow turn south. He had lost the others but he knew he would come up below them eventually. It was an anxious two full minutes before he saw one, then two, already spreading out at 1000 feet. He climbed and closed on Rudi to about a mile, staying much lower. He was calm now and again he wished he'd thought to grab a beer from the cooler.

Rudi was pulling away. Hauling ass now, Eric thought as he pushed on more throttle.

Once he was confident of his bearings Theo scanned his instrument faces automatically and gradually increased throttle. The 109 sailed south-southwest true and swift. Building airspeed, he tuned his senses to the steady roaring pulse of the Daimler-Benz just a few feet from his knees, its vibration transmitting power to each of his nerve endings. There was a fleeting satisfaction that the craftsmanship of the great engine lived on in the thousands of Mercedes in this fat country of America. He was elated now, confident. There was minimal risk to the mission, this brilliant mission that would in thirty minutes achieve what he had set out to do. It would be a triumph that would surpass any other in his life. The war, the careful building of an empire, the wealth, the acclaim – all would pale in just thirty minutes in this rose-gray dawn in America. As if from the faintest nervous tic, sublime pride lifted the corners of his mouth. *Follow me,* he thought back to the pilots behind him, *and they will write books about us.*

Slightly less than two miles behind Theo, Walther Kesler guided his 109 with cold concentration. He also sensed the magnitude of their mission and whatever fears he had were displaced, by discipline, with a delectable tension. His was the excitement of battle. And of supremacy. This mission would be the turning point, the reward.

From his tension there came a taste of retribution, retrieved and awakened. There was a day over Germany in 1944 when he realized the war was over and he had cried – no one knew, would ever know – when the B-17s came without end, to the limits of vision, dark dots streaming contrails, dropping deadly blizzards of bombs, raining fire on the square and the cathedral and the farm, all gone in acres of ash, mother and father and both sisters.

And now the last word would be theirs. From then to now it was worth everything to be alive at this moment. Kesler picked out Theo's 109 ahead and raised a gloved hand to his brow in salute.

Anton Rendel, third in line, calmly checked and rechecked every detail of his aircraft in flight. It required attention to keep increasing airspeed and he repeatedly peered ahead to keep Kesler in sight at the proper interval. He was sure he was going to die in the next hour. He had learned long ago the formulas of irony and he had had a very clear premonition that the moment he made the decision at the airport to return to the Staffel he had signed the writ for his death. But it was far preferable to the spectre of drooling and tottering like the old man. And so it felt now. He was clean and shaved and combed and his scarf was tied perfectly and his flying suit pressed and zippered properly. He had been a good fighter pilot then and he was a good fighter pilot now.

All his life he was sorry about the Spitfire pilot that had fallen into his prop over Kent, that terrible sound that would haunt him for thirty-five years, that terrible debris of burst pomegranate. And he never forgot the Mosquito that burned mysteriously in level flight after his twilight attack over the North Sea. It just turned into an inferno, no one coming out, the skin burning away to reveal the wooden structure of the tailfin, the plywood body. He had flown alongside, screaming at them to get out, but it just kept flying and burning. The war seemed incomprehensible now, as he looked back, but he had done what was expected of him, done it well.

Such a vast and desolate place below, he mused, looking out. It was a good place for the end. He wished he could somehow have just one more good cigar.

Fourth in line, Gustav Beissemann adjusted his Space Cadet cap, poked a gloved finger at the bottom rim of his sunglasses, and broke into a wide grin. His tension was now mixed with nervous amusement; it seemed hilarious, what they were doing. He began almost uncontrollably to laugh aloud, his laughter a pleasant quivering in his chest, drowned in the engine's roar. They would pull it off, just like Chino, in and out, wonderfully outrageous, invincible in their madness. They would zip through without a scratch. In less that fifteen minutes they would be over target. Today, he thought with relish, they were going to make *Time* and *Newsweek*.

He believed Theo now, believed they would all live in secret notoriety, famed mystery fighters nameless but glorified. Though the only nameless glory Beissemann wanted when this was over was that BOAC stewardess based in London, a velvet-voiced German girl flying British whose first name always escaped him; Eichenthal was her last, the one who put her warm stockinged foot at his throat in the taxi from Heathrow that night. That was nameless glory. Take her to the Bahamas, he decided. Beissemann had now successfully transformed the heavy pressure under his sternum from apprehension to lust.

Fifth in line, Schilling had no premonitions of death, no particular fear that the mission against Williams would be, in itself, especially dangerous. Rather, Schilling's fear of catastrophe, of dying, was far outweighed by his fear of spending the rest of his life in prison. He still carried the bitter resentment of those years of internment in England and he found it all too easy to imagine himself growing feeble in a tiny concrete cell, until he came out in a box. He touched the almost imperceptible bulk of Marta's scarf in his pocket. There would be no one to care if they hauled his ass off to jail. Always alone. Pleasant and temporary. Even now he had a peculiar illusion of solitude, hurtling over the godforsaken heaps of rock below, only the speck of Bison's 109 ahead to remind him of reality.

He thought about the target aircraft. Would they be sitting ducks, standing silent with no defense, no secret system that would erupt and swallow any armed attack? He imagined hitting the jets with 20 millimeter, remembering all too clearly the Milwaukee Air Show the year before when he saw a Hawker Harrier VTO auger in from sixty feet in front of the crowd during a demonstration flight at Mitchell Field. Damned thing blew to hell with a fireball the size of a two-story house. Jets went big, all that fuel, not like the piston-engine fighters he had strafed in Russia. He reminded himself to stay off the deck, maybe fifty feet, no less.

Sixth in line, one mile astern, Rudi was keeping Schilling's 109 clearly in sight, glancing back and forth from his compass to the little dark shape silhouetted ahead in the gray-blue dawn.

He kept alert for civilian air traffic, searching each quadrant of sky. Running into some slow and wandering Cessna at this speed would be just the sort of unexpected disaster one could expect. All they had to do was think clearly and fly smoothly and they would all be back – he checked his watch – in fifty minutes. He watched Schilling ahead, trying to ignore the recurring fantasy of standing in court as a traitor charged with master-minding an attack on his own country. Again and again he had weighed the odds. How many airbases had they all hit before? Without flak, nothing to it. And they did have the advantage of complete surprise.

But he knew the attack was not the worst risk. The real risk was Luke; they were up to their ass in hardware over there. God help us all, he thought, and keep us from any error. And from death.

Seventh and last in line, Eric skimmed the mountains about a mile behind and below Rudi, keeping his brother-in-law's aircraft clearly in view, knowing there was no way Rudi could spot him. He was strung out high, wired as tight as any mission in Nam, he realized. In the roar of the cockpit he spoke aloud to himself, not hearing, his voice resonating in his throat. 'One hour.'

His hands were sweating under the gloves and he glanced nervously at the rock ridges flashing under him, the 109 lifting and dipping as he followed the contours of the ragged terrain. He thought of Schilling somewhere up ahead, picturing him cool and deadly calm in the cockpit, his lip curled in that pouting look he had. 'Right back here behind you, Major Three,' Eric called out. 'Gonna get some! All *right*!'

He checked his watch; 0559 hours. One hour of brave. Fifty minutes to go. Ten minutes – less – to Willie. They'd push it to the wall as they came in, he reminded himself, and it would be better to stay tight on Rudi. At a quarter-mile he tucked up low and behind where he could now see the dirty blue under-surface of Rudi's 109, the blue tear-drop belly tank and flat twin oil cooler boxes under each wing. He studied the 109 for a moment, thinking how menacingly beautiful a weapon it was still. He knew every inch, every rivet, every wire in that aircraft, had even stenciled and spray-painted the big insignia crosses so perfect black, so perfect white.

He saw Rudi lift a little now, leaving a thin dark exhaust trail that hung like a smear of soot against the flawless flat gray-blue sky. Rudi was getting on it. They were getting close. Jesus. God, they were all mad, man. Bowling balls. His stomach knotted.

'All right-o-Rudi,' he called, careful to keep his finger off the mike button. 'Right behind you, man! Der Leutnant ist gekommen, Willie! Gonna get some! Der Leutnant und der Oberstleutnant und der Oberst und der Majors ist gekommen, Willie, so all you fighter jocks get to hell out of the way! All der Katzenjammer kids ist gekommen, Willie, mit der Messerschmitts und ve ist going to vaste all der Tveets und der T-38s! Blow your *mind*, Willie!'

And he suddenly remembered reading an article in the newspaper about a new program at Willie to train women pilots and he hoped to Jesus none of them would be anywhere near that fucking base today. Women pilots, Jesus what a half-assed idea that was. How terrible to think about any honeys getting wasted. What faggot maniac in Washington had that harebrained idea? Goddamnit, keep the honeys out of the shooting, protect them forever. Marta sleeping popped into his mind, remembering crawling tipping drunkenly into bed, throwing one arm heavily over her ribcage, burying his face in the scented tangle of her hair, wanting to awaken her and say 'I'm sorry' though he didn't know then, or now, for what. While you are sleeping, Marta, I am here.

'Right here,' he called out. 'All right-o-Rudi, Major Three, I am here!'

As if in answer, startling him, Theo's voice came over the R/T. '*Zwanzig-Meilen Marke. Feurt Gewehre zum Test!*'

Shit, Eric thought. He had overlooked the small detail of not being able to understand what the hell they were saying. Then, a hundred feet ahead and above, Rudi's 109 trailed thin white smoke past the fuselage and Eric saw red embers and white fireballs spewing out ahead. The spent shells whipped past Eric's plane, some of them clinking sharply on his port wing surface. All right-o-Rudi, he thought, I got it; test fire. He reached for his gun arming switches, then stopped. No way he could test fire without Rudi seeing it. Calm and easy now.

'*Fünfzehn-Meilen Marke,*' Theo's voice in German came again.

Rudi was still pulling ahead. Eric swallowed, pushed the throttle. Airspeed 375 mph . . . 380 Damn, if only he knew what Theo was saying! Never mind, man. Just hang loose. It means that you're going to do Willie. Hoo, Jesus. He remembered Slim Pickens riding the bomb in *Dr Strangelove*.

'Ve ist gekommen, Willie,' he screamed suddenly. 'Der Messerschmitts ist gekommen!'

Cresting the last ridge at 0609 hours Theo came rocketing down the slopes of the Superstition Mountain range at 402 mph, tearing through a paper-thin layer of gauze haze and trailing a sooty line of exhaust. He saw before him a vast clear plain.

'Twelve-mile mark,' he said into the R/T in German. 'Beginning run.' Red gun lights stared from the instrument panel. The earth rushed under him in a wide blurred band. There were acres of farmland spread out ahead and as he reached the plain he eased the stick back smoothly and leveled off at 150 feet. He recognized huge brown fields of cotton, corn in even green lines, great rust-colored expanses of irrigated land in dizzying patterns of silver where water lay between geometrically perfect rows of tilled dirt. Remarkable in this desert, he thought, scanning the horizon left to right and easing down to 100 feet without looking at the altimeter. His eyes swept the center portion of horizon at the end of the 109's nose. A gray line, highway, whipped under him.

'Four-mile mark,' he said into the R/T. 'Crossing airfield boundary road.' He pushed a little more stick, settling to eighty, sixty, forty, twenty feet, then eased it back. He picked out the tiny spike of the control tower just a little to port. Right on line. Runway coming . . . green grass . . . he crossed the runway in a flash . . . another coming now. He kept his eyes locked on the tower. His gloved thumb lifted the gun-button shield. Square shapes of hangars materialized beyond the tower. And then the white dots of the target aircraft. There seemed to be hundreds, a solid line of white tailfins and fuselages. Every round would hit. He eased the white shapes into his sights. Range closing . . . 350 . . . 300 . . . 250 yards. He could see now that the aircraft were parked in rows of about ten each, one row after another, wingtip to wingtip, across and beyond his sights to either side. *Now*.

He squeezed his fingers. Banging clatter shook the cockpit as smoke whipped back along both sides of his windscreen and the tracers zoomed out, arrowing into the white aircraft, sparking flashing. And then he clearly saw, as if in some heart-stopping dream, that one was *moving, two were moving*, red beacons flashing in the center of their tailfins, not white planes but mottled blue-green, taxiing nearly broadside into his fire, and too late he saw his shells striking one moving jet aft of the double cockpit where the twin canopies were raised, two white helmets visible, and he was past, streaking but several feet over the tailfins. He stopped firing, flashing by the control tower painted gaudily in big red-and-white squares, swooping upward. A thin vein of dread oozed into Theo's tripping senses; he had struck *moving aircraft*. He glanced back. There were two more aircraft, one on the taxi strip, one out on the runway. They were blue and green, not white.

'This is Oberst Leader,' he snapped into the R/T in German. 'There are target aircraft moving on runway left of tower repeat left of tower. Fire on them repeat fire on them!'

Another decision, he thought. The jets would kill them if they got up. Or they would follow them. They were fighters, not trainers. As he climbed and turned he weighed the next decision. Should he make another pass, fire on them? Were they armed? He decided to follow the original plan, knowing that any change could cause a fatal confusion.

At that moment Kesler's 109 cleared the boundary road and he was watching the diagonal concrete band of runway sweep toward him. He had sighted the tower and was locked on target at an altitude of twenty-five feet when Theo's warning came over the R/T. Automatically he made the instantaneous decision to rudder left of the tower. He too was astounded by the lines of parked white aircraft filling his sights. Kesler opened fire, his shells and bullets chattering across the taxi strip early. He could see that his fire would savage one line of aircraft after another. It was a mirage, he thought then, blinking as two planes, not white, seemed to be moving. They were blue, with blinking red lights on the tails. In the part of a second it took to pass over the moving planes, Kesler realized that they were manned and that he had hit one, seeing his cannon shells tear away the rudder and most of the square tailfin. He kept firing because there were more target planes, no way to miss. It was chaos. The trainers were so close together the whole line would go, one setting off another.

As Kesler's 109 howled by the tower, banking and climbing, he glanced out at the runway, his eye catching a rolling jet. It was then he understood Theo's message. Instinctively he put the jet in his sights. It was about to lift off – he could see the white furnace of the after-burner in the blue morning light – and in seconds it would accelerate up and out of range. And turn on them. He fired well before he was within range, his tracers sparking down the runway in pursuit. The jet was off the ground now, its nose rising, and Kesler's hail of shells and bullets spattered across the fuselage and both wings as he passed over. Climbing, he looked back once to see the jet still nosing up. A thin sheet of gray smoke began to stream out of the tailpipes. Kesler headed home.

Third in line, Rendel had no need to search out the target area. Dead ahead of the blunt nose of his 109 the horizon sparkled with orange flashes. He came down on the deck, alert to Theo's message, but confused. Awe-struck by the sight of multiple explosions and the thick rolling smoke ahead, he leveled off at sixty feet and set up for the attack. He was fearful of the exploding aircraft, and he steered further left. Then the white shapes took form and he saw there would be plenty of target. He opened up early, watching his tracers sail ahead and curve downward into the white planes. In another second he was tearing into the flight line. His steady fire, deadly accurate, lashed the parked trainers in a storm of debris. He kept on the buttons, seeing distinctly one aircraft, no *two*, unlike the others, blue-green fighters, moving among the white trainers, red tail beacons flashing, now one skidding and tipping like a giant toy as its landing gear collapsed and two pilots leaping out of the double cockpit, their white helmets and olive-drab flight suits clear in every detail. He caught a glimpse of pools of burning fuel spreading under the trainers. *Get up, get out*, he thought, lifting past the control tower, then seeing ahead of him the extraordinary sight of an airborne jet streaming white, lifting off the runway. He was closing on it. Fascinated, he kept on the throttle, and drew closer. It was not white but blue and green and he could see its odd Coke-bottle shape, the stubby razor-thin wings and low tailplanes, the wide squarish fin, the twin tail-pipes spewing smoke. He could see numerous rents in the metal skin of the fuselage and across the starboard wing surface. He did not need to shoot; he could tell the jet was in trouble. Even as he watched, a tiny glowing line of fire trailed out from beneath the fuselage and the jet began a slow roll.

'Get out!' Rendel muttered anxiously. 'Now get out.'

Both of the jet's canopies popped off and tumbled back and first one pilot and then the other was ejected in a flash of flame and puff of white smoke, spreading apart still in their seats, small bright orange drogue chutes blooming dragging out streaming orange main chutes. They would be OK, he thought, climbing and looking back and then seeing the jet rolling completely over and sailing down into a hangar where it blew up in a massive double explosion.

Fourth in line, Beissemann saw the flash of the hangar going up from a distance of less than two miles. He knew from the size of the flash that it was something other than the explosion of stationary aircraft, perhaps a fuel supply. He was alarmed by the strange explosion and all the rising smoke ahead and now he had a premonition of disaster. He was hurtling across the runways at 410 mph at an altitude of forty-five feet and had already made the decision to keep to the right of the tower, regardless of Theo's message which, after all, was not an order. By habit, Beissemann made decisions like a computer, quickly and irrevocably, especially when under any stress. He would do exactly as they had been told at briefing. The tower was clear now and the flight line was horrendously clear, an inferno, and he would fly on course, fire on target, turn to port and get out.

He was closing on range and he saw more orange flashes and he spoke aloud into the R/T – '*Wir haben uns vermessen*!' – as the white target aircraft grew in his sights and he opened fire, suddenly realizing he had somehow lost about twenty feet of altitude and finding himself lower than he had planned, the ground whizzing blurred under his wings, and in his rapid-fire flash-flow of thoughts there registered the fact that he had made a minute error; the decision to stay right and to speak had cost a slice of a seconds – *not good*, he thought as his Messerschmitt screamed over the first row of trashed smoking trainers, his belly tank barely clearing the white tail-fins, seeing another explosion to his left hurling flaming pieces higher than he was flying, thinking god*damn* those babies blew up with a hell of a larger fireball than piston fighters; Schilling had said they did. Then one went up just ahead of him billowing up bright orange and he saw he was going to fly through the top of the fireball and he braced and hauled back on the stick, knowing it was going to be a jolt. The shock wave slammed under the starboard wing and tipped the plane, banging his head against the canopy, jerking his gloved hand holding the stick, heaving the entire aircraft up and over. The port wing dipped, all balance upset, and he saw the ground out the port side, saw the horizon tip crazily. *Not this way*, he just had time to think as the wingtip caught on the concrete and hurled the 109 into a cartwheel the nose slamming in first compacting the engine into the cockpit and shearing the port wing off cleanly as the tail came around and the fuselage collapsed midway behind the cockpit buckling and then exploding in a roaring mass of junk disintegrating in a long avalanche of broiling orange flame that rolled 300 feet down the taxi strip and into the grass.

Trailing by four seconds, Schilling was confused by Beissemann's message, '*We have misjudged ourselves*', not knowing if he should laugh or be warned. He was level and stable at sixty feet and was perfectly set up to fire. Equally confused by Theo's message, he also made the decision to remain to the right of the tower like the original plan. *Concentrate*, he told himself. Range closing 300 . . . 250. Then a flash in his peripheral vision, rolling flame at ten o'clock that looked like a plane going in . . . 200 yards. *Fire.* Explosions blossomed left and right, two, three, even as his guns opened up filling the cockpit with the cordite smell, shaking him in his seat. God what a mess, he thought, watching the target planes quiver as the shells slammed in and there was a blue one angled oddly one wingtip on the ground someone moving white helmets two pilots as he flashed over them in a blink seeing in astonishment one of the pilots half-crouched by his plane defiantly giving him a gloved finger and he knew then it was all going wrong and pulled back on the stick and let go the gun-button and trigger banking to port passing the tower thinking *no more*. It was like the Fourth of July – those pilots? and what the hell blew up over here? – as he passed over all that smeared fire then a still-skidding wingtip bright sky-blue and black-and-white cross *no* and a bright blue belly tank still tumbling end over end *no* and with curious horror he glimpsed one of the 109's wheels still flying free below and alongside his wing. The wheel was sailing flat like a saucer and it arced and dropped and was gone. Like Major Bison was gone. Schilling felt his stomach rise and turn and he slumped in his seat with the stick pulled back, the engine pulling lifting him away. Without thinking he kept a wide left turn and headed north-northwest instead of north, to A route instead of B. It wouldn't matter, he realized, inhaling sharply; not now. He never looked down or back.

Rudi had closed the gap behind Schilling to scarcely a quarter-mile and when he came in range of the decimated flight line he was so stupified by the nightmate of exploding aircraft and rising black-gray smoke that he never thought to open fire. There were at least two dozen planes burning that he could see and another dozed tilted on collapsed landing gear like broken-winged birds. And there a whole hangar going up, a *hangar*. How the hell could 20 millimeters set off a goddamn *hangar*? He felt light-headed, strange, a mix of elation . . . and apprehension.

In slightly less than three seconds Rudi passed over the blazing wreckage of the flight line, piercing walls of smoke in a flutter of dark and light, smelling fuel and oil and rubber – the charred scent of war – his memory spinning backwards. We have indeed misjudged ourselves, he thought darkly, intrigued with Beissemann's message. He began his left turn about a half-mile past the tower, keeping the throttle wide open. He glanced once more over his shoulder at the hangar boiling in smoke and then down at his compass. Looking at his watch he realized the attack had taken less than seven minutes . . . All we have to do now, he thought, is make it back.

Eric had let Rudi pull ahead as they came down onto the plain. He knew he only had to follow Rudi and they'd skate right into Willie like two toys on a string and then sky out. No sweat. Then the highway whizzed up and flashed underneath and he dropped to fifty feet and leveled off. He quit watching Rudi then and looked ahead to the dark smoke and orange flashes. *Uh-oh*, he thought.

'Your turn, Big Time,' he said aloud. Ho boy, calm and easy now.

He was momentarily hypnotized by the holocaust on the horizon now sweeping closer. No trouble finding a target. Man, what a mess, a real Numbah Ten. He touched his thumb and forefinger lightly against the gun-button and cannon trigger. He would do everything exactly right, though there was that gnawing growing pressure inside as if he was going to heave his guts: it was fear, a fear that something had gone wrong in all that smoke, something he wouldn't know about because he couldn't understand the transmissions in German. The runways came up, zipped under his wings. Red gun lights glowed . . . airspeed 415 mph . . . the destruction ahead was now mind-boggling . . . Numbah Ten for sure . . . they had blown Willie's flight line to pieces. Don't puke now, he thought, feeling cold sweat, seeing the tiny white rectangular chips of tailfins against the dark smoke. Calm and easy now. He was closing on range, doing everything right everything right, nearly crawling out of his skin, God, seeing one of the target planes bloom orange and vanish in the fireball, debris sailing. Now coming up fast on dozens of the little side-by-side two-seater T-37 Tweets scattered like blasted burning broken geese in pools of flaming fuel and then an odd blue fighter tilted on one wing, double canopies open, tailfin shot away and now the rows of odd long-bodied white needle-nosed T-38s flaming tilted burning in acres of smoking junk. Now roaring through boiling rising soft black clouds, flashes of dark then light then dark like blinking, smoke smell sweat smell, the tower came up in red-and-white circus paint and whisked past to port and Jesus a hangar over there gone to hell the roof collapsing showering sparks like a steel mill, and now calm and open air, joy at being alive, awe for the destruction below and a wash of relief and then curiosity for what looked like two orange parachutes, yes, drifting to the ground out by the runway. Eric began his turn, thinking I did it just right all right-o-Rudi. And then realizing he'd never fired a single round. It is a most Numbah Ten mess, Oberst, and the shit is going to hit the fan. Better pray there are no fly-boys in that mess and God help us please no honeys. Lifting away he used all the throttle he had. Now beat feet, he thought, most ricky-tick.

CHAPTER THIRTEEN

Once out of his turn south of the field, Schilling slid his canopy back to let the fluttering turbulence whip his face cool. *Think now*, he reminded himself harshly, *and forget Bison. You have already made one error by turning right instead of left, and small errors become big ones when you are flying. Check gauges . . . all OK . . . airspeed 280. Altitude 800 feet . . . plenty of fuel . . . bearing check from the sheet once again . . . wrong, they were* wrong, damnit; he had transposed west and north, incredibly, and was flying *west*-northwest instead of *north*-northwest. He slammed the canopy shut to ease his concentration, steering right and climbing to 1000 feet while he worked out the correct course. He figured he had lost at least five minutes off-course and would not only be on the wrong return route but last as well. He decided to check it out once more, remembering how he had been lost a dozen times over Russia, losing a 109 when he had run out of fuel coming back from covering the 6th Army leaving Stalingrad. When he crossed Route 60 he knew by the map he was OK, and he then calculated that Rudi was ahead of him and that he had forty minutes to the field. He was not about to be both last and late. He pushed on more throttle.

Rudi had come out of his turn south of the field and then slipped into the heading home, trying to put aside in his mind the destruction behind him. Now it was important only to get back quickly, on course. He flew at 1000 feet and 300 mph, anxious to raise the open expanse of desert north of 60. As each minute ticked off he became less tense. Major Bison would be five, six miles ahead and Schilling would be over Apache

Junction, bringing up the rear on B route. The air was clear and he could see the desert flat and endless, the mountains like islands in a pale pink sea. He estimated twelve minutes over the desert to the turn into A route and another fifteen minutes to the field. When he crossed Route 60 he began to ease off, overcoming the temptation to fly faster. He leveled off at 100 feet when he reached the desert. He was very thirsty.

Eric was on course at 1200 feet and 325 mph. He didn't want to be seen by Rudi, though he resolved to try to get him in sight as they neared the field. He grinned, thinking of how the others would react. Then he remembered he had not fired his guns. Would they think he had been afraid to fire? Would it be enough that he had just flown the mission? Or worse, yet, would they not believe him? He could empty his guns over the desert if he decided to do so . . . but he wasn't sure.

He wondered if they had called up the jets from Luke. He didn't let himself calculate how far Luke was, though he guessed 50 miles, and he didn't let himself calculate how long it would take jets to get over to Willie and then make some decision on how to search. He knew Rudi was right; they all had a good chance of getting back. Gotcha, Major Three, he thought. I was right behind you guys all the way. He grinned again. Most definitely the Herr General would go *dinky-dau*. And Rudi would give him a ration of shit for sure, but no matter . . . they would know he had done the mission. Especially Schilling. And Marta. That was enough, it was all he needed.

Glancing below he picked out familiar landmarks and boosted his airspeed to 350, watching for Rudi. He decided not to empty his guns when he got to the desert. It would be kind of a lie to do that. He had done everything perfectly and now he would not jeopardize that, not for anything. He thought about debriefing – that would be a trip; he'd get a cold beer like the others and smoke the joint right in the briefing room while the Herr General and Rudi chewed his ass out. Schilling and Major Bison would grin at each other like they always did. He leaned forward in the cockpit and looked back on both sides, surprised to see a long thin cloudbank southwest. Probably coming in from California, like all the weather did. It stretched for miles and miles at about 20,000 feet, behind and around Willie.

His watch read 0629 hours. He wondered if the Air Force

was up and around. He grinned again, imagining the pandemonium at Willie, all the airmen leaping about in their skivvies, thinking the Russians had hit them, all kinds of screw-ups in the confusion. He dialed the radio, searching for Air Force channels. There was light, steadily-hissing static, like a dirty record on a turntable.

Schilling had the 109 wide open, watching the instrument faces. The desert was in sight and he began a descent to 600 feet. He had checked his map and compass repeatedly and though he was sure he was on course he was troubled over his error, recalling his botched landing. That's why there were no fifty-year-old fighter pilots, he reminded himself. Maybe Bison screwed up, too. He found himself trying to imagine how he might be wrong about Bison; maybe it was someone else. It was a 109 for sure, that sky-blue wingtip with the cross, the tumbling blue belly tank. No, there was no mistake, no hope. He had learned long ago about hope, about how, whenever the news came – a telephone call, a letter, the face of the doctor walking toward you – you always hoped first that there was some mistake someplace. But there never was.

Fly faster, he thought, and maybe you'll leave some of the pain behind. He was over the desert now. He descended still further, no longer watching the altimeter but concentrating ahead. The engine howled in an even piercing tone, setting up a vibration, a resonance in the airframe that tingled like a mild electric current. Schilling watched the dark clumps of desert bush and the weird green fingers of saguaro cactus whip beneath him. He was not apprehensive anymore; no radar of any kind could pick up aircraft this low.

'—is Cobra Leader. Do you copy, Three?' the voice leaped out of the headset in Eric's ears as if the pilot were sitting beside him. The voice jolted him and he could hear the whining of a jet behind the pilot's words. His heart quickened. 'Affirmative, Three. Down to one thousand, so it's tough. Got some bad static. Can you raise Willie Control for me, Three? Over.'

Eric began to feel cold. It was Air Force that voice. Static crackled. He listened intently, eyes sweeping ahead and above, waiting, knowing he could only hear the pilot sending, but not receiving.

'Roger, Three,' the voice resumed. 'Relay message Cobra Leader section four coordinates' – static and rumble garbled the voice, then vanished – 'zero five estimate four two miles. I've got a visual. One bandit repeat visual one bandit. Request instruction. Over.'

Calm and easy now, Eric repeated to himself. A visual meant the pilot could see, and thus be seen. He searched the sky above, behind, ahead. Nothing. Nothing anywhere in a perfect crystal sky – then there should be no static. Was the Air Force tracking someone on B route? He remembered the weather front.

'Yeah I copy, Three,' the voice came back. 'No question. Piston engine, German markings and some outstanding camouflage. Estimated airspeed three-nine-zero knots and way down on the deck. Am closing, repeat closing. Advise quickly repeat quickly. Over.'

Oh God, Eric thought, they've got one of the guys. Numbah Ten now, most definitely Numbah Ten.

Rudi was staying level and very low, watching ahead as the terrain swept under him like an insanely fast-moving belt of painted scenery . . . airspeed 275 mph . . . altitude thirty feet. He felt safe because he knew how good the camouflage paint was, and there was a comfortable security in holding his speed and altitude even and steady as the seconds ticked by. Ahead he could see the mountains where he would make his turn.

Off the starboard wing the ground was rising gradually, as if he were flying alongside a banked high-speed track. He could see his own shadow skipping over the sand and as the ground swelled more steeply the shadow became more clearly defined. It was rather fascinating, like flying with another 109, like having company. He could recognize the long tapered fuselage, the heavy nose, the belly tank, the high rounded tail. Ahead, the mountains were growing closer. He checked his watch; 0649 hours. The turn would be coming up in just a few minutes. He glanced to starboard again where his shadow darted.

There were two shadows.

Rudi felt his heart stop, then trip and resume, pounding. The new shadow was clear and dart-like with a wide cropped fin and it hung above his own clear shadow; two dark rocket-fish skimming the sand bottom of an endless sea of open air. He would never have believed he could be pierced so horribly by fear. He was unable to breathe. His bladder began voiding warmly, and he sank weakly in the seat.

'Yeah I copy, Three,' came the voice in Eric's headphones, 'but you got some bad static over there. Tell Willie Control I got my bandit cold, right on my wingtip, clear as day. Fuselage carries a big number Two. And we're right down on the deck, trimmin' the cactus. Relay to Willie Control Cobra Leader proceeding as instructed. And stand by, Three. Over.'

Ahhh Jeeesus, Eric moaned, it's Rudi. Panic came crawling uncoiling like snakes awakening in his flight suit. Real Numbah Ten. Rudi and the jet would be dead ahead. He squinted to the left and right of his thick armor-glass windscreen. Make it a recon plane, he prayed, or a T-38 unarmed, please. He pushed full throttle.

Rudi forced himself with agonizing effort to turn and look up and back. The jet fighter hovered above and behind some fifty feet away, weaving. It seemed smaller than he would have expected and it was silent – no roar, no whine, – its noise trailing eerily behind. From his viewpoint the jet was dramatically foreshortened; all nose – flat black and needle-tipped – and fuselage, painted in wide jagged bands of dull olive and bright yellow-tan, swelling up to the canopy bubble and back to the fin. Dark twin cannon barrels protruded above the nose – 20 millimeter, he knew, like his own single nose cannon, except these could spit out shells like a berserk machine gun, thousands of rounds in seconds. It would be quick. The jet hung nose-high as if in landing altitude and there were two squarish flaps – air brakes, he guessed – hanging under the fuselage that, like the undersurfaces of the wings, glowed gold-pink from the reflecting sand rushing below. And, most ominously, as if it were the only sign of life, in the tall sharkfin tailfin a red beacon pulsed, rythmically in time with the muscular thumping cadence of his own heart.

Finally the transparent acrylic bubble of the canopy, the pilot's white helmet and black visor barely visible – *Angel of my death*, he thought – so impassively faceless it might as well have been a robot riding, guiding.

He turned back, looking ahead. Automatically he scanned the instrument faces, reading nothing, hollow, nearly numb. He understood now that there was no escape, that it had all come down to this moment – secretly he thought it might, was not surprised – and that it was his time to die. *Well, if it was the time then it was the time.* Small surprise that his life did not begin to spin out in reverse like some memory tape gone amok. Nothing. There was instead a feeling of surreal clarity that came easily, naturally, a single thought, it was a long life and a short life. And by unchangeable design – destiny – his had all come finally to this. Like some Zen puzzle. It was simply the end.

'Bandit Number Two,' came the pilot's voice in Eric's headphones, 'this is Air Force Cobra One sittin on your ass. Acknowledge. Over.' The voice was not so calm now, Eric noted. He looked above, left, right and behind. Could he be ahead of Rudi, somehow off course? Should he say something over the R/T? Was Rudi receiving the pilot? Sweat beaded his forehead. Blinking, he scanned the desert ahead.

'Bandit Number Two. Acknowledge, repeat acknowledge, by waving or lowering your landing gear. Over,' came the voice again.

Then Eric had his visual. He blinked, stared . . . yes, a shadow, darting movement . . . aircraft, deceiving in its elusive camouflage, flash of sun reflection in the brown sandscape, eleven o'clock . . . two shapes – he thought of the hummingbird – two aircraft, and he was closing on them. His breathing grew quick and shallow when he recognized the jet, rocket-shape rocking wings slightly, twin tailpipes glowing white, sitting nearly on top of Rudi's 109. He was still closing, watching them sailing over the sand rises . . . 400 yards maybe . . . there they are, for real, asshole-to-bellybutton. Numbah Ten.

'Cobra Three, this is Leader. I'm not receiving you. If you can hear me, tell Willie Control I'm getting no response from Bandit. Over.' The voice paused and the whine of the jet was clear. 'Bandit Number Two . . . you are ordered, repeat ordered, to lower your landing gear. Acknowledge *now*. Over.'

Rudi realized that he was no longer thinking; he was merely steering, riding. Paralysis. He had no thought of landing, of . . . just nothing. He glanced back again at the jet's canopy, remembering what Eric had said. *The kid's going to get you*, Rudi, he thought. This is for real now. Like over Europe. Think . . . think or die. The pilot would be young, green . . . no combat time, no kills. *Think*.

Eric was closing fast at 300 yards. He could see the jet clearly now, nose up, the odd swollen Coke-bottle shape painted bright olive-tan, the blue wingtip rockets, twin exhaust ports glowing. He swallowed, feeling just below his throat his heart tapping as if someone knocked impatiently on a door.

'Bandit Number Two. Acknowledge repeat acknowledge now or I open fire repeat I will fire.' The voice. The jet whine.

Eric knew then that Rudi wasn't receiving. Please, he thought. Please, Jesus. This is a fucking nightmare. Please don't look back, he pleaded silently with the jet pilot. As if it were something separate from his arm or body or will, his gloved hand moved up and flicked the gun-arming switches. The red lights came on.

Schilling now had his visual contact. Not a shape, just a flash of reflected sunlight at one o'clock, low and ahead. It had to be Rudi. He steered right, staying low, a little relieved to have the Oberstleutnant in sight. And then he saw the long charcoal smudge hanging above him in the air. He grinned. Now he could just follow Rudi's exhaust trail all the way back.

Then the 109 ahead snapped into focus, weaving along a sand ridge very low. He was closing too fast, he realized, and he was reaching out to pull back the throttle when he saw two other shapes. Two aircraft ahead of the first. He blinked again, not believing. *Three* aircraft. And then he saw that one was a jet fighter and that it was sitting on top of the second 109. A chill rippled down along the insides of his upper arms. Blinking as he stared, Schilling held the throttle open, closing quickly. He could smell the exhaust of the 109s, and kerosene . . . jet fuel. He knew something incomprehensible was about to happen to Rudi and to – who? And he remembered Marta saying *If you want to do something for me don't let anything happen to Eric or my brother*. We aren't all going to get back today after all, he thought. Bison was only the first, and goddamnit underneath he knew it would come to this, from the beginning. *Act. This is for real. Act.* Mechanically his gloved fingers flicked on the gun-arming switches, and with the red lights came the yellow ones this time: ammunition expended. Or nearly so; he knew there were usually a few rounds left. Maybe enough.

He estimated the three aircraft to be about 400 yards ahead. Even at full throttle it would be several seconds before he was in range. With empty guns. Mindless of altitude he hurled the 109 forward, engine off the tach, propwash raising dust as he whipped over the sand a dozen feet below his belly tank – *belly tank* – he reached down and yanked the release lever and the 109 leaped forward, relieved of the tank's weight and drag. Mesmerized, his heart lunged against his ribs, he drew closer, the three aircraft weaving in his sights. The jet then skidded upward to the right, lifting and turning in one quick smooth maneuver. And then opened fire, pouring a stream of fiery scarlet-orange embers out of the nose.

In his cockpit Rudi twitched convulsively as the glowing tracers filled the air in front of his cowling, his scalp rising with the sound, a demonic Godless groaning howl so terrifyingly loud that he thought some massive structural failure was folding the 109 around him. *Death now*.

Behind him Eric nearly fainted, as horrified by the howling moan of the jet's cannon as he was by the burst of tracers, none of which struck Rudi's plane. Hundreds of spent shells showered glittering dully out of the belly of the jet thick as locusts and came whizzing past him in a metallic hail clinking cracking off his windscreen and wing surfaces.

Schilling, prepared to see the 109 vanish in a ball of fire, watched incredulously as instead it flew on untouched. The jet slipped smoothly back into place. Warning shots. He thought of the jet pilot ahead and he thought of the other jet pilot crouched on the ground under fire at the air base, raising his gloved finger at the 109s as their fire stormed around him. The Air Force was still choosing them tough and he thought *don't let this one get hurt* because we want plenty like him when the Russians come over the hill. Schilling set his teeth. He was closing . . . 350 yards . . . and then, not believing, he realized that the first 109 was in firing range behind the jet. *No*.

Eric watched the jet weaving 100 yards ahead and slightly above. He knew now what he was going to do and then he remembered that he hadn't test fired, a thought that came and vanished. *Get away*, he raged at the jet, *get away. Don't look back*, he prayed then to the pilot, shrinking in his seat as if he could make himself smaller huddling below in the jet's blind spot . . . 250 feet . . . His gloved thumb lifting shield, forefinger curling, heart beating its way out of his flight suit. Transfixed he stared up at the rear of the jet growing larger, all pipes and high tail with red light winking pulsing in the center, huge black soot twin exhaust pipes the size of culverts, glowing white. It was an F-5 he knew; deadly 'monster bastard, titanium' aluminum rocket, death dealing Sidewinders and 20 millimeter AP or HE take your pick, or napalm remembering Nam the F-5s ear-splitting overhead loosing pods of jellied gasoline sailing tumbling end-over-end into the bush bursting booming billowing flare-bright orange monstrous rolling searing fire roasting Charlie everywhere hey roasting *everyone* everywhere even the wretched peasants slopes mama-san papa-san baby-san Jesus hideous scorched smoking stinking roast meat the children charred little monkey corpses oh you wished they weren't but you knew they were why didn't they not be there? no children no children never have any ever . . . Now 150 feet . . . The 109 bucked in the jet's turbulence. *Get closer. One chance.* Damn the napalm the bombs the airplanes all of them and this one too damn them all they keep building these things more planes more jobs goddamnit stop building them you never sea the roast monkeys . . . 100 feet . . . Don't want to hurt the F-5 pilot he is someone's child as Marta is someone's child as Rudi is someone's child don't die motherfucker your splendid rocket so sleek huge tail olive-tan red eye winking he could read the numbers 01401 on it *don't kill Rudi* ugly mother all huge black twin pipes ugly mother ugly mother mugly other he could see up inside shimmering furnaces smell heated kerosene eyes burning *don't kill Rudi don't look back just hold on now hold on now* . . . 50 feet.

'Bandit Number Two,' came the pilot's voice, 'you are—'

'*All right-o-Rudiiiiii,*' Eric screamed, locking thumb and forefinger firing, jackhammer detonation shaking the cockpit, white fire red fire flaring sparking black junk flying banging off his cowling firing *ram it kill it!*

Schilling, from 500 feet directly behind, saw flashing white strikes cover the rear of the jet, thrashing the tailfin, chewing at the fuselage, tearing off one air brake, sparkling in the exhaust ports. Like a space rocket triggered from standstill, the F-5 lifted its needle nose and launched itself vertically with awesome acceleration, spewing sparks and steam-like smoke from the tailpipes, then chips of disintegrating turbo fan, shedding debris, rising from the smoke of the attack like some great sea beast sounding, wounded, its smooth olive-tan skin holed along the spine bleeding fire. The cockpit would be lit up like Christmas.

'Get out,' he said aloud. 'Get out! *Get out!*'

Twisting as it lifted into a vertical roll, the jet was shaken by an internal explosion aft, gouting more debris out the tailpipes as the canopy whipped off tumbling flashing sunlight and another flash catapulted a dark form outward at two o'clock, the pilot sailing a hundred feet followed by the orange dart of the drogue chute.

Schilling crouched reflexively as pieces of the jet banged off his canopy, the bitter stench of burnt metal and jet fuel filling his nose, his eyes riveted upward on the jet now inverted, straining, quivering once, then blowing apart from the middle in a great white flash that hurled the unscarred forward half of the fuselage smoking outward while the aft portion exploded violently in boiling fire, showering hundreds of black smoking pieces out and down.

Turning hard left to bank away from the gauntlet of cascading junk, Schilling felt the flat roaring *boooom* shake the 109, push its tail to port, press at a wing. Correcting under full power he caught control, climbing and looking back to see the F-5 pilot's chute bloom bright tangerine beyond the descending litter.

Good Christ.

For almost two minutes the three Messerschmitts flew without radio contact, forming up in loose echelon. Still shaken, Schilling was confused to see the other plane bearing the number Seven, until he made out Eric's face through the canopy. Lifting a gloved hand, Eric waggled his fingers. Schilling gave a loose salute in return, wondering what the crazy bastard was doing there and wondering which of the two of them had taken out the jet to save the other. He turned to look at Rudi above on his left, deciding to break radio silence in English.

'This is Major Three to Oberstleutnant. Do you read?'

The response came hoarsely, 'Oberstleutnant here, Major Three.'

'Are you hit, Oberstleutnant?'

'Negative, Major Three.' Rudi's voice was slow and weary. 'Did you hit the jet, Major?'

'Negative,' replied Schilling. He realized then, that Eric had miraculously appeared – from where? – and done something truly heroic. 'Seven hit it. Over.'

'Seven,' Rudi repeated.

Schilling turned to Eric. Number Seven 109 was very dirty and battered. Dents and scratches were clearly visible on the cowling and wing surfaces and the entire plane was filmed over light-gray with smoke residue.

'Seven, this is Major Three. Acknowledge.'

'Seven here.'

'Are you hit, Seven?'

'Negative, Major Three.'

'That is you, Leutnant,' Rudi spoke without emotion; it was a statement, not a question.

'Yo,' came the response.

'We have missed . . . our turn,' Rudi said. 'Form on me, Major Three, line astern . . . Leutnant, form on Three. Stick tight . . . and let's go home.'

The telephone jangled both Lowen and Webb awake in the semi-darkness. As Webb picked it up from the bedside table, Lowen stirred in the other bed and squinted at his watch: 0658 hours. Morning light seeping in soft blue bands from the top and bottom edge of the opaque motel drapes.

'Yeah?' Webb rasped into the telephone, groping for his eyeglasses on the nightstand. 'Yessir, yessir I can hear you.' He paused, listening, then slowly lay back on the pillow, putting on the tinted glasses.

Seconds passed as Lowen watched him, waiting, amused at the dark glasses. Webb already looked regulation and he wasn't even out of bed. Even his goddamned hair looked perfect, like actors in a film waking up perfect. He wondered how Webb did that.

'*God*,' Webb breathed finally, getting up on one elbow and pulling on the light, cradling the phone with his shoulder. Lowen watched, awake now.

'Yessir,' Webb said tensely. 'Were there casualties?' There was another pause. 'Yessir, he's here . . . right here in fact. Yessir . . . I'll try, yessir . . . maybe six hours, seven. Yessir. And thank you.' Webb hung up slowly, staring a moment at the telephone and then up at Lowen.

'That was the Base Commander . . . at Willie.' Webb's expression seemed bemused, dumbfounded. 'The Messerschmitts, all seven of them . . . hit the base, Williams. Less than an hour ago. Like here yesterday.' Webb looked at his watch and then sat up in the bed. 'They came in at ground level and made one pass down the flight line and took out maybe thirty planes . . .'

Lowen sat up then, too, feeling exactly as he perceived Webb to be feeling: dumbfounded.

'One of the Messerschmitts went in, too. Wiped out.'

Lowen grunted, a small sound in his throat, not so much for the 109 pilot as for the incredulous unreality of what he was hearing.

'They took casualties at Willie,' Webb went on. 'Maybe a dozen.'

Lowen shook his head. *Godamighty*.

'They've got fighters up now, from Luke, looking for them.'

Lowen tried to imagine that.

'We have to hurry,' Webb said then, getting up.

'We?'

'Ah, yessir . . . The CO, Colonel Butler, asked if you would be good enough to come back to Willie with me.' Webb headed for the bathroom in his shorts.

'You mean right now?'

'There's a meeting this evening, a Task Force to work on this. Special.' Webb paused at the bathroom door. 'We need your assistance, Colonel. The CO said you would be compensated, and that they would cover the repairs on your Mustang and have someone fly it over to Willie for you as soon as it was ready.'

'So, I'm conscripted?'

'No sir.' Webb grinned just a little, clearly relishing every word of Lowen's reaction. 'I was merely ordered to, ah, persuade you. Sir.'

'I see.' Lowen rubbed the stubble on his jaw. 'Well, Captain, I've had worse offers.'

'Yessir. I'm in charge, too.'

'In charge. Of what?'

'Executive Officer of the Task Force, sir. Under Colonel Butler.'

'I see. Well Captain, you've had worse offers, too.'

'Yessir. And thank you. For coming along. I'm glad.'

'I'm glad you're glad, Captain. Maybe we'll both learn something.' He watched Webb vanish into the bathroom, hearing the shower burst on like heavy rain. He sat on the bed waiting, thinking. Six left now. Jets up from Luke looking for them – he looked at his watch – an hour. It was probably all over now. Lord, not a prayer. They'd never get away. And then, strangely, unexpectedly, he realized he hoped they would. Somehow.

The three pilots on the ground, watching anxiously as they maneuvered the 109s into the hangar, heard the triple growl of the approaching aircraft and looked up to see one break and drop low, roar down the strip at eighty feet and turn gracefully belly-up into a smooth roll as it passed overhead. The numeral Seven was clear on the fuselage.

Puzzled, Theo watched it turn and bank to come around behind the other two 109s now on landing approach. The first plane down was Two – Rudi – and then he made out Schilling's number Three. Had Beissemann somehow switched to Seven? And why was the bloody fool doing a victory roll?

Hurriedly, sweating wet with tension, they had put the first three 109s in the hangar by the time Rudi taxied up. Theo came up to the side of the plane as Rudi cut his switches and slid the canopy back. Theo climbed up on the wing. Rudi was slumped in the seat. He made no move to release his harness.

'Ah, we worried for you,' Theo shouted over the rumble of Schilling's engine pulling up alongside.

'Are you all right?'

Rudi nodded dumbly.

'Here, here,' Theo said impatiently. 'Your harness.' He reached down and unbuckled Rudi's belts, noting the stench of burned paint, kerosene and urine. Rudi stared ahead, not moving.

'He will need help, Oberst,' came Schilling's voice from below on the ground.

Schilling called for Rendel to come with him to meet Eric now taxiing up, prop whickering down. Schilling crawled up on the port wing, Rendel on the other. Eric slid the canopy back and shut down the switches.

'Hello, Seven,' Schilling said.

Eric looked as if he had not heard. There was a false grin on his sweating smoke-darkened face. His hand snapped loose his harness and he shrugged off the shoulder belts.

'Here.' Schilling reached for his arm.

'No help,' Eric said. 'I'm OK, OK.' He placed his gloved hands on both sides of the cockpit and rose shakily. Schilling stepped down, ready to catch him as he slid over the side, guiding his foot to the step aperture. Eric's flying suit was soaked brown with sweat and he smelled of kerosene. Schilling reached up to help him down from the wing.

'I can manage,' Eric mumbled, shaking his head. He stepped down and collapsed smoothly on his knees, holding to the trailing edge of the wing. Schilling and Rendel lifted his upper

217

arms and propped him against the fuselage. Still grinning vacantly, he watched Schilling's fingers as they placed a damp cigarette in his mouth and lit it. He stared at Schilling. Schilling stared back, lighting up his own.

Eric took a long drag, then tried to step forward. 'Let's go, Major Three,' he said staggering along the wing.

Rudi and Theo came up then. Eric stopped, looking at Rudi and then hesitantly reaching out. Without words they embraced, exchanging solid slaps across the back. The others looked on curiously.

'Watch for Major Five,' said Theo. 'We must get these aircraft under cover. Now! Quickly!'

'Bison is down,' Schilling said absently, wiping his face. 'He won't be coming.'

Marta had taken tomato juice and black coffee out to the pool, and then swam for a while, grateful for the empty house and the quiet, but puzzled that the Staffel had gone flying so early on a Sunday. She didn't worry over it until she was back in the kitchen in her bathrobe and heard the radio bulletin about Williams Air Force Base.

The bulletin was brief and clear and she heard every word of it and understood exactly what had happened. It said that one of the attacking pilots had been killed and that there was extensive damage and that there were casualties.

Stunned, she sat down at the kitchen table and thought about the word *casualties*; it was also the word the books used when they described what had happened at Cologne, where they were called civilian casualties. She remembered some of the faces that became civilian casualties, and their names. The bulletin had said that there were seven attacking and it confused her because there were only six pilots. Surely it was an error, she decided. And then she thought about the pilot who was killed and decided not to expect it to be Rudi. Neither did she want it to be Schilling, or anyone, so she sorted out each of the pilots in her mind, assigning them an order in which she would be most grieved if they died, and wrote the names on a scratch-pad: Rudi, the Major, Beissemann, Rendel, Kesler, and Theo. Then she crumpled up the little paper, and calculated how long it would take them to return. She decided it would be any minute now.

It seemed absolutely incomprehensible that Rudi and the others could have done this. She stood up, a little faint, and went over to the counter and leaned her head against the cabinet and crossed her hands tightly around her upper arms. She wondered if there was no one to stop them, no one but her. Someone would come looking for them now, all of them . . . all of *us*, she thought.

Now another one of them was dead. She shook her head, began to rock back and forth. What was to be done? Rudi saying *yes, that is what is done* . . . what? She tried to remember. She looked at the stove clock that was twenty minutes fast. They would come, less one. She moved suddenly, walking in bare feet to the bedroom where she put on a yellow sundress and sandals. Then she set the dining room table for nine, as usual. Rudi had told her to always set Franz's – but not Weinert's – place, something they did in the war when a pilot was lost, and as she set the plates around, thinking now two of them would not be used, she began to cry silently.

When the table was set she made a Bloody Mary with lemon and drank it, and then made another. She put out cold diced fruit and opened a pink cardboard box of croissants that she could heat in the microwave. Still crying silently she broke a dozen eggs into a stainless steel bowl and mixed them evenly, watching the clock. When there was nothing more to do she took the Bloody Mary out to the table and sat at her place and opened a pack of Eric's Marlboros and smoked while she drank. It was the first cigarette she had had in two years and ten months. By the third cigarette she heard the automatic garage door opener and the gutteral putting exhaust of the van, and then the door opened in the den and Rudi came in. She bit her lip to keep from crying out.

Schilling reached down under the bed and pulled out a large wine-colored leather suitcase; it was finely crafted, expensive-looking. He put it on the bed and opened it and sorted quickly through the contents, separating the clothing from everything else. Then he took Beissemann's civilian clothing from the closet and folded it neatly in the suitcase and closed it.

Left on the bed was a shaving kit, a bottle of French liqueur, several paperback books, stationery from various hotels, a small leather notebook which he did not open, a package of letters which he did not open, a leather case containing sewing materials and silver grooming articles, two bottles of after-shave cologne, and a small photo-case holding two dozen snapshots in a plastic sleeve that folded like an accordion.

He rubbed his forehead slowly, noting that it was less than twenty-four hours since he'd packed up Franz's suitcase. So this is how it ends for Bison. Just like that. He opened the photo-case and let out the accordion sleeve and looked at the snapshots. They were all of pretty girls, women; some were in stewardess uniforms – of different airlines, he noticed – and some were in beautifully tailored clothes and some were in bikinis and some were in nothing. The backgrounds were New York, London, Paris, Hong Kong and beaches that could have been Australia or Jamaica or Miami or Tahiti. He wondered how many women Bison had had. A hell of a lot more than his share. Well, there was nothing to be envious of now. He hoped he had had hundreds.

Bison really didn't seem gone yet. But he would. Schilling knew very well that he would. Maybe he should print cards, dozens of them, announcing Bison's demise. And then send one to every name in the leather notebook. Stewardesses in tears from Rio to Rotterdam, Sydney to Surrey. He almost smiled.

He supposed they would gather at the pool for Bison when the sun went down and he wondered if the Herr General would deliver the eulogy this time. Or Rudi. Rudi had done very well. He wondered if whoever it was would say Bison did good things for mankind. Good things for womankind was closer. He almost smiled again. If he were delivering the eulogy he knew Bison would want him to say he was good for womankind and to hell with the men, let them get their own. You didn't run a string of women like that without having a talent for it, without patience and effort. Or so he guessed. Bison had done good things for mankind, too, flying them all over the world for years. He'd asked Bison if he'd ever had a crash and he'd said yes, twice, all in training, wrecking two 109s. Until today. Make that three.

Whatever they said about Bison at the pool wouldn't be accurate though, Schilling knew, because no one knew Bison, no one in this house. The thing about Bison you never noticed unless you were around him, close enough, often enough, was that he never talked about the past and he never smiled with his eyes.

Schilling took a long nap in the empty room.

220

BOOK III

PURSUIT

CHAPTER FOURTEEN

Colonel Butler stood at the conference table in the Meeting Room of Headquarters Building. Seated at his right, a young woman in Air Force uniform operated a tape recorder to which were connected small microphones for each of the six men seated around the table. He walked over to the wall, where a large map of the southwest portion of the United States was mounted and covered by a transparent plastic sheet.

'As Base Commander, I have been authorized by the United States Government to appoint and direct this Task Force, with the objective of investigating a recent series of armed attacks upon civilian and military airfield facilities in the states of Arizona and California.

'To summarize. A group of unidentified and capable pilots flying eight restored German fighters of World War Two vintage, with Luftwaffe battle markings, has conducted armed attacks on civilian and military aircraft, property, and personnel in Arizona and California, inflicting death, injury, and great damage. We are charged with terminating their activities, and apprehending the six surviving pilots and anyone else involved.

'The basic division of the responsibilities of this Task Force will be that the Air Force will conduct search operations in the air, and civilian agencies will conduct search operations on the ground.

'It is understood that each of us has a defined role in this investigation. We are more likely to succeed if we function as a team, and share with each other our information as we proceed. To this end, we will meet here daily at this time. Transcriptions of tapes from each meeting will be available the following morning.

'Sergeant Evans—' Butler turned to the airman seated behind him by the wall – 'is with Public Affairs here on base and will serve as adjutant to Captain Webb. Airman Harper will assist Sergeant Ward, keep notes and tapes, and oversee your needs such as typing, telephone, whatever, for these meetings, especially the reports.

'These fact sheets—' Butler motioned to Sergeant Evans, who began passing out papers – 'contain basic information on these proceedings and will serve as a model for our daily reports. This meeting is adjourned. Thank you. And we'll see you tomorrow evening. Captain Webb, Colonel Lowen, if you would stay on, please.'

Webb and Lowen remained in their seats, watching the others file out. When Sergeant Evans and Airman Harper left, closing the door, Butler took off his uniform jacket and hung it neatly over a chair-back before sitting down across the table from Webb and Lowen. With thumb and forefinger of his left hand he rubbed both temples slowly, studying the wall map. 'What group were you with in Europe, Lowen?'

'Three-fifty-seventh. Suffolk.'

'How many missions?'

'Eighty-nine.'

'Kills?'

'Six confirmed. All 109s.'

Butler nodded. 'I flew with the Three-twenty-first Bomb Group, Twelfth Air Force. Sicily. B-25s the whole time. Shot at so goddamned many 109s I couldn't count.'

Lowen looked down at the yellow pad on the table where he had written the names of the Task Force members: Col. Edwin Butler – CO, Capt. James Webb – Exec, Sgt. Emrys Evans – Adj., Gene Koontz – FAA, Michael Montgomery – FBI, John Stratton – Sheriff.

And below that, the name *Osterhoudt, Franz-Munich*, the name of the 109 pilot downed at Chino received by the FAA from an anonymous caller.

'Did you see that flight line out there?' Butler was still staring at the map. 'Millions,' he said tiredly. 'Millions. And I've got six airmen missing and presumed dead, and eight injured. We lost thirty-one aircraft destroyed, twenty-seven damaged, and a whole damned service hangar gone . . .' He turned to Lowen and Webb. 'Those people over in California lost – what was it, twenty-two ships?'

'Plus my four,' added Lowen.

'Jesus.' Butler turned to Webb. 'You get any photographs, Captain?'

'Yes, sir. I'll have them tomorrow.'

'Colonel,' Lowen said then to Butler, 'you should know that the Captain was shooting pictures alone, out by the display aircraft, when they came under attack.' Here he turned and gave Webb a contemplative look. 'One of the emergency crew, a fireman, was coming to warn Captain Webb away and he was hit by machine-gun fire. I went after him, the fireman, and the Captain saw this and came to help. He assisted me, under fire, with courage. Together we dragged him out of the line of fire. Then an Army ambulance came out for him.'

There was silence in the room. Outside they could hear a car alarm chirping briefly in the base parking lot. Butler shifted his attention from Lowen to Webb.

'I see,' he said finally, studying Webb. 'Well, Captain, I hope you have a good camera.'

Webb sat up a little straighter. 'The best, sir.'

'I talked to Washington this afternoon. You can imagine what that was like.' He paused. 'Expedite . . . terminate by force . . . maximum effort . . . were some of the words used. They want this thing cleaned up in hours, hours. They consider this . . . this mess, solely the responsibility of the Air Force. And if those 109s hit anything or anybody again, *anywhere* . . .'

Butler turned back to the map. 'We've got the whole Southwest on standby. By tomorrow this base and Luke are going to look like war zones. Photo recon flights begin tomorrow at first light – the darkroom team is setting up right now – and the Marines have a chopper assault team coming over from San Diego.' After a moment he turned once again to Lowen and lifted his chin, looking at the ceiling. 'What do you think we've got here, Lowen?'

Lowen shifted his pipe in his teeth. He was still thinking about the 109 pilot being from Munich. 'None of the warbird people could put together eight 109s without it getting around.'

'Don't you have any idea, any theory?'

'Not yet,' Lowen answered truthfully.

'Well,' Butler said, 'that's one direction we should take, the warbird people. And it's all yours. If you can give me a theory, an idea, Lowen, then I'll give you whatever you need. Jesus, we've got to have something to get a handle on.' He stood up. 'I appreciate your help, Colonel. I've got a bunk set up for you in BOQ and perhaps you'll have dinner with me?' He turned to Webb. 'Captain, do you wish to join us, or do you have something to do?'

'I've got quite a lot going on, sir. But thank you.'

'Yes.' Butler began buttoning his jacket. 'You do.'

Marta remained quietly alert during the Staffel's leisurely dinner. Both Theo and Rudi had steered the conversation away from any mention of flying, as if the day's events had never happened. At previous dinners she had usually excused herself after dessert, though they always asked her to stay and then always stood formally together in unison while she left the room. This night, however, she had decided to sit tight, even until they drank themselves under the table.

There were roses at two places at the table, for Franz and Beissemann, both of them to her left and to Schilling's right. The twin piles of flowers, white and yellow, seemed a disconcerting bridge between them, and during the evening she had glanced several times across it but never did she catch Schilling looking back.

They lingered over lemon-pineapple sherbet with much wine, frequent cognac, and coffee. Marta neglected her dessert, watching it turn to pearl soup.

'Now,' Theo said from the end of the table, announcing in that single word and its firm delivery, timed during a lull in the talk, that he would speak. The others ceased to stir and turned toward him.

'It is customary, I know,' he said quietly, 'for the Commanding Officer to address his men standing. This evening I will not stand, except once . . . though I have something of importance to say.' He paused to take a sip from his cognac and then held it out and studied it. 'This has been a day of triumph . . . and of tragedy . . . and of courage. The mission against the airbase proved more . . . hazardous than the Oberstleutnant and I had expected. There was bad luck.

'It is our best estimate that Major Beissemann was struck by debris to cause his crash. He took his chances, as we all did. We will remember him.'

With these words Theo looked up at each pilot in turn, his small fierce eyes resting last upon Eric at the far end of the table.

'This was also a day of courage,' he continued, keeping his

gaze on Eric. 'Courage,' he repeated, in a voice that in its rich inflection seemed to give the word a lustrous solidity, like that of finely sculpted marble. 'The Leutnant, aside from his role in reconstructing the aircraft, has been a valuable officer. No one needs to be reminded of this, his ... contribution.' Theo paused, still watching Eric. Marta felt as if he were looking at her instead of Eric to her right. 'This morning, the Leutnant took it upon himself to fly the mission. Secretly. I do not know why he did this ... but he must have had a very good reason. Any wisdom is not apparent to me.

'But then if the Leutnant had not flown the mission ...' Theo's voice trailed off a little. 'If the Leutnant had not followed instructions perfectly ... had not navigated precisely ... had not saved his ammunition ... then Oberstleutnant Felbeck and Major Schilling would not be sitting here with us now. And we would have lost three ... instead of one.'

He turned to look first at Rudi and then Schilling. 'It is mysterious how these things happen, yes? But this is how they happen. As you know, part of the wisdom of experience is to expect the unexpected ... and to abandon the search for the reason why.' Theo then stood up, slowly, as if to avoid disrupting the quiet informality that held them all in comfortable reflection.

'None the less, the Leutnant found himself in a crucial situation ... faced with crucial decisions ... to be made at great risk. He acted with exemplary skill and in my opinion with extraordinary courage.' He looked down the table at Eric. 'Leutnant, would you step forward?'

As Eric rose, Theo went on. 'For this reason, extraordinary courage, I believe he is deserving of recognition ... and as Commanding Officer of this Staffel—' he turned to Eric as he came up and stood at relaxed attention – 'I award him the rank of Major ... and—' here Theo lifted the ribbon from his own collar and held it in both hands, the small Maltese metal cross swinging from the ribbon and reflecting a wink of burnished light as it spun slowly— 'I award him the German Cross.

'It is only a medal,' he said directly to Eric though his voice was unchanged. 'Only a medal. It is as valuable as any medal, no more valuable, no less. It is a symbol ... a symbol that the wearer of it is deserving of respect wherever he goes among other pilots, other men.'

Theo placed the ribbon over Eric's head and straightened the cross at the bottom of Eric's collar. Then he gripped Eric's hand.

'It is an honor, Major,' he said, then turned to the others. 'Your glasses gentlemen. To Major Nine.'

The others stood quickly, including Marta. They drank together, then came up each in turn to shake Eric's hand.

Marta remained standing at the end of the table, empty glass in hand. Schilling found it amusing to watch her expressions and try to identify each emotion as it appeared: curiosity, coolness, surprise and indecisive pleasure. When Eric had sat down beside her, Marta leaned over and whispered in his ear what seemed to Schilling at least a dozen words.

Seated once more, Theo raised his chin to await silence and attention.

'And now I will tell you what we – Rudi and I – have decided. With the mission this morning, a successful mission, a brilliant mission, we have without doubt achieved . . . what we set out to do, what I promised you we would do the night we met together out at the hangar.' He looked around the table and a thin smile passed across his tanned lined face, never reaching his eyes, and then faded. 'The cost,' he said then quietly, 'was high.'

In the silence that followed, it seemed to Marta that each of the men paused, as if in some religious ceremony, to contemplate Franz, Beissemann, themselves alone.

'But we have done what we set out to do,' Theo went on. 'It will be an odd glory, but we will have it, all the rest of our lives. You are brave and loyal men, Graue Adler. And you are a credit to the business of being a fighter pilot.

'The authorities will search for us, and sooner or later—' He shrugged. 'You do not need to fly the third mission. Now it is not necessary. You may leave, before there is risk of being imprisoned.'

'What is the third mission, Theo?' asked Rendel.

'Rudi and I will engage the American Colonel. In the air,' Theo replied promptly, as if it had been obvious all along. Rendel smiled and took up his cognac, puffing on his cigar.

'Are you ordering us to leave, Oberst?' asked Kesler.

'I am merely pointing out that there is no need to stay. We have achieved our objective.'

'Then,' Kesler said, leaning forward with hands together, 'we may choose to leave or stay?'

Theo paused in thought before answering, 'Of course.'

'I stay.' Kesler spoke as if to himself, then tossed down his wine, set the glass firmly on the table, and looked over at Rendel beside him.

'As I have said . . .' Rendel turned to Kesler as if only the two of them were having the conversation. 'I stay.'

Together the two men stared across the table at Schilling, who had seen what was happening, but not quickly enough to have weighed his own reply. Impassively he looked back at Kesler and Rendel, and at Theo and at Rudi beside him, and finally down at his own cognac.

He decided to take whatever time he needed to decide. He knew now what Rendel had felt at the airport when he was looking at the old man. He glanced around at each of them again. They all looked like almost-old men. We are all almost-old men, he thought, wondering if behind this little drama there was, for them, the bravado of the last act? Not for me, he thought. None of this Going Out in a Blaze of Glory crap.

Where was reason? Were these heroics the inflexibilities of aging men tethered – terminally – to tradition, to Teutonic stubbornness, Prussian pride? Theo and Kesler and Rendel had not seen that Air Force jet hovering like some monstrous malevolent metal insect, lethal, a glowing spacecraft in the sky. Schilling smiled faintly, grimly; before this was over they would.

Or did he hesitate because he had become an American, wondering if reason could become an easy substitute for courage? Had such things changed, like so many others, in thirty years? Had the age of overkill, the age of air-lifted holiday dinners and supply tents full of Scotch and prophylactics for combat troops, made such a noble posture – if it was noble – outdated? He looked up at Rudi, Rudi the other American, watching back curiously through his pipe smoke.

What mattered here? History? Screw history; it would bring him nothing if he was dead. What mattered was not any other time but *now*, and the people at this table.

He realized then that he did not, not ever, think of himself as a car salesman, but as a racing driver and now, again, as a fighter pilot. And he realized he was living on the edge every moment here, that getting caught up in this Staffel was the experience of his life, just as Rendel had said. And here he sat in the candlelight, at a crossroads, in the company of men with whom he felt more intimate than any in his life. And in the presence of a woman who might alter his life.

They would see his leaving as desertion, as dishonor by default. He would vanish like Weinert, with no place setting at the table. They were going all the way now, Eric included, upping the ante as in some mad poker game, some hyper-exquisite test of pure don't-give-a-damn warrior *machismo*. And at that moment he knew how each of them felt, that charged vicarious excruciation watching him face this test, each one secretly glad he himself wasn't dancing on that dreadful bed of embers indecision. How easily each of them had escaped, quickly throwing in rather than risk dishonor in any form.

Schilling stared at the candle flame. Let them wait. He could feel the shifting form of his decision taking shape now.

He thought, just for a second, about Marta and he overcame with considerable effort the temptation to risk a glance toward her. It was a bad card for him to hold, her presence at this most intimate council of war, watching. Damn her. Inevitably she too would judge him.

Finally he looked up at the others. We all keep taking these little tests, and the big tests, he thought, until finally – like Bison – we fail one. Schilling had never failed one.

'Stay,' he said as he lifted his glass, and looked at no one over the rim as he drank.

Lowen lay awake on a narrow cot in a small room in the Bachelor Officer's Quarters. The dinner with Butler in the Officer's Club had not been unpleasant; the beef was half-decent and they talked about the war during the first half of the meal, until Sergeant Evans had called. When Butler returned to the table he told Lowen that another anonymous call had come in with the name of the second 109 pilot, and a Stuttgart address. And that the wreckage on the strip had included the 109's rudder, intact, with thirty-one kill markings. So it became even more difficult to keep silent about his conversation with the 109 leader over the R/T the day before. He sensed, for no reason he yet knew, that the time for confiding in Butler was not right and he was relieved when the Base Commander chose to skip dessert and retire early.

Lowen stared at the ceiling in the semi-darkness, thinking

about two dead pilots from Munich and Stuttgart, one with twenty-nine kills and one with thirty-one, knowing that the kill markings were accurate and that they would both turn out to be Luftwaffe veterans. And that among the eight, two would be just who they had said they were. Sure as God made little green apples. It didn't seem so fantastic anymore; just very strange now.

He wondered what each of the two pilots had done for a living in post-war Germany during the last thirty-some years and he wondered if either of them was one of the pilots he had attacked, so long ago. With just a little effort he could remember the mission – Target Regensburg – with the Mustangs on escort. His flight still had plenty of ammunition by the time they had to turn around, so they went down to beat up whatever they could find. He remembered the victorious feeling he had, hedge-hopping flying with the other three Mustangs over the hills and forests of Nazi Germany great blade-winged shining silver torpedoes hunting hungrily for prey, lusting for troop concentrations, convoys or – the biggest prize of all – an airfield.

He remembered the thin low overcast, misting wet, flying under it, dark pines and empty muddy roads. And then they had stumbled on the airfield and he turned tight to come around on the strip, deciding they could nip in without worrying about flak because – *Hot Damn* – there were Jerry fighters landing. He remembered the excitement, seeing three 109s on approach, two of them smoking, and he remembered going in ahead of his wingman even though he hadn't gotten up much airspeed. It was too good a chance to pass up, catching them setting down like ducks, and he was so excited he couldn't decide which one to shoot at so he shot at all of them – from the hip; a burst here, there, surprised at his luck hitting one in the air, one almost on the ground, and the third still rolling on the strip. And then seeing the unexpected scarlet fireballs spitting up out of the mist from the right.

Looking back he remembered more than anything else how furious he had always been with himself for being so stupid to go in so slow, to take the chance. And now . . . could it be? This wide-awake nightmare coming to haunt him.

What could drive them, these madmen, to come this far, to attack an airbase, *this* airbase? What had brought him to this tin cot in this tiny room, mere hundreds of yards from where they had attacked, where one died? Two from Germany . . . they were real.

He wondered then how long it would take the Air Force to find them. He wondered what he would do if he were the German commander. They were probably holed up in a good place . . . mountains, desert, Mexico maybe. Hell, you could hide anything in this kind of country if you were smart. If the Air Force didn't find them, they'd wait it out . . . and find him. He wondered if they were crazy enough to go to Texas to get him and he decided they were. The Air Force wouldn't look in Texas . . . No, he'd get back down there and sooner or later those crazy Krauts would show up. He knew it. He felt very much alone.

On the trip back from Williams, Webb had stopped at a drug mart to pick up a school compass, protractor, and ruler. The trip had taken over an hour and when he got to his apartment door he heard the phone ringing.

'Hello?' He began unbuttoning his shirt.

'Cap'n, this is Sergeant Evans.'

'Yeah, Evans. Whattaya got?'

'Couple things you ought to know. First of all we got a couple film couriers from California. News film, other stuff—'

'*My* film. What about *my* film?'

'Yeah, it's done. They called a few minutes ago. I told them to special messenger it right to your house.'

'Good, good. What else?'

'Okay. First, the crash team that went up north where the F-5 went down brought back a belly tank from one of the German planes, intact and empty. Plus a whole bunch of empty shells. From the one that crashed this morning they got another belly tank, intact and empty, too. Plus the rudder, which has thirty-one of those bars painted on it.'

'Thirty-one?' Webb wrote the numerals on a pad.

'Yes sir. Now hear this. We got an anonymous call, about thirty minutes ago, with the name of the 109 pilot that crashed this morning. Got a pencil?'

'Shoot.'

'Beissemann, Gustav. Spelling B-e-i-s-s-e-m-a-n-n. With address in Stuttgart.'

Webb printed the name on the pad. 'Where'd you get all this, Evans?'

'We're typing the FAA guy's report. I passed this on to Butler over at the Officers' Mess with Colonel Lowen, too.'

'Outstanding. Anything else?'

'Yeah. Revised casualty report. Four of the six individuals listed as missing have turned up, all EMs. Hell, I knew that. They just didn't sign out for the weekend. They're thinkin' the other two are still in the hangar, but I'll bet not. Injured still stands at seven. They guy on critical was changed to satisfactory. That's it.'

'Outstanding, Sergeant. I appreciate the call. Let me know if anything else comes up, no matter how late.'

Webb took the scrap of paper with the pilot's name and the numerals 3 and 1 and studied it a moment before placing it on the desk. From the kitchen he got a cold beer and drank it while he stripped down and took a long hot shower. As he was soaping his arms and legs he thought about the sound the bullets had made smacking off the concrete all around him and then whining away with exactly the same sound they made in western movies. He was glad he had all his arms and all his legs and all his fingers and all his everything else. Just a few nicks and scratches from concrete chips. God. Now he had learned a little better the meaning of terror.

Out of the shower, he put on a sweat shirt and gym shorts and went to the kitchen to make a ham sandwich and brought it to the desk with another beer.

He spread his Triple-A road map on the desk, folding the creases backward so it would stay flat, and he set out the school instruments and some pencils and the papers from the Task Force meeting. His mind was working so fast one thought tripped over another. All the little pieces were already starting to flutter down. In the desk drawer he found half a joint and he lit it up and took two hits and immediately felt more calm. He decided there were two things to do. One was to prepare his report, and the other was to think . . . to think it all out. The report would come first. He would get all his books and dig up all the stuff on the 109 and put that together for the first part of his report.

He set to work.

CHAPTER FIFTEEN

Schilling took off his uniform jacket and hung it over the back of a pool chair and picked up the vodka bottle by the neck and unlocked the high wooden door and stepped out into the desert night. The moon was glaring bright, a translucent ivory wafer illuminating every little stone, and each twisting stem of brush, casting sharp shadows, and gleaming off his boots as he placed one foot in front of the other, stepping carefully. The soles of the boots were thin and he could feel each piece of rock underfoot.

The heat still came up from the sand and he was sweating, whether from the drinking or from the walking he couldn't decide. There was a ridge ahead. He had seen it numerous times during daylight and had always wanted to see over the other side. It rose like the back of an alligator from the desert, perhaps sixty feet, and it seemed made of granite slabs stacked on edge against each other. It was brutal-looking rock and he had to climb cautiously, careful not to mar the finish of the fine boots.

When he reached the top he was fairly winded. He found a place to sit and he opened his white shirt to welcome the weak night breeze. The ridge dropped away sharply to a shallow valley of bush-dotted sand, then rose to another higher ridge that stretched away on both sides. Beyond this second ridge he could see the lights of Phoenix, a gleaming grid of multicolored lights symmetrically set like so many precious stones. How marvelous it would be, he thought, to fly at night here.

When his wind had settled he lit a cigarette and unscrewed the cap of the vodka bottle and took a long pull, loving the way it burned down inside and pushed tears out of his eyes. He thought about Bison and Franz then and the tears kept on coming. He didn't wipe them away when he smoked the cigarette and he was careful not to make any noise except, finally, a deep grunt of release – it seemed stuck in his chest and had to be let out – which made him angry, even though there was no one to hear, because he didn't want to hear himself.

The service for Bison had been at deep sunset, when the sky glowed cherry like forged iron. They had lined up around the pool with Theo at the end, Rudi and Kesler and Eric on the right, and Rendel and himself on the left. They waited for Theo to speak, but the time passed and Theo still said nothing, just stared at the water as if he were in some sort of trance.

Finally they no longer waited for Theo to speak. They stood for the sunset, glancing sometimes at each other, sometimes at the sky turning plum. Behind Rudi and Eric, Marta stood in a white dress and held an open yellow rose, as patient and motionless as any of them. Eventually she stepped forward and tossed the flower on the water and, as if that were his signal, Theo finally spoke so suddenly that it was jarring.

'Where is our usual manager of mirth?' his voice came clearly. 'This man, our comrade, who spent most of his life, even to the last moment, in the sky. Gustav Beissemann . . . Space Cadet. Each of us will smile to remember you. Gustav Beissemann . . . Godspeed.'

That was all. They had saluted, turned and walked away.

All the good people kept dying, he thought. They kept dying for stupid reasons or for no reason at all and it always bothered him that there wasn't any sense to it. Even in the war most of them went in stupid ways, because of stupid mistakes, random chance, accidents. Those who went down in battle he would understand; it was skill or it was luck, not enough of either one.

He drank some more of the vodka until he was numb in the face and the feet. He began thinking about women, the ones who had died, and he was curious to realize that he felt as badly about Franz and Bison as he had about any woman. The men he cared about stayed in his life until they died. But the women he cared about stayed until they left and when they left it was the same as dying. They were as good as dead then, like the ones who had died. In either case, one hurt as much as the other and it didn't matter what sex they were. God, how he hated the finality of it all, the absolute finality. When they were gone they were gone. Period.

A big crap shoot, all of it, which sounded like something Bison would have said. Bison had the right idea about the women. If you had to decide what made it all worthwhile – if anything did – it was the women. Better than airplanes or cars or money. And they were the biggest crap shoot of all, the women. They came and they went. None ever stayed. Pleasant and temporary. They left because they got tired or bored, or because they found something or someone better. And sometimes they went for no reason he knew. No one stayed with anyone anymore. He didn't know why this was but he didn't want to be a part of it, not the part of it that caused it, and especially not for someone who had saved his ass. Twice.

There was another point of view about such things, he reminded himself, which came from knowing that if you wanted something badly enough, more than anything, you could weigh the price, and then pay, do whatever you had to do to get it. It seemed very strange that he could sit on a rock in the desert in the middle of the night and know, without thinking it over, without deciding, that Marta Felbeck-Malzahn was what he wanted. More than anything.

Webb was reading over the first typed draft of his report:

Messerschmitt (Me) 109
1. *General*
   The eight identical Me-109s involved in these incidents are apparently well-restored and updated G models, the fastest and most effective of the 109 series produced from 1935 through 1945. The Me-109 comprised the bulk of the Luftwaffe fighter force in WWII and was produced in greater quantity (est. 34,000) than any other fighter. It was/is comparable in combat performance with other top fighters, such as the British Spitfire and US Mustang P-51, and was/is considered deadly in the hands of an experienced pilot.

2. *Specifications*
   Wingspan: 32 feet. *Length*: 29 feet. *Weight* (loaded): 7498 lb. *Engine*: Daimler-Benz 605A liquid-cooled, inverted V-12. *Horsepower*: 1475-1800 (with boost). *Speed* (est): 400+mph.

Ceiling: 37,000 feet (with oxygen & pressure cabin). *Range* (est): 350 miles (internal fuel-88 gallons). *Armament*: Nose cannon(1): 20mm/60 rounds. Engine-mounted machine guns(2): 7.92mm/1000 rounds.

3. *Observations*
    (a) These particular aircraft are 'clean' versions; without wing guns, with enlarged tail fins and late-model Galland-type canopies, indicating high performance.
    (b) They carry auxiliary belly tanks (est. 300 liter capacity) which could contain fuel or water/methanol for higher engine boost. The added weight and drag reduce speed, however.
    (c) Because of the unique fuselage-mounted landing gear and the resulting narrow wheelbase, plus certain handling characteristics at very low and very high speeds, the Me-109 was/is notoriously difficult to handle (particularly on take-off and landing) unless the pilot is experienced and skillful.
    (d) Although the Me-109 was produced in great numbers, very few remain. Less than a half-dozen are in flying trim anywhere in the world, and no more than that are on static display in aircraft museums. The value of the Me-109 on the collectors' market is estimated to exceed $250,000.

Good enough for a start. He pushed the books aside and put the portable typewriter on a chair and took up the ruler and the compass and began to study the map.

The range would be the first matter. From the books he figured the range of the 109G at 350 miles, divided by two for each way, thus 175 miles from base. With the point of the compass at Chino he scribed a circle on the map for the internal fuel range of 175 miles. He then drew the same circle with the point at Willie. Then he stopped, putting down the compass. So what? They'd figured this out tomorrow on the big map. A highschool kid could figure out the goddamned range. No shortage of brainpower to do that.

He needed to think of other answers. Which meant he had to think of other questions. It was his intuition that if he could somehow think beyond such things as fuel range, he would discover far more important clues.

He finished off the joint, which meant he would have to roll a new one. The grass was in a Ziploc bag in the desk, and he took it out and held it up. Less than a quarter ounce, but it was very good Colombian, even though it smelled like moldy mule crap. Cleaning grass was just the sort of mindless task he needed. It would help him think while he fooled with it and then it would help him think while he smoked it. He took out a sheet of the Air Force stationery they sold at the PX and placed it on the desk and dumped the grass on it. When he had shaken every particle out of the Ziploc, he lifted the corners of the paper each in turn until the grass was mounded neatly in the center of the sheet. Then he slid the paper back and forth gently on the desk-top until the seeds rolled free, quivering around the edges of the mound. Deftly he picked out stem pieces and the little olive-colored egg-shaped seeds and put them in the ashtray.

In one of the aircraft books he had found a color photograph of 109s flying over the Tunisian desert, shot from above to show how the camouflage worked. The camouflage paint was very familiar indeed. That meant something.

He separated and broke apart the larger pieces, kneading the little clumps apart into manageable fragments like tobacco, then using a business card to scrape the cleaned grass aside. When he had enough for a joint he rolled one slowly and carefully. Webb always liked to roll his own, like the cowboys did, and he was secretly proud of his dexterity in making them tight and slender.

He lit up with a match and took a deep drag, holding it and watching the escaped white smoke curl up and drift under the desk light.

Just before the Task Force Meeting he and Lowen had gone over to the 425th to look at the flight line. They were still cleaning up at dusk. Those Messerschmitts had just wasted the Trainer Squadron: turbine engines smoldering in ash-covered heaps, Tweets all shot to pieces, T-38s now big fish-like fuselage skeletons. So many of them. And the Service Hangar wiped out, still smoking, eleventeen jillion dollars worth of engines and parts. Whew. Why, he wondered, did they do that? That meant something.

He cleaned enough grass to fill a 35mm film canister; it was Japanese, transparent plastic. Leave it to the Japanese to make clear plastic film canisters, he thought, so you could read the film type inside – or see how much dope you had – instead of opaque canisters like Kodak's. The details, with care and thoughtfulness. Like the Z-cars, like his camera lens, like his stereo. Crafted. He wondered if the Mitsubishi Zeros during the war were crafted. Funny Mitsubishi was making cars for somebody in Detroit now; Dodge wasn't it? And Kawasaki – builder of the B-29 killer Ki-61 with the engine copied from the DB605A in the Me-109 – now making rocket motorcycles. Funny. He'd always wanted a motorcycle, a Harley-Davidson XLCH . . . the ultimate, man. One of these days.

Webb picked up the sheet of pale blue paper and dumped the rest of the grass back into the Ziploc and sealed it. Why would they hit Willie? It seemed so stupid. They must have taken the trouble to learn that the flight line and the tower would be down on Sunday. Except for the ferry pilots. Surprise. And then they went and knocked down that F-5 from Luke. Man. The balloon was up now. He thought about the F-5 pilot. Poor sonofabitch would go through life notorious as the only jet fighter pilot knocked down by a Second World War German Messerschmitt. Haha. He'd be a sort of hero anyway, a celebrity. Not all bad.

Webb had a little blue box of wooden matches from the Buena Vista. He lit up the joint again. He liked wooden matches. He imagined they were more real, like the cowboys used, more rugged. You wouldn't see the fuckin' Marlboro man lighting up with a gold Dunhill lighter or a paper matchbook for crissake. The pioneers didn't have matches, did they? Or did they? Did Kit Carson and Daniel Boone and those guys have matches? What did they light their pipes with, flint?

This is bitchin' stuff, he thought.

The Messerschmitt pilots would know that hitting Willie would send the Air Force straight up the wall. No joke. They knew that going in. And they sure as shit must have known about Luke, and they sure as shit knew that when the US-of-A Air Force went ape there was no place on this planet to hide. It was merely a matter of time. They had fucked with the System. Serious. And the System would eat them alive. The FBI and the Air Force had a little war now. Firepower, man. Get the fighter jocks to sic 'em, waste 'em. Every mother air-to-air missile at Luke was probably all set out and polished up. You bet.

And you, my man, are in the catbird seat, part of the System, Executive Officer of The Machine. Far out. What a weird responsibility to come to him, what bizarre and astonishing good luck. A gift.

Webb had made only two serious commitments in his life; the

first was the Air Force and the second was marriage, and of late he had begun to fear that the first was sliding downward in the same direction as the second. Now he decided to make a third: to find them. And to find them first.

He took another hit. It would be the last because he was cookin' now. He could just drive his brain right out there now, right to the edge. Just get down. He was in a perfect position to find them. He had every conceivable means at his personal disposal to find them, every conceivable advantage. He would be thoughtful and thorough and persistent and he would take advantage of his advantages. He would figure it out and find them. Before the others. Before the System chewed them up. Screw the FAA and the FBI and the Air Force too, he thought. I want them. I want them even more than they do.

Get down.

The door buzzer sounded. Startled, Webb jerked upright in the chair, then laughed at himself. It would be the messenger.

Webb began tearing open the wrapping as he returned to the desk. He had already set up his Kodak Carousel projector and focused the lens on the wall some six feet from the desk. Opening the three film boxes, he inserted each slide in numerical order, upside down and facing front, in the individual slots of the circular plastic tray. His heartbeat increased. He was sure that the tiny squares of film sandwiched in cardboard would hold answers for him that no one else yet had.

He turned off all the lights and lifted the projector switch, throwing a glaring bright square of light on the wall. He clicked the forward button and projected the first slide. His heart jumped.

'Outstanding,' he breathed aloud slowly.

It was a primo slide, full of airplane, stunning in its detail, and perfectly framed. Webb stared as if hypnotized.

There were two perfect 109s in the frame. Both were banked to starboard so that he could study them in perfect detail and in perfect light. Numbers Six and Seven in big white numerals behind the cockpits. Flawless, flat camouflage paint in brown and tan. Black-and-white crosses. Heraldry! Both pilots wore tan caps and sunglasses and tan flying jackets and bright orange scarves neatly tied. And both of their faces – it gave him a wonderful slight chill – were looking straight at the camera. They were tanned, definitely older-looking, and though it was

240

not entirely clear, both seemed to have blond or gray hair. *Outstaaaanding*, he thought again. Such incredible presence, such life, those two pilots had, the detail, with the canopies back ... The canopies back? The 109 canopy didn't slide back; it lifted over. He studied both canopies. They were of the later design, called the 'Galland hood', he recognized. And they were obviously retractable. He made a note on the paper: Check retractable canopy.

Below and forward of the cockpits there was some sort of squadron insignia on the fuselages of both aircraft; within a bright orange disc an eagle of Germanic design was painted in gray. He had seen the design before somewhere and he made another note – Check heraldry – and continued to study the slide. The belly tanks were not visible because both planes were tipped laterally toward the camera. Then he noticed something new. On the far – port – side of the engine cowling, just forward of the ammunition feed fairing, was the upper surface of what appeared to be a rectangular fixture attached to the carburetor air intake. He could only see the top edge of it and he made a note to check this as well.

The next slide was very similar to the first but at a somewhat further distance. These two 109s, numbers Eight and One, were in the same tipped position and were identical to the other two except for the white numbers. The upper edge of the intake fixtures was visible on both planes.

The third slide was nothing but a blue rectangle, sky, as were the fourth, fifth, sixth ... he clicked the forward button, cursing, remembering then that he had been trying desperately to pan with the 109s on their first attack run. The tenth slide had a tail section, the eleventh a nose, the twelfth half of 109 Number Four and the thirteenth more sky.

Of the remaining twenty-three slides Webb found nine of value; the other seventeen were useless. And of the nine, eight were splendidly sharp profiles of the 109s on the attack runs. Every aircraft but Number Seven was captured perfectly, most with gun and cannon muzzle flash, even the scattering patterns of ejected shells like tiny dark sticks falling away, and hazy smoke streaming back. With each pilot in profile as well.

The ninth slide was fascinating; it showed the four Mustangs parked out on the strip. They were under fire, taking hits, and all around the four silver aircraft there were grass clots and shining fragments of debris suspended oddly in the air amidst dust and tiny pinpoint sparks. He stared at that slide, taking another hit off the joint. Outstanding . . . outstanding . . .

Webb culled the blank sky slides out of the tray, discarding them, arranged the remaining eleven in sequence and began to go back through them. On the profile shots the detail was so clear he could, with effort, count the kill markings on the rudders. Number One had some glare on the tail, but there seemed to be twenty-two, Number Two had twenty-eight, and Number Three had nineteen. There was no profile of Number Four. Number Five came on the screen and he counted thirty-one; this must have been the one that crashed at Willie. The pilot – Webb had begun to drink from his beer can, but it stopped at his mouth. He blinked – the pilot *What the hell*? the pilot . . . was different; his head was massive, black. Webb lowered the beer can, groped at the focus knob, leaned forward as if it would help him to see more clearly. The picture was in focus. Webb squinted, kept blinking . . . no cap, no sunglasses, great black bushy . . . bulging overhung brow, flat flared nose . . . Webb gasped. In profile there was no mistake. Gorilla. The pilot was wearing a gorilla mask.

An incredulous giggle escaped from Webb's throat. Eyes fastened on the picture, he lifted the projector, knocking books off the desk, backing up holding the projector, enlarging the image until he was against the far wall. He placed the projector on top of a bookshelf, pushing books and magazines to the floor. He refocused the picture, now five feet wide. Clearly in focus, there was no mistake: gorilla mask.

Webb began to laugh, a little and then more, then harder and then with such stoned and weeping hysteria that he slid to the floor, tears running, his stomach quivering. He laughed for minutes and minutes, until he was exhausted. Then he crawled back to the desk and got the beer and the joint and sat on the floor looking at the gorilla in the cockpit of Number Six covering his wall. He had no idea what to make of it. No idea at all. More than anything Webb wanted to find them. First . . . and alone.

Again seated at the desk he took a pen and a sheet of PX stationery. The paper was light blue, about six by eight inches, with the Air Force Wings badge reproduced in silver ink at the top and little jet planes flying across the page. How weird, he thought, momentarily preoccupied with the paper. The sheet was marked in thin horizontal pale blue lines – he smiled – as if it were designed for someone too clumsy to write straight. Or too stoned. He then wrote *(1) Who are they?* and then sat back, looking at the words.

Think, turkey. You're stoned out there right to the edge. So think.

The kill markings meant something. The two empty belly tanks meant something. The devices on the carburetor intakes meant something. The eagle heraldry meant something. Everything meant something. Perseverance, he thought. Perseverance, man. It always worked, always. When you locked on, and hung in, you usually got what you wanted. Like Pamela, slippery glorious Pamela, such sweet reward for those weeks on end of cruising without a score. And wasn't it worth it? Amen. Webb weaved a little in his chair, his thigh muscles twitching as he thought of her stripping in the candlelight, freed breasts bobbing loose, hair tangled dark over shoulders. Oh man. And of sword-blade legs scissoring around him. God, he thought suddenly, your mind just goes leaping all over the goddamn place on this stuff. He hooked back onto his train of thought as if he had been running alongside.

The airplanes themselves, he sensed intuitively, those lovingly crafted 109s, were the most obvious clue of all. Outrageous, beautiful and sinister in their perfect war paint, black crosses so bold. Nothing reticent about swastikas so blatantly evil, or the kill markings. Someone demanded that degree of authenticity for good reason. It was a statement, surely. The Messerschmitt 109 was an odd choice. Incredibly rare, difficult to handle, but ... *the* Luftwaffe fighter of all time. They had to have come from Europe. Who would have the resources to find them?

How did they get here? Webb took a last slow hit from the joint. Answers darted, flitted, like teasing shadows in the midnight jungle of such questions.

Money was a prerequisite. Men of wealth, of means, to find the pieces, reconstruct and transport them to ... California, Arizona, Nevada? Or transport the pieces and *then* reconstruct? *Bingo*. And they would be men of skill, obviously good pilots, former fighter pilots? Eccentrics surely. Who could find and organize eight nutball eccentrics all of the same bent warp? There had to be some central passion which could be, which would be, linked ... in that unity of ... eight identical planes, those particular planes, and the caps and scarves and numbers and kill markings and heraldry. Like former Luftwaffe pilots. *Bingo*! Oh how wonderfully mad and perfect, Webb exulted. Osterhoudt of Munich! Beissemann of Stuttgart! *Bingo*! Twenty-nine and thirty-one kills. *Bingo, bingo*! Luftwaffe aces, the real thing, survivors of an era in history gone forever, a vanishing species. Webb could barely contain his excitement.

And the machines – vanishing as well – once the mightiest of the Luftwaffe, disappearing until there were only a handful, their engines stilled and dry frozen in carbon, resting in museums ... except for these eight – now six – alive and shining, meticulously restored, bright battle colors flashing in the sun, their grace and menace and motion and sound alive once again, soaring wheeling prowling over desert wastes, hunting, striking ... just once more, warplanes making war. First Chino, then Willie; a masterful one-two punch.

Below the question *Who are they*? Webb wrote *Real Luftwaffe fighter pilots*? Then he added *aces*. He sat back staring at the words. If it was far-fetched it was still no less bizarre or unlikely than any other possibility that had so far come to mind. Plus, he loved it. It was outstanding.

Returning to his notes Webb began with the device on the carburetor intakes. One of his books provided the answer: tropical sand filter, like the ones fitted to 109s in the North African campaign. Sand filter ... which meant that they were operating on a sand strip; no point in having filters otherwise. *Bingo*! Surely they flew from a hidden field and surely it would not be paved. Which meant that all the effort checking out paved strips would be pissing in the wind. Webb grinned. Let the FAA and the FBI look for paved strips. It would give him that much more time.

He ran across another small clue concerning the belly tanks, which held either fuel or water-methanol mix. The water/meth was for extra boost at high altitudes, which required the standard round carburetor airscoop. A sand filter negated the round scoop, thus the tanks were for fuel, range. He could make bigger circles on the map, he noted. Cookin' now.

Another book confirmed that the canopies were never retractable. Since these obviously were, it meant that someone had taken the extraordinary effort to redesign and build retractable canopies, no small feat, without departing from the original design.

And since he found no squadron insignia to match those on the planes, he found one emblem using a similar eagle design, black on yellow, for 1/JG54 Focke-Wulfs. Probably the orange and gray eagle heraldry was designed just for these 109s. Another nice detail.

Webb finished off the beer, then he picked up the pen and wrote *(2) Why did they hit Chino?* They had picked up on Lowen and followed him. Why? Why wouldn't they have just gone in without Lowen? He wrote *(3) Why did they intercept Lowen?* and then went back to thinking about Chino.

Chino ... an airshow of warbirds, a most excellent event at which to dazzle the troops ... showmanship ... showing-off-man-ship. That's what airshows were, showing off in the air. What better place to come out of the closet ... the closet; what was that? Some cavern hangar carved in the side of a mountain up north in Nevada like in a James Bond movie? Showing off their beautiful 109s to a crowd that would go absolutely batshit over them, of course. Webb recalled the wave of applause as the 109s came over on the slow first pass. Hey, nobody would ever forget that. Outstanding. Destroying the Mustangs, and the other WWII fighters, the war all over again in microcosm; was that the word? And Lowen's plane untouched ... accident? No. Deliberate? Yes. Why? It was a question for which he could not imagine an answer. Not yet. There had to be a reason for that too. Below his second question he wrote *War – microcosm.*

Webb took off his watch, deliberately not looking at the time, and placed it on the desk. He got up and made a cup of instant coffee with plenty of sugar, thinking every moment as he went through the steps of heating water, pouring, stirring.

After Chino, the questions got tougher. They could have vanished and gotten away with it. Why did they hit Willie? They had to have had a reason. It had nothing to do with Lowen and they weren't showing off. No one to see them, the field and the tower deserted, no photographers, very high risk. What did hitting Willie *get* them? Why would they do something so suicidal as screw with the Air Force? Jesus, like whacking a hornet's nest with a two-by-four. What, besides enormous kicks, could it get them? Simple now ... simple. Literally, what did it get them? Jesus, what what *what*? Webb knew what it got them, but he couldn't articulate it. What could you call it? *Notoriety?* ... yes. *Identity?* ... yes. He struggled with the words ... *Reality?*

245

. . . yes. They were tough, these dudes. Chino was tough, but you couldn't get no tougher than hitting Willie, no way. And knocking down an F-5. Hoo boy. Most certainly they would be taken seriously after that. They had reality all right, in spades.

Then he understood. It was so simple and so clear and so . . . outstanding. Exalted, he understood. They did it to establish what they were, that they were really . . . real. They did it to re-exist, once more, exactly as they once were, complete and perfect in every detail.

He wondered what they would do next. Perhaps nothing. They could vanish now, escape, and they would have achieved . . . their reality. Maybe they were packing up right now.

He set the clock and turned off the lights and stripped down and got into bed, sleepy from the grass. As he drifted off he remembered the pilot in the gorilla mask. They had screwballs in the Luftwaffe too, always a comedian . . . Outstanding, outrageous. A gorilla mask. Webb smiled in the dark. Then slept.

Getting back down the ridge to the house was far more difficult than Schilling had anticipated. Twice he had lost his footing and dropped the vodka bottle which, to his amusement, refused to break. When he reached the patio he noticed that the pool and Jacuzzi lights were still on under the water. It seemed like a very good idea to be in one or the other. Noting that the house was dark except for a small light in the kitchen, he decided it would be OK to take his clothes off. He moved first to the pool, where for minutes he stood staring down, intrigued with the patterns shimmering on the bottom like blown sand. The water was so clear that the pool seemed to be empty, its color bright aquamarine. During the day it seemed to be much more blue. He wondered what the reason for this was.

He chose the Jacuzzi because he was stiff and aching. He peeled his clothes off, having great difficulty with the boots, and turned on the waterjet switch. Holding the chrome rail he lowered himself into the steaming water, the heat crawling up his body in itching rings as he slipped below the surface. He sat and then spread his legs out, the water up to his chin, head resting on the edge. It was wonderful, wonderful. Overhead the stars were so remarkably brilliant, more gems. He closed his eyes, listening to the bubbles hissing soothingly around him.

With his eyes shut, the vodka made him dizzy, nearly nauseated, so he opened them now and then, drifting. He didn't know, didn't care, how much time had passed and he was half-asleep and so relaxed that when two hands, from behind and above, slipped suddenly softly down both sides of his face, palms on each cheek, he wasn't very startled. He knew whose fingers they were because they touched his mouth a moment and he could smell-taste perfumed soap or perfumed something and he thought dully then that he probably had her if she would do something like that. He let the fingers work his jaw and neck and then push his head forward a little and massage his hair. He closed his eyes, wishing he were not so loaded.

'Well, Major,' Marta's voice came finally, quiet and calm, 'it seems as if this time our positions are reversed, yes? Now it is my turn to peek?'

'Peekaway,' he said thickly, drifting on a thin tide of sensual pleasure, his eyes closed. God but her hands were wonderful. Whole minutes seemed to pass before she spoke again.

'I am truly sorry about Beissemann. He was your friend.'

'Um,' he managed to reply. Bison seemed just gone away now, on a 747 to Tahiti with a dozen sun-browned stewardesses in black string bikinis. The thirteen of them frolicking on some atoll forever more forever more. Perhaps that's what heaven was, he hoped, getting dizzy again.

'At dinner tonight,' she began in a voice slightly changed, 'when they asked if you were going to stay, you took a long time to decide.'

'Um.'

'For a moment, I thought you had some sense after all.'

'You were wrong. I had no sense.'

'Why?'

'Why what?'

'Why did you decide to stay?'

'Hard to say.'

'Because of me?'

'Not the main reason.'

'What is the main reason?'

'Hard to say.'

'Nobody's going to give in, are they?' She dropped her hands from his hair. He could feel the exasperation in them as they flew away. 'Not you, not Rudi, not any of you. The whole

247

damned house is full of heroes now. Including Eric.'

Schilling laughed, finding it peculiarly humorous that this particular woman was complaining of heroes. He laughed alone.

'For some reason,' she continued, 'neither my brother nor my husband has been willing to tell me what it was that Eric did today. Since you were the only other person there, will you tell me?'

'He shot down an Air Force jet fighter.'

'He shot down an Air Force jet fighter,[2] she repeated after a pause. He had heard her breath go in, which made her voice sound shallow. 'How . . . could that be?'

'He followed Rudi, last, without anyone knowing, and flew the whole mission. On the way back, the jet caught Rudi and was trying to get him down. Eric caught up with them . . . just as I was catching up with him, so I saw it all. Rudi was ignoring the jet – I don't know why – and the jet fired on him, warning shots, and Eric attacked the jet. Shot it down. The pilot bailed out.'

'My Christ,' she whispered.

Schilling was not pleased that the conversation had turned to the heroics of Marta's husband, though he realized with perverse pleasure that she would view it as something more, or less, than heroic. He rummaged through the drunken disorder of his thoughts to find a new sentence. Her presence, though he had not turned to see her, charged him. Now was the time to push a little.

'Ah yes,' he said then, 'Major Nine . . . is a hero.' He turned his head slightly, as if to find her. 'Did you reward him?'

'Don't turn around.' She put her hands on his head to prevent it and then said, 'He rewarded himself.'

'Bet that was nice.' He was glad to have her hands back.

'It depends.'

Schilling decided not to ask 'upon what?' and reached for his cigarettes which were just beyond his fingertips. Marta's bare brown arm appeared and lifted the pack, along with the lighter. She lit one and he could hear her taking a long drag from it before her hand came around and put it between his lips.

'Tell me . . . What did you whisper in Major Nine's ear when he was awarded his medal at dinner? If it was something intimate, of course you—'

'It was very intimate, Major. I told him if he ever got into one of those fucking airplanes again I'd kill him.'

'That's all?' he asked, glad that she couldn't see him smile.

'That's all.'

'Ahh . . . well, then I bet he won't.'

'That's what Rudi said before all this started, too. We'll see.' She reached down and took the cigarette out from his mouth and it disappeared behind him. And then came back after a moment. 'My God . . .' her voice had changed again, 'what kind of . . . crime is shooting down a jet plane?'

'In my experience the Air Force tends to frown on it.'

'Be serious, please.'

'Don't worry about it. After this morning one more isn't going to make much difference. Just remember that nobody knows it. Except the people in this house.'

'The pilot?'

'The pilot was too busy to get a license number. Believe it.' Schilling moved a little sitting up. He was very tired and very drunk.

'If you left . . . if you had decided to leave, it wouldn't stop anything, would it?'

'Fraid not,' he answered. 'Try to relax. We'll be out of the house tomorrow. Then the rest of it will be over in a few days. Rudi and the Herr General won't let Eric fly again; I'm sure of that.'

'You won't be out of the house tomorrow.' Her voice was absent again. 'Eric and I decided. You'd all die out there in the heat. You really can die out there,' she assured him. 'Rudi was crazy to even suggest it.'

'I'm truly glad to hear that.'

'He thinks they couldn't find you, us, within a week . . . so what are a few days? Besides, it makes the everyday sort of interesting, wondering if at any moment the Marines might come crashing through the door with machine guns.'

'Um,' Schilling grunted.

'I'm going back to work tomorrow,' she went on. 'At least if anybody is watching us, I'll be doing my normal thing.'

'Rudi is right. It's a little too early to get paranoid.'

'I've never broken the law, really, in my life.'

'You still haven't.'

'Major, I am feeding and housing the pilots of those planes!'

'What planes?' Schilling sat up, leaning forward. 'I don't see any planes. Neither do you. We go off and fly out of some field every day. You know nothing more.'

'But I do.'

'But you don't.'

'God,' she said helplessly. There was silence for a few moments.

'Busted up your glassware tonight,' he said then.

'It wasn't exactly Lalique.'

Schilling wondered what 'lah-leek' was but he wasn't going to ask. And he was finding himself still much too drunk to maneuver the conversation.

'How I wish . . . you would leave,' she said.

For a moment he thought that she meant he should get out of the Jacuzzi and go to bed. Then he leaned back, wishing for her hands.

'What would it take, Major, to get you to leave?'

'Is that a proposition?'

'Is that what it would take?'

'It's a nice offer,' he answered, 'though it would make a rather busy night for you, wouldn't it?'

'Somehow that seems like a very improper thing to say.'

'We're running out of time to be proper.'

'Then let's just make a deal, Major. Man to woman. Just an unemotional deal.'

Schilling began to laugh. He could feel her recoil behind him.

'Well, fuck you,' she snapped. 'What's so funny?'

'I'm not sure,' he said truthfully, still laughing.

'You're indifferent now, I see.'

'Not indifferent.'

'I'm not blind, Major. I'm not stupid. You are indifferent.'

Schilling stopped laughing. 'No.'

'Forget it. It's not that big a deal anyhow, Major. Believe me.' The anger was gone from her voice now, he noticed. 'I've lost my . . . nerve already. God, I'm thirty-eight years old and I still can't handle this sort of thing, still can't make up my mind whether to get laid or not.'

'Relax.' Thirty-eight. She was older than he had thought. Good.

'But I could handle it, Major. And don't laugh at me.'

'I'm not laughing.'

'Think you could handle it, Major?' She began to massage his head. Was she smiling, he wondered? Was she screwing with him again, in her own weird way? The hot water had sapped his strength. He wanted sleep. He wanted her.

'I could handle it,' he said, feeling – surprise – some evidence that he could.

'Sometimes . . . I feel old.' It was as if she were speaking in her sleep and the way she said the word old seemed to give it an echo. 'I look in the mirror . . . and I see lines in my face that weren't there before. I don't want to be old. I'm nine years older than Eric. I didn't think of it before. It didn't seem to matter.' Her hands dropped away.

'It doesn't matter.'

'It matters to me. It's not your problem. Eric is not your problem.'

'Lots of problems here.'

'Yes. Eric is my problem. You are my problem. Rudi is my problem. All—'

'Pick one,' Schilling cut in. 'You can't handle all of them. Pick one. Pick me.'

'Pick me. Pick one. Pick you.'

'About your deal, an unemotional deal.'

'Yes, Major. Yes, Major.'

'I'll leave, when this is over. And you leave with me.'

He waited for her to answer, but she didn't. 'Milwaukee's a good place,' he said. 'Or anywhere else.'

Still no reply. Around his shoulders the bubbles swirled and popped apart silently. The noise of the waterjets boiling the surface reminded him suddenly of a trout stream in Germany. Staring at the water made him dizzy again so he leaned back, head resting on the tile rim, growing impatient. She was taking her time, but that was good; she was dealing with it, deciding. Then, after a while, he sensed that she might be gone, so he turned. She was. He had heard not the slightest sound of her retreat, until now – the bedroom door to the patio sliding shut.

How strange it felt; he had never seen her.

CHAPTER SIXTEEN

'The heat will be a sonofabitch today,' Rudi said to the other pilots seated before him in the briefing room. 'Drink a lot of water and don't overexert yourselves. We have a lot to do so we'll get to work . . . and then break during the hottest hours and go back for lunch, a swim or a nap, and then work until dark.'

Already he could feel sweat trickle down his back as he spoke. He glanced at the air-conditioning unit whirring laboriously at the covered window, wishing he could will it to produce cooler air.

'Major Malzahn will oversee each of our projects, which I have listed on the board here.' He turned to tap each of the numbered tasks as he spoke: 'First, we will clean and check and reload all gun assemblies. Second, refuel all aircraft and test and replace the drop tank for Number Three. Third, check all systems, especially engines, and test the Freon fire systems. Fourth, replace seats in all aircraft with original steel seats. And fifth, install armor back headrests.

'This should take two days at most. When we get that done, we must repack and recrate all pieces and parts, then bury all remaining ammunition stores. Finally, we must clean both hangars thoroughly, every single scrap of paper, every cigarette butt, every empty beer can. Everything.

'Perhaps this afternoon, when the Oberst and I have studied it a little more, we will brief you on the final mission plan.' Rudi looked over to Theo, who nodded once, then he turned back to the others. 'We've got a lot to do, so let's get to it.'

During the morning drive down to Willie, Webb had another Bingo about the whereabouts of the hidden airfield. It came as he was thinking about the fact that they had hit the flight line at Willie at the very first light of dawn. It was not likely that the 109s would fly at night or even during predawn dark. And the day before, they had intercepted Lowen late in the morning. He reminded himself to ask the FAA inspector, Koontz, if they had found lights of any kind on the 109s. If he could decide that they didn't fly in the dark . . . then their field would be within thirty minutes of Willie.

Webb was unusually tense. His hands seemed to want to tremble on the wheel as the Z-car propelled him south on US Ten at 65 mph. It occurred to him that the cause of this heightened excitement, no doubt of it, was that he was now hunting the Germans both as Task Force Officer and – he smiled at the word – investigator. Go get 'em, Double 0 Seven. He had wrestled with, and made, the conscious decision to say nothing about the sand filters until the next day. There was some comfort in the rationale that he was not guilty of withholding information so long as he acted upon that information. It seemed hazy, but defensible. Similarly, he would not yet mention his new theory about night flying. If he delayed these tidbits just twenty-four hours it would give him enough time to check them out alone.

And another part of his tension, he realized, was the excitement of taking risk. Webb almost never took real risks. There was no escaping the fact that there was some risk, however slight, in playing this thing both ways, in withholding *anything*. And he could barely stretch his imagination far enough to imagine finding the airfield, of coming face-to-face with real Luftwaffe. The fantasy, even more forbidding in the light of day, set his pulse higher. He would have to be extremely careful. Screwing up would screw up everything, his entire career. Webb weighed these matters back and forth all the way to the entrance gate of Williams Air Force Base.

Sergeant Evans greeted him with an inch-thick stack of paper. 'Coffee and rolls in the Meeting Room, Captain. Colonel Lowen's in there now. He's been on the telephone since seven-thirty.' Evans yawned. 'And stop by Public Affairs on the way. They've got reporters ringing the phones off the hooks. The CO said for me to tell you not to release anything until he

253

got here, which –' Evans looked up at the wall clock – 'should be any time now.'

'Thanks, Sergeant.' Webb concealed his interest. Interviews. The press. Webb had never been on radio or TV, never even been in a newspaper. 'Anything else new?'

'Yessir. Wait till you see the newspapers, especially the ones from California. They're in the Meeting Room.'

'When you get some time I could use some help working on the map. I'll be in there with Colonel Lowen.'

'Yessir. Plus,' Evans said, raising his finger, 'the first recon flights are in and they're already processing film, I heard.'

'Yeah?' Webb stopped at the door.

'Yessir. Plus . . . the switchboard is getting calls from people who saw the Messerschmitts yesterday.'

'Yeah? Is someone logging them, taking names, numbers?'

'Yessir. Plus . . . one of the two AWOLs turned up, in jail in Tuscon. Drunk driving. That leaves one.'

'Yeah?'

'Yessir. Plus . . . there's a *Newsweek* reporter all pissed off because he couldn't get anyone to talk to him. He's in Public Affairs.'

'Yeah?' Oh man, he thought.

'Yessir. Plus –' Evan's telephone rang at his elbow. When he picked it up, Webb ducked out the door and down the hall, stopping to soothe the reporter by promising him a short wait. He found Lowen on the telephone in one corner of the Meeting Room, looking ready for a round of golf in khaki slacks and a white knit shirt. Webb poured himself coffee and selected the breakfast roll with the least frosting before sitting down at the table. He began reading the newspaper from California.

There was no shortage of pictures, grainy in black-and-white printing, of the 109s, the P-51s burning, the fire fighters at work, even the downed 109 smoking in the grass. Webb felt it was his responsibility to read every word so he plunged in. To his delight he soon found mention of his rescue, with Lowen, of the wounded fireman. The reporter had called them 'two daring pilots, who could not be found or identified'. Sonofabitch hadn't looked very hard, Webb thought, reading on.

In mid-bite of his cinnamon Danish, Webb ran into a paragraph where the reporter was interviewing witnesses. The

254

words he read stopped him cold. He read them again to make sure, then set the paper on the table and watched Lowen, studied him, until he hung up the phone.

'Morning, Captain,' said Lowen briskly, jotting on a pad of yellow paper.

'Morning, sir. How'd you sleep in the BOQ?'

'Not bad. Not great.' Lowen continued to write.

'Colonel? Have you read this stuff, the papers, from Chino?'

Lowen looked up, setting his pen aside and taking up his pipe. 'No, Captain. But I will.'

'I think you should, sir. Here.' Webb got up and brought the newspaper over to Lowen then returned to his seat. 'Page five. Bottom left-hand column, the last couple of inches,' he directed, sitting back in the chair, watching Lowen begin to read.

'Could you read it aloud, please, sir?' Webb asked. 'Where it begins "One of the Texas Mustang pilots—"'

'One of the Texas Mustang pilots,' Lowen read, 'said that he thought the eight German aircraft were piloted by warbird owners on their way to the Chino Fly-in, until the German flight leader told their flight leader, Colonel Roger Lowen of Brownsville, Texas, that they were ex-Luftwaffe pilots who had survived an attack by Lowen in 1944 at a German airbase. The pilot said he didn't take the matter seriously until the Chino attack. Colonel Lowen could not be found for any comment.' Lowen stopped reading aloud but continued to read the balance of the article silently. Then he looked up at Webb, who was finding himself a little more nervous than he expected. Lowen set the newspaper down and leaned back in the chair.

After a moment or two, Webb summoned the nerve to speak. 'Is that true, sir? Did the German flight leader say that?'

'Something like that,' Lowen replied, shifting his pipe in his teeth and looking away as if through the walls.

'But that wasn't . . . wasn't mentioned, yesterday, at the meeting.'

'What you mean to say, Captain, is that I didn't bring it up. Isn't that right? What you also mean to ask is why didn't I bring it up. Isn't that also right?'

'Yessir.' Webb mustered a firmness in his voice. He was puzzled. And very much intrigued.

'Yes, well . . .' Lowen paused. 'I should have known. Have you had breakfast, Captain?'

Webb held up his half-eaten Danish.

'No, I mean breakfast – eggs, toast, bacon. A real breakfast.'

'No sir.'

'Then—' Lowen stood up, adjusted his shirt and shuffled his papers together – 'let's go have some. Somewhere off base.'

Marta found welcome sanctuary in the cool neatness and hi-tech sterility of the office. There wasn't much going on, just another Monday, and her week's absence had drawn only a dozen call-back messages. It was the heat, probably; August was not the best time in Phoenix for the real estate business. The whole summer had been less busy than usual. Money. Lucky that Eric did so well.

Once settled at her desk, isolated by the glass partitions, she found it blessedly easier to think more calmly. She was still thinking about the Major. She had been thinking about the Major since awakening, while she showered and while she made coffee alone in the kitchen and while she dressed for work. Pulling on her panty hose she had had a fantasy of being watched by the Major and she wondered how she would feel if he had been standing there. Some men seemed to like stockings very much. She wondered if he was like that. She was sure he was, while Eric was not, not particularly. She found herself beginning to think of Eric, and then she began to think of the two of them at the same time, which was confusing.

It was very difficult to think of either of them outside the context of the past nine days – it seemed more like a month – while so much was happening, faster than she could follow. Before she could cope with one thing, something else over-whelmed her. She felt inadequate, stereotypically timid, as if she should have had enough foresight to see what was coming. And now it seemed too late.

This business with the Major, right from the airport, along with everything else, had gathered more momentum than she could manage. The truth about the Major, she admitted reluctantly, is that you are falling on your ass for an obviously self-centered drunk, while everything else is going to hell. Being asked to leave with him had caught her cold, shocked her. He had won another round of this little bout where they danced

256

around each other with clever words and a little grab-ass now and again. This time he had shaken up her little world, asked her to *leave* – not just get laid but leave, asked her away . . . from this. She had looked around the bright sunlit bedroom almost furtively, feeling the entire house, the pool, the cars, her clothes, around her. Like prizes she had won on a game show. And Eric.

She thought about that kinky business in the hangar. She still didn't quite understand why he had acted so obsessed. It wasn't like him, yet it was like him. It reminded her that she had once read that all men, unless something tamed them, got to killing each other. She remembered being very surprised that underneath he wasn't so tamed after all. The Major wouldn't be tame either. Too late for that.

Marta had never, from the beginning, expected a lot of polish from Eric. He was tough and strong and good looking. And sexual. He did the things men in the movies did: hunt, work on fast cars, drink, smoke dope. She hadn't had much polish either, not when they had met. Neither of them had had schools and all that went with that, but it wasn't the sort of thing Eric ever mentioned or seemed to care about.

But she had come to know what polish was and to think about it now and then, even care a little about it. She acquired a little, then more. She paid attention to it and the more she paid attention to it the more she wanted more. She knew men who had it. They had gone to famous schools and they dressed well and drove new cars and made money. They were interesting to talk with because they knew something about everything and they were often charming and occasionally clever. Yet, you always knew they could be tempted away by other things if there was enough money in it. Or sex. Such men were, in other words, her words, subject to change. Susceptible. And they were, in her experience, not given to adoration. Marta adored being adored. She preferred it, slightly, over money. And polish.

She reminded herself that Eric did in a way adore her, had adored her from the beginning, but it was different now . . . though she didn't understand how or why it had changed. She did not need to remind herself that the Major, polish be damned, would adore her. A little adoration sounded pretty good and a lot of adoration sounded even better. It was a pleasant thought, a warm and pleasant thought, being adored.

What would he be like, the Major? Somehow nothing she

knew of him from Rudi or nothing he had said about himself had given her a very substantial impression of what he was other than what he was here and now. He wasn't rich, wasn't polished. What was he that seemed to overcome such things? She wondered if he was ever dull in whatever life he led, selling cars, racing cars. She found it difficult to imagine him standing in a showroom in a tie beside a new car. Probably had four women waiting for him. At least two.

Perhaps his charm was that he didn't intend to have any charm, didn't care. And he alone among the others had seemed to give some thought to getting out before the roof came in on all of them. So he wasn't entirely without some sense. She supposed that he had been through enough to know when he was overextending, which was something that Eric seemed to be getting further away from, rather than closer.

Eric, Eric, Eric. Sometimes he did those things, though, those things with her and to her that she wouldn't want to train someone else to do. Strange things and delicious things and sometimes indescribable things. Like in the hangar. A new man . . . no. It did not seem – she paused – likely. Yes, that was the word. Not in nine days. Such foolishness.

All these things happening, the television, the newspapers. They flew away and come back – less one – and then you find out they've launched some little war. Franz . . . small frail Franz with the tired tired eyes. It was beyond her understanding how he could have flown those airplanes. Gone, gone. God care for you, Franz. And Beissemann – what did they call him? Bison, yes. You and Franz the only ones not so grim, so possessed. Gone so suddenly, sudden-death losers in this mad bravery contest. Crazy bastards, with their fucking war toys. What kind of God made things this way?

She then thought about the envelope, at home in the desk, that Rudi had given her at the beginning of the week. He said it contained signed documents that made her the legal owner of all eight – now six, she thought darkly – airplanes, in case something happened to him, and that it was not be opened unless something did. It was like Rudi to do that, she thought, wondering what they were worth. She remembered Rudi saying, 'a lot'.

There were newspapers in the office and she had seen the headline 1 DEAD 7 MISSING IN BIZARRE WAFB RAID and a lot of

large photos that she refused to look at, and a subhead reading
WWII GERMAN PLANES REPEAT CALIFORNIA ATTACK. Two of
the salesmen were talking about the airplanes. She could hear
them in the other room. She found it strange that they seemed,
from what she could tell, to be very excited and very interested,
talking about it in the same enthusiastic manner as they talked
about football. She was afraid to look at the newspapers and as
she sat at her white curved plastic desk staring out at the cars
passing in the glare of high heat she became increasingly
agitated, fearful. She took another Valium and methodically
made several phone calls to keep her mind occupied. She was
sweating in the coolness of the perfectly air-conditioned
orange-walled office. In her purse she had the list of record
albums from Franz. On the way home she would buy them. And
the newspapers.

'What do we have?' Rudi asked Eric.

'Got our hands full,' Eric replied, looking at his clipboard.
'Got some cooling problems in yours, Three, Five . . . Leaking
fuel in Seven. All the plugs look lousy. Lots of cleaning to do.'
Eric wiped his hands with a greasy rag. 'And One is missing a
bit, and I think Eight has a manifold leak. Not sure. But I'm
starting on this one and working through them all.'

'Best way,' Rudi agreed. 'I'll join you.'

After they had worked for a few minutes, Eric spoke.
'Numbah Ten yesterday. Bison.'

Rudi fitted a plug wrench over the last plug on his side.

'Guys went like that in Nam,' Eric said, not looking up. 'Bang,
gone. No sense to it. Numbah Ten. You wonder why somebody
gets it, somebody doesn't.'

'Bad luck.'

'Yeah. Don't mean nothin'.' The two of them worked on for a
few minutes.

'When I saw that jet,' Rudi began out of nowhere, 'I couldn't
do anything. Not a thing. I just kept flying . . . ahead. And when
it fired . . . I thought I was . . . I thought it was over. I never
heard a sound like that cannon in my life.'

'Yeah. Tell me.'

'You really did a job on the Air Force.'

'Sumbitch went off like a rocket, didn't it? Jesus!'

'What do you think Schilling was going to do?'

'Hell, Rudi, he was going to shoot.' Eric looked up, leaned over a little. 'I checked his guns. He had two rounds of cannon, maybe a dozen rounds machine gun.' Eric shook his head. 'Man he's crazier than me.'

'Why in the hell did you do that, fly that mission yesterday?'

'Don't know,' Eric answered. Rudi saw his manner as deliberately nonchalant.'

'Must have been a good reason,' Rudi said.

'Must have been.'

'Why?'

'Just keeping in shape.'

'Is that anything like keeping up?'

'Sort of.'

'Who are you keeping up with?'

'Keeping up with me,' Eric responded, not looking up from his work.

'Anybody else?'

'Everybody else.'

Rudi thought this over a moment. 'Well, the point is . . . I can't fault you for pulling my ass out of the fire, but you—'

'Yeah man. I understand.' Eric glanced up once. 'You guys are going after that Colonel, huh?'

'It's being discussed.'

'This is where I get to drive the tank truck to Mexico, right?'

Rudi looked up, then around. 'If it works out that way. I don't know.'

'Can't wait.' Eric made a small smile.

'How fast will this thing go, Captain?' Lowen asked when they were five minutes down the road.

'Hundred-plus, easy.'

'Japanese, isn't it?'

'Yessir. Datsun.' Webb almost reminded him that they had had this very same conversation on the drive from Chino. He knew exactly what Lowen would say next.

'I have a Corvette. Seventy-three. It's American, Captain. Chevrolet.'

'Different strokes, sir.'

'There,' Lowen said suddenly. 'Pull in there.'

Webb saw only a dusty roadhouse with two sun-bleached

pickups parked in front. He down-shifted and leaned on the brakes.

'Gonna drink some breakfast, Captain. Sometimes it beats bacon and eggs.'

'Yessir.' Webb eased the Z-car over the potholes in the parking area, raising a cloud of talcum dust.

Inside, they needed a few moments to adapt their vision to the cool gloom. There were only two other customers at the far end of the bar, wearing straw hats. Lowen ordered coffee and Jack Daniel's, and Webb ordered coffee and a beer.

Lowen said nothing until his shot came and then he put it down immediately, using the coffee as a chaser. Webb wiped the mouth of his beer bottle with his handkerchief before taking a pull. He sensed that Lowen was working up to something and he itched inside just waiting to hear it. Lowen fastidiously loaded his pipe bowl with tiny shreds of tobacco. Webb glanced at his watch again, then stirred his coffee and lit up a cigarette. The bar didn't smell very good.

Lowen lit his pipe, then motioned for the bartender.

'These pilots,' Lowen said, as if he were talking to his empty shot glass, 'these Messerschmitt pilots, when they intercepted us Saturday morning, said they were – two of them – the Krauts I shot down at that airbase. The newspaper was right.'

Webb was so surprised at this that he stayed quiet.

'And I think they are,' Lowen added. 'It's not something anyone else would know.'

Webb watched the bartender bring Lowen's shot and set it slopping on the bar. He motioned for another beer, even though he hadn't finished the first.

'And before you ask –' Lowen put down half of the second shot – 'I believe the other pilots are Luftwaffe vets, too.'

Oh man, Webb thought, instantly elated that his conclusion about the pilots was accurate. It was true then.

'This is gonna blow Butler's mind,' Webb said half to himself.

'Yeah. He'll read that paper and get his pants in a bunch because I didn't mention it before. So . . . we'll go see him when we get back.'

Lowen finished off the second shot and raised his hand for another. Webb hurried to keep up. Got to keep up. Six Luftwaffe aces hunting for this guy. Unbelievable. Webb drank

261

all of his beer at once. The telephone? He had the weird feeling that everything was speeding up. He turned to Lowen. 'Where do you think they are?'

'Mexico probably.'

'They're in the desert, for sure,' Webb said. 'They all have sand filters on the carburetor intakes.'

'Ahh, yes.' Lowen squinted and raised his chin. 'That's what those things are. I wondered about that.'

'I've figured their range; 350 miles maximum, one way.'

'Mexico,' Lowen repeated.

'Maybe they're gone now,' Webb suggested, surprised to realize that he hoped they weren't. He was comfortable now, feeling a fresh and conspiratorial strength in being the recipient of Lowen's confidence. He could barely sit still on the stool. Outstanding.

'Don't bet on it.' Lowen began relighting his pipe. 'But we'll know soon. It's their move, I figure.'

'Sir, those 109 pilots couldn't fly five miles now without getting spotted.'

'Horsecrap, Captain.' Lowen lifted his chin again and rubbed his throat. 'They managed to find me in the air, they managed to shoot up Chino and get away, and they managed to turn Williams into junk and get away. So I think if they want to fly again, they'll figure out how.'

Webb finished his beer. He was feeling weird, light, not sure if it was the beer or—

'They want a fight,' Lowen said.

Oh Jesus Bingo, Webb thought, the word *fight* flowing cold and quick just like the beer down his gullet.

'That's why they didn't take me out Saturday when they had the chance. I didn't have any guns. And that's why they didn't shoot up my Mustang on the ground. They want a fair fight.'

'A fair fight,' Webb repeated. It sounded silly in his own ears. The German pilots wanted, yes, a fair fight. Just like it was. *To re-exist*. Again.

'I'll need your help, Captain.' Lowen knocked the ashes out of his pipe in the little tin ashtray on the bar.

'My help?'

'We're gonna go back and work on your Commander, Captain, and I'll need you to back me up.'

'Back you up? For what?'

'You gotta understand how these things work, Captain. You can float around forever in the service during peacetime and nothing will happen to give you a boost. Just one gray office to the next. That's why everybody gets all excited when there's a war of some kind. Everybody gets a chance to perform. Now, your CO is in this godawful desert one day and the next day he's getting obscene phone calls from Washington. It's his turn.'

'It's like "Take it away, Colonel Butler"?'

'That's it.' Lowen nodded.

'And it's like "Take it away, Captain Webb"?'

'That's it.' Lowen nodded again. 'So your Colonel is in the spotlight now. And so are you. It's his big chance. And your big chance. He's wound up tighter'n a whore's garters, Captain. All this arming up, red alerts. Everybody gets to run around with their pants zippered up and their safety off. On the other hand, he's got this Twilight Zone thing in his lap and he doesn't know quite what to make of it. On the surface it seems simple; all he has to do is find the Krauts, call in a real honest-to-God airstrike, and he's a winner. And so are you. But,' Lowen paused, chewing on his pipe stem, 'he needs a solution. You need a solution.'

'Yessir, he does. We do.'

'Quickly.'

'Yessir.' Webb wanted to hold his breath.

'What they want is a fight. So, they get a fight.'

'Sir?'

'A few more Mustangs, some ordnance. Simple. Save time, save money, save looking for them for weeks. Just slug it out.'

'With . . . Mustangs?'

'Well now they worked just fine on those 109s in forty-four now, didn't they?'

Webb drank more beer, at a loss for words until he finished the bottle and set it down and looked up again. 'You're saying,' he spoke slowly, 'that you want Butler to arm your P-51 . . . get some others . . . and let you shoot it out with the Germans?'

'That's right, Captain.'

'Oh man.' Webb reached for the new bottle. 'And you want me to lay this on Butler?'

'That's right, Captain.'

'Oh man. They'll ship my ass to a SAC base at the Arctic Circle. By next week.'

'Not if it works, Captain.'

'Oh man.'

'Damnit Captain, I'm telling you how it works. I'm telling you how it's done. We go in there and give Butler his solution and you get a gold star on your report card. You get the credit because he gets the credit. That's how it works. It's simple.'

'Oh man.'

'This thing could drag on for weeks. And the brass in Washington will squeeze Butler tighter and tighter. And *you* Captain, are out on point. So your ass is going in the grinder, too. That's the way it will be.

'And I can tell you right now, there will be casualties. You've been around airfields long enough to know that. They've got airplanes all over the damned Southwest today, while we're sitting here. They flew the first recon missions this morning. Then there'll be low-level patrols and then there'll be chopper recon patrols. The longer it goes, the more hardware they'll throw up in the sky and with all that going on, somebody's going to have an accident. Those guys will be flying in and out of every damned mountain and mesa in three states and Mexico, and one of them will sure as hell plaster himself into a rock. You just watch.'

Webb thought about the pilots from Willie who went down in the mountains while training. Something nobody talked about.

'In the meantime,' Lowen continued, 'the Krauts are hiding in Mexico and the brass in Washington are grilling your CO on a spit. And while he cooks, Captain, so will you.'

Webb wondered if maybe this was a crazy streak in Lowen that he simply hadn't seen before. All of the German pilots were crazy. Maybe you got a little more crazy with age. Webb decided there was nothing more he could say. He stared at the frail bubble that covered the mouth of his beer bottle like a transparent dome.

'Something else I should add.' Lowen leaned over, waiting a second until Webb had to look up, eye-to-eye. 'There's another side to this coin. What I said about your CO is true, as I see it. From my experience. He seems like a decent sort of a guy, sincere . . . Now you remember that he has spent his life in the service of this country, moving from one gray office to the next

264

. . . from a bomber gunner in Sicily to the middle of Arizona. While you were growing up in – where you from, Captain?'

'Ohio, sir.'

'While you were growing up in East Overshoe, Ohio, fat and safe and dry and warm, your Commander was sweating blood up in one of those tin crates, behind a fifty-caliber, watching 109s come at him.' Webb had a sudden recollection, perfectly clear, of the surprisingly thin aluminum skin of the B-25 at the Chino Airshow.

'Your Commander,' Lowen went on, 'was laying his life on the line to keep the Krauts from doing to you and your family what they did to millions across Europe and in England. You know about all that.'

'Yessir.'

'And his responsibility – training fighter pilots – is a serious matter, something nobody thinks about until there are someone else's fighter pilots – enemies – to deal with. I just don't want to see him lose any people in this thing, Captain, and I wasn't knocking your CO. Get that straight. I'm just giving you another perspective.'

'I hear you, sir.'

'Now, Captain.' Lowen stood up, picked his wallet out of his pocket, and thumbed several bills onto the bar. 'Let's go see the man.'

CHAPTER SEVENTEEN

Schilling's airplane was clean and tuned and fueled and loaded with ammunition and a new belly tank had been fitted. He wiped at the finger smudges around the cowling with a clean rag and then leaned wearily on the leading edge of the port wing, drinking his third beer in the last hour. He and Rendel had loaded the ammunition for all six planes and his muscles hurt, all of them it seemed.

The metal of the wing was hot under his arm. He looked over the Messerschmitt from nose to tail, pleased with the wicked camouflage paint and the dramatic white-and-black crosses and the swastika and kill markings on the tail. In a few days this would be all over. He would be gone. The airplane would be gone. The others would be gone. Marta.

He rubbed his hand over the wing paint which showed the abrasion of the sand and the scratches and dents from the debris. He realized he had become very attached to the aircraft. This was the last one he would ever fly. It was a splendid sonofabitch. When he was in the air he felt as if he could do anything with it; fly upside down, sideways, straight up, straight down, roll, split-S ... or pull out of any dive, out-fly and out-land and out-run and out-turn anything. Or nearly anything. He flashed back on the death-throes of the F-5 climbing away from Eric's fire. It seemed as if the spectacle of the exploding jet might have been nothing but a bad dream, the worst of nightmares inspired by the worst of fears.

He wanted to keep it somehow. It was strange how you could feel that way about a machine. He had felt that way about certain automobiles, particularly if they were racing cars. Like this

Gustav, machines you trusted your life to, machines you risked your neck with, machines that carried you through whole, alive. It was sad that he couldn't keep this airplane. There were so few, almost none, he had heard. In this hangar, and the other, were now most of the operational 109s in the world. It was his first, the 109, and like the cherry red MGA Twin-Cam he had started racing with, the 109 would always be special. He smiled, remembering the dinner in Milwaukee when Rudi had asked him if he truly loved to fly.

When the work was well under way and they had inspected all the engines, Theo and Rudi took their first beer of the day into the briefing room, leaving the door ajar so that none of the others would be reluctant to come in to cool off. They had scheduled a conference on the third mission plan. All morning he had been apprehensive, a feeling that had bothered him much of the night. He had fallen asleep with his mind turning over the details of the mission, and in particular the question of whether Theo would persist, in spite of all that had happened, in flying the third mission as planned.

He had sketched a rather crude but proportionally accurate map of the southwestern states on the blackboard with blue chalk. Then with red chalk he had made X-marks to indicate their own field, Lowen's field, and two more spots south of the Mexican border. Seated at the opposite side of the little desk, Theo smoked a cigarette as he reviewed the notebook for several minutes before looking up at Rudi.

'So,' Theo said. 'We now look at our third mission. Proceed, Oberstleutnant.'

'We are here.' Rudi tapped the red X centered in Arizona. 'And Lowen's field is here.' He tapped the X at the bottom tip of Texas on the Gulf Coast. 'Our first leg, from here to Chihuahua where we refuel, is 458 miles.' With the chalk he tapped a red dotted line across the border southeast into Mexico. 'We fly at night, land at dawn. Eric will leave the day before with the fuel truck and be waiting for us.'

Theo waved his beer bottle. 'The next leg, distance?'

'Next stop is 300 miles. Unfortunately our range is still too limited to make the target and return to—'

'Yes, yes. Another fuel stop . . . which will give us plenty of fuel and time over target.'

'As you can see,' Rudi pressed on, confused by Theo's irritability, 'the problem is fuel. We need 1500 gallons in addition to the fuel carried from takeoff. The distance one way is just over a thousand miles.'

'What is your feeling, Oberstleutnant, about . . . the plan?'

Rudi put down the chalk, studying the blackboard until he gathered his thoughts. He was relieved now, pleased by Theo's question. He would have to phrase his answer carefully. 'Suicidal.'

'Suicidal?'

'We haven't got a chance. We'd never even make the border, even low-level, even at night. Even without all this Air Force, the FBI hunts dope runners everywhere down there. It's just too far. There are just too many risks. If Eric breaks down in Mexico, we're out of gas. Out of luck. Sitting ducks.'

'Isn't the truck properly prepared? Isn't he a mechanic?'

'Yes, of course. But if any one of us has trouble, has to set down . . . And navigation will be critical, especially at night. If one of us gets lost—'

'If. If!' Theo snapped. 'Are we not prepared to navigate? Yes! As for trouble, it is the normal risk. Bettter than the Channel, yes? Not so wet, ha ha,' he laughed suddenly, confusing Rudi for a moment.

'If you turned around,' Rudi said without smiling, 'and looked up the cannon barrels of an F-5, Herr Oberst, you'd learn about getting wet another way.'

Theo's laughter, again sudden, was prolonged. He wiped a tear from one eye and beamed at Rudi. 'It was a good plan, if we had used it first . . . but now, as you say, suicidal.' Rudi was profoundly glad to hear what Theo was saying.

'Now what do we do about our Colonel Lowen if we are not able to destroy his airplanes?' Theo was still smiling.

'As you said, we have done what we set out to do. Each day now the risk increases, Theo.' The vision of the F-5 hovering above him would be his nightmare, Rudi was sure, for the rest of his life.

'Do not overestimate the Americans. All they have to work with is our range, Oberstleutnant. What do you think they are doing with their big maps? They are drawing big circles around the two airfields we attacked, and then staring at them.' Theo looked very pleased, amused. 'What is that province, that state, above this one?' He pointed at the map.

'Utah.'

'Yes, Utah. For all they know, we could be based in the southwest corner of Utah. Or that peninsula in Mexico. I have studied the maps, too. Do you think they have enough imagination to look for us on their doorstep?'

Rudi made a small shrug. 'Sooner or later.'

'Perhaps—' Theo stared at the map – 'the question is: Do we want to destroy the Colonel Lowen?'

'Perhaps it is . . . not feasible.'

Theo turned. 'You remember what Hans looked like,' he said. The remark was a reminder, Rudi knew, not a question. He needed no reminder; even after thirty-two years he remembered. Just the lower jaw was left.'

'Ah,' said Theo, looking up at the ceiling, 'I like to think about what the Colonel Lowen is thinking . . . Hour by hour . . . Day by day.' He smiled, then looked over at Rudi. 'It is exquisite, that kind of punishment, yes? Do you think he wonders when the Luftwaffe will attack his Confederates Air Force? Do you think he waits for the telephone to ring at any moment? Exquisite.'

'If we were to disappear now . . . he would wonder about us for weeks, months.'

'Would that be enough for you, Rudi? Enough revenge?'

Rudi was not quite sure what to say. Nor was he quite sure what he was feeling. It had seemed such a significant coincidence to discover Lowen's picture, to discover he was still flying a Mustang, a coincidence of such impact, such irresistible potential, that there was no way it could be ignored. How easily it could be interpreted as some mysterious God-sent opportunity for retribution.

Now in the light of the Staffel's existence and success, of the real experience of Theo's vision, there was no way to avoid Lowen. It seemed a mission at least ordained. Were they in the realm of predestination after all? He thought of Theo's speech in the hangar. Destiny.

'No,' Rudi replied. 'No, it is not enough.'

'Of course it is not enough!' Theo's words exploded in the tiny room. 'To engage this Colonel Lowen in the air would

269

complete what we have done. In the most perfect way, yes?'

'Win or lose?'

'We cannot lose!' Theo slammed his hand on the desk. 'We tell him we will destroy his Confederates Air Force – even if we cannot – if he does not come up to fight, yes?'

'And if he refuses?'

Theo looked away. 'Then we go home.'

Rudi studied Theo closely to be sure he was understanding what he was hearing. 'Do you think he will fight?'

'Will he fight? Of course he will fight! He is *still* flying his Mustang, Rudi. Still! He has never stopped being a fighter pilot, in his own mind.'

'How will we persuade him?'

'We will tell him to meet us halfway. His range is twice ours. He can refuel anywhere.'

'Tell him?'

'Of course.' Theo grinned. 'The telephone. Like before, yes?'

Colonel Butler finished reading the part of the newspaper article that Webb had outlined in red pencil, then he looked up across his desk at Lowen.

'Roger, why didn't you mention this before?'

Butler's voice was more perplexed than angry, Webb noted with relief.

'What's the difference? I'm telling you now.'

'Do you believe ... that two of these guys are the same Luftwaffe pilots?'

'Nobody else would know about it,' Lowen replied, 'unless someone dug up a mission report from thirty-two years ago.'

'Jesus,' Butler breathed after a moment.

'Sir,' Webb said, 'no matter who they are, it doesn't change anything.'

'True,' Lowen said. 'Because they want me.'

'Want you?' Butler seemed a little dazed. 'Revenge?'

Lowen shrugged. 'It's logical in a way.'

'Jesus.' Butler rubbed his forehead.

'Get my ship patched up,' said Lowen, 'and let me get back home. They'll get in touch.'

'In touch how?'

'On the telephone. Like they did before.'

'On the *telephone*?'

Lowen explained how he had received the call from the *LA Times* reporter, and that he had given him the time and altitude of their route over Phoenix.

'*Jesus*, this is getting out of hand,' Butler said half to himself. 'What do you think they would, ah, say? Over the telephone.'

'I think they'll want a fight.'

'Jesus, a *fight*?'

'Or else they'll come down to my field and do what they did here and at Chino.'

Butler stared at Lowen, watching him fill his pipe. Webb watched both men, intrigued. Butler was visibly startled at this new possibility of yet another attack materializing a thousand miles east and Webb was beginning to appreciate his Commander's situation much more clearly now. He tried to imagine what kind of pressure Butler was feeling, having the brass in Washington calling daily, waiting hourly.

'Your Mustang,' said Butler to Lowen, 'will be flown here tomorrow evening. Then you can go home.'

'Colonel?' Webb was starting to feel more like a spectator than a participant. 'We think we have a new, ah, approach. To finding them.'

'What new approach, Captain?'

'Let them contact Colonel Lowen. Then we'll know what they're planning to do, at least.'

Butler appeared to think this over. 'Then what?'

'Then we'll know if they're heading for Texas. Or they'll ask for a showdown.'

'Showdown? This sounds like a goddamned western.'

'It is,' Lowen said. 'Them and me, and whoever I can find to help.'

Butler was looking confused again. 'What are you talking about, some sort of dogfight?'

'It's what they want.' Lowen slowly blew out a small cloud of white pipe smoke.

'Are you telling me – ?'

'I'm telling you, Ed, I want some Spam-cans and some ground crew and some ordnance.'

'And then?'

'And then we go slug it out.'

Butler sat back in his chair. 'Are you serious?'

'It would smoke 'em out, sir,' said Webb quickly.

271

'Do you think' – Butler kept staring at Lowen – 'that I'm going to set up a combat situation, a *duel*, between you and these . . . these terrorists, over civilian property, Roger?'

'Well, set it up over government property if that's—'

'No way.'

'What are you going to do then, Ed? Set up more patrols? Put all the bases in the western United States on combat alert? For six piston fighters?'

'What I'm going to do, Roger, is find them.'

'Forget finding them! We don't have to find them. They'll find me.'

'And you'll just go up and shoot it out?'

'I have done that sort of thing a few times before, if you recall.'

'No way.'

'Sir?' Webb sat up in his chair.

'No way,' Butler repeated.

'Sir?' Webb tried again.

'Listen,' said Lowen 'let's suppose the Krauts go up again and your boys catch them in the air. What are you going to do, shoot them to pieces? Over civilian territory? You don't really want a combat incident. Just turn off this firepower stuff and let me handle them. You said you'd give me what I needed. Now give me what I need and I'll end it. Mission accomplished.' Lowen stuck his pipe back between his teeth. 'Do they still use that term in the Air Force?'

'Jesus.' Butler shook his head.

'Sir?' Webb put an edge on his voice. He was agitated now; the discussion had gone haywire, out of sequence, and they were arguing the solution before discussing the reasons. 'It may take weeks to find them. We're building an operation here: aircraft, support personnel. Like a war game exercise. With all of this, isn't it likely we'll have accidents, casualties?'

'It's a built-in risk, Captain, but the answer is yes.'

'And the expense. It is expensive.'

'Yes, Captain. It is expensive.'

'Then, sir, if we had a solution that bypassed these risks, these costs, you would consider it.'

'Captain, I cannot imagine any solution that would preclude flying patrols and photo recon missions or having aircraft on standby alert to prevent further attacks by these lunatics who have already – speaking of expense – cost the government seventy-two million dollars. Can you?'

'Yessir. Just what Colonel Lowen proposed. We quit looking for them. We let them make the move.'

'They'll call,' Lowen said.

'We set a trap,' said Butler finally. 'Have our people waiting.'

'You mean combat aircraft?' Lowen leaned forward. 'You mean maybe a little air battle, air-to-air missiles? Over civilian territory?'

'Twenty millimeter, not missiles. When they appear.'

'Ed, how will you know when they will appear?'

'They'll tell you. Isn't that—'

'They'll tell *me*,' Lowen cut in. 'They want *me* and they're gonna tell *me*. And I'm not gonna tell *you* when they tell *me*!'

'What do you mean?' Butler growled. 'Why wouldn't you tell me?'

'Because that's my ace, Ed. That's my card in this deal. I'm just making a deal.'

'Why?'

'Because I don't want to lose any of your boys, that's why.'

'A deal . . .' Butler shook his head.

'A *good* deal,' Lowen insisted. 'A good deal and you're too damned . . . *bureaucratic* to snap it up. Those Krauts are smart, if we have to be reminded. They're not going up now for a joyride so your fighter pilots can use them for target practice. They're not sitting out in a field waiting for your photo-recon planes to take their snapshots. They're all covered up down in Mexico, waiting for me. If I don't show up, then they'll jump out and plaster my field, damnit. I want some defense.'

'Defense,' Butler echoed. 'Like a war.'

'It is a war! Unless you can think of a nicer name for it. You've lost thirty-one planes, I've lost four, and another twenty-two over at Chino. And we've had casualties. If that isn't combat then you tell me what is.'

'Sir,' said Webb. 'I think we should consider it.'

'You said you'd give me what I needed,' Lowen said.

Webb loved it now; a one-two punch.

'Can you imagine . . .' Butler looked away, 'what Washington would think about this?'

'So *what*?' Lowen's voice split with exasperation. All they want from you is those Krauts on a platter. And I'm giving you

273

the answer. Hell, I'm doing it for you. And *quickly*, Ed, quickly!'

'I cannot sanction civilian pilots engaging in armed combat.'

Lowen watched Butler through a drifting wreath of his pipe smoke. 'Well, then draw up a damned paper or something, whatever makes you feel right. Doesn't the Air Force still have lawyers?'

'This is nuts.' Butler shook his head. 'If those lunatics call you up . . . then you call me and we'll handle them. Period.'

'Horsecrap, Ed. There's no way you're going to use me as bait for your fighters, no way I'm going to be up there with those damned rockets flying around. Just let me handle it for you.'

'Jesus,' Butler groaned.

Fascinated, Webb watched the two men staring at each other, holding tautly, as if pulling at opposite ends of a single strand of wire.

'It's not that complicated.' Lowen's voice was relaxed now. 'Just pick up the telephone and find me a few P-51s. The National Guard must still have a bunch of them. Pull some strings, Ed. Call in some favors. This is the time.'

Butler continued to study Lowen, his expression blank. Webb sensed the scales tipping slightly.

'Ground crew,' Lowen continued. 'Ordnance. The taxpayers get a break, you've made a smart strategic decision. And the Confederate Air Force gets to keep the Mustangs. Simple.'

'It's no deal, Roger.'

'Sir?' Webb leaned forward.

'It's no deal, Captain,' Butler said.

'If you knew . . .' Lowen spoke carefully, 'that the Krauts were going to meet me at a specific place and time, would you do it?'

'Perhaps,' Butler answered.

'Cover yourself, Ed. Get me my airplanes and keep it a big secret. We'll be ready just in case. Insurance, Ed. If it doesn't work, you take the Mustangs back; is that fair?'

Butler rested his forehead in his hand, elbow on the desk, still staring at Lowen. 'We'd base you here.'

'No sir. Texas. My base. My command.'

'Texas,' Butler repeated.

'Secret,' Lowen added.

'Jesus,' Butler muttered.

'What have you got to lose, Ed? It's a reasonable protective measure, maybe a bit unorthodox, but—' Lowen shrugged. 'What's the worst that could happen? Hell, ten damned P-51s don't cost half as much as one of those rocketships you've got.'

'Why are you doing this?'

'Because it's a good idea.'

'Sir, I think it's a good idea,' said Webb solemnly.

'Secret,' Lowen said. 'Nobody knows.'

'I'm not stopping the photo-recon flights.' Butler now had a decisive tone to his voice.

'No need,' agreed Lowen. 'Just let me get back to Texas.'

'You really believe they'll fly to Texas?'

'Sure as God made little green apples.'

'This is crazy, all of it. Crazy.' Butler's hands massaged the back of his neck.

Then to Webb's discomfort, Butler turned his attention to him, as if he were weighing the matter solely upon Webb's support. It was, Webb decided, a most disquieting sensation.

'I'll tell you, gentlemen,' Butler said finally, his eyes still on Webb, 'how it's going to be.' He then looked over at Lowen. 'First, this conversation is not to go beyond this room, not under any circumstances. Second, I'll get your P-51s, Roger, and a ground crew. And you agree not to move, unless I know about it. And if we find them first, in Mexico or wherever, the P-51s come back without a word.

'And you, Captain . . .' Once again Butler's eyes reached out to Webb's. 'I expect you to find these . . . Germans, if they are anywhere near here, before they leave for Texas. The moment you do, you'll be a Major. And if you don't . . .' Butler let the word hang in the air. As if for punctuation, he lit another cigar and snapped his lighter shut with a small chrome click. 'Now that's my deal, gentlemen.'

Lowen tapped his pipe bowl empty on the edge of an ashtray and stood up. Webb stood up, too.

'You won't regret this decision, sir,' Webb said.

'I regret it already, Captain.'

'Courier brought a package for you, Captain.' Evans pushed a large manila envelope across the desk. 'From the FAA office in Phoenix. Koontz.'

'Thanks, Sergeant.' Webb lifted the package. Several pounds of paper.

'Plus . . . reporters ganging up in Public Affairs. One's from *Time* magazine, insists on a short interview with somebody.'

'No way.' Webb began tearing open the package.

'It's a woman. Good-looking.'

'Call over and say I'll be there in ten minutes.'

'Plus . . . flight line personnel and pilots from yesterday are assembled in the meeting room. Waiting.'

'Damnit. Listen, Sergeant, will you please handle that? Just get everyone to describe exactly what they saw – on tape – and get the transcripts out, okay?'

'Can do,' Evans replied. 'Plus . . . we got forty-eight pages of transcript from the public telephone number. And it's still coming.'

Webb looked around the office. There were two more typists now, fingers dancing over their keys with noises like little machine guns, firing out reams of paper. We're all going to drown in paper by the end of the week, he thought. Lowen was right.

'Koontz said to tell you this stuff—' Evans gestured at the packet of paper in Webb's hand – 'is fresh from the FAA computer in Oklahoma City. Single-engined aircraft registrations.'

'I'm out of here, Sergeant.'

It was nearly another hour before Webb got free to retreat to his own office, a block down the street from Headquarters Building on the second floor of a converted barracks. He shared the space, and a secretary, with another OSI officer, now absent on vacation.

He completed his daily report and gave it to Sarah to type before closing the door, leaving her to intercept telephone calls. Two hours remaining until the meeting. Not, he thought, time enough. He pulled off his glasses and rubbed the bridge of his nose. He heard the Tweets and T-38s ripping up the afternoon silence, noting that Butler had somehow gotten trainers in the air already, those that were left. Remarkable.

He cleaned his glasses with his handkerchief, staring with blurred vision at the stack of paper from Koontz and wondering whether it was just another roadblock – or another clue. He placed his glasses back on deliberately, deciding to study it until he was satisfied either way. He could afford to overlook nothing.

The stack of printout seemed like an endless single piece of light green paper, folded back and forth. Reading from left to right, each line began with the name of the aircraft manufacturer, followed by the aircraft name, the engine displacement, a code of letters and numbers he couldn't decipher, and then the name and address of the owner. Webb shuffled the edge of the stack. There were hundreds, thousands, of listings in alphabetical sequence. He skimmed at random through the manufacturers' names, finding many he had never heard of, others that rose quickly with familiarity to his eye: BEECH, BRISTOL, CESSNA, DE HAVILLAND, FALCO, GARRETT, HAWKER. Then two penciled check marks on the margin beside a MESSERSCHMITT type 108 and the single type 109 registered to C PAYNE of HARLINGEN TX – one of Lowen's group. It would take hours to run through the damned list. If the only two Messerschmitts were checked, then what could be found? Would the FBI screw with a list like this? Yes, he decided, they would wring it dry; every scrap . . . every possible scrap.

He leaned back in the chair and began to scan down the page: AERONAUTICA D'ITALIA SA (FIAT), AERONAUTICA MACCHI, AEROSPATIALE . . . Damnit, damnit. Keep going, he told himself. Persevere. Every scrap. Keep going. AGUSTA . . . ANSALDO . . . ARMSTRONG WHITWORTH . . . AVI . . . AVIATIK . . . AVION CAULDRON-RENAULT . . . AVRO . . . four pages of A's now, and there were the B's and right off there were the words BAYERISCHE FLUGZEUGWERKE. They seemed to spring right off the paper – something clicked – and they were followed by T109G MFR GERM 1943. Oh Jesus Bingo; *Bayerische Flugzeugwerke*! He couldn't pronounce it but he knew exactly what it was; the name of the manufacturing concern licensed to build for Messerschmitt. The 109 was sometimes called the Bf-109 by purists, but Me-109 was almost always used in the aircraft books. And this was clearly a 109. Webb sat up in the chair, rereading the line carefully. The date of registration was over five years old and the owner listed was R O FELBECK with an address in EL SEGUNDO CA.

He stared at the name for a moment, disappointed because it wasn't very German-sounding, then copied it down, along with the address, and took the scrap of paper out to Sarah and asked her to get the number for him. Then he went back and copied down the code letters and numbers that he didn't understand.

'Captain?' Sarah's voice came around the half-closed door.

277

'No listing at that address for that name and no listing for that name anywhere in El Segundo. And it's not an unlisted number.'

'Try every section of the Los Angeles metro area then, please. There can't be that many R.O. Felbecks.' Webb looked at his watch. The meeting would begin in forty-five minutes. If he turned this over to the FBI they'd have it in no time, he thought. Damn, there was no way he would let go of a lead like this, no way.

He dialed Sergeant Evans and read off the codes and asked him to call Koontz for a translation.

'Sarah,' he called. 'Get the County Sheriff's Office and tell them I need the number for that address. There's something called a reverse directory and those people can get it quickly.'

Webb sat back and lit a cigarette and watched the second hand sweeping around his watch face. The telephone buzzed. It was Sergeant Evans.

'Captain, Inspector Koontz has already left. On his way here. But I got your information. The codes indicate certain modifications of the original aircraft to racing trim, then the serial numbers, registration numbers, and the inspector's identification.'

Webb turned this information over in his mind. 'Call back, Sergeant, and see if you can get the name and address of the inspector, okay?'

When Webb hung up he let his hand rest on the phone, thinking. Racing trim. Five years. Not promising. He knew that some warbirds were dramatically changed from original form for racing purposes. The P-51 was a perfect example. And the plane could have changed hands several times. He wondered if the 109 was very suitable for racing and he decided it was a strange choice, especially with the goofy landing gear. He recalled hearing that somebody had ground-looped an E-type 109 with a Spanish engine up at Reno the last year or so.

'No luck, Captain,' Sarah called. 'The address has a number but it's a company, not a residence.'

'What kind of company?'

'It's called Sunwest Aviation Incorporated. Want the number?'

In two minutes he was speaking to Felbeck's secretary, who informed him that her boss was on vacation and, no, it was against company policy to give out either his home address or number and, no, not his vacation address or number either.

Three minutes after that, Webb had reserved a seat on a morning flight to LA. He looked around the little office with gray walls, feeling as if he were lighting up, glowing again, the way he had felt in the bar with Lowen. Felbeck's secretary had finally, under Webb's best effort at polite persuasion, revealed that her boss was vacationing in Phoenix.

CHAPTER EIGHTEEN

The second Task Force meeting began with the screening of more news film from Chino, some amateur movie film, and an assortment of slides taken by spectators. Among the slides, Webb's ten close-ups of the 109s were far superior. As he watched the screen he felt in his uniform shirt pocket for the gorilla slide. He did not know what he would do with that one, if anything.

When the lights came on, Butler had Sergeant Evans distribute copies of the group's typed reports, then requested that each member give their report verbally. He began with his own, standing in front of the map.

'As of this morning we have photo reconnaissance flights twice daily. The film is processed here on base. We already have prints from this morning's flight over the northern Baja peninsula and Southern California. We will photograph all of the area indicated there on the map.'

'Colonel?' Lowen raised his hand. 'How long do you estimate it will take to photograph that area?'

'Two days at best. Perhaps three.'

Case rested, Lowen thought. Before he left the meeting he intended to drive home his point.

'Daylight patrols by armed fighters,' Butler went on, 'have been initiated in assigned sectors from various bases, primarily Luke, where we also have a Marine assault team standing by in the event we get something hot. We are also setting up chopper recon patrols.'

As he listened, Webb had a surprising sense of delayed recognition: he was seeing. The Machine – he was *part* of The

Machine – gather strength to strike: The aircraft assigned and assembled, the flights scheduled and flown, the missiles armed and fitted, the cannons loaded. Link by link, the chain of action was being forged by the words and decisions created in this room.

And if Butler was the pilot of this deadly force, then he, Webb, was the co-pilot. Armed jet fighters and Marines with loaded weapons were poised even now, awaiting the command of the officer who stood at the map with the pointer stick, talking.

How could something so horrible be so simple? He had seen the training films, rockets arrowing in flight – a single slim metal tube no longer than a shower rail – blasting a tank, a truck, a decoy plane into flaming flying wreckage. They never showed people, human beings, in those films. Something you were expected to overlook in your imagination: heads and limbs flying, charred meat, real people, real death. Oh man.

'Considering their estimated fuel range,' Butler was saying, 'their base is probably within this area – 215 miles in diameter – from a point midway between Chino and here.' Butler's pointer traced the circle that included Southern California, the southern tip of Nevada, the western half of Arizona, about half the Baja peninsula, and the northwest corner of Sonora.

Lowen was right, thought Webb; this could easily take a week or more. Time. This whole thing was a race, he realized. Butler running The Machine and me trying to find the Staffel before The Machine, before Lowen goes off on his own mad little mission. A three-way race, and only he knew it. Oh man.

Butler was nearing the end of his report.

'—pleased to announce that all seven of our missing personnel from yesterday's incident have been accounted for.'

Webb looked down at the papers before him on the table, at his notes on top. His report would be next. He looked at the clock. What chance would he have alone? Persevere, he said silently to himself. Persevere calmly.

Lowen, as he listened to Webb's report, was selective in the notes he made, recording only those bits of information that might be of use to him. He found himself thinking ahead. Webb's presentation strengthened his theory that the Staffel was in Mexico, and that the Task Force wouldn't find them before they went to Texas.

He shifted in his chair and deliberately appeared to be attentive. Somewhere up there his Mustang was on the way in. He tuned his ear beyond, knowing he could pick up the growling of the Merlin engine if it flew anywhere close overhead, but he heard only the sound of jets, like fabric tearing evenly in the early dusk.

'Another theory,' Webb was saying, 'is that the entire group of pilots are West German nationals, perhaps Luftwaffe veterans. Colonel Lowen will describe an exchange over the radio between himself and one of the pilots last Saturday.' He nodded to Lowen before taking his seat.

While Lowen was talking, Webb watched and listened with new-found fascination. He was sorry that Lowen would be leaving. Being around him was . . . reassuring, yes. There he was, the real thing, in a damned golf shirt and slacks. And wasn't it outstanding how he had leaned on the CO to set him up with more P-51s? What was that, crazy? Or brave?

'I am virtually certain,' Lowen was saying, 'that no builder or collector among the various warbird groups in the continental United States has any knowledge of these eight aircraft. I have contacted over two dozen of these people, most of whom I know personally, and asked them to continue to contact others among these groups for any possible leads.

'And finally, the restoration and testing of eight aircraft of this type would be such an extensive project – months, years – that it could hardly be kept secret unless extraordinary means were taken. This fact also leads to the conclusion that these aircraft were probably brought into the States, or Mexico, secretly and then assembled, and that the assembly and testing and flying were carried out in a remote location. Such as Mexico.'

Next to report, Sheriff Stratton had collected sighting reports from public telephone calls and had marked each of the sightings on the wall map with colored pins. There were scattered blue pins in Southern California strung out in basically easterly patterns from Chino and there were scattered yellow pins north of Willie in both northeast and northwest patterns. Stratton then announced that the Public Telephone Number, with 24-hour tape recording system, was pulling calls regularly. He was recommending the prompt establishing of a cash reward for such tips when Airman Harper slipped quietly in the door, came over to Lowen, and handed him a note: *Call holding. 'Most urgent'. Mr Becker. LA Times.*

Lowen read it twice, then stood up and left the room and walked down the hall to Public Affairs and picked up the telephone indicated by Airman Harper. He took a deep breath. 'This is Lowen,' he said curtly, pressing his forefinger against his left ear to shut out the typewriter clatter.

'Colonel Lowen? This is Becker. *Los Angeles Times.* Do you remember?'

'I remember. How are things at the *Times?*'

'Your wife gave us the number there.' The voice was clear and without accent. 'I hope we aren't interrupting.'

'Are you the Commanding Officer?'

'Executive Officer. Now we —'

'Get your Commanding Officer on the line, Becker. If he speaks English. I'm only talking to the CO.'

There was a pause. Lowen listened closely, hearing only Becker's muffled voice speaking to someone else. A moment later there was a new voice: 'Yes, Colonel. Good evening.' The accent was noticeable but not heavy. Good evening your ass, thought Lowen.

'What do I call you, a name?'

'I am the Commander, Colonel. My rank is Oberst.'

'Give me a name, Oberst. Or I'll call you Kraut.'

'Oberst Kraut, if you wish, Colonel. I am hardly in a position to give you my name.'

'Go ahead, Oberst. I'm listening.'

'Who is your commander, sir? Of the Confederates Air Force.'

'Colonel Jethro Culpeper is the commander, Sir.'

'And is he in Texas?'

'No, not exactly. Meanwhile, I'm in command.'

'We will meet you on Thursday, Colonel. Five of us.'

'Thursday I will be in Texas.'

'Yes. You will have four other aircraft? You will be armed?'

'I'm not sure.'

'Either way, Colonel, we will visit your airbase.'

'That's quite a distance for you people, isn't it?'

'Yes, but we are prepared.'

'Prepared . . . ah, how about meeting, say, halfway?'

The Oberst paused a moment. 'Yes. A good suggestion . . .

Perhaps the southwest of the State of New Mexico. We will let you know exactly when and where. Until then, Colonel. Good-bye.'

The telephone clicked off abruptly. Godamighty, Lowen thought, replacing the receiver. Southwest New Mexico.

When he returned to the meeting room he felt a little flushed. Koontz from the FAA was speaking, still in his seat, looking like a professor. Lowen took his chair and pretended to listen.

'—list might be expanded to include aircraft material suppliers, engine rebuilders, et cetera, but this would take weeks and is, ah, beyond our jurisdiction, of course.' Koontz adjusted his glasses and cleared his throat. 'Within our time framework, Colonel, it is my feeling that pursuing this direction is, ah, pointless.'

Lowen had the feeling that he had returned in the middle of a football game just in time to see the home team score. Koontz was the sort of wonderfully exact and tenacious bloodhound that would lead them all to the very front door of the Staffel. Guaranteed, if they had months.

So those Kraut bastards were all set to hit the field at Harlingen. He knew it all along. Now he knew they were in Mexico. Five of them. He wondered what had happened to the sixth. Probably had cardiac arrest when the F-5 showed up. Five. He wondered how many pilots he'd need to go up against five crack 109 aces. It was a sobering thought. And he wondered how many P-51s Butler would scare up and how quickly.

'— and it is confirmed that the Chino aircraft was definitely downed by gunfire. Cannon and machine gun. Our reports on both downed aircraft will continue to expand well beyond . . .' Koontz paused for no apparent reason, as if he had lost his place, '. . . well beyond what I have summarized here, but I should, I think, point out that I do not, we do not, anticipate finding anything that would be meaningful, or would assist, in locating the remaining six aircraft.'

Lowen stole a long look over Koontz's head to the wall map, picking out New Mexico and noting that one of Webb's red circles took in the whole western half of the state. The center of this particular range circle was Willie, he remembered. He wondered if there was some further clue to be found in the map now that he knew the Krauts could reach southwest New Mexico.

'From the remains,' Koontz was saying, 'such as they are, of both pilots . . . extensive forensic efforts could provide identification to match those that were provided – confirm, I should say – those names that we have . . . though it will be painstaking. And time-consuming.'

'How much time, Mr Koontz, would be consumed?' Butler's voice sounded weary.

'Weeks,' Koontz replied promptly.

Lowen glanced at Butler. The home team had scored again.

The real problem, Lowen was thinking, would be getting pilots. He'd call Fitz right after the meeting and lay out the program, get him to start looking up other pilots who were still flying, still hot. It would take some digging. Easy now, he thought, one problem at a time. Thursday. Three days. Lord.

The FBI guy, Montgomery, was on his feet now. Today he had on a powder blue suit, Lowen noted, while it was a beige suit yesterday. But the same maroon tie. 'We have identities of both deceased pilots by name only, pending positive identification of remains, as follows: First pilot killed at Chino Field, California as Osterhoudt, Franz, resident Munich, West Germany. Age fifty-six, occupation musician, Munich Bach Orchestra. Luftwaffe veteran, served 1938-1945, awarded German Cross March 1942. Second pilot killed Williams Air Force Base, Chandler, Arizona as Beissemann, Gustav, resident Stuttgart, West Germany. Age fifty-five, occupation senior pilot, Lufthansa Airlines. Luftwaffe veteran served 1940-1945, awarded German Cross June 1943.'

Listening intently, Lowen had filled his pipe bowl and was lighting it.

'Confirmation of both individuals,' Montgomery continued, 'as West German nationals would seem to support the premise that the six surviving pilots may also be from West Germany. I have advised our people in Washington of this.'

Twenty-four hours now, Lowen thought, and they've got zero. Texas. Now a good ordnance crew wouldn't need a lot of time to install the Brownings, and then they'd have to sight them in and test in flight. Couple of days maybe. He dismissed the temptation to count the years since he'd last fired in flight. When he was doing it then, he did it well. And so it should still be. Why not?

'Our ballistics people confirm that shell casings collected

here, at Chino field, and the location where the jet fighter went down are all of the same specification – 7.9 millimeter and 20 millimeter. Montgomery glanced up at Butler before turning the page. 'We have assigned individual agents in California, as well as here, to –'

Lowen heard his Mustang then. It was far off, maybe a mile, but he knew the sound – nasty dog snarling, deep – as sure as he knew his own breathing. It made him feel very good. If it came overhead low enough it would rattle the windows. He glanced up at Butler, whose attention upon Montgomery wavered a moment, then switched with his eyes across the table to Lowen.

Forty minutes later Webb and Lowen were out on the 425th flight line to see the Mustang. Some of the trainee pilots and ground personnel were hanging around the plane which, in spite of its age, appeared sleek and fierce alongside the T-38s and F-5s. Lowen walked around his newly delivered fighter, peering over and under, touching the aluminum surfaces wherever he went, and reaching out once to touch the huge white star painted on the side of the fuselage. Webb watched curiously. The sun was sliding down and the pastel orange light painted the P-51 in soft glowing color.

'Well, Captain, she looks ready to go.'

'Yessir.'

'It's a good ship.' Lowen patted the wing.

'Colonel, we're gonna find those people, the Germans.'

'Good,' Lowen said without looking at him.

'I'm gonna find them is what I mean. Soon.'

'Good, Captain. Then what?'

Webb shrugged. He was holding Lowen's attention by only a thin thread. 'I don't want any of them to get killed.'

'No?' Lowen appeared to smile.

'You don't want anyone to get killed either. You said so.'

'Not our boys. No need.'

'No need for them to get killed either.'

'They're looking for it, Captain.'

'There aren't any more like them,' Webb said. 'Not many like you, either.'

'What does that mean?'

Webb groped for words. Could it be that Lowen had no concept of what he was? Of what the Staffel was? 'Fighter pilots. World War Two fighter pilots,' he said simply.

'What are you planning to do; save them?'

'What are you planning to do; kill them?'

Lowen seemed to regard Webb with renewed interest. 'Yes, Captain. That's exactly what I'm planning to do.'

Webb did not reply, did not let whatever it was he was feeling – disappointment was the only name he could give it – show. He felt Lowen's eyes on him.

'Captain, do you have any idea how many died in Europe during the war?'

'Yessir I do. Millions.'

'Millions, Captain. That's right; millions. That's a lot of people.'

'Yessir.'

'Children, Captain. They bombed children. Everywhere. In the middle of the night they tried to level London. The Krauts were one big death machine.'

'Yes sir, I know.' Webb was not comfortable in what was becoming a defensive posture.

'Those people were members of an army that systematically murdered, slaughtered, millions of innocent people. These pilots fly the swastika, Captain, and the swastika is the symbol of the greatest evil in the experience of the civilized world. Whether a man wears it on his arm or on his aircraft, the meaning is the same.'

'I understand,' said Webb. And he did.

'It must be erased, Captain. Everywhere.'

Webb nodded silently, knowing it was time to keep his mouth shut.

'I'll tell you something, Captain. I'm going back to Texas tomorrow morning and get some more aircraft and then I'm going to meet them. That's the way it's going to be.'

Webb looked up, watching Lowen chew on his pipe stem.

'And if you get lucky, Captain, and find them first, then you would be doing me a great favor if you told me where to find them. It might save a few lives.'

Imagine that, Webb thought. The crazy bastard wants them all to himself. The last dogfight of World War Two, thirty-one years after. Great God. He'd give his left arm and his left nut and his left eye to see that if it happened. Outstanding.

'Yessir,' he said finally, wondering if Lowen believed in God.

CHAPTER NINETEEN

Roger Lowen believed in God, though God was not on his mind as he climbed away from Willie over the Superstition Mountains, awed as always by the expanse of desolate country beneath his wings. The early light below was still ghostly cool blue, the dawn as yet unbroken over the gnarled landscape tinted lavender, sienna, ochre. Then as he climbed the sun struck the aluminum skin of the P-51 with golden-white heat, lifting his spirits like a silent chorus. The aircraft hummed with vibration of brute power as he ascended, its high-pitched roar steady and strong and even, its thrusting torque pressing him firmly in the seat. Reclining comfortably at his angle of climb he watched his gauges each in turn, pausing at the revolving white altimeter needle. What a splendid sensation, this lifting, being propelled above the earth by the huge 12-cylinder engine at his feet, its power at the fingertips of his gloved left hand resting on the throttle, this slim silver craft holding him, embracing him.

Lowen never tired of his journeys into the sky, of the solitude of height when the P-51 became his companion, when the horizon began to bend, the colors and textures below taking form like the photos taken from orbiting space cameras. You could feel as if you were the only soul alive over country like this, the miles unreeling below with no sign of man. It made you think about God sometimes, perhaps because being a flier gave you a better view of God's work, a cleaner view, a simpler view. Lowen hadn't always believed in God. When he went over to the war in Europe he thought he believed, but what he was doing then was sincerely hoping that there really was a God. During those moments of death clashing in the skies over Germany he had had more than one occasion to call upon or otherwise recognize a Deity, but he didn't really know what believing, really believing, was until years later, when he was in his forties, when he finally saw that there was always some sort of grand shit-fight going on between Good and Evil – any fool could clearly see that – and that they seemed pretty evenly matched.

Since this was true, there had to be a name for whatever was Good and so he had decided it might as well be God. He wondered which word had come first, Good or God, and whether one was a derivation of the other. It seemed right. After he had accepted that, he believed with all his heart. But with a jaundiced eye. You could be on the side of God, but you'd damned well better be wide alert. And quick on the draw.

Lowen felt much too old to be thinking about such matters, especially when he didn't know the answers. Nobody he knew seemed to have any answers eithers; perhaps that was what was meant by 'blind faith'.

It seemed he'd read somewhere that most Germans were Catholic. Or was it Protestant? He wondered how many of those eight – now six – maniacs believed in God. When you were closing on each other head-on at a combined speed of 700 mph with guns loaded, just whose side was God on then? He never could figure that out. Maybe when two men were busy at committing the ultimate sin – trying to kill each other – God just sat back and watched, neutral if both fools were believers, and let 'em have it. No answers there.

Lowen leveled off at 12,000 feet and loosened his jacket collar. He then steered on a heading due east. He found himself scanning the sky above and around him, then searching below to each quarter, his eyes narrowed, all senses alert. Reason told him it was senseless to expect the 109s to be up in daylight this close to Willie; they were far too smart for that. With some discomfort he willed himself to feel safe, realizing then that he was again a fighter pilot. Watching for 109s – absurd – over Arizona.

Fighter pilot. Those dim gray mornings in England, the endless rain, cold fog, wretched mud. Steaming coffee in tin cups and the tension in the stomach, sheepskin jackets and flying boots, the briefing hut in the haze of morning cigarettes, the wall-sized maps. Nerve-racking take-offs in the soup, the rubber taste of the oxygen gear, the sweat trickling itching under layers of clothing, frost inside the canopy. Fighter pilot. One-on-one. What had Webb said? Not many left. The good Captain thought it such a glamorous fraternity. True, there wasn't anything quite like it and there was pride in that. Nothing you talked about. The Krauts had that esprit routine down pat right from the start, the First War, and the Brits weren't bad at it either. It was all right, no denying that. Pride was fine, honor was fine, fairness was fine. He thought about the 109 pilots, their orange scarves and their heraldry on the fuselage, those beautiful 109s. Hell, it was a class act. They really got into that business in a big way. Even today the Luftwaffe vets were still big heroes over there. Lots of honor . . . respect . . . admiration. The way it should be. Not like here, where no one wanted to know about it. Not like here, where you had to be a damned movie star or a damned rock star to get recognized. Horsecrap. Here you could be the first damned man to land on the damned moon, for God's sake, and everyone forgot your damned name a year later. It was true; who remembered Neil Armstrong? And Buzz Aldrin and Mike Collins?

Lowen realized that his neck was beginning to chafe . . . the looking back and forth, the reason you wore a silk scarf . . . then. Very often the sky was magnificent over Europe, so bright, so powder blue, it bruised the senses. And clear, so clear, when you got up above the clouds, high in the cold blue, you could see farther than your eyes were able. When you could get your mind off staying on course for a moment, you thought about the beauty of it but you always had to share such thinking with vigilance. Death was on the way. And you watched for it until your eyeballs hurt, searching for little dark specks.

When the Luftwaffe fighters came they were like tiny black gnats and you had to spot them quickly because they came terribly fast, and every second was an incremental advantage gained or lost. You saw them swarming up miles away, or much closer – sometimes diving on you or coming head-on – and you had to act; turn, dive, climb, fight or flee. But you were a fighter pilot and the job was to fight so there was seldom any fleeing, even when the odds were crazy. There was no place to dig a hole up there; when they came, you fought. Then all the beauty and all the business of being special or elite changed to something else. You were quick and lucky or you were dead. It seemed so clean up there, another world, but there was such carnage in that sky, all happening fast, all over in minutes; ten dead, a hundred dead, a thousand dead. No battlefield vista photos from that part of the war. No glamour then. No glamour to puking into your oxygen mask or pissing your pants. No glamour to roasting alive trapped in a whirling whipping cockpit. Or to bleeding to death, or falling without a chute. Terrible things in the memory . . . the B-17 crewman trying to climb up the straps of his burning chute . . . the Jug winging homeward straight and level with the cockpit solid glowing yellow flame . . . the Mustang ahead to port on a strafing run that took a direct hit and came apart in a silent white flash, its wings cartwheeling like playing cards and the smoking engine still travelling at 350 mph turning end over end and all the rest little pieces showering down.

All that stuff had to come to earth somewhere. You could imagine Europe being littered with that hideous junk, especially Germany, and you wondered who it was that pried through the thousands of aircraft hulks and the thousands of corpses that rained down. What a hell-hole that beautiful country must have been at the end, between the air battles and the ground fighting and the death camps. Forests and fields carpeted with pieces of the dead.

And five damned years later they were strewn frozen over the damned hills of Korea and twenty damned years later they were moldering in the damned jungles of Vietnam. It would never end, as any fool could see. That much was certain.

And now what about this? Thirty-two years later, like 1944 all over again. Sitting in the sky in a P-51, a few pounds heavier, a few less teeth, looking for damned Messerschmitts over Arizona. Godamighty. It was too inconceivable, too weird, to be without some reason. He felt abnormally driven to face them, as if there were supernatural forces at work, forces in the realm of such mysteries as destiny, as fate. Though it seemed beyond his reach, what he struggled to grasp was the term 'divine retribution'.

He had indeed attacked them, the three of them. It was his mission to attack them, his duty. There was no wrong in that, not in war. They would have done the same. And now they were back, looking for him. Absurd. There was a pattern he could sense, yes . . . as if some impartial judge had ruled it was to be this way. Lowen pictured a judge-like figure in black – no, white – robes and a long white beard and tiny square eyeglasses, seated in some celestial court, poring over a huge book of some sort. Absurd.

What if there really was some old goat of a judge up there, wherever up there was? Where was up there? How did you know? How did you know God himself in some form wasn't sitting here jammed into this damned cockpit – a spirit, a spark, a bug? Nobody, but *nobody* knew that. Hell, anybody knew that nobody knew that. And what if it was decided by this official judge that it *was* 'divine retribution', that he was to be challenged by men he had tried to kill, that they were to be given a chance back? Thirty-two years later was he being called to account for his attempt on the lives of others? Or was he somehow chosen . . . chosen to defend his country, his personal honor, the very side of Good . . . once again against the Evil of Nazi Germany?

Lowen could believe in all these things, for each had the ring of mysterious and unfathomable truth. They all could be.

Webb was right; so few of us left. And those damned Krauts had set it up so perfectly. All in honorable order. Lowen was not without admiration for that. Let it be some test of courage, of honor. Let it be so. There was already some little bit of history being made, sure as God made little green apples. The Krauts were making news, making history.

History. Well, let history also record that those arrogant sonsabitches started another weird little war right smack in the middle of God's Country. And let history record that they got their asses whipped again by Americans, by the very same tough sonofabitch that shot holes in their ass to begin with and by the same tough sonofabitch made-in-the-USA North American P-51 Mustang fighter and not some supersonic squadron of rocket jockeys.

And you, Roger, he thought. How would you feel? Would you feel like . . . a soldier of God? . . . a warrior of Good? . . . a defender of democracy?

Well surely. And he felt this through and through. It was exactly the right thing to do.

At an altitude of 29,000 feet James Webb, Captain USAF sat buckled into a window seat on the earliest flight from Phoenix Skyharbor to LA. In one hand he held a styrofoam cup of black coffee, the other he raised to read his watch; with luck, the entire round trip would see him back at Williams shortly after noon.

He hadn't worked out in four days now and he was feeling it. His eyes hurt from working late into the night before. He was, he knew too well, barely keeping up. Thin ice. And now he was reminded of that silly line Is This Trip Necessary? Whatever else it was, it was an extravagance in both time and money. Unless of course it paid off. This Felbeck character had to be it, had to bust it open. Yet gambling half a day – to hell with the money – could get tight if he was wrong. No, he couldn't afford anything but success.

Failure of any sort did not go down well. He'd lost a lot of life's little contests, enough – so he felt – to be in danger of becoming one who was seen by others as being one of life's failures. Would they say secretly, *poor fellow*? Christ, what a horror, what a nightmare. Failure. One gray office to another. Lowen was right; you had to have a break. And here he was in the middle of it. It had to work. He could in time learn to deal with the failure of his marriage, but a failed career would put him under. He was sure.

He leaned back in his seat, loosening the safety belt, and stared out the window into a perfect blue sky. He thought about Lowen flying alone in the opposite direction and he felt . . . he missed him. A genuine good guy. Hell, he even looked like a good guy, that tanned lined face, wavy gray hair, that look of total alertness, even the pipe in his teeth. Webb couldn't remember ever meeting a man who looked that right, who just plain looked honest, like he had bags of guts, like he could be trusted, and like he loved his country. Maybe Butler was kind of like that, in a way, but he didn't know anyone else who was. It was a little out of date to be patriotic, it seemed. Or to be trustworthy, honest. The new way was to have no rules, every man for himself. How the hell could you be otherwise if everyone else was living like that? Oh man. He wondered if he would ever be like Lowen, whether it was even possible to be like Lowen. Webb shook his head. Funny how he actually missed him; it was like he had made a friend. Well, Webb resolved, when this craziness was over he would go visit him in Texas, meet his wife, go drinking beer and Jack Daniel's.

Breakfast came in a little yellow plastic dish covered with foil. Webb unwrapped the silverware rolled in a cloth napkin. He tucked one corner of the napkin behind his brightly polished belt buckle and then spread the other three corners neatly across his lap. Good it was cloth; when he finished eating he could use it to dust off his gleaming shoes before getting off the plane.

When Lowen taxied up to the hangar at Harlingen the first thing he noticed was a brace of olive-drab military six-bys with canvas covers parked by the operations building. He climbed down from the Mustang, chocked the wheels and carried his bag over to the trucks. When he drew close he saw a Sergeant of Air Police in the cab of the first vehicle. The AP looked up at him.

'Sergeant?' Lowen saw the AP was reading a copy of *Playboy*.

'Morning, sir.' The AP put down the magazine.

'My name's Lowen, Sergeant. Colonel Lowen.'

'Yessir,' the AP replied quickly, stepping down from the truck as his arm went up in salute. 'Been waiting for you, Colonel. I'm with Lackland Air Police, assigned to security for these vehicles. My orders are to report directly to you.'

'As you were, Sergeant. What have you got here?'

'These two vehicles and two sedans, sir. Got three pilots and four ground crew checking in a motel down the road right now. These vehicles have parts, oil, and ordnance. And there are some papers to sign, sir. One other pilot is due in later today. They'll bring him down.'

Lowen gave the trucks a pleased scrutiny. Good for Butler, he thought. 'I'll see those papers.'

'Yessir.' The AP reached into the cab and withdrew a large sealed envelope and handed it to Lowen. 'Nice plane, sir.'

'Thank you, Sergeant.'

Lowen opened the packet and skimmed over the papers. Listed in typescript, he tallied two dozen cases parts, six cases tools, fifteen drums 1120 grade oil, eight drop tanks size 92 gallons, six K-14 gunsights, thirty-six M2HB .50 caliber Browning machine guns and fifteen cases .50 caliber AP/HE ammunition. He calculated the ammo, with each Mustang aircraft at 1880 rounds, to be more than sufficient. This, he thought, is another reason we win wars.

'I'll sign these when we unload, Sergeant. When your people get back here they can set up in the second hangar over there.' Lowen pointed.

'Yessir.' The AP looked at his watch. 'It should be about –'

Over their exchange of words Lowen had picked up the distant growling of an aircraft engine – piston fighter – but had paid little attention. Now he locked onto the sound curving closer, low and fast. Both men turned. Lowen picked out the airplane a mile off and coming on much too low, rooftop level. The AP crouched instinctively. Lowen resisted the impulse. In the next second the fighter was on them, fifty feet above, and Lowen recognized a Spitfire as it howled overhead in a smooth roll, showing first the upper-surface camouflage paint of green and brown, with blue-and-red roundels on the tapered elliptical wings, and with yellow-red-blue-white flank roundels and white call letters on the long slender fuselage. As it completed the roll, the Spit showed its pale blue under-surface, belly tank and wide black-and-white D-Day invasion stripes. It was, Lowen noticed, a very clean aircraft.

The wave of noise washed over the two men in the wake of the sleek British fighter, as it went leveling off into a shallow climb. Lowen shook his head, watching the Spitfire bank to port and throttle back. He'd never seen that Spit before; it wasn't one of the CAF ships, but if the screwball flying it was coming in, it would be Lowen's aggravating responsibility to chew him out for buzzing so low. But Lord it was a lovely kite, and the pilot was no amateur either. He wondered who it was, shading his eyes as he watched the plane come around the far end of the field.

Hearing and seeing the Spit made him think again of being in England and of being in the air with the Spits and of how he always admired their deadly curving grace – decidedly feminine even in earthen war paint – and their shining history; defender of the UK, victor in the Battle of Britain, its pilots rewarded with Churchill's immortal blessing: 'Never in the field of human conflict was so much owed by so many to so few.'

'Gawd,' said the AP.

Lowen tucked the papers in the envelope and picked up his bag and walked off to the ops building.

Once inside, he watched through the windows as the Spitfire taxied up and stopped alongside his Mustang, noting the contrast between the dully-painted slimmer smaller plane and his bigger brutish shining P-51. It made him wonder once again what there was about things American that they were always bigger and louder and more ostentatious than anything else. Like his Corvette parked next to any British sports car.

He watched the Spitfire pilot flip down the quaint little access door to the cockpit and remove a leather flying helmet with goggles and then replace it with a khaki RAF officer's cap. Then the pilot crawled out, lifting a bag with shoulder strap, and stepped down on the wing to the ground. He walked over to the USAF truck, spoke briefly with the AP then headed toward the ops building.

With some haste Lowen tried to tidy up the desk in front of him, then gave up and lighted his pipe instead.

The man who came through the door wore a khaki uniform which Lowen recognized an RAF issue, at least in style. And there were battle ribbons over the pocket and officer's badges on the epaulets. Much of the pilot's sunburned face seemed covered by large aviator's sunglasses, but the yellow mustache and white sideburns and the lines from mouth to nose marked the man as well over fifty. He tucked the cap under his arm.

'Are you Colonel Roger Lowen, sir?' The voice was quiet, British. The pilot seemed yet another flashback in time for Lowen, as RAF officer in summer issue whose subtle bearing and controlled manner prompted Lowen to stand straighter himself.

'I am,' he replied.

The pilot stepped closer to the desk, letting down the bag with his left arm, and stood straight. 'Wing Commander J. P. Redmond-Donleavy,' he said briskly, sweeping his right hand up in the palm-out extra-quick British military salute. 'DFC,' he added.

'Commander.' What the hell? Lowen wondered, returning the salute and then holding out his hand. 'Welcome to Harlingen.'

'Thank you, sir.' The pilot's grip was dry and tight. He was neatly trimmed and starched, solid as a fire hydrant.

'What can I do for you?'

'Perhaps I might smoke, Colonel?'

'Please, Commander. Feel free. This isn't a military unit,' Lowen answered. Or is it? he thought, regretting the remark. 'Not yet, anyway,' he added.

'Ah, not yet.' The Wing Commander lit up a cigarette which had no filter. He flashed Lowen a quick mechanical grin.

'Fine-looking ship, that Spit. Saw you come over.' Lowen paused. 'Can you fly that well a bit higher, Commander? You've heard of the FAA, I take it?'

'Sir, I can fly that well at any bloody altitude under 41,000 feet and above thirty feet. Getting tuned up, you see.'

'For what, Commander?'

'For Jerry. Word's out, you know.'

'Word? What word is out?'

'That your taking on those Jerries. Or you wouldn't be looking for fighter pilots now, would you? Wouldn't miss this. Not for anything.' He flashed the quick grin again, then added, 'Thing like that gets around fast, you know.'

Lowen rubbed his ear slowly, staring at Redmond-Donleavy to buy a little time. He was not surprised that 'the word' had traveled among the warbird people. He wished the Wing Commander would remove his dark sunglasses so he could see his eyes. And he noticed then that both the man's arms carried burn scars.

'Where are you from, Commander?'

'Chicago, a bit north, place called Racine, actually.'

'Is that your Spit?'

'Not exactly, sir. Though just about. The owner's a friend of mine. From Milwaukee. In the beer business. He's on his way down for the show. Should be here tomorrow.' Redmond-Donleavy turned to glance out the window at his airplane. 'The ship's a Mark Five-B. I helped him put it back together and I keep it up for him, taught him to fly it. She has a new four-blade prop and there's thirty-two hours on her since the last overhaul. She's quite tight, actually.'

'Is it armed?'

'Two twenties,' said Redmond-Donleavy with cheer. 'Ready to go . . . other than, haha, it's a bit short on ammunition.'

'How old are you, Commander?'

'Born in twenty-two, sir.'

'Horsecrap, sir.'

'Eighteen then it was. Cranwell in thirty-eight. I've got papers here in my kit – credentials, if you need them – and then Sergeant Pilot in forty. Two years in Hurris, three in Spits.'

Redmond-Donleavy let the cigarette smoke out of his mouth and pulled it back up through his nose. Lowen understood why the mustache was yellow while his hair, thick but cut short, was white.

'Unit?' Lowen asked, relighting his pipe.

'All Eleven Group, from the start. Seventeen Squadron, Debden, then down to Tangmere with 601 Squadron. Did, ah,

389 missions. Eighteen kills. Stayed on after Armistice over at Middle Wallop. Heard you were over there in P-51s.'

'Not far away.' Lowen remembered, puffing slowly. 'Down the road a piece, maybe sixty miles. Leiston on the coast, with 357th Group.'

'Ah yes.' Redmond-Donleavy nodded. 'Yoxford Boys wasn't it? Escort. You got a few 109s, I'd imagine.'

'A few. Not enough.'

'Thought we had it all cleaned up ... funny. Looks like they're at it again now, doesn't it? Are they Luftwaffe boys?'

'Looks like it.'

'Remarkable, those bastards coming round like this.' Redmond-Donleavy crushed out his cigarette and rubbed his hands together. 'Now Colonel, what's Jerry flying? Which 109s?'

'G models, all of them. And in mint condition.'

'Gustavs. Bloody hell. Nose or wing guns?'

'Clean wings. Nose cannon, machine guns on top.

Redmond-Donleavy began nodding again, as if his head was on a spring. 'Well, now what?'

Lowen stared at the Wing Commander, at his battle ribbons and burn-scarred arms, the opaque dark glasses, the starched and tailored uniform, and then over to the old leather flying helmet and RAF goggles. He was thinking he should make some sort of protest, even if for – for what? It was the Krauts who had opened the door on this time-warp, and here was another character, out of the blue. Literally. He knew that Redmond-Donleavy wouldn't go away. Any fool could see that. And Lowen didn't want him to go away.

'Well, Commander ...' Lowen said. 'We'll put you up with the others at Howard Johnson's down the road. I'll drop you off. We'll all be getting together later this evening for dinner.'

'Ah,' Redmond-Donleavy beamed. 'Then I'm with you then, is it? May I say, sir, I'm glad to be joining up?'

'Yessir, you may. And I'm damned pleased to have you.'

At an altitude of 29,000 feet Webb sat buckled in an aisle seat on the noon flight from LA to Phoenix. He was a changed man. This, he thought, must be the way you feel after hitting a jackpot at Vegas, sitting on top of the world in a plane going home. For he had indeed hit a jackpot.

The president of Sunwest Aviation, Inc. had received him

graciously. The Air Force, Webb had said truthfully, was seeking an expert consultant for a classified project and Felbeck's name had come to their attention. Within twenty minutes his every question concerning Sunwest's Executive VP, R. O. Felbeck, was answered. Rudi Felbeck was an expert in fabrication design *Bingo*, an active pilot *Bingo*, and a Luftwaffe veteran *Bingo* with security clearance. He also had two daughters living on the East Coast and had lost his wife eight years before in an auto accident. He was vacationing with his sister in Phoenix *Bingo*, and his 'engine wizard' brother-in-law *Bingo*, who had helped him convert numerous aircraft into racing trim *Bingo*.

Webb came away with the sister's telephone number and a feeling that, finally, the Gods were favoring him.

Roger Lowen basked in the familiarity of his kitchen and of his wife's presence as she prepared brunch. And of the taste of the coffee and of the blue cup hot in his hand. Through the windows the trees and vines and flowers of his yard seemed to glow intensely green. On the table in front of him the roses he had picked up for Jean were spread as if sprouting from a too-large emerald vase, the fragrance of their pink-magenta petals mixing with the fresh coffee smell. As he often did, he imagined himself in a TV commerical; even the floor shone like a wax commercial. What he smelled and saw and felt in the kitchen of his home made him pleased to be alive.

'Thank you for the flowers. Again,' Jean said from the stove.

'Seems silly. Damned garden's full of them.'

'Not roses.' They always said these exact words to each other whenever he brought roses. 'Say you missed me.'

'Missed you.'

Somehow the added familiarity of this exchange seemed to dovetail perfectly with the feeling of magnified detail of all that surrounded him. He wondered what it was, this impression of everything being extra-real. It was difficult to reconcile what felt real and what felt unreal, like the telephone calls he had just made to seven of the CAF pilots who had flown combat in Europe, asking each of them to meet him at the Amigo Club in – he looked at the wall clock – five hours.

Now reality was seeing the USAF trucks unloaded in the hangar, of getting the ground crew to work, of seeing two more

P-51s come in by ferry pilots from Oklahoma.

Reality was climbing in the Corvette at the field with the Wing Commander, who wasn't real yet, and finding that it didn't start all that quickly. On the road it rumbled with a new loudness, like the P-51, and there was a new rattle; he knew the sound, something in the intestinal steel tubing of the exhaust system had come unstuck again. Now he'd need new pipes or maybe another damned muffler. It seemed as if leaving the car to sit while he was gone had caused it to develop another new ailment o ut of spite. More damned money. That was reality.

Jean was reality. Looking at her made him feel fortunate. He liked the healthy thickness of her waist, and the tight flatness of her butt. And the chaste whiteness of her skin. On the rare occasions when she wore black, particularly underclothing, the eggshell paleness of her thighs and arms and the rust-red brown of her hair always reminded him of Rita Hayworth, his favorite beauty.

Now she came over and set a blue plate of bright yellow scrambled eggs, still-sizzling bacon, and sliced wet tomatoes before him, followed by toast. Lowen knocked out his pipe and spread the napkin on his lap.

'It seemed you were gone a long time.' She seated herself, poured more coffee. 'Are you all right?'

'I'm all right,' he answered, buttering a piece of toast.

'You didn't say much over the phone. What's going on?'

'Well, I'm still involved.'

'Involved how?'

'In finding those people, the German pilots.'

'Are they real Germans?'

'Two were identified. They figure the others are West German nationals, too.'

'What do you have to do?'

'Let's say I'm temporarily reactivated. The Base Commander over at Williams has got the big brass all over him to clean this up. I've made an agreement to help him out, help the Air Force.'

'How can you help if you're here?'

'It's a . . . strange situation. Complicated.'

'I've got all afternoon to listen.'

Lowen finished his scrambled eggs and pushed a scrap of toast to the side of his plate and put the fork down and then folded his hands together and looked up at his wife. He thought how clear and sea-green her eyes were. 'I don't want you to worry. Or be afraid.'

'What is it?'

There was no other way, none that he could think of, than to tell her the truth as it appeared to be. That two of the German pilots were the ones he had attacked in 1944, that one had posed as a newspaper reporter over the telephone, that they had planned the interception over Phoenix, and that they wanted a rematch. And that he had made the deal with Butler to mobilize a flight of armed P-51s. When he explained that much, he stopped to see how difficult the rest was going to be.

She suprised him by standing and going over to the sink. She turned, looking at him, then crossed her arms over her chest. 'You absolutely cannot be serious.'

'Come and sit down.'

'I don't believe this.'

'Come and sit down.'

'Are you telling me that a bunch of German pilots from the war are going to call you on the telephone to arrange a shooting match with real bullets, real bombs?'

'Bullets, no bombs.'

'Forgive me. The distinction is somehow lost.'

She sat down across from him. Her face was subtly distorted, quizzical. 'What about all those people, the police, the FBI? Aren't they looking for them?'

'In three states, night and day. No luck, not yet. The Krauts will come out, you see, if I agree to meet them.'

'And if you don't agree to meet them?'

'Well, they'll probably come over here and attack the field. Like they did over there.'

'This is insane. Insane.'

'I know it's difficult to understand.'

'Difficult? It's impossible! You're going to agree, agree to meet these . . . these madmen? Is that right?'

'Right.'

'And then the Air Force – what? – catches them when they come out?'

'I am the Air Force. I catch them when they come out.'

She stared at him for what seemed a very long time. He stared back. She licked her lips twice before she spoke again in a deliberate voice, 'Roger, what do you mean, "you're the Air

Force"? Where is the . . . the real Air Force?'

'I told you. It's very simple. I made a deal with the Air Force.'

'Roger, where will the Air Force, the real Air Force, be when all this is going on?'

Lowen shrugged. 'They won't know.'

'Why won't they know?'

'Because I'm not telling them.'

'Not telling them.' She studied him. 'In other words, you could avoid this whole thing?'

'I made a deal, I told you.'

'Why, why? Is this some act of, of patriotism? What?'

'Maybe.'

'Maybe means yes, coming from you.'

'Okay, yes. It's fair.'

'Fair? Fair? Like a gunfight at high noon? Is it that sort of thing? Pride? Honor?'

'Close.'

'Roger, how can the Air Force give you airplanes, guns, bullets? How could they let you do this?'

'They can. It makes sense.'

'It makes sense? Are you crazy? Are you expecting me to—'

'I'm expecting you to leave it alone.'

'I don't know what to do . . .'

'Don't do anything.'

'And if you . . . lose?'

'We won't lose. We didn't then, we won't now.'

'For God's sake, you talk like it's the war all over again.'

'It is. In a way.'

'I can't let you do this. I'm not going to just stand here and let you do this.'

'What will you do, leave on the noon train?'

'What are you talking about?'

It was quiet in the kitchen then, except for the nervous tick from the coffee percolator, which made Lowen want another cup. Instead, he sat silently.

'Well,' she said finally, looking down at her hand tracing zig-zag patterns on the tablecloth, 'we've had eight good years and hardly ever a bad time. I've been lucky.'

'We've been lucky.'

She looked up. 'Because we tell each other everything, share everything. We resolved to do that, remember?'

'I remember.'

'If anything happened to you—'

'It won't.' He saw then that she might begin to cry.

'You can't say that.'

'Nothing will happen to me.'

'You do love me?'

'I do love you.'

'Then don't do this! Let the Air—'

'Jean, listen to me.' He took her hand; it was trembling, tense. 'Maybe I can't explain it so you'd understand. But can I ask you, please, to understand . . . without explaining it?'

'No . . . yes. I mean, try to explain it. Just try.'

'In my life,' he spoke slowly, thinking, trying to be truthful and clear. 'In my experience – besides the kids, and you – the best part of it was being a pilot, a fighter pilot. It was the only real glory I've ever felt. I know it was a long time ago, the war, but I'm still . . . who I was then.' He paused, pursing his lips in search of the right phrases. 'This, ah, business with these Germans . . . is for me a kind of test. I don't know what else to call it, but it's something I know I have to do. It just is.

'And I can tell you – and it's true – that I believe I might keep a few young pilots from getting killed.' He looked up. 'Stick with me?'

She watched him for a moment and he could see that she wasn't going to start crying after all. Though it was pretty close. Her fingers went to her temples and then rubbed at her hairline, then at her cheeks.

'You're a horse's ass anyway,' she said through an attempt at smiling, 'and if anything happens to you, I'll kill you.'

Webb grabbed a quick lunch at the Offices' Club, then went over to Headquarters to check in with Sergeant Evans.

'CO was looking for you, Cap'n. He's gone now but he left a few messages,' Evans said, grinning as he pushed more paper across the desk.

'What's hot? Anything?'

'Everything, from what I hear. We got a recon chopper down this morning, up north where that F-5 went down.'

Oh God, thought Webb. 'Are they okay?'

'Don't know yet. They got a search team out. Plus . . . we got an outhouse full of calls on the public telephone number. Two

303

days worth. It's all been transcribed off the tapes but most of it seems useless.'

'Like what?' Webb leafed through the papers.

'Well, most of it is from people calling to ask about the Nazis.' Webb looked up. 'Hey.'

'Sir?'

'Sergeant, I don't think the term "Nazi" is, ah, appropriate.'

'Cap'n, if those guys got swastikas painted on their tails that's about as Nazi as you can get.'

'Yeah, but I don't like the word. Use something else.'

'Like what? Sir.'

'Like . . . Germans, I guess. Now, what else?'

'Well, there's about thirty calls from civilians who say they saw the German aircraft. And the rest from crackpots who have some theories, but haven't seen anything. There's one call from a woman who knows this guy who travels out of town a lot and likes to dress up in those boots and play with whips and—'

'All right, all right. Where's the tape report?'

'Being copied for the Task Force Meeting this evening.'

'You'll get me a copy? And the tapes, too?'

'Easy. The FBI guy, Montgomery, glommed Tuesday's tapes, but I can get you the rest.'

'I'll be over in my office all afternoon.' Webb placed the papers in his briefcase and then looked at his watch, noting that he had less than three hours to prepare his own daily report. The little jaunt to LA had really put him behind.

In his own office Webb collected half a dozen messages from Sarah and closed the door and sat down at his desk. After a moment, he buzzed Sarah to have her run R.O. Felbeck's Phoenix telephone number through the Sheriff's office and the reverse directory, then asked her to get Koontz on the line at the FAA. He sorted through the papers, placing Colonel Butler's messages in a separate stack to tackle first. He wrote out a few notes before Sarah buzzed him with the FAA on the line. Still writing, Webb asked Koontz to check the registration listings under *Bayerische Flugzeugwerke* back beyond five years.

He then buzzed Sarah again and asked her to contact each of the other Task Force members. It seemed proper for the Executive Officer to call for a chat. The buzzer sounded. He lifted the phone.

'Captain Webb, this is Stratton, Sheriff's office.'

Two down, Webb thought, 'Yessir?'

'Captain, they tell me Colonel Butler is off base. And we have a hot one.'

'A hot one?'

'We've located an abandoned airfield about forty miles south of Phoenix where aerial photos show vehicles and evidence of current use. Montgomery wants to go in right away and we've got our units rolling. If this is our German bunch we may need some back-up. I want some of that Marine detachment Butler offered. And we need to go *now*, Captain. How about it?'

Oh man, Webb thought, his pulse picking up. 'Stand by, Sheriff. I'll have someone back to you immediately.'

Webb hung up, sat back. He felt something like momentary paralysis. Oh man, call out the fucking Marines? Quick, quick! The hot sheet. He scrabbled through his briefcase. Could he do this? Where the hell was Butler? There was the hot sheet. Number number for alert alert. Oh man. He dialed, his hand was shaking, and got an immediate answer.

'Ops seven-seven. Sergeant Ward speaking, sir.'

'Sergeant, this is Captain Webb at Willie, Executive Officer on the Task Force on those Messerschmitts.'

'Go ahead, sir.'

'Sergeant, our CO is off base and I'm in charge. We have a Code Two alert, County Sheriff and FBI requesting a Marine chopper unit as backup on location of, ah, German suspects.' He heard the Sergeant yell something to someone else before he came back on the line.

'Location, sir?'

'Ah, forty miles south of Phoenix. Call this number, Sheriff John Stratton, for details.' He read off the number.

'How many units, sir?'

'Ah, one chopper for now,' answered Webb nimbly. Oh man, how many men in a unit? Why don't you *know* this sort of thing?

'First unit airborne in three more minutes, sir.'

'Sergeant, how many men in each unit?'

'Each assault team has ten troops plus crew, sir.'

'Thank you, Sergeant. Keep me advised. I'm standing by.'

Webb hung up. He was trembling a little. Three minutes! He imagined ten Marines in combat gear scrambling into an olive-drab chopper, all pumped up, weapons at the ready. Just like in the movies. He remembered Lowen's grim prediction about accidents, casualties, and he pictured the helicopter exploding against a mesa, spewing orange flame, hurtling burning bodies down onto the rocks. Oh man. He pushed the call-button for Sarah.

'We've got an alert, Sarah. Break in if I'm on the phone and a Sergeant Ward calls from Luke.'

'I have the confirmation from the Sheriff's office, the number you wanted traced, Captain. The listing is for Malzahn, initial E, at the following address.'

Webb scribbled the name and address, noticing that his handwriting had gone wobbly. Three of the four remaining telephone lights came on at once. He glanced at his watch. The buzzer again, Sarah's voice again:

'Sergeant Ward at Luke on three, Captain.'

Webb stabbed a finger at the blinking button. 'This is Captain Webb, Sergeant. Go ahead.'

'Captain, Sheriff is requesting two more assault teams. Will you approve? The first is on the way.'

Webb's pulse picked up again. Oh man. Decide quickly, he thought; yes or no? Thirty Marines plus crew in the air?

'Negative on two teams, Sergeant. Let one go, until they confirm they've actually located these people, the Germans. Twenty Marines can handle damn near anything. What's going on down there; do you know yet?'

He heard the Sergeant yell something, then come back on the line. 'No sir, but we have a communications vehicle on the way so I'll be back to you with the situation. Roger on that second team. It's on the way.'

'Keep me posted, Sergeant.' Webb hung up.

Now he imagined both helicopters colliding over the desert. Twenty-plus-crew funerals ... coffins covered by flags ... weeping wives and little children in Sunday clothes. Oh man, he thought, I didn't want any part of this part of it. The tiny office seemed to shrink around him like a cell.

The next call buzzed at his elbow. 'Captain, this is Sarah. Colonel Butler is en route to Luke for lunch with their Base Commander. I've left an urgent call-back for you.'

'Thank you, Sarah.' He hung up.

Another call buzzing, light blinking. 'Captain Webb speaking.'

'Captain, this is Sergeant Ward at Luke.'

'Go ahead, Sergeant.' Oh man, what now?

'Captain, we now have two teams dispatched to location forty-eight miles south-southeast of Phoenix near Picacho. Also, a Medevac chopper is packing up to go. That's SOP in case we take casualties.'

'OK Sergeant, thanks for letting me know. Sergeant, our CO Colonel Butler is supposed to be on his way over there to meet with your commander. Have you been in touch with your CO?'

'Negative, sir. We've been a little busy, but I'll give it a try.'

'I understand. If you locate Colonel Butler, have him call me.'

Webb hung up. He stared at the phone, lighting a cigarette without thinking. Then he stared at his scribbled notes, none of which seemed to be important now. Had they really found the Staffel? The phone buzzed again.

'Captain, this is Sarah. The FAA called regarding your request on those registration lists while you were on the other line. Their office in Oklahoma City is closed down for the day.'

'Call back and tell them . . . get Koontz, tell him to tell them to open it to hell up regardless. This is urgent.'

He hung up. The phone buzzed, light blinking. Oh man. 'Captain Webb speaking.'

'Captain?' Never had Webb been so glad to hear Butler's voice.

'Sir.'

'Captain, I'm in touch with operations over here, now. Good work getting those teams out quick. And good work holding back on the third unit. Those people just got a little over-excited. I just talked to Montgomery and he thinks it looks like a dope bust. Anyway, I'll pick it up from here and I'll be back to you shortly.' Butler hung up.

Webb slumped in the chair, his hand still resting on the receiver. He waited for the next call but none of the buttons lit up. He thought about the dope runners looking up to see themselves surrounded by armed Marines. Haha, poor bastards. Then he wondered what the Staffel was doing and he realized that what he was feeling was . . . relief. They're just waiting for you, man, he thought. And for Lowen.

Lowen watched the bartender pouring Jack Daniel's for him and then for Fitzgerald. The color of the whiskey – reminding him of a TV commercial – was a deep translucent maple in the soft late afternoon sunlight that pried its way onto the long mahogany bar of the Amigo Club.

'Cheers,' said Fitzgerald, raising his glass.

'Right,' Lowen replied, raising his own.

'How much time before the others show?'

Lowen studied his watch. 'Hour.'

'This is happening pretty fast, Roger.'

'I was thinking the same thing.'

'I was thinking it when I saw those two six-bys full of fifty caliber Brownings. With the ammo. Like the war.'

'It is the war, Fitz.'

'What I'd like to know is how you twisted the arm of that CO over at Willie to set you up.'

For some reason – it felt like a premonition – Lowen didn't care for the *you* in Fitz's sentence. He took another sip of whiskey without replying.

'Those guys aren't exactly amateurs,' Fitzgerald went on. 'This is getting just a little out of hand.'

'Yup,' Lowen said, glancing at Fitzgerald. He now had the distinct feeling that whatever he expected Fitzgerald, as well as the others, to feel about this adventure might not be what he would get. Not at all.

'Roger, maybe this isn't the best idea in the world. Maybe you should let the Air Force handle these maniacs. Those Krauts are playing hardball, Roger. They're crazy, you have to admit that.'

Lowen contemplated his friend, the expression of his face, the tension of his voice, the fluttering of his fingers, and he realized that Fitzgerald wasn't going to go up. It was a rude and sudden recognition. What if Polk and Meredith wouldn't go up either? How foolish, he thought, that he'd never considered whether any of the other pilots would—

'I mean you don't have to do this,' Fitzgerald was saying.

'I do. You don't.'

'Well . . .' Fitzgerald stared at the last of his drink.

Yes, it was clear. He would have to move quickly to motivate the others, inspire them. Esprit, the very root of the art of command. Damnit, how could he have been so slow? Minutes counted now. These people would have to be directed, forged as a single unit, a team. And he knew he had already lost Fitz. Even

Butler's hired guns would have to be handled carefully.

'Fitz,' Lowen said. 'I bent that CO's arm over at Willie for this job, this mission, but I'm not bending yours. Either you're in or you're out.'

Fitzgerald rubbed mechanically at the back of his head for a full minute before replying. 'I don't think I'm that . . . fast anymore, Roger. You know?'

'You think they're any faster?'

'Well, they're certainly crazier.'

'It doesn't matter.' Lowen was losing his patience. 'Fitz, you just do it or you don't do it.'

'I'm sorry, Roger. It's not easy. We're friends.'

'Nothing to do with friendship. They're crazy and I'm crazy and you're not. That's probably exactly right.' Lowen paused to bang the ashes out of his pipe into an ash tray. 'Fitz, listen. If you don't want to go up, then will you help me put it together?'

'Hell yes, you know that. Anything.'

'Get some paper, a pen.'

Fitzgerald fumbled in his jacket and produced a leather pocket secretary and a silver pen.

'Major Fitzgerald.' Lowen looked up at his friend. 'From this point we are functioning as a military unit of the Air Force, under my command. And you are the Executive Officer of this squadron.'

'Yessir.' Fitzgerald held the pen poised.

'You will oversee the ground crew twenty-four hours a day. Get the ships tuned and checked out. That's first. Make a roster, a schedule. Run it. Will you do that?'

'You know I will. You sure as hell know I will.'

'Set up the first practice flight tomorrow morning first thing. We've got to get up in the air. You can get the guns in, bored and sighted, at night.'

Fitzgerald wrote his notes slowly and neatly.

'Get a painter. I want everyone's kill markings painted on tomorrow. Paint the noses red and the rudders – no, the whole tail – blue. Find a dozen good silk scarves, red, while we're up tomorrow. And get everyone's glove size when they show up and get good gloves, the best. Get some of our CAF guys to help you.'

Fitzgerald was nodding as he wrote.

'Check out every crate in those trucks against the packing list and then I'll sign it. And get red caps for everyone.'

'Got it.' Fitz looked up. 'What else?'

'You figure what else, Major. I'm open to suggestions. I just want this unit combat-ready in twenty-four hours.'

'Do you think the Air Force will get to them before we do?'

There, Lowen thought, that's the way it works; 'before *me* do.' He thought his answer over for a moment. 'Yes,' he lied. 'But we're gonna get ready just the same.'

'You got it,' Major Fitzgerald said, as if he were writing that down, too.

'And get ahold of every pilot you can. Tell them to evacuate our CAF aircraft by noon tomorrow. Don't answer any questions; just tell'em to get'em out fast.'

'Yessir.' Fitzgerald scribbled away.

'Check with Garcia on the dinner setup. Get the best red wine they've got here. Bird-dog him on being ready at seven-thirty. We're in the back corner, that room.'

'Right.'

'I need to do some thinking, Major. Alone. When each of our CAF guys come in, send them over one at a time here to me. And keep the rest away. I want to talk to each one alone. Got it?'

'Got it.' Fitzgerald scooped up his pen and pad and glass.

'Major?'

Fitzgerald turned. 'Sir?'

Lowen held out his hand. 'Thanks.'

Fitzgerald shook his hand and moved off down the bar. The club was filling up now, the after-work gang with their ties loosened. Roger Lowen liked the colors of the bar, wood and brass, the maroon carpet, even the phony high-tone atmosphere the owners perpetuated in the hope of drawing a high-tone crowd. The Amigo had its own flavour of exclusivity merely because the clientele never changed much. In many ways it was very similar in feeling to the many Officers' Clubs he'd frequented. An easy place to get a little loaded. He looked at his watch. His own pilots would show up first, as he'd asked them to, in about half an hour.

Pull them together, tighten it up, make it run, make it happen. Just like the war. He'd never paid much attention to how it worked back then, but he knew it was definitely a structured process. Men had to be set in motion. Someone made the plan, a lot of arrangements all along the line, and the line started when you were sworn in, and then trained, and then put in an airplane alone. You got on a train and you got on a boat and then it was another bus and another train and another truck to an airfield in England and then you walked out on the flight line and climbed into a fighter plane and flew where they told you, until you ran into other pilots who were very determined about killing you. Simple.

Not so simple. Left alone, men would not do something so insane as that, not to mention such other things as crossing a rice paddy under fire or retaking a ravaged hill for the *nth* time when it was already littered with corpses. No one in possession of all their marbles would do such things unless they were motivated. Not so simple at all.

The four guys that Butler sent ... what motivated them? Meredith, Polk, Gardner, the rest – and the P-47 ace from Houston; would they decide like Fitz that they weren't fast enough anymore? He'd have to think of the right words. And soon. What was there to say to men of their age, in peacetime, to get them to walk out on the concrete at Harlingen and climb into those P-51s to mix it up with six Kraut aces? What would motivate these men? It seemed reasonable, he decided, to trust what it was that motivated him. And to go from there. He ordered another whiskey.

The first of his six CAF pilots that showed up was Reynolds, a big man, neatly suited, drink in hand. Lowen recalled that Reynolds had had eight kills in six months over Germany. He was an active flier and handled CAF business.

'Glad to see you, Roger.' They shook hands. 'Wait till you hear what the insurance people have to say about the P-51s we lost at Chino. Not good.'

'We aren't done yet.' Lowen tempered his reply with a false grin.

'Well, welcome back. Glad you're in one piece. What's going on?'

'This is absolutely confidential, Paul. We've got something going on with these Luftwaffe crazies. Time is short. I have been authorized by the Air Force to assemble a combat unit of P-51s here at the field, and to prepare for a mission against those 109s in the next several days. This is an armed combat mission. Is that completely clear?'

Reynolds drew out a gold cigarette case. 'Hey.'

311

'We need volunteer combat pilots, Paul.'

'Well, Roger, I—' Reynolds looked confused like he had lost something.

'Paul, I know we're friends. This thing is hot. Either you're in or you're out. If you want a little time to think it over, you've got twenty seconds.'

Reynolds squinted at his opened cigarette case as if it were a little book in which he could read his decision. Lowen was sure that he used every one of the twenty seconds before replying. 'I'm out, Roger. You know Marian's been having—'

'Thanks for stopping by, Paul. I'd be happy to buy you a drink, but chow is for the Squadron only.' Lowen held out his hand. 'If you can help us out otherwise, check with Fitzgerald. He's our Exec.'

Reynolds looked at Lowen for a moment, his expression so dazed that Lowen felt genuinely sorry for him. Snapping closed his cigarette case without having taken a cigarette, he said finally, 'Good luck, Roger. I mean that.'

'Thank you, Paul.' Lowen watched him moving away.

The next pilot declined. And so did the third. Lowen's hands were sweating. Meredith was the fourth and – as Lowen expected – he accepted. The fifth pilot did not. Polk was the sixth and he accepted. The seventh, and last, did not accept and in fact seemed speechless, looking at Lowen as if he had lost his wits, backing away and then glancing over his shoulder twice as he walked toward the door.

Fitzgerald came over then. 'How'd it go?'

'Nearly down the toilet. Meredith and Polk.'

'The four guys from Lackland are here. All Colonels.'

'Any of our guys offer to help you out?'

'All but the last.' Fitzgerald hesitated. 'The guy from Houston, the P-47 ace, called. Couldn't make it.'

Lowen nodded tiredly. 'With the Air Force people we have eight. That's enough, I guess.'

'Dinner is about ready, Roger.'

'Okay Major. Sit'em down and mix'em up; our guys in between each of the Air Force guys. Put me at the end, you on my right. And cut off the booze. Beer and wine only. I want that roster before dinner, Major.' Lowen looked up at Fitzgerald. 'I'll be along shortly.'

Lowen was the only one among the nine men who didn't eat

much of the meal. They had the privacy of a small area partially closed from the bar noise by a plastic accordion divider. The table had been set for twelve when Lowen entered and he ordered Fitzgerald to have the other four settings removed before he seated himself at last. There was plenty of steak and ribs and barbecue beans and the table talk, mostly war stories, was easy and lively. Dressed casually as they all were, Lowen noted, they could have been a group of Brownsville civic leaders convening for an informal meeting. He wondered what the Germans were eating tonight; sauerkraut, sausage, strudel?

He'd taken a few bites of the choicest part of his prime rib and of the chunks of baked potato he had mashed into the beef broth, nibbling at some cornbread which he figured would help soak up the Jack Daniel's. Fitzgerald had hand-printed a squadron roster on the back of a paper place mat and as Lowen listened and watched he matched each man to the name on the roster. The four USAF pilots, aside from WW Two combat, had all flown P-51s in Korea – ground attack – rough duty in the early part of that war. All were aces. Lowen felt a little more confident now. Experience was everything, what counted. He watched the waiters clear the table and begin pouring coffee.

'Gentlemen.' Lowen's voice rose above the conversation. 'If we could come to order.'

The others turned quiet and watched as Lowen held a match to his pipe bowl. He was undecided about standing up to address them and he finally leaned forward with his arms crossed on the table.

'Most of you know pretty much about our situation here but I'll review it in detail because there are some things you don't know. You're aware that these 109 pilots are now thought to be Luftwaffe veterans. You're also aware of the mess they made at Chino and Willie. And that they managed to bring down an F-5 out of Luke. They're pretty well organized and they're pretty good fliers and their aircraft are in top shape.

'At this point, the Air Force and law enforcement people are tearing up three states and Mexico looking for them. So far, no luck. Nobody's arguing over whether this incident is a military or civilian matter, but you can understand that the brass considers these jokers their fair game, exclusively, and they've got a good head of steam up by now to nail them. It's only a matter of time.

'What most of you don't know is that two of these Kraut pilots got in front of me in Germany, in forty-four, on a strafing run. I shot'em up as they were setting down at their base and got hit by their flak at the same time. I went down in their backyard and ended up in the base hospital – with these two pilots, and they identified me. And now, crazy as it sounds, they've come looking for me.'

Lowen paused to look around the table. His audience was – what was the word? – yes; captive.

'What they want, is to meet in aerial combat at a pre-arranged time and place. And if we agree to this, this dogfight, they will supposedly come out of hiding. We'd be the bait. The Krauts come up, and the jets hit'em.

'That's the way it's set up now. And that's why the Air Force has authorized this unit and supplied it with P-51s.

'Major Fitzgerald, our Executive Officer, and Colonel Meredith and Colonel Polk here, were with me on the flight to Chino when we were intercepted by all eight 109s and they heard the conversation over the R/T. The Krauts have kept in touch in a simple way; they just pick up the phone.'

Which means, he realized suddenly, *that they couldn't be in Mexico after all.* Godamighty. How *stupid* he'd been. He puffed at his pipe and leaned back in his chair, looking over each of the seven pilots in turn.

'Seem pretty simple to you, Recchio?' he asked one of the USAF pilots, glancing down at the roster by his coffee to read; 55th FG, 343rd FS, 8th AF, Wormingford, England. Eight kills.

'Seems pretty strange to me.'

'Colonel Lowen?' Another USAF pilot, Warner. 'Do you mean those people put together a whole damned unit of 109s and came over here just to get you?'

Lowen looked again at the roster for Warner's ETO record – 352nd FG, 486th FS, 8th AF, Asche, Belgium. Five kills. 'I don't know how to explain that, Colonel. They had the chance at Chino to take me out ... but –' he shrugged – 'I was in California when they hit Willie. At any rate, the Krauts have made their point, whatever it is.'

'Damned people are all over the news, now,' Polk muttered.

And thank you Colonel Polk, thought Lowen, waiting.

'You actually spoke with the Jerry commander, did you?' asked Redmond-Donleavy.

'Yup.'

'And Jerry just wants to slug it out. Like the war.'

'Yup. Provided there's no Air Force.'

'Can't say as I blame them for that,' said Meredith. The others laughed.

'What did you tell him, then?' Redmond-Donleavy peered at Lowen through his dark glasses which, Lowen recalled, he had not taken off once yet.

'Well Commander, first he asked if I could find some other pilots who weren't too old, too senile, to come up and square off. In so many words. Said we Americans had it too soft.' Lowen was pleased with the way the words *senile* and *soft* seemed to hang in the hazy air over the table. It was just the right white lie. He nibbled at his pipe stem for a moment. 'I told him, this Kraut, that we were ready when he was.'

'How many of them?' It was Spangler this time; 15th FG, 45th FS, 7th AF, Iwo Jima. Nine kills.

'They said five, but they've lost two so I think it's six.'

'So they'll come out when we agree to meet them?'

'Yup.'

'When, do you think?' asked Meredith.

'Few days. They're giving us a little time. They'll call back to set it up.'

'Then,' said Willett, another USAF pilot, 'when we go up, the jets bounce them?'

'That's the way it stands now,' Lowen replied.

'Bit of a jolt for Jerry,' mused Redmond-Donleavy.

And thank you Wing Commander, thought Lowen. He watched the other pilots before he spoke again. 'How does that sound to you people?'

'We sit and watch Jerry get the chop, do we?' Redmond-Donleavy looked up at the ceiling and launched a smoke ring. The others were still quiet.

'Doubt if we'll see anything.' Lowen made an effort to sound casual, just a little disappointed. 'Once the Air Force knows where and when, they'll spot those 109s before we even get close.' He skipped a beat. 'Hell, they don't want us old farts gettin' in the way of their shooting match, gentlemen. You can understand that.'

'Don't see any old farts at this table, Colonel,' said Willett.

And God bless you, Colonel Willett, Lowen thought, glancing down at the roster to read: 352nd FG, 328th FS, 8th AF, Bodney, England. Twelve kills.

'That's not much of a shooting match.' Polk was toying with his beer bottle. 'Jets and 109s.'

'Colonel Lowen,' said Spangler, leaning forward. 'I agreed, like Warner here, and Recchio and Willett, to fly this assignment . . . which Butler described as anti-terrorist, requiring combat experience in prop fighters, against the individuals flying these Messerschmitts. Possibly Luftwaffe. But I didn't know this part of it, about being bait. Now I've made my agreement, Colonel . . .' Spangler lifted his brown bottle of Lone Star and moved it with a small circular motion. There seemed to be nearly a dozen empties around him. 'But I want to say I think it sucks.'

Thank you Colonel Spangler, thought Lowen.

'I feel the same way, Roger,' said Polk.

'Don't like it either,' said Meredith.

'Well gentlemen . . .' Lowen raised his hand. 'As it happens, those are my feelings, too. We do have an alternative, if we decide unanimously –' he let the word linger a moment – 'to handle it differently. This is my command and it is my right to exercise any decision that I feel will achieve the objective of the government of the United States, which is to get these Krauts.' He paused to relight his pipe. 'My feelings are, since they want a fight, they'll get it. Put our 51s up against their 109s any time. Whip their asses.

'My feelings are, since they came over here looking to fight the war all over again . . . they're gonna lose it all over again. My feelings are also that I, we, don't need a dozen jet fighters loaded up with computer missiles to do this job. It's my feeling we should take'em on. Without the Air Force. And each of you are free to accept these terms. Or not.'

'Hear, hear.' Spangler raised his Lone Star.

'Ha ha,' chortled Redmond-Donleavy. 'Any old farts can leave now, can't they?'

'I'm for it, Colonel,' said Willett.

'Now who'll be leaving?' Redmond-Donleavy looked around at each of the others, grinning wide beneath the mustache.

'In other words,' Recchio said, 'we're just not telling the Air Force when the Krauts call?'

'If it's unanimous,' Lowen replied.

'It's unanimous then, is it?' Redmond-Donleavy looked once again around the table. All nodded.

'Flying uniform with badges of rank will be worn at all times when we are on duty,' Lowen said. 'Report to the field at 0600 hours tomorrow morning. That's all for tonight.'

'Except for a little drinking,' Colonel Spangler added.

'Except for a little drinking,' Lowen agreed.

CHAPTER TWENTY

Webb sat cross-legged on the couch, wearing gym shorts and sipping at his third vodka tonic. He watched the smoke from his cigarette curl upward in the warm orange light of early sunset that tinted the apartment walls around him. A half-smoked roach lay in the ash tray and the stereo played Linda Ronstadt's *Love Has No Pride*, to him the most beautiful song ever recorded. And though it called up images of Cecille, he listened to it repeatedly for the serene pleasure of its special sadness.

> Love has no pride when I call out your name.
> Love has no pride when there's no one but
>   myself to blame.

He sought control again. The day's events tumbled through his head. It was all moving, he knew, all moving faster. And he found it so difficult to concentrate until he was alone.

> But I'd give anything to see you again.
> Yes, I'd give anything to see you again.

He finished the vodka, drifting. The alert had netted the Sheriff and the FBI eleven hundred pounds of Mexican marijuana without a shot being fired. No helicopter had crashed. Neither Stratton nor Montgomery had made the Task Force meeting, which had been brief. Sarah had walked into the middle of it with an envelope, he remembered suddenly.

He got up to get it, recalling that he had folded it in his uniform pocket. He brought it to the desk, where he opened it to read: *Reply from FAA Oklahoma City concerning registration of aircraft manufactured Bayerische Flugzeugwerke lists one owner MALZAHN, E., address 15066 Cactus Lane, Phoenix, AZ 85028 Registered 13 June 1971 as converted racing type. No other BF listing within last ten years.*

Webb stared at the typewritten name, distinctly feeling the clicking into place of great invisible gears. *Bingo. Bingo!* It was the *same name!* He flipped through the papers on the desk. It was the same name, yes, that was listed for Felbeck's vacation telephone number. He put the two pieces of paper side by side on the coffee table and lit up the roach, trying to stay calm. Oh man, now what?

He had it, no question about it. He had two registered owners of Me-109s, two registered owners who happened to be related, two registered owners who happened to be at the same address. At this very moment. On his Triple-A road map he found the address in the northeast section of Phoenix and made a mark on the map.

He looked at his watch; 0840 hours. He would spend the rest of the evening getting his paperwork pulled together. Then check out the Malzahn address in the morning.

Lowen was getting loaded. The nine pilots had taken over one end of the bar, divided where the bartender had placed a Reserved sign between them and the other patrons. Lowen studied each of his pilots, particularly the new four. In spite of their age and the differences of physique, each one was tanned and trim and athletic-looking. Somehow that youthfulness remained, as if they were aged copies of the kind of quick young men he had seen in the Officers' Club at Willie. Remarkable how they could be pushing sixty and still look, unmistakably, like the pilots they were. Just like yourself, he thought; go look in the mirror and see.

Between war stories from Europe and Korea, Lowen's own CAF pilots were relating in vivid detail their experience of being bounced by the 109s over Phoenix, being tailed to Chino, and then watching the Messerschmitts tear up their Mustangs and the other warbirds. Lowen had avoided any detailed description of the mess the 109s had made of the flight line at Williams. No point in making the damned Krauts appear any more superhuman than they already seemed to be. Bastards. The damned media were responsible for that kind of crap. Everyone in the damned country knew about them now. Well – he glanced once more at the others – maybe we'll get our pictures in the damned papers, too. If, he reminded himself, you see to it. Your responsibility.

'Fitz,' he spoke to Fitzgerald's back, next to him.

Fitzgerald turned. 'Roger?'

'More notes.' Lowen raised and waved his forefinger. 'Get a reporter, couple of them, at the papers. Somebody who can get on the wire services, and tell'em to stand by. Tell'em to have photographers and tell'em they'll get a story in about forty-eight hours. As soon as we get everything pulled together.'

'Got it.' Fitzgerald scribbled a little loosely, Lowen noticed.

'Pulled together,' Lowen said again. 'That's all.'

He went back to drinking alone, watching Redmond-Donleavy and the four new pilots. He had spoken with each of them and he was satisfied. They were plenty tough enough. Let 'em get half-snapped up now. Good for morale.

Lowen contemplated his own half-empty glass of good morale, humming in his mind *That ol' Jack Daniel's that I know so well . . . ol' Black Daniel's got me in its spell*. Rubbish, he thought. Like the good Wing Commander was fond of saying. Like the good Wing Commander said when he finally slipped off his dark glasses to clean them and Lowen saw that he had one bad eye, odd and flat and oyster-like.

Godamighty . . . *Down and down we go . . . round and round we go . . . in a spin* . . . He wondered for a moment if any of the USAF pilots might get it into their heads to tip off Butler. Then he dismissed it. *Lovin' the spin I'm in*. No more for you, he thought. Then he wondered if the Air Force would get the Krauts first. Or that gung-ho Captain Webb.

He didn't want the Air Force to get them first now. He wanted to get them first. Those damned Heinies doing it just right, right down to the spit-and-polish. You could bet that's the way they were. If they walked in the damned door here this very damned minute, they'd all be wearing Luftwaffe uniform right down to the last damned ribbon and button. And their boots would be mirror-black.

Involuntarily, Lowen glanced down the bar toward the entrance. Can't let the bastards get to you, he reminded himself. You could get spooked by this sort of thing. You bet. But you could do the same thing back, too.

'Fitz.' Lowen tapped at Fitzgerald's shoulder, watched him set down his drink and fumble at pen and pad.

'Roger?'

'More notes, Major.'

'Yessir.'

'Ged a good artist, Fitz.' Lowen spoke in a half-whisper. 'Ged one of those damned hippies that spray-paint those weird things on motorcycles and vans. He'll have to work at night. In the hangar. We'll pay him. Whatever it takes. Tell him I want ideas, a sketch, of . . . of a damned skull. With a damned swastika on it. In twenty-four hours. He oughta be able to do that with his eyes closed, huh?'

Fitzgerald looked a little confused as he began scribbling.

'That's all, Major.'

One more Black Daniel's, he thought. If the Kraut bastards want to play Halloween, well we can do that too. Do it better right here in the United States. Do everything better, dammit. Everything. After all, who invented the damned Mustang, the damned B-17, the damned atomic bomb? You bet. Don't see anyone else inventing Coca-Cola either. Kraut bastards coming over here, knocking out his P-51s, calling up his house on the damned phone like it was some sort of a damned party invitation. Bastards, making him sweat like this, screwing up his life. Sonsabitches.

They'd come down here, too, even find a way to get across a thousand miles of desert to tear up his damned field. They were crazy enough to do that, to fly right in the window of this damned bar, cannons blazing, and blow the damned shit out of it, if they wanted to. Or walk up to his damned door with Lugers, land in the damned front yard, strafe his damned house. Coming into this country and pulling this crap. Well, there was—

'Roger?' Fitz was leaning close enough so that Roger could smell his breath. 'Roger, you all right?'

'Yup.'

'Isn't that true, Roger?' It was Polk talking to him.

'Isn't what true, Colonel Polk?'

'Isn't it true the Kraut pilots wore orange scarves?'

'Yup.' Lowen reminded himself to order coffee.

'Haha, really, Colonel.' Redmond-Donleavy was grinning across the corner of the bar at him, his mustache frothy with beer foam, his eyes hidden behind the opaque lenses. 'Really, Colonel, now don't you find it all a bit amusing?'

'Don't I find all of what a bit amusing, Commander?'

'Jerry doing this. The lovely Messerschmitts. And such splendid jobs on the two airbases. Really now, bloody bright all along. What do—'

'Hey, Donleavy,' Meredith cut in. 'See how amusing it is when one of those lovely 109s is pumping twenty bloody millimeter up your ass, ha ha.'

The others, including Redmond-Donleavy, himself thought this was very funny and Lowen, though he balked drunkenly, could not help but laugh with them.

'Ah, come on now, chaps. Really. You have to give Jerry his due, now. There'll be time enough to get serious when we're up there with him. It is a good show Jerry has. Very proper. Just like it was then. Now there aren't really many of us left, are there?'

Redmond-Donleavy's words seemed to quiet the others; they looked at him over their glasses and bottles. Lowen, hearing Webb's words once again, watched them looking.

'Now then.' Redmond-Donleavy raised his beer mug. 'I say the Jerry bastards have put on a good show and let's have one for them. Just one. Because the poor buggers are going to get their ballocks shot off now, aren't they?'

Another chorus of drunken laughter. Lowen hesitated.

'Come on chaps. Just one for Jerry then, for a good show!' Redmond-Donleavy waved his mug, some of the beer sloshing out and spattering on the bar. They all drank, including Lowen who was last.

'And now one for them that are going to give Jerry bloody hell.'

They all drank again.

'And one for the US Air Force, the Eighth that came over.'

They all drank again.

'And one for the RAF now.'

They all drank again.

'And one for the CAF now.'

They all drank again.

'And one for all the lads that didn't make it back.'

Webb saved for last the half-inch-thick report on telephone calls taped from the public number. All the calls were transcribed but he had the tapes in his briefcase. Skipping the categories headed Theories and Questions he settled into the list of Reported Sightings. Most of the messages were brief, giving location, time, direction, and an assortment of odd little comments that were so amusing he decided to play the tapes and listen rather than read. He listened for nearly an hour, entertained by the voices: hesitant, self-conscious, rambling, indignant, angry, excited, and frequently a little stupid.

He had marked the sightings on his road map in the same manner that the Sheriff had used the colored pins on the big map. He noticed that the sightings were concentrated northeast and northwest of Willie, like the Sheriff's pins. He also noticed that all the sightings fell within the football shape created by his penciled circles indicating maximum fuel range. And there were no sightings south of Willie...which placed all the various marks he had made – including the Malzahn address and the spot where the F-5 went down and the spot where Lowen was intercepted – in a triangular area surrounding Phoenix.

Webb sat back. Those bastards were north of Phoenix. Had to be. He turned the tape back on and listened. The ninth call caught his attention and he took up the transcription to read along as he reversed the tape and listened again: *Ah . . . uh . . . My name is Vern . . . I saw those German airplanes . . . up north . . . way out in the desert . . . last week . . . Is there a reward for . . . for this? We saw them very clearly . . . Ah . . . my telephone number . . . if there is a reward . . . is . . . ah* – Webb laughed aloud.

The voice was slow, slurred, a little vacant. And that momentary lapse when you couldn't recall your own telephone number. Ol' Vern was a doper.

He replayed the tape again. The word *airplanes* . . . plural. *Last week . . . way out in the desert . . . saw them* – plural again – *very clearly*. Webb played the tape back once again. It was the only message he recalled that mentioned more than one aircraft, and the only message that mentioned sightings prior to either attack.

The FBI would be all over that stoned dude by tomorrow afternoon. To hell with the doper, he thought. No . . . no, that bulldog Montgomery would hunt down every single call, every single scrap. Nothing would escape the FBI, nothing. He remembered Montgomery saying, 'We do it inch by inch, Captain. Airstrip by airstrip. Name by name. One blind alley after another. But,' and he smiled, 'sooner or later—' The fucker busts some dope runners one day and gets a commendation, and the next day busts the Staffel and gets a promotion. Webb sat up. No way, Jose, he thought. He reached for the telephone and dialed.

The phone rang eight, nine times before someone picked it up and said nothing. Webb could hear music – the Stones doing *Satisfaction* – in the background. 'Hello?' he said after a moment.

'Yeah,' came a male voice, relaxed but guarded.

'Ah, is this Vern?'

'Yeah.'

'Vern, my name is Jim Webb, Captain, Air Force.'

'Yeah.'

'I'm assigned to check out telephone calls received through the public telephone number, for information on those German aircraft.'

'Yeah.'

'Well, I'd like to talk to you about it.'

'Okay, Cap'n.' He said Cap'n just like Evans, Webb noticed.

'We have to, ah, be sure you saw these planes, you understand. I mean, a lot of people get them confused with—'

'No confusion, man. No confusion.'

'Are you sure? Did you see them clearly?'

'Yeah. Clearly.'

'How may? Two?'

'Four.'

'Four? You saw four aircraft, together at one time?'

'Four of those German aircraft, Cap'n. Bombs and all.'

Webb sensed the Bingo feeling close by again. The 'bombs' would be the belly tanks. 'Okay,' he said. 'Has anyone else called you about this?'

'No. What about the reward?'

'Reward,' Webb repeated. Yes, there was a reward, cash. He could not recall how much or how it worked. 'Ah . . . look, the reward is for valid information leading to the apprehension of these pilots and must be—'

'We are leading to the apprehension of bullshit,' said Vern.

'—must be verified before the reward is paid,' Webb finished stubbornly. 'However,' he continued in the same breath, 'before the FBI comes to see you tomorrow, I would be agreeable to laying some cash on you tonight.'

'Valid information,' said Vern after a pause. 'We saw something valid all right.'

'We?'

'Yeah. My ol' lady was with me, man.'

'Is she with you now?'

'Sure, man. Wanna talk to her?'

'No, listen . . . If we can meet right away, tonight, I'll lay the cash on you. Cash.'

'How much?'

'Ah . . . fifty and—' Webb grabbed his wallet off the coffee table and counted bills '—and another fifty if the information is really hot.' Just like Vegas, Webb thought; the Captain puts a hundred on a stoned freak.

'A hundred.' There was satisfaction in Vern's voice.

'A hundred. What do you say?'

'Far out. Bring beer.'

'What kind?'

'Don't matter.'

'Okay. The address?' Webb copied down the address, in Mesa, with instructions on finding the house.

It took him fifteen minutes to get into his uniform, fifteen minutes to find the beer, another twenty minutes to run to Mesa, and another aggravating ten minutes to find the house, one of many all alike in a rundown neighborhood of grassless plots and collapsed fencing. Like the others, the house was a small tinted adobe – Webb thought it to be pale green in the light from the street – and there were no numbers visible. Dogs barked in the dark from neighboring houses. He pushed through a sagging gate and crossed the sand yard, careful of his polished shoes, clutching the now-soggy bag of three six-packs.

Even before he reached the darkened porch he heard music, more Stones, and the door opened. The silhouette was definitely feminine, a woman in white. 'Captain Webb?'

'Yo,' he answered, feeling for the step with a cautious toe.

'Come in.' She pushed open what was left of a screen door.

In the soft interior light cast from a single small lamp and an assortment of candles, Webb saw a voluptuous young woman, her great length of dark hair parted center and flowing through a white cloth headband. Beneath her robe-like gown he sensed the shifting of generous breasts. She had a truly lovely face, oval and cinnamon tanned, that reminded him of some Egyptian princess. He found himself feeling self-conscious in his perfectly pressed uniform. He removed his cutter cap.

'I'm Terry,' she said, lifting a bangled arm from beneath the robe. She smelled very good. Her chin lifted as if she expected Webb to perhaps kiss the proferred hand, each finger shining dully with rings. Webb grasped it lightly, then looked over to her companion. 'And this is Vern.' Terry closed the door, took the bag of six-packs.

Vern, thin and slight, peered up from the couch where he sat cross-legged. His full beard – was it gray or blond? – seemed that of an aged man, such was the thickness and width of it, covering more than half his face and blending into frizzed shoulder-length hair that was bound like Terry's with a red cloth band. Vern's clothing was well-bleached denim, the shirt loose and buttonless. One thin foot poked out, crossed over the opposite calf.

'Come in, Cap'n. Good, you brought the brew.'

'Don't know if it's your brand.'

'Don't matter. Come and sit.'

The room seemed to Webb as if it were set up for a garage sale. No single piece of furniture looked untorn or unbroken, all of it covered with blankets of striped bright colors. Books spilled from makeshift shelves of boards and bricks. A row of vertically stacked records lined one wall on the floor. What appeared to be an expensive stereo receiver radiated a mixed green-blue light that seemed to flicker with the Stones' music crossing back and forth between two huge speakers in opposite corners of the room.

Webb sat down on the edge of the couch. Terry snapped open the beers. Vern looked up at Webb, his hands moving independently at the task of running a pipe cleaner in and out of the stem of a tiny pipe. Both of his wrists were circled by stunningly intricate silver bracelets set with turquoise.

'Thanks for seeing me.' Webb extended his hand. 'I know it's late.'

'Not late, man.' Vern continued to stare at him with light amusement crinkling his eyes. Then he raised his hand to Webb's, shaking it but once. Then went back to cleaning the pipe.

Terry handed a beer to each of them and settled on the floor. Webb was then aware that his sense of everything moving in slower motion came from the recognition that his host and hostess were themselves geared to a slower motion. He sipped at the beer, gearing himself down with them, looking around. The room smelled of herbs and strange blossoms, of dried clay and clean spices. He saw no hash or grass on the littered coffee table, its surface concealed by books, papers, mail, and cigarette packs. Terry was watching him, wide dark eyes appraising him. She was splendid-looking, he thought again, and like Vern she seemed to emanate a cool distraction, an aloofness. Neither of them were children; Webb guessed early thirties, perhaps older than he.

'Are you a cop, man?' Vern asked without looking up. His hands were still busy.

'This is an Air Force uniform.'

'Yeah, well you could dress up in anything, couldn't you?'

'Here—' Webb fished his wallet out and opened it with the ID card under Vern's face.

'We expected a cop.' Terry spoke rather cheerfully.

'Or FBI,' added Vern, glancing at Webb's ID.

'Well, the law enforcement agencies are working with us,' said Webb, 'but since we're looking for airplanes it's an Air Force deal, you know?'

Vern watched him as he put the wallet away; his wrinkled eyes examined every seam and button of Webb's uniform. Webb was glad of the uniform then. Plain clothes would have been the wrong choice. Still rather ill at ease, Webb lit a cigarette, choosing a matchbox from the table rather than his gold lighter.

'He's not a policeman,' Terry said to Vern without taking her eyes from Webb.

Vern finished cleaning the pipe, screwed the stem into the tiny metal bowl, and placed it with studied slowness into a carved wooden box on the table. 'Fifty dollars,' he said then, still staring at the box. The words seemed not so much a question as a distant recollection.

'Fifty.' Webb reached again for his wallet and picked out two twenties and a ten, placing them on top of a copy of *Horizon* magazine.

Vern seemed not to see the money. He looked instead at

Webb, studying him with the remote half-smile people wore while being entertained. 'Do you have a little smoke, Cap'n? Maybe a stray roach?'

'No. Sorry I don't.'

'We'd feel so much better if you did,' Terry said.

'Well, I'm in uniform. You know, regulations.'

'You can take it off then,' Terry suggested. Vern sniffed, giggled.

Oh man, Webb thought. He glanced at his watch.

'Have a little hit now and then, Cap'n?' asked Vern.

'Now and then, actually. Off duty.'

'Now and then,' Vern repeated. 'Well this is now, man. Tomorrow is then.'

'Right,' said Webb promptly, ordering himself to go with it. In the line of duty.

Terry snapped a lighter, the flame's glow illuminating her eyes. Between glistening lips she drew on a roach held in a silver clip, then held it out to Webb. He took it without hesitation, pulled a long hit, and passed it to Vern. Vern smiled, took a slow toke and handed it to Terry without taking his eyes from Webb.

'How do you like the Air Force, Cap'n?' he asked.

'It's all right. I like it.'

'Do you fly an airplane?' asked Terry.

'No.' Webb tapped his glasses. 'My eyes.'

'I used to watch those F-4s goin' over—' Vern spoke without emotion '—layin' napalm on Charlie. And wish I was up there. Until one came down right in front of us. Watched it burn.'

Automatically Webb identified the F-4 – Phantom – and watched Vern take a long pull of beer, some of which sparkled down his beard.

'Well.' Vern finished the beer. 'In one end and out the other.' He put the can down and moved to stand up, swinging his legs out. Webb saw then that Vern had but one foot; in the other denim pantleg there was nothing below the knee. He watched him reach beside the couch and pick up a pair of aluminum crutches and get to his feet and make his way toward the back of the little house.

He looked over to find Terry watching him. Without moving her eyes she took the last hit off the roach. They could hear Vern's water – it seemed endless – and then the toilet flushing.

'He makes these.' Terry held up her arm, flashing bracelets

and rings. 'And I sell them. We do all right.'

'They're beautiful,' said Webb lamely. He was beginning to sweat.

He finished his beer, resisting the urge to look once again at his watch. Vern came back, swinging nimbly between his crutches and then tossing them to the floor as he settled back on the couch and popped open a new beer. 'Now,' he said brightly.

Webb was wondering how wounded men could attract lovely women, wondering if he were ever war-wounded whether he would have the same magnetism, any magnetism, if that's what it was. It was something that hurt to think about.

'Well, Cap'n,' Vern said, nodding slowly, 'I've seen your airplanes.'

'I saw them too,' said Terry.

Webb found himself nodding. 'I hope you have.'

'No hope, man . . . not hope, but truth.'

Webb nodded on, knowing nothing better to do.

'A hundred dollars,' said Vern. 'Whose money is that, the hundred?'

'The government's,' Webb replied.

'The money you're offering me is the government's?'

'In a way. The government pays me, so—'

'So it's your money, man? Your own money? Why is it worth a hundred dollars of your own money, man, to hear about these airplanes, when you don't even know if it's the truth?'

'I'll know.'

'Would it be worth two hundred?' Vern lit a freshly rolled joint.

'I have limits. Christ, I don't make—'

'What are your limits, man? Two . . . three . . . four? I'm not an extortionist, man. I just want to know your limits, is all.'

'Like I promised,' Webb said patiently, hiding his confusion. 'Fifty down, and fifty more if it's real. Then maybe the reward. If it works out.'

'Works out? Maybe, maybe, maybe.' Vern sighed. 'Well, I said a hundred was cool. I always keep my word, man.'

'It's important,' said Webb. 'Very important.'

'Yeah, man, I know. It's all over the papers, TV. Messers-chmitts, man. Like the war . . . Second World War. Far out. Right?'

'Right.'

'I mean to *you*, man. Why is it important to *you*?'

Webb took a very small hit from the joint, holding it in to give himself time to think. 'Because . . . I'm part of the search team.'

'Part of. Part of. What are *you*, you alone? Not *part* of, man.'

Webb wasn't quite sure what to say.

'Why is it important to *you*, man?' Vern persisted. 'If you find them will you be a hero? Get a promotion? What?'

Webb shrugged. 'It's possible.'

'Well man, now I can under*stand* that! I can under*stand* wanting to be a hero. See, that's what I want to know! That's all. Hey, a hero is a good thing to be.'

'Yeah . . .' Webb was relieved that he was back on track. 'Well, I've never been one.'

Vern smiled suddenly. 'Me either.' The smile faded. 'Now, you're one of the official guys looking for them, right? There must be *hundreds* of guys looking for them, right?'

'Right. Hundreds, almost.'

'Outasight.' Vern slowly shook his head. He seemed to drift, as if he were seeing by some secret camera the panorama of hundreds of searching men. 'Which one are you?' he said then, looking up at Webb with childlike anticipation.

'Which one?'

'Yeah man. You know. Are you a big guy or a little guy? In all those hundreds of guys you have the big shots and the go-fers, you know, like everything. There's the Number One guy and on down, you know.'

'Yeah . . .' Webb sighed with strained patience.

'Well, which are you?'

'Big guy,' Webb answered after a pause.

'Big guy! Wow!' Vern began nodding again. 'All right!' He smiled.

Webb began nodding again, too. He was still confused but he knew enough about being stoned to expect that their route would be circuitous.

'This is exciting, man!' Vern was beaming now. 'How big?'

'How big . . . what?'

'How *big* a guy? Like you said. Number Twenty? Number Ten?'

'Ah.' Webb kept nodding.

'I mean I have to know this stuff, man. It makes it real. You're gettin your information, man, guaranteed. So you can tell me this stuff. That's what I need.'

'Okay. Number Two,' Webb admitted with some reluctance.

'Number *Two*? Number *Two*?' Vern seemed in danger of falling off the couch. Even Terry began to giggle. 'Far fuckin-*out*! Wow, you're going to go ape when I tell you about the airplanes, man.'

'Okay, I'm ready.'

'Who are they?' said Vern as if it were a quiz.

'Who are . . . who?'

'The pilots, man.'

'Ah . . . we don't know. That's what—'

'I know, man!' Vern tapped at his thin chest.

'You do?'

'Yeah man. Of *course* I know, man! They're German pilots, real Luftwaffe, man. Very cool dudes.'

'Where . . . are they from?' asked Webb tentatively.

'From Germany, man. Of course.'

'Germany?'

'Of course, man. Of course!' Vern's voice was barely patient, as if he were talking to a six-year-old.

'How do you know this?'

'How do I *know* it? How do I *know* it?' He paused, incredulous, then leaned forward and whispered, 'Because . . . they have those swastikas and because they're flying real Luftwaffe fighters, man.' He sat back with the air of having presented Webb with a splendid revelation.

Webb stared at him for some ten seconds, feeling all of his optimism, his patience, his tension draining out. It was like watching the little whirlpool as the bathtub emptied. He began to think of how to leave.

'How do you think . . .' Webb pointlessly said, 'they got here, from Germany?'

'I don't know, man.' Vern looked as if he were concentrating. 'Most likely they flew.'

There was nothing more Webb could say. He was dead-ended.

'You ever do psilocybin, magic mushroom, man?'

'No.' Webb was trying to decide how to get the fifty. Goddamnit. Should he say something? Or just grab it and walk?

'We had some really good mushroom.' Vern spoke as if he were miles away. '. . . so we decided to pack a picnic, you know?'

'I packed the picnic,' said Terry.

'Right. Terry packed the picnic. Some wine and some fruit and some chow mein and some marshmallows and some Coke and some chocolate chip cookies and some feathers . . . and I forget what else.

'Anyway, we packed this stuff up and we got in the van and we drove way to hell out in the desert. Man, it's a great place, great place. High . . . high. You climb and climb, and when you get there, it's a little ledge, like. You can see for miles . . . miles. And you do the mushroom. The rock is almost hot, still warm, and when the sun goes down it bathes you in golden light. Bathes you. And the rock glows, man . . . orange, gold . . . And you take your clothes off and sit in the hot sand and bathe in this . . . this golden light.'

Vern began to rock slowly backward and forward. Webb, now caught up in this unexpected narrative, put together a very satisfying image of Terry bathing nude in the rays of the setting sun, seated like an Indian, eyes closed, auburn hair streaming over those tits. Oh man. He glanced over at her and she smiled back.

'Beautiful,' she said dreamily. 'It's so quiet. So wonderfully perfectly quiet. You can hear the silence, like a noise that isn't a noise.'

'I don't know . . .' Vern went on, 'how long it was then. We were really flying . . . just sitting, not moving, just getting into it.' Eyes closed, he continued rocking slowly, his legs crossed, hands on knees. 'You couldn't hear a sound, man.'

Webb watched them both.

'We could look down on the van,' Terry said, 'below in the valley. It was the only thing, the van, that was out of place. We even talked about it. Funny, we actually wished somehow that it would go away.' She herself seemed to drift away even as Webb watched.

'We heard the first . . . airplane,' said Vern then, 'but we didn't see it. It was just a noise, above us. And then it was gone. We . . . to tell the truth, we decided it wasn't real, you know? Like we were hallucinating noise, too.'

'Um,' Webb grunted.

'And so we got it back together . . . maybe for a few minutes . . .'

'Maybe half an hour,' giggled Terry.

'No, it wasn't long, I don't think.' Vern's brow wrinkled with concentration. 'It wasn't long ... and then, man, the first one comes, Jesus *howling* man! Those motherfuckers were loud, man!' Vern's eyes popped open and his body tensed as he leaned forward. 'This plane man, comes by man, I mean right even with us man. I mean we didn't even have to look up! And it was smoking and clattering, right in front of us, man. And you could see the muzzle flash and the shells ejecting coming out the bottom underneath man, they sounded like twenties man, tracers sparky white and sparky red right out of the nose man *bambambambambam* and I saw all this shit flyin' up around the van, man they were shootin' up our van, man, our van. What do you *think*?'

Vern finished in a rush of breath, his eyes resting wide on Webb, his body halted, poised for an answer. Webb, staring at Vern, was unable to think of what he thought. Speechless.

'And then the next one came, man! Right in front of us again, man, right behind the first, shooting man. Our goddamned van was being wasted, man, sparks and glass flying man and we could hear the bullets hitting man *splak splak splak splak*! And then the third one comes right behind the second, man, banging away. We were freaking ... shaking, man, pissing all over ourselves man! I couldn't believe my eyes! They were shooting my fucking van abso-fucking-lutely to *pieces*, man, and it blew up man, just blew to hell and gone *BALAAAM* big ball of fire. Pieces flying every which fucking way! Wow! And then the fourth one man, still banging away man, that fuckin van was wasted man – junk ... junk! Scattered for a hundred yards man. Four fighter planes man we were blown *away*!'

Webb continued to stare at Vern, who continued to rock back and forth, reminding Webb of one of those little Japanese wind-up toys. Terry was nodding along like another toy.

'Is ... this *true*?' Webb said finally.

'Is it true? Of course it's true, man! Could I make that up?'

'When?'

'Last Tuesday, man.'

'You could see these four airplanes ... how close?'

'Hey, hey, about from here to the street, man. About a hundred feet, maybe fifty yards. They were flying right by us, man. The noise would split your eardrums, man. We could see everything. Every pilot. They all had tan caps and sunglasses and orange scarves. All alike.'

'And they had bombs underneath,' said Terry. 'Blue bombs.'

'Yeah,' Vern said. 'Or they were tanks, I think. Just like the TV and the papers. They were all the same, man. Far out. Pink.'

'Pink?' Webb grimaced.

'Yeah man, the most far out pink on top, and bright blue underneath. Pink and blue airplanes, man. Wastin' my van, man.' Vern popped open another beer.

'*Pink? Pink?*' Webb began to feel crazy.

'Yeah, pink.'

'No crosses? No swastikas? No markings?'

'Just pink and blue.' Vern was thinking. 'Oh, and numbers. Big white numbers right behind the cockpit. Number One ... Six ... Number Seven ... and Number Eight, man. Big white numbers.'

Webb's mind was boiling. Oh man. '*Pink?*' he said again, wanting to shake Vern.

'Yes, they were pink, Captain,' said Terry. 'And blue.'

'But ...' Webb looked back and forth between them. 'Those planes aren't ... *pink.*'

'Yes they were, man. I could see them on TV. Pink with brown spots painted over. They weren't painted yet with the brown or the crosses, man. I figured that out.'

'I figured that out,' Terry said.

'Terry figured that out. They were the same planes, man. I saw Number Three on TV. You could see the number Three easy. Same planes.'

'Bingo,' said Webb, leaning back on the couch.

'Right, man. I keep my word.' Vern was nodding again.

'So ... the wreck, the van is still there?'

'Right, man, of course.' Vern relit the joint and took a good hit. 'It took us five hours to get back, too. It seemed like we walked a hundred miles before we got to a road and got a lift. Whew, we were blown away, man. I couldn't put my clothes on right for two days.'

'Did you tell anyone else about this?'

'What, are you serious, man? I didn't believe it myself. Neither of us did – except there was the van – until they tore up Willie, man. Then we knew.'

'You can show me where the van is?'

'Right, man.'

Webb took his wallet out and counted out another fifty and placed the bills on top of the others. 'How much more to take me there? How much more money?'

'No much more money, man. I said a hundred is a deal. I keep my word. But I can't take you there because I don't have wheels, man. The Luftwaffe wasted it, man. *Blooee*!'

'I'll get a Jeep,' Webb said. 'In the morning. I'll pick you up. How far is it?'

Vern seemed puzzled.

'About thirty miles,' Terry offered.

'A Jeep is fine, man,' Vern said.

'Five o'clock?' Webb was calculating how to get a motor pool Jeep. 'Five-thirty latest I'll pick you up.'

CHAPTER TWENTY-ONE

Webb drove in a hurry. Like most of the desert roads north of Phoenix, this one was straight but full of roller-coaster dips, which made for a violent ride at any serious speed. Fiercely he gripped the wheel, flying through the dove-gray dawn with headlights ablaze, knowing the Jeep would track true so long as the road didn't curve.

Vern hung on beside him like a monkey, leg braced, clutching the windshield frame, his bearded face in the wind, his headband rag and long hair whipping back. When Webb crested a hill and the Jeep lifted and their stomachs dropped, Vern would let go with a long rebel yell. It made Webb laugh.

They were a good hour north before Vern motioned for him to slow down. 'Gotta use the map now,' he yelled.

'Do you know this country up here?' Webb yelled back.

'Hell no, man. I'm always zonked when I'm up here. But a map is all you need, man. Maps are miracles, man. You can go anywhere with a map!'

'But you're sure this is the way?'

'Yeah man, I'm sure.'

The sun was breaking and the heat was coming up. They drove deeper into a range of rock-strewn hills, more slowly as the road surfaces grew rougher. Vern stood, squinting ahead like a cavalry scout, directing Webb to yet another turn. The Jeep ground along in low gear down a twisting sandy trail, then into a narrow valley between high orange-rock mesas. Vern called for Webb to slow down, shading his eyes as he searched, then pointed. 'Over there!'

It took several minutes to cross the shimmering expanse of

sand – more white than pink, and as fine as any beach. Webb could see shapeless black pieces, sharp against the light sand, scattered for yards. He pulled the Jeep alongside the largest piece of debris, a chassis and engine block. Three of the wheels were still attached, their tires burnt away.

Webb turned off the ignition. Silence settled around them, so palpable that for a moment Webb thought he had lost his hearing. He lifted off his fatigue cap and fanned his damp matted hair. Vern was standing beside the Jeep, staring at the remains of his van.

'That's it, huh?' Webb asked.

'Gonna be a hell of a repair bill, man.'

Webb laughed as he climbed down. He walked around the burned chassis, looking at smaller pieces scattered nearby. Not far away he found a door, apparently torn free in the explosion. The chrome handle and the blue paint were still shiny but the surface was sieved with bullet holes, some so concentrated they formed jagged gaping rents of shining metal.

Webb looked up at Vern. 'When the planes came, which way were they flying?'

Vern pointed to the end of the valley, then drew an arc with his crutch over their heads to the other end.

'Where were you and Terry?'

Vern pointed up the side of the mesa closest to them, perhaps a hundred yards.

'Let's go,' Webb said, standing.

They got back in the Jeep and Webb moved forward down the valley, crawling in low gear and hanging over the side with his eyes on the ground. After about thirty yards he stopped the Jeep and jumped down, kneeling, picking at the sand.

Vern came around beside him. 'Whatcha got?'

'All I need, buddy. All I need.' He held up several small metal cylinders then tossed one to Vern. 'Souvenir.'

Webb collected a dozen shell casings – they were of two sizes – and stuffed the thigh pocket of his fatigues with them. As he turned the last one over in his hand he thought *Somebody screwed up here, finally*.

'Hey Cap'n. Can I ask a favor?'

'Sure. What?' Webb looked at his watch; 0720 hours.

'Can we take the door back? That's the souvenir I want.'

'Yeah, it'll fit in the back.'

'Well, whattaya think?' Vern spread his arms over the debris.

Webb shook his head.

'Outstanding.'

'Good. Hey, this is exciting, man. Now what are you going to do?'

'Take these shell casings back. Have them tested.'

'That's it?' Vern looked a little panicked.

'That's it.'

'Man, you're the Number Two Guy, right? Aren't you going to call out the Air Force, man? On a red telephone? Call them out like the flying monkeys in Oz, man?'

Webb stared at Vern, startled by the genuine disappointment in the man's voice, his very body as he raised both arms. Then Webb laughed, picturing the wonderfully bizarre flying monkeys, each in uniform with red fez, swarming in the sky . . . and then he pictured them changing to jet fighters, low over the desert, hunting like titanium-aluminum sharks, wings laden with rockets – yes, he could call them up – and his laughter left him. He was very thirsty again.

'No red telephone,' he said then. 'Just black.'

'No, man. Gotta be. I know it,' Vern insisted, his eyes unusually bright under bushy brows and headband.

'Maybe the CO's got one I haven't seen,' Webb said, trying not to sound as if he were dealing with a madman. 'Ready to go?'

'We've got red phones, man. We've got everything, man!'

Webb nodded, looking pointedly at his watch. 'Right.'

'Hey man.' Vern's tone was strong, staying, and he moved forward carrying himself in a posture of demanding anger. Webb came alert.

'Listen man . . .' Now the voice was insistent, angered. 'This country is mad, man. They're all getting ready for the Big One, man. You know that, right?' Now his tone was secretive, conspiratorial. 'It's all gone to power, man. And everybody's trying to build the biggest weapons, man. Right?'

'Right,' agreed Webb solemnly, thinking how it actually was right.

'So . . .' Vern relaxed now.

'We must be thankful. I am thankful. That we have more. More missiles. More bombs. More airplanes . . . And more fine military gentlemen like you, Captain.' He extended his hand as if in some religious fervor.

Startled again, Webb grasped the hand and found himself caught in a vise-tight grip. Vern's face was close now, the eyes hot-bright. Oh man, thought Webb, thankful that his own eyes were hidden by his sunglasses.

'It's an honor, Captain,' Vern almost whispered. 'An honor to meet you. An honor to help you. An honor to know a man who gives himself to the service. Of his country.' Vern's voice was as sincere as any Webb had heard in his life.

'Our country,' Webb corrected.

'Our country, yes!' Vern renewed his grip. 'Our country first. We do have more, don't we, man? You're one of them; you know. We do have more. Of everything. Don't we, man?'

'Yeah.' Webb nodded. 'Truly.'

'It's a problem. I understand that now. A problem within a problem. We keep making more because they keep making more because we keep making more. Ahh . . . just round and round. Lots of missiles, man. Lots of flying things, right?'

'Right.' Webb nodded. 'Truly. More.'

'The best, man. The best Air Force, best Marines, best Navy, best Army. The best in all the world, on the whole fuckin' planet, right?'

'Right.' Webb nodded. 'Truly. The best.'

'Ahhhh . . .' Vern relaxed his grip with the of decreasing pressure of someone falling asleep. 'What a relief, man. I love to hear it.' He seemed to drift away again, his grip growing weaker. 'I love to hear it . . . from someone who really knows.'

Webb lowered his hand. 'Come on,' he said with care. 'Let's get your door loaded on.'

'I've been looking forward, Captain, to hearing of your progress,' said Butler from behind his desk. 'I mean the progress you're not telling anyone about.'

'Sir?' Webb replied as if he hadn't heard.

'Cut the crap will you, Captain?' Butler tapped a stack of paper on his desk, his forefinger sounding like someone knocking lightly on a door. 'I've read your reports, no problem there, except half the time I don't know where the hell you are. Know what I'm saying?'

'Yessir.' Webb was feeling rather vulnerable and sloppy in his sweaty fatigues.

'Captain, I'm not accusing you of screwing off. You're a

bright guy, which is why I put you in charge of this operation. But don't think you're so much brighter than the rest of us that you don't have to share what you're doing. Do you follow?'

'Yessir.'

'Each of those Task Force people has specific skills – some that you don't have, believe it or not – and each of them, like you, has certain responsibilities. This is a team, Captain, and I'd like you to reassure me that you comprehend, and accept, the team concept.'

'Yessir, I do.'

Butler glared expectantly at him. 'All right, what have you got? What's going on that you haven't found the time to include in your reports?'

'So far, sir, bits and pieces. But it's coming together.'

'What kind of bits and pieces, Captain?'

Webb dug in his fatigue pants pocket and dumped a handful of shell casings on the desk. Butler picked one up, turning it over in his fingers.

'Where'd these come from?'

'In a valley about eighty miles north, where four of the Messerschmitts used a parked van for target practice a week ago.

Butler continued to examine the shell casings.

'And I've got two people who saw the 109s, four of them, from about a hundred yards. No mistake. And I want these witnesses, Colonel, to get that cash award.'

Butler looked up. 'Okay, Captain, put it on paper; name, address. And now tell me what this means.'

'Sir, I've only got theories.'

'I expect theories, Captain. That's part of your responsibility.'

'Those 109s wouldn't travel very far for practice, would they? Every time something shows up – the pin patterns after the attack here, the F-5 getting knocked down, now this – it shows up north of Phoenix.'

'All right, all right.' Butler rubbed his fingertips in the center of his forehead, then looked up. 'Listen, you should have sent the FBI after this. Do you see my point?'

'I see your point,' Webb said with just the right touch of respect.

'All right. Now what about this little joy-ride to Los Angeles?'

'I had a lead. Guy registered a 109 six years ago. I took a

chance on finding him. No luck over the phone. He was on vacation.' Webb stopped a second, trying to decide something. 'I'll have all this in today's report, sir.'

'And you will turn these names over to Montgomery.'

'Yessir. It's just that I've been moving pretty quickly.'

'All right, Captain. I appreciate that. But use these people; that's what they're for. Let the Sheriff and the FBI run around.'

'I understand, sir.'

Butler looked away, out the window. His attention seemed to sail away with the Tweets lifting off outside, their engines tearing finely-drawn lines across the hum of the window air-conditioner. He spoke to Webb without looking at him. 'Have you by any chance heard from Colonel Lowen?'

'No sir.'

'Well, he got his P-51s. And his pilots. And his ammunition. Yesterday.'

Webb waited a moment, having decided to say nothing about Lowen.

'You'll keep me informed,' Butler said, turning back to Webb. 'On everything now, won't you?'

'Yessir.'

'That's all, Captain.'

They exchanged salutes.

After stopping by the photo lab to order a set of aerial map prints of the area just north of Phoenix, Webb checked out one of the motor pool sedans and then drove over to the lot where the Datsun was parked and transferred his dress blues, gym bag, and shoes into the sedan. He then made one more stop to draw a .45 automatic with holster, web belt, and two clips of ammunition.

Within the hour he had located the Malzahn address, north of Phoenix in open country. He passed the house at normal speed, checking the number on the mailbox by the road, and then parked on the shoulder about 300 feet away. From the gym bag he pulled out binoculars and focused them in on the house.

It was isolated, a fairly large Spanish adobe, with plenty of palm shrubbery and a high wall. Webb studied every foot of the house that he could see; small arched vestibule beyond the gate, large clay pots of desert plants, a three-car-wide garage door, and a battered sun-bleached Jeep.

He put down the binoculars. Screw the FBI, he thought. I can do this sort of thing, too. Taking off his fatigue shirt, he settled in and lit up a cigarette. Then the garage door opened.

He grabbed up the binoculars in time to see a blue Buick sedan backing out. Before the automatic door closed again he had seen a light-colored van. And a silver BMW coupe with blue California plates. He could also see that the Buick driver was a good-looking blond in sunglasses. He decided not to follow. He would wait.

At 1120 hours the garage door lifted again. Webb yanked up the binoculars. The big van backed out. The van's side windows were shaded with suntint, but he could make out two men in the front. And the tires were oversized, with monster treads; a serious vehicle. Webb started the engine without taking the binoculars from his eyes. The van pulled away and Webb followed. Now we're getting somewhere, he thought, checking his odometer.

The van driver was in no hurry, he discovered, staying well back. Until they got onto 87 north. Then the big van moved out. Webb stayed a dozen cars away, thankful for traffic to hide him. They'd be paranoid as hell by now. He knew it was them. And the BMW with California plates. Felbeck's. Had to be.

He made a mental map of their route as the van's speed picked up and the traffic thinned. Running at sixty-five now, Webb hung back. Half a mile ahead the van flashed brake lights and turned. Keeping the gap, Webb followed onto a secondary two-lane and discovered that the van was still accelerating. It was a damned roller-coaster road again. He was pushing seventy and he fumbled for the seat belt with his right hand. The sedan topped then, wrenching his stomach as it lifted and dropped. Webb let out a long rebel yell like Vern's.

He had nearly caught up when he saw the brake lights flare again, less than a quarter mile away. As he closed, Webb saw the van kicking up a high cloud of powder dust to his left. Sucker was really hauling now. Webb flashed by the turn-off, hit the brakes and skidded into a U-turn. Now almost half a mile away he could see the dust cloud moving out across a huge level expanse of cactus-dotted desert. Cursing, he wrenched the sedan into a slewing turn and roared down the sandy trail, wishing he had had the simple common sense to have kept the

342

Jeep. The sedan wouldn't take much of this, he thought, lurching in the seat. Oh man.

He charged ahead, hanging on to the wheel. The dust cloud of the van seemed a mile off now. The road grew rougher. In spite of his seat belt, Webb was thrown back and forth against the door. Something crashed in the back seat. Ice cubes and tin tea cans rattled. Something else clunked in the trunk. The car groaned as it was flung over the desert trail. Bushes lashed against the flanks and dust and boiled up behind.

Desperate to keep the van in sight, Webb roared forward, driving beyond the edge of control, heedless that the trail was often blind as it turned, obscured by brush. He charged ahead.

Then the trail hooked suddenly right, into a wash. Webb hit the brakes, cranked the wheel to the left to keep the car straight. He was too late; the sedan nosed down and hit hard and bounced back up, flinging him into the door, slamming to a stop. His head banged against the window, spreading a spiderweb of white crack lines.

Dazed, he shut off the ignition and leaned back in the seat. He shook his head, realizing then that he had severely bruised his upper left arm against the door. He felt a bead of sweat drip off his nose. He closed his eyes. He massaged his arm. Opening the door, he heard a sound, a long steady hissing that seemed to come from under the hood.

Webb looked down to see steam vapor wafting from the left wheel well. Leaping out, he fell to his knees and looked under the car, watching a steaming green liquid dribble into the sand to be instantly absorbed. He heard another sound then; a louder hissing, then a rush of steam.

Webb stood up slowly. Clouds of vapor whispered up around the front of the car and drifted away, dissolving. Oh man; it was over now, he realized. Should have gone back and called someone instead of chasing across the mother desert in this tin-shit fuck-bucket sedan. *Idiot.*

He kicked the crumpled front fender with his boot, then leaned against the car – only to recoil from the hot metal. He then crawled up on the hood with the binoculars for another look. Nothing but desert, endlessly repetitive, shimmering in the silent broiling heat. He began to feel the heat and he decided to sit in the car with the doors open and decide what to do next.

343

With a still-cold can of iced tea retrieved from the jumble in the back – the spilled ice had already melted – he relaxed in the driver's seat. His arm was hurting, throbbing now. And he had a mother of a headache. He pushed his fingertips through his hair to feel a rising goose egg and they came away bloodied.

Wonderful, just wonderful, he thought, staring at the heat waves undulating across the hood. This sort of stupid crap never happened to James Bond, you could bet. No way. Bond wouldn't have a headache, wouldn't have crashed the car, wouldn't be sweating like a pig; he'd have a chick right beside him with her blouse half-open and her legs crossed with her skirt halfway up her thighs while ol' 007 figured out what to do next. He wondered if the men who made movies all had an agreement to make everything appear so simple in life, so easy, when it never was. You had to sweat and grind and hang in and keep flailing at it, keep pushing. Like the women he hunted. All the doggies and dipsticks you worked your way through until you got somebody like Pamela.

Goddamnit, his arm hurt. And the mother heat. He looked at his watch; three minutes rest was enough. It was 1235 hours, definitely not the best time of day to be stuck in the mother desert. He remembered reading newspaper stories of tourists who had perished in the desert. Oh man.

Refreshed momentarily, he got out and rummaged in the back seat. First he put on his fatigue cap, then straightened his dress uniform and hung it back on the hook. The cooler had dumped all the water and ice and there were four cans of tea left. Just these efforts made him sweat. He paused to think.

He couldn't be in much danger. He could walk out. Or, he reminded himself, walk in. It was several miles back to the road, perhaps four or five; he wasn't sure. The car wasn't going anywhere . . . so it was wait or walk. Screw it, he decided. He wasn't going to sit and cook. Press on regardless. Lock up the car and move out.

He took his fatigue shirt and folded it in a long rectangular shape so it would fold over the web belt in case he needed it later. Already he felt his skin crawling with dryness, as if it were shrinking.

He remembered then that nobody knew where he was. No one could find him. Except the people in the van when they came back, if they came back. From the rear seat floor he retrieved the web belt with the leather holster and the .45 automatic. Folding his shirt over the back of the belt he pulled it around his waist and hooked it tight. Damned .45 weighed a ton. He moved the belt, wincing from the pain of his bruised arm, so the pistol hung over his right haunch. Two of the tea cans went in the fatigue pockets along with the two clips of ammunition.

Only then did it occur to him that the Triple-A map might be of use. He traced the route out of Phoenix, but when he fixed his position as being somewhere between the Fort McDowell Indian Reservation and the town of Sunflower, he discovered that the map showed no secondary roads.

He leaned back in the seat and took off his glasses and cleaned them with his handkerchief. Then he checked the coordinates – K-14 southwest – and refolded the map and locked up the car. Then he started walking.

The second hangar was completely cleaned. Three of the 109s and a dozen ammunition crates remained, but nothing else, not so much as a cigarette butt or stray rivet.

Miserable in the heat, Schilling and Rendel tied up the last of four large trash bags and dragged them over to the first hangar where Eric and Rudi were making final electrical tests on the other three planes. The original steel seats had been replaced in all six aircraft, as well as the armor headrests. There was nothing more to be done on the 109s; tested, tuned, armed, cleaned, and fueled, they waited.

The first hangar, including the briefing room, had also been tediously scoured of anything that would reveal their presence, every scrap of paper, bottle cap, and beer can. All spare parts, all paints and fluids and most of the tools had been packed for removal.

Schilling leaned against the rear fuselage of his own Number Three, drinking another beer. He was gritty and sweaty and tense and half-drunk. It was past noon and the worst of the heat was on them now.

He had begun to wonder if the Herr General had slipped over the edge, from the heat or some emerging madness, holding them waiting. Or whether he was even more daring than anyone suspected. Eric had told him about the mission plan to Mexico, which sounded truly mad. Schilling had to give Theo credit for some sanity after all, for the simple reason that he had cancelled it. Though it seemed hardly less bizarre to be sitting and waiting for that P-51 pilot in Texas to get his act together for a good ol' times dogfight. Christ.

So it was not so much the heat that weighed on him as the tension. Now he endured every hour that passed. Since the raids, it was like living in a vacuum; there was never any sign that anyone was looking for them. And here, where you could look across the silent vastness of the desert and see no other living thing, you could easily imagine that no one was.

But he knew they were. Each hour someone was getting closer. So each hour it grew tighter, this feeling – fear in some form – though no one spoke of it. They had earned the undivided attention of the FBI and the military machine, which was certainly nothing to be calm about. You carried the weight of this around in your chest, a bad dream all day long. The sheer psychological presence of these invisible pursuers was as terrifying as a tidal wave at his running heels.

He wondered – if he found himself in court – what exactly he would say in his own defense. What words could explain those emotions that had overcome – if only by a thin margin – his sense of station, his respect for order, and his abhorrence for hurting other human beings? No words he knew; he would be helpless.

Was it Marta who had tipped the scale in favor of his staying? Christ, how angry he was with himself for wanting her. It was a stupid business you never quite learned how to avoid. There was always so long a time between good women and it had been so long now that he didn't trust himself to handle it wisely. What terrible curse was it that caused a rational man to come unstuck over the shape of a slightly crooked nose, the ripple of tendons in a foot, the texture of a whisper?

Yet, he had come to terms with himself about Marta in the last day or so. What he was going to do about Marta was to do nothing about Marta. He had done and said all that he could, perhaps more than he should have. There was no way he was capable of doing more.

If only women were like the prizes of victory, if only you could fight for them, simply take them by force, capture them, keep them. But there was no way to make them love you if they wouldn't. Sometimes you could try everything, and nothing worked. And then sometimes you could try nothing, and nothing

346

was what worked. So what Schilling was doing now was doing nothing. It wouldn't take her long to pick up on that either. He just wouldn't give a goddamn. Whatever happened, happened. She could take it or leave it now.

'You know . . .' Eric's voice from behind him.

He turned and looked over the waist-high fuselage to see Eric with a beer in one hand, his other hand touching the black swastika on the tailfin.

'. . . in Nam, those fuckers never told us about these.' He was studying the swastika, tracing the pattern with his forefinger.

Schilling could tell he was loaded.

'Never could forgive them for that,' Eric went on. 'To the civilians in Nam, the swastika – just like this, with a circle around it – is a religious symbol. Like the Christian cross.' He seemed to be talking to himself. His eyes were heavy-lidded, and he held an unlit joint along with the beer can.

Uncertain, Schilling remained quiet.

'So they had these . . . swastikas . . . on the grave markers. There were graves everywhere, like in their yards. Everywhere. No cemeteries. A kind of custom. But they never explained that kind of thing to us, about civilians. When the green troopers came in, they always reacted to those swastikas, on the grave markers, like you would expect anyone to react. Perfect for target practice, see?'

Schilling said nothing. He had never heard of such a story.

'Winning hearts and minds—' and here Eric made an empty smile— 'was not so easy when the saviours were potting at family grave markers all the time.'

Schilling still didn't say anything, didn't want to listen, not because he was hearing the catharsis of yet another man's war but because every word from Eric's mouth was yet another fragment to the mosaic of the man Marta had married.

'So, how you doin'?' asked Eric.

'Okay,' Schilling was startled to be asked.

'I didn't mean to lean on you, about Nam. You had your own war.' He chuckled dryly. 'Still do.'

Schilling moved his head instead of replying.

'You think those P-51s will show?' asked Eric.

'They'll show.'

'You don't think they'll tip off the Air Force?'

'Christ, I hope not.'

347

'How do you feel?'

'Impatient.'

'That's all?'

'That's all.'

'I can't believe what you guys are doing, man.'

'Sometimes I have the same problem.'

'Well, Major Three.' Eric grinned.

'Well, Major Nine,' Schilling responded automatically, touched by the memory of Bison, and then touched with amusement by Eric's little trick.

'Are you screwing my old lady, man?'

Schilling looked over at Eric's eyes to see if they were angry. 'No.'

'Okay.' Eric took a long swallow of beer.

'Relax, Major Nine.' Schilling finished his own beer. 'In twenty-four hours this will all be over.'

CHAPTER TWENTY-TWO

The walking was not unpleasant at first. It was easy to follow the tread marks which, Webb noticed, indicated that two vehicles used the trail. He had no doubts that it would lead him to the Staffel field. He patted the bulky leather holster on his hip.

The reddish-pink sand under his boots was coarse and loose, and in the heated silence the sound of his steps scuffing rhythmically seemed unnaturally amplified. He was sweating under his cap and under his armpits and he could feel the heat weighing hot on his shoulders.

The desert brush was sparse, mostly clumpy frail bush-trees; some gray and skeletal, some willowy and green with delicate fronds. He recognized cholla plants, and the occasional yucca with its ivory stalk sprouting from a spiky palm base. And the big saguaro, vertically ridged green sentinels sometimes thirty feet high. Webb was surprised at the life around him. Ordinary flies and sand flies cruised by, and a black butterfly now and then. Long little lizards skittered across his path, tiny birds darted among the cactus and brush, and every so often some creature stirred scurrying through reed-like twigs that rustled like paper. He knew the rattlers wouldn't be out on the open sand in the high sun and he knew there was no other creature very dangerous. Except the men he was seeking.

He patted the .45 again, reassuring himself that his decision to keep going was wiser than trying to walk back to the highway.

The trail wound through the bush clumps, which were high enough so that he could never see very far ahead. There was a ridge that looked about a mile off but after an hour of walking it didn't seem an hour closer. He was growing light-headed and, at times, a little faint. Somewhere during his training he had learned about heat exhaustion but he couldn't remember any of the rules.

He decided to take a short break and he looked in vain for some shade. He sat down by a bush and lit a cigarette and drank one of the cans of tea, now almost hot. He took off his boots and found that his socks were almost dry to the touch. He finished the cigarette, looking around in the silence. There was a little thin grass here and there – greenish with long thin shafts like wheat – and there were tiny yellow flowers as perfect as miniature daisies, very bright, with leaves that looked like gray velvet. And larger lavender flowers with yellow centers. It struck him that it didn't look very much like a dangerous place to be.

When he put on his boots, his bruised arm began to hurt again, but he ignored it. When he stood, he brushed against the bush and caught a thorn in the tender crook of his elbow. It was a little black spike of a thorn, unexpectedly painful. He picked it out and resumed walking. He noticed that his forehead seemed to sweat but that the moisture never ran down his face, and his armpits were damp, but not his back or chest. Though he was perspiring a lot, it was evaporating just as fast. So he was losing water.

He looked at his watch – 1305 hours – which seemed later than he expected. He wondered how far he had come; it was impossible to tell, since everything seemed the same and nothing in the distance seemed to be any closer or any farther than before. He studied the tread marks as he walked, reassuring himself that he wasn't lost. Soon he began to feel dizzy. And confused. Not a good sign. He wondered whether he could possibily die; how long would it take? Was it better to keep moving? Or should he rest more often? He had the feeling he had forgotten something important, left it in the car. No there was nothing else. He had the .45 and two clips, and the binoculars and one can of tea.

What was Lowen doing now, he wondered? And he remembered Susan – no, Pamela – saying as she moved her hands up over her ribcage, 'Do you like these?' He remembered drinking big drinks with crushed ice in the Buena Vista with Pamela. Cecille. He didn't want to think of Cecille. He didn't have anyone to think about. Gone. He could think about Pamela, but he didn't really believe she would care whether he thought about her or not. So that didn't count. Persevere.

Oh man. What in hell was he doing out here in this desert? Oh man, what was he doing out here in this *life?* Cecille was gone how long now? Cecille was something, someone, that had had meaning, some purpose, some . . . structure. It seemed impossible that anything with structure and purpose and meaning could fall apart. Even now it still hurt, losing her, losing the whole act. Failure, clear and simple. It was what people meant when they said, 'It didn't work.' Shit-fuck it hurt, so bad you cried about it, though no one ever knew. No one ever saw him cry.

He was not feeling well. His skin seemed to be dry-heated like sunburn, though he had enough protective tan. Didn't he? He wondered about that, thinking how foolish it seemed to remember sunning by the pool to keep his tan. He thought of the aqua pool and the condensation on a cold brown glass cylinder of chilled beer. He looked at his watch; 1325 hours. Something was wrong. He couldn't remember what time he had started walking. Cecille always left her watch on, he recalled. It seemed stupid and they had argued about it. An expensive gold watch. Even when she was making love or in the shower. She said it was waterproof.

The van tracks under his feet went on, and on and on. Webb looked ahead. If the trail continued in a straight line it would go on for miles more, not to the ridges he could see to both sides. The air was so clear. It was so quiet. All he could hear was the soft *chuff-chuff* of his polished boots coated now with fine pink dust. A huge fly, or bee – he couldn't tell which – cruised by.

'Hey!' he called out to it, 'Bee twenty-five!'

He looked around at the endless acres of dead-looking brush. He knew he couldn't make it back to the car now. No way. Weird how he felt light-headed, light-bodied, as if he had lost weight. And itchy, sort of hot-itchy.

Forty minutes later Webb fell down between the van tracks. He'd been shuffling along on automatic for a while, his mind disengaged, watching his boot tips moving forward one after another. He remembered not wanting to be in the Army so he wouldn't have to do this. They walk, we fly. Haha. Then his ankle had turned in the soft sand and both his knees – to his slow surprise – hit the ground together, not hard at all. Just kneeling. It seemed humorous, as if he were supposed to pray.

351

He decided it was okay to be resting for a moment. And that it was better to fall backward rather than forward. So he just relaxed. And found himself sitting.

He worked the can of now-hot tea out of his fatigue pants pocket and drank half. Then he took his handkerchief out and cleaned his sunglasses; the frame was almost too hot to touch. Shade, he needed shade. He remembered his fatigue shirt then, folded over the back of the web belt. He pulled it out and opened it up and covered his head and shoulders with it. Must look silly, he thought. Certainly feels silly. It was all silly. Everything was silly.

There was something not right with his vision; it came and went, fuzzy and clear. His tongue felt odd, swollen, and the tea tasted like metal. He could feel it tracing down his insides and reaching his stomach. He wondered again if he had made the right decision, to walk in. It was the right decision if he found the Staffel – it seemed to be difficult to keep remembering that – and the Staffel . . . was at the end of this road. He had to be close. No more than a few miles maybe. What was a few miles?

Webb was not so sure then about being able to stand up. If he sat there long enough the van would come back and run over him. This thought gave him enough energy to crawl out of the tracks. He raised his wrist to look at his watch, blinking. The glare off his watch face, a flash from the sun overhead, seemed near-blinding. Not well, he thought. Jesus, this could be serious.

He sat in the sand, baking, looking dumbly around, wondering if he should worry about the time, wondering what it was that he had been unable to do to keep Cecille from loading up the Mazda and driving back. If he'd known what to do, he'd have done it. If he found the Staffel then somehow he knew it would all be fine. In this case he knew what to do. All there was to do was to do it. Persevere.

He looked around again, surprised to discover his fatigue cap upside down in the sand a few feet away. Oh yes. He picked up the dusty cap and studiously polished the double silver Captain's bars with the shirt sleeve hanging over his shoulder.

He managed to get on his hands and knees. The shirt hanging over his head felt like a tent. The pistol and the holster seemed incredibly heavy around his waist and he thought about taking it off and leaving it. Like in the movies when those poor wretches lost in the Sahara left a trail of gear for the vultures to follow. He looked up suddenly, feeling a volt of panic. There were always vultures out here, everywhere; he often saw them from the car. But there were none cruising above, none casting their fringed-wing shadows over his silly-looking form. Such a silly thing, vultures. Such a silly business, being out here just a stone's throw from air-conditioned Phoenix in the US-of-A. If he found the Staffel . . . he would be a Major . . . and Cecille would read about it in the papers. Even up there in Ohio. If he died here she'd read about that too, haha. He thought about Vern and smiled. Pain etched his lips; they were cracked, splitting. Oh man. If Vern was here, he'd be helping him up, cheering him on, limping along.

'Now get up, you sonofabitch,' he mumbled. 'Get your regulation ass in gear, Captain!'

Webb stood, weaving. He put on the cap to hold his shirt-cape, and hitched up his web belt a little.

'Persevere, you sonofabitch,' he whispered. 'And if you fall on your ass. And can't walk . . . then start crawling. Because . . . because—'

He felt like crying and laughing at the same time. Because he now understood one thing above everything else; if he didn't succeed this time he was going to die. For real. He staggered forward.

It was Rendel who saw the tiny red light blinking on the wall by the door to the briefing room and called it to Rudi's attention. Now they could hear a faint pulsing beep. Rudi climbed down from the wing of Number One.

'Don't be concerned,' he said, wiping his hands on a cloth. 'Keep going so we can leave soon. The pool will feel good today.'

He walked over to the alarm unit and stared at it a moment before pressing the switch. 'It's all right,' he said to the others, all of whom were watching him. 'Sometimes a jack rabbit sets it off. Sometimes even a tumbleweed. I'll check it out.'

They went back to work and Rudi went behind the door in the briefing room and brought out binoculars and a Remington twelve-guage. He pulled off the sweatband from his forehead and put on his cap and then broke open the breech, inserted two brass-green shells, and clicked it shut. Then he walked outside, squinting in the glare, dreading even a short walk.

He made his way slowly up the ridge, parallel to the descending road, with the shotgun over his shoulder. He had long ago chosen a vantage point from which he could see the approach road even before it reached the wire gate with the alarm. He always checked here first because the gate was the most likely place for a trespasser to come in. Several times in the past he or Eric had responded to the alarm and found nothing but a tumbleweed lodged in the wire. This time if there was nothing at the gate he would walk the perimeter of the fence, more than a mile along the ridge. And this time he was apprehensive.

When he reached the observation point he stayed low and set the Remington level and raised the binoculars. He was somehow not surprised when he saw a solitary figure trudging up the road. From what he could tell, the man was alone – his magnified form quivering in the heat waves through the glasses – wearing an odd garment which Rudi made out to be a shirt draped over the capped head. He was a lean and fit man, not very tall and not very old, and the sunglasses and gray T-shirt and olive pants – were they fatigues? – caused Rudi to study him even more closely. No gloves, his arms bare, glint of a gold watch. Not a dirt-bike rider, not some scruffy dune-buggy jockey.

Rudi watched him reach the top of the ridge, seeing him stagger, attempt in vain to keep his balance, and fall. He took a long time to rise and his head hung like a drunk's to one side. Rudi saw then a tiny flash of reflection off the cap; twin silver bars of a Captain. *Goddamnit*, thought Rudi, *goddamnit, goddamnit*. Now on his feet, the Captain pulled the shirt and cap off his head with a loose careless gesture and let it fall. Then he moved forward with the motion of a marionette, stumbling slowly up to the crest of the ridge where he fell, first to his knees and then to his elbows.

Rudi crawled up a little higher so he could see the prone officer more clearly. For a second or two he thought the man had fainted, but then, the Captain rolled to one hip, lifting up a pair of binoculars. Then Rudi saw the holster and web belt. God damn the luck; what was this fool doing, coming down the road with a side-arm? Rudi swept his glasses back over the road, looking for a vehicle or other men. Nothing.

He focused again on the Captain, who was sweeping his own binoculars back and forth. Rudi crouched down, thinking; the

Captain knew exactly what he was looking for. When he edged up and looked over the rock again, the Captain was studying the hangars below.

Rudi was glad that Theo and Kesler were back at the house. He knew there was no way he could get down to the hangers now without being seen. He waited. Well, he thought, we may have some real trouble after all, though it was puzzling that an officer would come walking in alone.

The Captain took a long time with the binoculars. Rudi began to squirm in the heat.

Webb lowered his binoculars, blinking. His eyes burned, but would not water. His back and shouders and forearms seemed to radiate heat. Swollen in his mouth, his tongue was starting to push between his teeth. There was a sound he could almost hear, a vague high-pitched hum; the vibration of heat and silence. He knew that the two large wood buildings with the camouflage netting could only be the Staffel base, yet he had to remind himself that he had succeeded. Dulled to stupidity, his senses discarded the excitement, tuned only to the proximity of life-sustaining shade and water. There was no hesitation about going in. There was no choice about going in.

He eased over on his left hip, making an unintelligible noise from the pain of his left arm. And from the fear of death. Unfastening the holster flap, he withdrew the .45, the grip hot in his hand, and rolled over on his back. The .45 seemed enormous and beautiful. He fumbled for the clips in his thigh pocket; they felt like hard heavy candy bars. *Some candy*, he thought. *Haha, eat lead.* Everything was going to be all right now. He pushed the clip up inside the grip and then lowered the weapon onto his chest, to rest just once more. There seemed no strength left to summon. He would have to remind himself of every move, command himself to rise and go. His thoughts meshed, then disengaged, melting into blankness. And then engaged again. How curious that there was no strip, no runway. Perhaps the crazy bastards just took off in the sand, bouncing through the mesquite and joshua.

He saw the vultures then. Lying on his back with the sun broiling his face he watched the six dark birds soaring effortlessly in a silent circle sixty feet above. *Real vultures. Sonofabitch. Haha, too late, motherfuckers.* He fingered the .45 – it was almost too hot to hold – and rolled over on his belly and eased up, grunting, to his knees, feeling his pulse pound at his temples. Here we go, he thought.

When Rudi saw the Captain load the .45 he crouched back down and rested his head against the covering boulder. At fifty yards, there was no use for the Remington. This was trouble all right. The crazy sonofabitch was going in alone with a .45, which was no weapon to take lightly. He peeked around the boulder with the binoculars. The Captain was on his knees, and then he stood so precariously that Rudi was sure he would topple where he was. Holding the .45 slackly at his side, he staggered over the crest, moving as if every joint in his body was unhinged and with the kind of drunken forward speed that had no control. Or fear, Rudi realized, watching the Captain shamble down the slope toward the hangars.

Goddamnit, he thought again, picking up the shotgun. He broke the breech and plucked the two shells out and put them in his pocket. In the burning silence he could hear the scuffle of the Captain's boots from thirty yards.

Conveniently for Webb, he caught all three men close together. He had heard them talking and laughing inside the hangar and then the snap-hiss of opened beer as he edged around the door into the briefing room and then looked through the crack of the half-opened door that led into the hangar. All of them were sweat-soaked, shirtless, with headbands. Two were much older, grayed and tanned. The third, lean and hard-looking, had thick dark hair and a mustache. They were standing no more than twenty feet from the door, drinking cans of beer. God, that beer looks better than gold, Webb thought as he cocked the hammer of the .45 and stepped out, spread-legged and crouched, arms out stiff with both hands holding the pistol.

'Freeth!' he croaked.

The sound of his own voice and the odd way the word came out made him feel foolish. He expected the three men to laugh. But no one laughed and no one moved. The younger man with the black mustache stopped still with a can of Coors at his lips, staring at Webb over the aluminum rim.

Webb cleared his throat. 'No one move a fuckin' muscle.' No one did. He could feel his temples pulsing insanely as he took a cautious step forward, looking around, keeping the .45 leveled at arm's length. Satisfied that no one else was in the hangar, he moved in closer. His eyes were beginning to adjust to the shaded interior and he could see the 109s – three of them tight together. The sight gave him a ripple of goose bumps.

'Just stay put now,' he warned.

There was a peculiar gap between the sound of his own words and his hearing of them. And the floor of the hangar seemed to list, like the deck of a ship.

'You!' He waved the .45 at the younger one. 'Put the can down. Put the hands up high. All of you, get'em high!' Webb was grateful that they all complied. 'Now . . . turn around, backs to me. Good. Now, over to the wall . . . stay apart . . . right there *stop*!' Webb could feel his voice running out, dry.

'Okay,' he rasped. 'Spread the legs . . . little more . . . lean forward with your hands flat on the wall. Very nice.'

Webb side-stepped over to the cooler, glancing again at the three 109s which seemed huge; God, what a shock they were. With his left hand he pulled off his cap and then filled a plastic container with ice water and poured it over his head and shoulders. The water hitting the floor sounded as if he were pissing. He wanted to laugh. Then he fished a Coors out of the water and opened the tab with his teeth and poured it into his mouth. He could feel it coursing every inch down his gullet and then hit his stomach; he was surprised that it was painful.

'Now,' he said in a voice more clear. 'Just . . . stay put.' The hangar began to shimmer and tip around him. He began to panic. The .45 seemed too heavy to hold. He took several very deep breaths.

'Okay guys,' he said to the back of the three silent figures against the wall. Webb was confused; what was he to do with them now? And where were the others?

'Okay,' he said again. 'Put you hands . . . on top of your head. And sit down. Slowly. Facing the wall.'

Silent still, the three men obeyed. What had they done, these three? Why was he holding a weapon on them? Oh man. He should tie them up. Which seemed absolutely impossible. The humming came in his ears again.

He opened another beer and raised it to his cracked lips but it slid out of his wet hand and clunked on the floor, spewing foam. Webb sagged against the work table, turning to stare at the

Messerschmitts. How wonderful they looked, how ominous. Like dragons, blunt-nosed and reptile-colored. Vern was right, he thought; the base color was a kind of tan-pink.

Webb stared at the three aircraft and he stared at his hand holding the pistol. He was going to collapse. *Not now*, he thought, *not now after* – Webb sensed a movement behind, a scraping of sand under a sole, and before he could lift the .45 he felt something hard press against the back of his neck and he heard a calm voice – nearly in his ear, it seemed – say slowly, 'This is a twelve-gauge.'

Webb was not unconscious, because he was dimly aware of what was happening around him. He was conscious of voices in German, of hands supporting him, of a helpless resignation as someone pried the .45 out of his fingers, of water pouring down his chest and lap, of cool liquid being poured into his mouth, of an icy towel wrapped over his forehead and eyes, of hands removing his web belt and going through his pockets.

He was not afraid. The hands bracing his head were wet on his cheeks, cool and caring, and he imagined Cecille. *Oh babe, I loved you, babe.*

Rudi stared with tired exasperation at Webb's form as Eric and Schilling dragged him dripping from the pool in his shorts, his head supported by Rendel.

'Get him in bed, get him covered and make him drink,' Rudi said to Eric as they passed. 'And put some oil or lotion on his arms. Major Three, stay with him the first hour.'

He watched Webb's back receding, already beginning to hate him for bumbling into the field, for being an OSI officer. Now what would they do with him?

He arranged Webb's sodden fatigues over a pool chair and walked barefoot inside to the kitchen where Marta and Theo had been watching from the window. He made himself a drink and waited for Eric to join them at the table.

'He'll be okay,' Eric said when he returned.

Rudi handed Webb's wallet to Theo. 'He's an investigative officer for the Air Force.'

'No shit, Rudi,' said Eric. 'He's a federal agent.'

'What does this mean?' Marta asked of Rudi. 'Was he looking for you, for us, for the field?'

Rudi nodded as he filled his pipe bowl.

'Then he's a prisoner?' She stared at Rudi.

'We can't exactly drop him off down at Willie now, can we?' said Eric.

'He was alone,' Rudi said to Theo, 'in an Air Force sedan. We towed the car in and put it in the hangar, emptied it completely, and put everything in that plastic bag. He was carrying a change of clothing, shoes, dress uniform. And a map. He knew what he was looking for.'

'I have seen his name,' Theo said. 'In the newspapers. Do you have the newspapers, Frau Malzahn?'

Marta brought the newspaper clippings and Theo read one and passed it to Rudi. 'Executive officer, Task Force.'

'Oh good God,' Marta said.

'No, no,' said Theo. 'It may turn out to be good luck for us. We are taking very good care of the Captain, yes? Have we not saved his life, Rudi?'

Rudi was looking out the window as he puffed on his pipe. 'We must take very good care of him.'

'He can put us in jail, can't he?' Marta said to Rudi. 'He knows the field. He knows this house. Why did you bring him here? Now he knows—'

'Marta,' said Rudi patiently. 'He'd already found the house. He had papers; the address, my name, Eric's.'

'What will we do with him?' Marta asked, looking away.

'What we will do,' said Theo through a smile, 'is set another place at the table.'

Webb became aware of someone else in the small bedroom. He did not think he had slept, yet he found himself surprised to be in a bed, in fresh underclothing. His mouth was dry, his tongue still slightly swollen. His cracked lips, still painful, had been coated with something minty he could taste, and his sunburned forearms were oiled.

The room held two other beds and a bureau. His guard, the younger man with the thick hair and mustache, sat on chair near the end of the bed, looking very interested in Webb and holding the .45 resting on his thigh. Webb could see the muzzle, the dark hole of some dead eye; it made him feel prickly.

'That's loaded,' Webb said hoarsely.

'Don't sweat it,' replied his guard. 'Drink.' He waved the .45 toward the bedside table where a tray held an ice bucket, a bowl

359

of ice with four cans of tea and a blue violet glass pitcher of what Webb assumed to be ice water.

Webb's stomach contracted as he followed the pistol muzzle back and forth. 'Jesus buddy, quit waving that weapon around, okay?'

'Hey, how the fuck do you think I felt when you came busting in the fucking hangar, waving this mother around like James fucking Bond? Start drinking, man.'

'Right.'

Webb reached over and picked a can of iced tea. It took more strength than he expected to pull the tab. He lifted the can in mock toast and downed half.

'How you feeling, Captain?'

'I'd feel better if you'd put that weapon away. You ever handle a piece like that? It's a Colt automat—'

Without answering, his guard pointed the barrel upward, pressed the magazine release with his thumb, caught the clip in his left palm as it popped out of the bottom of the grip, then rammed it back up *click* in place. He then pulled back the barrel cover assembly, glanced in the chamber, released it – a much heavier *click* – back in place, and uncocked the hammer; all of this within three seconds and with such fluid skill that Webb could only stare.

'Right,' he said finally.

'Keep drinking, Captain.'

'Right.' Webb drank more tea, looking over his guard: he wore high polished boots, soft gray uniform breeches with a black stripe down the side of each leg, and a white cotton shirt open at the neck, with the sleeves rolled up to the elbow. It looked very much like a German dress uniform without jacket.

'What's your name?' asked Webb.

'Major Nine.'

'Major Nine?'

'Yeah, but you don't need to call me sir.'

'Really.'

'Drink.'

Webb finished off the can. 'Your name is Malzahn, initial E.'

'Major Nine.'

'What's the E for? Edward? Ernie?'

There was no answer.

'What we have here,' said Webb, 'is E. Malzahn.'

'What we have here,' said Malzahn, 'is your ass in a sling.'

'Tell me.' Webb reached for another can without lifting his head from the pillow. 'Oh man,' he said wearily, then after a pause, 'Thanks, you and the others, for fixing me up.'

'Your butt was broilin' out there.'

'Tell me.'

Malzahn was fishing in his shirt pocket, keeping his other hand on the pistol and his eyes on Webb. His fingers drew out a joint. He placed the pistol down on the bureau, to Webb's relief, and then lit up, still watching. He took a good drag, then held it up as if he had just discovered it.

'Hey,' said Webb.

'Don't suppose you'd do a doobie.' He picked up the .45 again.

'Not in uniform.'

'You're not in uniform, man.'

'Right.' Webb licked his cracked lips.

Malzahn released the smoke in his lungs and then held the joint out to Webb with two fingers. 'No hassle?'

'No hassle.' Webb raised his hands palms up, then reached out to take the joint between his thumb and forefinger. Their fingers touched briefly. Webb reacted to this touching, not so that it was evident, not knowing what it was he felt, but knowing that it was okay and not faggy. He took a toke and returned it, eye to eye with Malzahn. He seemed to be a good sort of guy.

'Thanks,' he breathed, leaning back. The grass had a good green taste. In several seconds he felt a wonderful light freshness settle smoothly over his head and chest. 'Outstanding. What is it?'

'Sinsemilla. Sonoma – supposedly.'

'All right.'

Malzahn took another hit. 'You based at Willie, huh?'

'Three years. Big mess down there.'

Malzahn exhaled slowly. 'Whew . . . Number Ten.'

'Number Ten?'

'Number Ten. Very bad. They're pissed down there, huh?'

'A bit.' Webb felt wonderful. 'Whoa, this is good shit.'

Malzahn passed the joint. The second hit took Webb up like an elevator.

'So, they got the Air Force looking for us.'

'Right.' Webb passed the joint back.

'Number Ten. The FBI, too?'

'Right.'

'The FAA? The Sheriff?'

'All of the above.'

'Wow.' Malzahn pulled another toke. 'Number Ten . . . but we got you though, huh?' He grinned.

'Yeah, right. Number Ten.'

They laughed together, then grew quiet, watching each other.

'You gettin' messed up, Captain?' Malzahn asked then.

'Well, I was a lot straighter a while ago.'

'This'll do it.' Malzahn again handed Webb the joint.

'I've had a busy day,' said Webb.

'And it's not over yet.'

'Number Ten.' Webb took another hit.

'The guy you gotta watch is the CO, man. The Oberst.'

'Right. The CO . . . the Oberst.'

'Right. We call him the Herr General.'

'Okay. The general of what?'

'All the planes, man. The Staffel.'

'Right. Whew, ripped. To the tits.'

'Right. It does that. Here, have another.'

Webb took another hit. 'Hey, I know you're E. Malzahn, man. Got to be.'

'Major Nine.'

'Bullshit. It's in the phone book. You're the brother-in-law.'

'Really.'

'I mean what's going on here, man?'

'You mean the planes?'

'I mean the whole *thing*, man.'

'Right.'

'They're all Luftwaffe aces, yeah?'

Malzahn stared back, stoned away. Smoke crept out of his nostrils. Eventually he passed the remainder of the joint.

'Did you ever wonder,' Webb asked slowly, staring at the ceiling from his pillow, 'why they did this?'

There was no reply.

'Would you know the reason . . . if you heard it?' He took the last hit. He was flying now.

Malzahn was watching Webb with a smugly vacant expression, nearly a smile. Then shaking his head.

'Me either,' said Webb. 'Though I thought I did.'

'Outasight.'

'Outasight is right.'

'So. How you doin', Captain?'

'Outstanding.'

'We got to get you dressed soon, man. Class A's for dinner.'

'I'm not exactly calm.'

'Right,' said Malzahn absently. 'What are we supposed to be doing?' He squinted at the wall.

'Getting dressed for dinner?' Webb suggested.

'Right. How long we got?'

'You're asking me, man? I'm the guest, remember?'

'Right. Eight, always at eight. What time is it?'

Webb found his watch on the little table. 'Eight-fifteen.'

'Okay, then we have fifteen minutes.'

Webb studied his watch again. 'On the other hand, we might be fifteen minutes late.'

'Oh Christ.' Malzahn sat up. 'Get dressed quick.'

'Right. Dressed.'

Webb got up and staggered off to the bathroom, with Malzahn's help. He found his kit there and he shaved, then took his uniform from the closet. The room seemed to tilt. 'Shirt,' he said.

'Right. Start with shirt.'

'Take shirt off hanger and . . . so on.'

'Right.' Malzahn watched. 'You messed up the buttons, man.'

Webb looked down. He rebuttoned the shirt, then pulled on his trousers. As he stood up, there was a quick knock on the door and Rudi Felbeck – Webb was certain – came in. He was wearing the same clothing as Malzahn and the gray uniform jacket of a German officer.

'Well Captain, how are you feeling? You look as if you've recovered.' Felbeck smiled cordially, inspecting him.

'Okay.' Webb was startled by the uniform. Like the movies.

'Good. Our officers are looking forward to meeting you.'

'Yessir.'

'Then—' Felbeck turned to Malzahn and seemed to inspect him too – 'if Major Nine is ready, we are ready.' As he went out the door he turned back to say, 'Now.'

CHAPTER TWENTY-THREE

With Eric leading, Webb proceeded down the hall, wobbly, using his fingertips on the wall to steady himself. He could feel his pulse at his temples. Stoned, he decided. On anticipation. Oh man.

When he entered the dining room, the sight of the five German pilots standing in line wearing gray dress uniforms and high black boots caused him to take a deep breath, brace his shoulders, and try to be just a little taller than he was. Was this what they called a receiving line? Across the long dining table, set with shining china, crystal, and lit candles, he saw a blond woman pouring water from a glass pitcher, her brown arms flashing gold bracelets in the candlelight. The one driving the Buick.

'Captain Webb.' Felbeck smiling. 'We are delighted to have you as our guest. May I present the officers of 76 Staffel.'

The proximity of the German officers seemed to rob Webb of his speech. Felbeck took him by the elbow as he turned to the first officer in line.

'Oberst, may I present Captain James Webb, United States Air Force. Captain, our Commanding Officer, Oberst One.'

Though he looked nothing at all like any Hollywood German officer, the Commander of 76 Staffel filled Webb with an immediate cold respect; grayed, tan, lean, and immaculately uniformed, the Oberst's squinted gaze and weathered visage revealed him clearly for what he was: pilot, military elite. No stranger to this aura among veteran Air Force officers, Webb nonetheless was surprised to find the architect of 76 Staffel chillingly familiar. Killer, man. Webb could not decide whether to offer his hand or do nothing; his indecision led him to nod once in acknowledgement.

'Ah, Captain Webb,' said the Oberst. 'Is it not customary to salute a superior officer in the Air Force of the United States?'

'I was not aware,' Webb replied carefully, 'that you were an officer of the United States Air Force.'

The Oberst kept his smile through pursed lips, curiously regarding Webb in a silence that Webb thought would never end.

'I see,' the Oberst said finally. 'Perhaps my English? However, this is a military unit, Captain. Under the circumstances you may choose, as an officer, to recognize military courtesy.' The Oberst paused. His voice, Webb noticed, had grown as brittle as his gaze. 'Your treatment as our guest may depend upon your attitude in this matter. Is my English good enough to make myself understood?'

Having won his point, Webb was now prepared to reply. 'Yes sir.'

The Oberst waited. Webb then felt a poke in his back just beneath his shoulder blades; he knew it was Malzahn behind him. Webb executed a precise salute.

The Oberst responded with an equally precise salute and offered his hand. '*Es freut mich ausserordentlich Sie kennenzulernen.*'

'The translation, Captain,' explained Rudi, 'is I am very pleased, very happy, to make your acquaintance.'

'We all speak English, Captain,' said the Oberst, 'though we do not all speak German. So English it will be.' He turned to the officer at his left. 'Captain, I present Major Five—'

Webb shook hands mechanically with the slight balding officer with thin white hair, odd flat eyes behind tinted glasses, and a smile that Webb sensed immediately was derived solely from the occasion of his capture.

'— and Major Eight.' Webb recognized Major Eight as one of the men in the hangar, the bearish one who had looked like a tired grandfather in sweaty clothes. In uniform, however, he was every bit the officer that his ribbons, and the Maltese cross at his throat, revealed.

'— and Major Three.'

Major Three shook hands tightly, smiled without showing his teeth. He was thin-faced and sharp-nosed and white-haired and his eyes seemed tired beneath dark brows. Webb remembered him from the hangar. Major Three was even more the epitome of a Luftwaffe fighter pilot, and Webb found him only slightly less fearful than the Oberst and Major Five. Major Three – as if he wore it like a mantle – was a gunfighter. Major Gunfighter.

'And our hostess, Frau—' the Oberst hesitated. The blond had come up on Webb to his right. He could smell her perfume.

'—Malzahn,' finished Webb with a hint of mischief.

'It's Marta, Captain, please.' She offered her hand and gave Webb a nervous smile; glossy lips and perfect teeth. Up close Webb found Marta Malzahn to be older than he expected, older than her husband surely. She was the type of woman one saw stepping from white Eldorados, rich brown legs flashing, in front of expensive restaurants. Webb resisted the temptation to drop his eyes below the delicate gold snake-scale necklace draped over tanned clavicles. Oh, such a nice pair. Over the hill, but slick.

'You will sit here, by our hostess, Captain.' Rudi guided Webb to the table like a *maître'd* as the others moved to their places.

After waiting for Marta to be seated, Webb put himself gingerly into his chair, finding his equilibrium coming and going. He unfolded his napkin. Bingo this all right, he thought. Oh Jesus Bingo. He was momentarily overcome by a profound sense of relief, of accomplishment. It wouldn't matter what happened now; he was *here*. With Marta seated alone at the foot of the table to his right, and Eric directly across from him, Webb then noticed the two empty place settings, to his left between him and Major – he was too ripped to remember the stupid numbers – Major Gunfighter.

At the head of the table the Oberst sat down last, in a chair larger than the others, with the Major that Webb didn't like – Five, he thought – on his right.

Webb knew that everyone at the table was looking at him, especially the Oberst. And Malzahn grinning privately. Webb reached for his water; mysteriously, it fell over at his touch. Malzahn laughed. Marta snatched up the towel from the wine bucket and tamped up the water from the tablecloth.

Major Five began to ladle out white soup. In the background, from another room, a stereo played slow and measured music, classical, that Webb found soothing.

'If we had known you'd be joining us, Captain,' said Rudi, 'we might have prepared something more traditional. Like schnitzel or sauerkraut. As it is, we will have to make do with vichyssoise . . . breast of chicken with mustard sauce . . . a variety of wines and, I think, some champagne for the occasion.'

'Fine. This is fine,' replied Webb. 'I am pleased to be here.'

'Oh right,' said Malzahn, looking down at his soup bowl as Major Five filled it.

'And how are you feeling, Captain?' Marta asked.

'Very well, thank you. And thank you all, for looking after me.'

'You would have done the same for any of us,' said the Oberst. 'Yes?'

'Certainly, sir,' Webb was quick to answer. He gave the word *sir* a carefully balanced inflection, neither too formal nor quite disrespectful. He knew it could be unsettling if one listened closely; it was one of his finely honed military skills.

'You were fortunate.' Major Five spoke with a strong accent as he moved behind Webb to serve his soup. 'The Oberstleutnant said that the vultures were keeping you company. You might have died, yes?' The hand and the ladle came before Webb and he recoiled from the brush of the gray uniform sleeve at his shoulder. He did not reply.

'You have to eat your soup fast,' said Malzahn, 'before it gets cold, Captain.'

Rudi was pouring white wine at each place. Webb noticed that he filled the two glasses at the empty places, too. 'Are you a career officer, Captain?' He asked, pouring Webb's.

'Yessir. Going for six now.'

'And how do you find it, the Air Force?' asked the Oberst.

'Fine, sir. Boring at times. Until now.'

'Ah,' said the Oberst, 'nothing is more boring than the military when there is no fighting. But the Air Force, any Air Force, is not boring when you can fly. Do you fly, Captain?'

'Not in the service. My eyes. But I have a civilian license.'

'Ahh, very good. Do you love flying, Captain?'

'Very much, sir. Though I can't afford it often. I have always wanted to fly a fighter, a piston fighter.'

'Well.' The Oberst reached for his wine. 'Perhaps you will.'

'Yessir. Someday.' Webb skipped a beat. 'I was at Chino last Saturday. On the flight line, by the display aircraft, taking photographs. It was sort of a grandstand seat, you might say.'

Major Five leaned forward. 'And were the spectators entertained, Captain?'

'Most were.' Webb was remembering the fireman screaming and writhing on the pavement, his blood pumping squirting bright cold red on the shiny yellow slicker. It made him a little sick. 'There were many photographs. Very impressive, eight perfect Gustavs . . . sand filters . . . retractable Galland hoods . . . the heraldry.'

'How is it that you know of a Galland hood?' asked Rudi.

'I am a student of aerial combat over Europe in the Second World War. It's my hobby, the aircraft, the history.'

'Hobby?' repeated Major Bear.

'*Es ist ein Amerikanisches Wort für Freizeit,*' explained Rudi.

'The good Willy Messerschmitt would have been pleased.' Webb was paying undue attention to finishing his soup. He was very hungry.

'Haha. Herr Messerschmitt would have been very pleased,' said Major Five.

'And,' Webb continued, 'if Colonel Lowen shows up, Mr Schmued would be very pleased, too.'

'I'm sorry, Captain,' said the Oberst. 'Mr Schmued?'

'Edgar Schmued. Sir. The designer of the Mustang. He's living in California now. I believe he is Bavarian.'

'Is this so?' asked the Oberst.

'Of course, it must be,' said Major Five. 'It is reasonable.'

'Well, gentlemen.' The Oberst raised his wine glass. 'We will have a drink to Willy Messerschmitt. And to Edgar Schmued. And to our guest, Captain James Webb.'

Glasses were raised around the table. Webb lifted his own, acknowledging the honor by nodding once in turn to both sides of the table and taking his sip last.

'Do you have a family, Captain?' asked Marta.

'No ma'am. Divorced. The soup was very good.'

'Thank you. Do have more.'

'And the music. Very nice.'

'Bach,' Marta said. 'Do you know Bach, Captain?'

'Ah, no ma'am. Not really.'

'What kind of music do you like, Captain?' Marta took up her wine goblet and leaned towards him. He again resisted looking at her cleavage.

'Ah . . . Pink Floyd, Eagles, Linda Ronstadt, Randy Newman . . . and, ah, the Stones.'

'Well, these are Bach's Brandenburg Concertos. This one, the sixth, is my favorite.'

'Very pleasant.'

'Bach,' Marta went on as if no one else was listening, 'was one of the greatest composers of all time. Like Beethoven, Brahms. All Germans. Germans wrote most of the world's greatest music. Did you know that, Captain?'

'Ah, I think so. Yes ma'am. Like Wagner?'

'Yes, Wagner—' She corrected his pronunciation to *Vogner*. 'All German composers.'

'Marta,' said her husband without looking at her. 'Why don't you have a hit?'

Marta ignored the question, or appeared to. Webb looked down at his empty soup bowl.

'Did you ever shoot down an airplane, Captain?' she asked, smiling.

Startled, Webb looked up. 'No ma'am.'

'This is a . . . a club . . . of airplane shooter-downers, did you know that? Every man in this room has shot down an airplane.' She looked around the table, holding her smile, her chin a little high.

'Except me,' Malzahn said quickly.

Rudi suddenly smacked his hand palm down on the table, jarring the conversation, and all movement, to a stop. He glared at Marta.

Webb watched, intrigued.

Marta, still smiling, resumed eating as if nothing unusual had been said. It was clear that some sort of feud was going on and Webb concluded that she alone was at odds with the others. She would be keeping house for all them; he wondered how long the pilots had been living under her roof, Malzahn's roof. Weeks? Months? *Years*?

When the main course was being served, Webb noticed that a lot of wine was going around – Major Five was plenty quick with those green bottles.

There was white chicken in mustard sauce, better than any food Webb could remember, and peas with tiny onions, and white buttered potatoes sprinkled with bits of parsley. He looked

369

around the dining room, feeling mellow and content. Through the glass windows overlooking the pool, the sunset dusted warm orange light over the white tablecloth. All very elegant, the crystal and wispy yellow flames of white tapers, the gentle metallic clink of cutlery and the fluid mechanical cadence of Bach.

'You know, Captain,' Rudi said, 'we are all rather curious about how you managed to find the airfield. And how you happened to be alone.'

'Yessir,' Webb replied, separating a chunk of soft chicken with his knife and keeping his eyes on the plate. He weighed his words as he formed them, wondering whether anything he said might somehow be interpreted as collaborating with the enemy. An odd enemy. 'There were aircraft registrations, the FAA. For Sunwest Aviation in Los Angeles.' He looked up at Malzahn. 'And for this address. I followed the van.'

'Ah,' said the Oberst, 'but why were you alone?'

Webb took a sip of wine to mix with the chicken and sauce – God, it was delicious – then halved one of the little potatoes with his fork. Deliberately he neither replied nor looked up.

'Interesting,' the Oberst went on, just as if Webb had answered. 'No helicopters . . . no Marines . . . no police cars. Just the Captain. His vehicle disabled. Braving the desert for miles.' He turned to Rudi. 'How many miles?'

'About six.'

'Six. Courageous of you Captain. Don't you agree, gentlemen?'

'*Aber der Fuchs hat den Hund gefangen,*' sniffed Major Five.

Major Gunfighter looked over at Webb. 'The fox has captured the hound,' he translated.

'Nonetheless!' said the Oberst with spirit. 'He deserves to be congratulated, yes? For courage, for somehow arranging events . . . in the sequence . . . where he now finds himself in dress uniform, sipping our fine champagne and dining at our table. You see, that is where he is, yes?' The Oberst's small eyes nearly crinkled closed from the width of his smile.

Major Gunfighter looked over to Webb, chewing as he spoke. 'I would say that the Captain is either very lucky or very clever. Which is it, Captain?'

'Both, Major.' Webb was pleased to see that his reply brought a trace of bemusement to Major Gunfighter's face.

'Or,' Major Five suggested, 'the Captain stumbled on the airfield by an accident.'

'Nonetheless,' said the Oberst, 'here he is. We cause our own accidents. So what is the difference, yes?'

'*Er ist ein verdammtes Problem*,' said Major Five, returning sullenly to his food. '*Ein Gluck dass er nicht sicher war die Andern zu fangen.*'

Webb glanced around, hoping for a translation.

'If he had gone back for the others,' said the Oberst to Major Five, 'we wouldn't be drinking champagne here, would we? And if the others knew where the Captain had gone, they would have been here by now. Isn't that true? So you see, everything is going well.'

Webb was beginning to have a very good time, maybe the most exciting time of his life. Even when he thought about being a prisoner, even when he admitted that it had been a brilliant and decisive blunder to come alone without telling anyone, he simply slammed his mind's door on such thoughts . . . since here they were and, as the Oberst had pointed out, here he was. So to hell with it. He thought about the prescription then.

Major Bear, who had spoken but once during the entire meal, stood and began clearing away the dishes. Major Five poured champagne. Webb noticed that Major Five poured with a less than steady hand. And that his own hand was less than steady. Getting loaded. Marta smiled; she was getting loaded, and looking better loaded. With dessert and coffee, Major Bear distributed small crystal glasses and then placed a bottle of clear liqueur on the table.

'Are you drinking man, Captain?' the Oberst asked.

'Now and again. Sir.'

'Do you know what schnapps is, Captain?'

'Of course. I happen to like it. Sir.'

'Good, good.' The Oberst smiled.

'Is this to be another contest?' asked Marta. 'To see who can keep from throwing up first? Why don't you leave this man alone? He nearly died today. That would have made three.'

Uh oh, thought Webb. Here we go again.

'Marta,' warned her husband.

'Fuck off,' she snapped back without looking at him.

'Really ma'am,' said Webb in haste. 'I'm feeling fine.'

'Yes, I know, Captain.' She smiled coldly. 'You're just like the rest of them. Another hero. You'll drink until you fall out of your chair rather than suffer the *disgrace* of saying no.'

'Well ma'am—'

'And you—' Marta looked past him to Major Gunfighter – 'quit grinning like a fucking ape! There's nothing funny about this!'

'Marta,' said Malzahn. 'Lighten up, for crissake.'

Marta turned to her husband, calmly, Webb thought, and then looked at the others. She took her napkin and folded it on the table. 'I am sorry . . . for my manners. Especially with you as our guest, Captain. I know you are completely *mortified* that a woman should come to your defense. But on the other hand . . .' She shook her head in a nervous bird-like gesture.

Webb waited for the last phrase which never came.

'Frau Malzahn,' the Oberst said then, 'Captain Webb is our guest. We are not forcing him to drink.'

'That's true, Marta,' said Rudi.

'I'm fine, ma'am. Really.'

Marta appeared to have heard nothing. Webb could feel the contained pressure of her anger and he consciously kept his knees a little to his left under the table to keep from bumping hers.

'Then drink,' she said. 'I'm not leaving this table.'

'It is a pleasure, Frau Malzahn,' Major Bear spoke up unexpectedly in a kindly voice. 'To have your company. A great pleasure. We are having . . . pressure, tension. This is a fine meal, a good experience. Try to be calm.'

Marta looked up at him without expression. Major Bear turned to the Oberst at the other end of the table. 'Perhaps, Oberst, the Captain is fearful of his safety, you see. But he does not seem so.'

The Oberst looked down the table at Webb. 'Are you fearful, Captain?'

Puzzled, Webb hesitated. 'Not at the moment. Sir.'

'Perhaps, Oberst,' Major Bear continued, 'the Captain feels like the prisoner and he would like to leave. Instead of drinking with us. Frau Malzahn is right; he has had the difficult day. He may be too weary . . . to drink.'

'He does not look weary,' said the Oberst. '*Wass planst du*, Rendel?'

'No, no, I'm fine,' said Webb. 'Really.'

'This is not a war, Frau Malzahn,' Major Bear turned back to Marta. 'There are no prisoners.' He then turned to the Oberst again. '*Oberst, sollen wir vielleicht den Feldwebel fragen, ob er gehen will.*'

'Captain,' the Oberst said to Webb, 'Major Eight suggests . . . that we ask you if you wish to leave. So we are asking you now: do you wish to leave?'

Webb stared at the Oberst, then at Rudi, and at Major Gunfighter, who still seemed amused. And then at Malzahn, who still seemed amused and stoned.

'Now?'

'If you wish. Though it would be a pleasure to continue to have you as our guest.'

'Just . . . get up and leave?'

'We would summon the taxi perhaps,' said Major Bear.

Webb was without words. Were they serious? What the fuck would he do then? Find a telephone? Call Butler? Call Lowen? Call out the Marines? Oh man.

'We can fix your car tomorrow, maybe,' Rudi said. 'And we will return your side-arm, of course.'

Oh man, thought Webb. Would they bail out of the house in thirty minutes? Leave the food on the table? The champagne still bubbling in the glasses? Would they fly the 109s away in the dark? Was this a trick? Would they shoot him down in the driveway? He pictured the scenarios; taking a taxi to the closest telephone and calling Butler; the Sheriff and FBI surrounding the house and finding it empty; the Marines piling into choppers; him leading a convoy of vehicles across the desert in the dark to find the hangars – empty. Oh man.

He looked over at Malzahn, making no attempt to hide his frustration. Malzahn shrugged. Just one thought then struck Webb with more apprehension than any other; if he left the Staffel, they would somehow vanish, escape. Such a possibility was enough to make his heart stop.

'You see,' said the Oberst, 'tomorrow evening it will be over. We will be gone. If you do not leave now, you must wait until then.'

It occurred to Webb that, so long as he stayed, the Staffel would not be attacked if they knew he was with them. If they knew . . . but they did not know, not yet. Oh man.

'I will leave tomorrow,' said Webb.

'You see, Frau Malzahn,' said Major Bear, pouring himself some schnapps, 'the Captain is choosing to stay. I will drink to you, Captain.' He raised the small crystal glass. 'You are a good officer of the Air Force. I wish you the best luck, but . . . not quite as much best luck as I wish to the rest of us. *Prosit.*' Major Bear drank.

'Captain,' Marta said, 'is it clear that you have been given the chance to leave? To leave tonight?'

'Yes ma'am.'

'Marta,' said her husband. 'Please.'

'Do you think, Frau Malzahn,' said Major Bear, 'that we will be attacked with shooting if Captain Webb is having our dinner together?'

'Captain?' Marta turned to Webb. 'Can we expect the Marines to descend upon us before dessert is served? It would be such an inconvenience.'

'No ma'am. I don't think so.'

Malzahn was grinning into his coffee. Major Gunfighter had poured himself some schnapps and now he held the bottle across the empty place settings to Webb.

'Captain, if you please.' Marta held up her glass. Webb poured it half full.

'Full, please,' she commanded.

Webb could smell the sweet peppermint alcohol as he poured. He looked up to see Malzahn watching his wife as he took the bottle from Webb, poured his own, and passed it on.

'To you, Captain,' the Oberst said. 'For succeeding in finding us.'

They all drank, including Webb.

'What a shame . . .' mused the Oberst, 'that the Colonel Lowen could not come to dinner with us as well, eh?' The others laughed – except Marta, Webb noticed. 'Do you know the Colonel Lowen, Captain?'

'Yes sir.'

'Ah . . . I wonder how he is, the Colonel.'

'He's pissed. Sir.'

The others laughed again – except Marta.

'Pissed?' echoed Major Bear.

'*Dass ist ein Amerikanishen Ausdruck für wenn mann die Schnauze voll hat,*' explained Rudi.

Major Bear laughed even more than the others then.

'Has he found some pilots, some guns for his wolves?' The Oberst was speaking to Webb, who was watching the schnapps coming around again.

'Wolves?'

'We called the American fighters wolves,' said Major Five. 'And the B-17s . . . elephants.'

'Charming,' Marta spoke up, 'how you all give such playful names to the weapons you use to kill each other. Like they were made by Walt Disney. Yes, Captain? Yes, Herr Oberst?'

Neither Webb nor the Oberst answered. Webb was watching Malzahn dump his schnapps over his ice cream; it seemed like a good idea.

'Rudi once told me,' continued Marta, 'that we called the English "Tommy", and that they called us "Jerry". Like the little mice in the cartoons. Yes, Rudi? And Eric called the enemy "Charlie", I think. And they fought with weapons called Blooper and Willie Peter. Even his helicopter was named Huey. Such fun.'

Malzahn, mushing his ice cream slowly with his spoon, gave Marta a weary look.

'Eric . . .' murmured Webb, staring at Malzahn. 'That's a nice name, Eric.'

Eric glanced up. 'Number Ten.'

Webb almost smiled. He liked Eric Malzahn. He also liked Marta, but wished she would go away because she was protecting him and because she would make a fool of herself with all the drinking. Or worse yet, *he* might make a fool of himself, might end up tossing his cookies in front of her, too. He watched Major Gunfighter refill his glass and pass the bottle over. Things were certainly going in that direction.

'Colonel Lowen went home. To Texas,' said Webb.

'He is a good pilot, this Colonel?' asked Major Five.

Webb hesitated before answering. 'Six confirmed in Europe.'

'Haha—' the Oberst grinned. 'Two of them are sitting at this table.'

'As I recall, Captain,' said Rudi, 'your group is called a Task Force.'

Webb said nothing. Less stoned, he was now more apprehensive.

'The newspapers said you are . . . what was it – Executive Officer?' Rudi looked up at him, raising the napkin to his mouth.

'And your Commander,' said the Oberst. 'He is a Colonel, yes?'

Still Webb gave no reply.

'Colonel Butler,' said Rudi.

'Your Commander Butler must be having a busy time.' The Oberst poured himself another schnapps. 'Maybe he is having a good time, a challenge. A reason to have an alert. To arm. A small war to fight, all his own. A relief from the boredom.' The Oberst watched Webb with a thin smile. 'And now you don't come back. Haha. Very busy time.'

'I think he is doing what he sees best to do. Sir.'

'No doubt! No doubt! I do not demean your Commander, Captain. Not at all, not at all. Obviously, he was shrewd enough to select you. And it is you who have found us.' He passed the bottle to Major Five. 'We are sitting here, having a fine time, while your Commander is wondering what has happened to his Captain the Executive Officer, yes?'

Webb glanced at his watch, wondering what Butler was doing. Major Gunfighter passed him the bottle.

'He must expect much from you, your Commander,' the Oberst went on, watching Webb. 'What does he expect from you, Captain?'

Webb gained a few seconds to think by pouring his schnapps slowly. He could feel his stomach doing odd things and his arms getting numb at the elbows.

'My mission,' he said, 'was to determine the location of your airfield. And to terminate your operation.'

'Well, you are halfway there, Captain,' said Major Five.

The others laughed. Loaded, Webb thought, all getting loaded. Oh man, and me too. He glanced at Marta, who was not laughing. Well if anyone was keeping score, he was keeping up. Marta held out her little glass again for him to fill.

'Tell me Captain,' continued the Oberst. 'Did you expect to round us all up, like the cowboys, and tie us all up with cowboy rope?'

'I don't know. Sir. I, ah, wasn't thinking too clearly.'

The Oberst nodded for what seemed a long time, reminding Webb of Vern, then he said, 'Are we the villains, Captain?'

'Sir?'

'Are we the villains . . . and you the secret agent?'

'Sounds close. Sir.'

'Ah, are we the Nazi villains?'

'Sir?' Webb felt the water getting deep.

'It must be disappointing. Not a monocle among us. Not even a swastika armband.'

'Not disappointed. Sir.'

'Is that the way your Commander Butler sees us? And the Colonel Lowen?'

'I don't know. Sir.'

'Is that how you see us, Captain?'

'I'm not really sure of that. Sir.' Webb remembered Lowen saying something about the swastikas on the tailfins . . . the same as being on the armbands.

'Well, we are!' The Oberst leaned back in the big chair. 'Or at least we were, as military fighter pilots, as the best in the world! . . . but—' the Oberst leaned forward with his elbow on the table, now speaking quietly—'but of course you are thinking of the campe, yes?'

'Yes . . .' continued the Oberst, 'as everyone inevitably makes the association. The three go hand in hand. German . . . thus Nazi . . . thus the camps, yes?'

Webb looked down at his glass, then glanced up. The Oberst's eyes were not, as he expected, on him or anyone else, but on his own glass.

'Well, Captain.' The Oberst paused, turning the liqueur glass by its stem, studying it. 'All there is to say about that . . . is that no German at that time can be innocent . . . but not all are guilty.' He looked up, across the table at Webb. 'You see, it is something – a curse – that all Germans must live with for . . . forever. Forever . . . forever.'

The only person at the table Webb could bring himself to look at was Eric. He found Eric looking back at him.

'The next time,' the Oberst continued, 'it will be Ivan. Your Air Force should worry about Ivan as much as we do; Ivan gained more in the war than anyone.

'And the Japanese, in the end, have beaten you. Because you let them. The second Pearl Harbor was in Detroit, yes? Haha, who would have imagined? Not fighters or bombers. Not tanks, but televisions! Not artillery, but automobiles! Datsuns and Toyotas and Hondas.'

'What a shame. What foolish . . . priorities Americans have. Letting any parasite into your country; the refuse of Indochina and Vietnam, the heathens with oil money from the Middle East. Money. Leeches to weaken you. None of them are required to do military service. No passion for freedom. Because they have not earned it.'

Webb had a sudden bitter flashback from the Chino airshow when he stood, hand to heart, for the national anthem while all around him others – half-drunk rocker punks and fat-gut men with expensive cameras – did not.

'This fat country where power is measured in money, in megatons, and not in the *integrity*—' the Oberst fired the word out of his mouth like an arrow – 'and in the *dedication* of its military . . . its people.'

The Oberst turned to Rudi. 'Am I not correct, Oberstleutnant? You would know.'

Rudi was fooling with his pipe, not looking up. 'For its faults, Oberst, it is still . . . a desirable system.'

'And you, Major Three?'

'It is a point of view, Oberst.'

'Well . . .' The Oberst picked a cigarette from a red-and-gold box. 'Ivan will wake you up someday. In the next war the Americans will be so busy airlifting hamburgers to their troops that they will lose the war while they are eating their Whoppers.'

Eric spoke suddenly, 'Well, they're gonna *waste* your ass, Theo. Those boys from Luke are gonna zap you. Or that Mustang ace in Texas. In either case, they're gonna come in swinging.'

'Major,' said Rudi tightly, 'you are speaking to your Commander.'

'They're gonna waste your ass, Rudi!'

'Major,' said Rudi more tightly, 'you will address me as Oberstleutnant.'

'Perhaps a more literal translation,' the Oberst said calmly, 'of the term "come in swinging"?'

'Major, you will control yourself,' warned Rudi.

'Hey, I'm just telling you how it's gonna be, man.' Eric put more respect in his voice. 'It means, Oberst, they kick the door in, right off the fuckin' hinges. Nobody says hello. And they start shooting. That business with the F-5 was only a taste; next time there'll be a dozen of those mothers. And they'll be hot. And that jockey down in Texas could show up with every goddamned fighter in the Confederate Air Force, loaded to the teeth. Like the man said –' he nodded at Webb – 'they're pissed.'

Webb was stirred by Eric's words, as if they had opened a vein. Eric was right and he knew he was right and Webb knew he was right.

And the Oberst's name was Theo; how surprising that it didn't seem like a German name.

'Then,' said Theo, 'aren't you glad that the Captain is with us?'

'It may not make any difference, when it hits the fan,' Eric said.

'Hits the fan?' repeated Major Bear, slumped in his chair, waving an unlighted cigar.

Oh man, thought Webb, a little more fear creeping in through his very comfortable alcoholic haze. *Think*. If there was a chance to make some sort of deal, anything that would keep them and Lowen from each other's throats, then this was it.

'He's right,' Webb said. 'There is time. We could . . . make a deal.'

'A deal.' There was sarcasm in Theo's voice. 'What kind of deal, Captain?'

'If this, your operation, was suspended . . . I could make some, ah, arrangement.'

'We have made the necessary arrangements, Captain,' said Theo. 'And you are in no position to make a deal.'

'I can stop the Air Force. I can stop Colonel Lowen.'

'You do not understand,' said Rudi. 'We don't want to stop Colonel Lowen.'

'No killing, no fighting,' Webb said, very drunk.

'Listen to him, Rudi,' Marta pleaded.

'Stay out of this, Marta,' said Eric.

'What is it you want?' she said. 'To kill each other, yes? Why? *Why?*'

'It is a contest, Frau Malzahn,' Theo said patiently. 'War is the ultimate contest. It has always been that way. Always there has been war. Always there will be. It is the way we are . . . All men.'

'It is the way *you* are, Herr Oberst!' she hissed. 'Not all men, *not all men*. If there is always war it is because of men like you, men of power.'

'Frau Malzahn, men of power, ultimately, always prevail.'

Marta paused. 'The Captain,' she said, barely in control, 'is asking that this be stopped. I am asking, *begging*, you to stop. It *can* be stopped.'

'Do you think so, Frau Malzahn?' Theo spoke with such calm sadness that Webb felt another cold quiver. 'Do you think the good Captain here can stop anything? Do you think I do not understand his Commander, the Colonel Butler with the jet fighters at his fingertips? I know what his orders are without seeing them, Frau Malzahn. And I know the Colonel Lowen who is flying his Mustang thirty-one years after the war, though I have not met him. Do you think he will stop? Do you think he will call for help from the Commander Butler to bring his jets? Do you think he will do that?'

'It does not matter what—'

'*Do you think he will do that, Frau Malzahn?*' Theo's words thundered across the tableware with such force that Webb cringed.

He glanced at Marta without moving his head. Never had he seen a woman look so helplessly enraged; her green eyes seemed to shoot darts of fury across the table at Theo. She said nothing back, only stared, motionless except for the soft shelf of her bosom rising with each breath.

'Now,' Theo said, composed, 'I will tell you that as long as the Captain is our guest . . . they will not attack us. And I will tell you, Frau Malzahn, that the Colonel Lowen will meet us tomorrow as we agreed.

'There is no need to be frightened. And there is no deal, Captain. We are doing exactly as we planned to do. And it is exactly as the Colonel Lowen wants to do, yes? And perhaps –' here he smiled – 'it is exactly what the Commander Butler wants him to do, yes? Who knows? It is a little contest, the last contest. And when it is all over, tomorrow, we will all be gone. So you may relax, Captain. And you, Frau Malzahn, may relax as well.'

Marta looked around the table, 'All of you could leave, this moment, and escape.'

'All of us know that, Marta,' said Rudi.

'Then all of you are insane.'

She arranged the folded napkin squarely at the side of her empty cup and saucer in a pointless gesture that Webb found . . courageous. Then she stood and repeated; 'Insane.'

The others stood, Webb last, swaying. Marta turned to him

380

and held out her hand. 'Goodnight, Captain. I hope you sleep well.'

Webb nodded. 'Ma'am.' Her hand trembled in his, electric, and then she turned and left.

Major Five took his seat, Eric and Major Bear staggered toward the bathroom. Major Gunfighter poured himself coffee. Only the Oberst Theo stood at his place, watching Webb. In the den Webb could see Rudi placing records on the turntable; he then heard the first bars of a familiar waltz.

'Strauss, Captain,' said Theo. 'The music of Vienna. Pleasant, yes?'

'Yes sir.' Webb felt for a second as if he were alone in the room with Theo. Major Gunfighter and Major Five leaned back in their chairs. Theo moved his head back and forth in time with the music.

It seemed impossible that the chance for making a deal with the Staffel had come and gone, dismissed in a sentence or two. No one seemed to be afraid of anything. Webb sat down, numb from the drinking, from disappointment. There was still schnapps in his glass. He braced both his elbows and rested heavily on the table, staring at the little goblet of clear liqueur. Now there was only the plan with the prescription. He looked at his watch: 2148 hours. There was no time left, just minutes. Anyone would know that any drugstore would close by ten.

Drunkenly, Webb tipped his head left and right like a metronome; the music made him both melancholy and happy. The others returned to the table. Eric was barely able to get into his chair.

'Major Three.' Theo turned to Major Gunfighter. 'There is a bottle in the freezer. If you please.'

When Major Gunfighter returned with the bottle – Webb saw it was Finnish vodka – Theo had him pour a round in fresh glassware. Now Webb counted six glasses at his place: water, two wine, champagne, schnapps, and now vodka. Oh man. Vodka seemed incomprehensible to him now. And now was the time.

'Drugstore closes,' he said thickly. 'At ten. Sir.'

'Drugstore?' echoed Rudi.

'Prescription,' said Webb. 'Request permission. To make telephone call. Medicine. They need twenty-four hours.' He took the orange plastic vial from his pocket and set it on the table. 'All gone . . . Friday. One telephone call.'

Webb was surprised to feel himself break out in perspiration, as if he were truly ill. Oh man. One telephone call. Butler or Lowen? Choose, Captain. Call'em up, call up the flying monkeys. Oh man. What had Lowen said? *If you get lucky, Captain, and find them first, tell me where to find them. It might save a few lives.*

Do it, he thought. Lowen was right. Helicopters whickering up dust clouds, Marines spilling out, F-5s cruising among the mesas, bristling with blue Sidewinders. Oh man. Lowen.

'One telephone call,' said Rudi, getting to his feet, his arm rubbery on the table for support.

Webb held up the orange vial so everyone could see it. He thought of praying. Then a gray-uniformed arm – Rudi's – placing a telephone in front of him. Oh man, give me a break, on the fuckin' table.

'One telephone call,' said Rudi again, weaving back to his chair.

Webb stared at the phone. It was beige and shiny and had pushbuttons. He looked up at Rudi, and then at the Oberst Theo, slightly hunched, his head settled drunkenly between gray shoulders. Through his cigarette smoke that rose upward and roiled at his face, the Oberst's small dark eyes were locked on Webb's.

'Make your call, Captain,' he said.

'Yes sir. Thank you.'

Webb picked up the vial and pretended to read it while he reached for the telephone with his other hand. He saw the Oberst lean back, shift in his seat, one hand sliding into his jacket and pulling out something he laid carefully on the table; a pistol, little and ugly and squarish. Webb could see down the muzzle. Oh God. Oh man, the Area Code, the *Area Code* please, 403 yes. Webb refused to look at the pistol. He dialed; the line hummed, clicked, buzzed, clicked, began ringing . . .

'Hello?' It would be Lowen's wife; he had forgotten her name. There was no way to ask for Lowen.

'My name is Webb, W-e-b-b, James Webb. Would you take down this prescription number for refill?'

'I'm sorry?' She had a very pleasant voice.

'Yes.' Webb held up the vial and pretended to read.

'A-A-A-K-14-S-W,' he said methodically, sweating now.

'I think you must have the wrong number.'

'No, no,' Webb said. 'Three As, then K-fourteen, then S and W. Got it? Okay, and thank you.'

He hung up and glanced at the Oberst Theo watching, one hand on top of the other, the pistol still there, his eyes like tiny marbles under shadowed gray brows.

Rudi got to his feet. 'One telephone call,' he said cheerfully, coming around the table.

'Thank you, sir.'

The Oberst Theo watched him still. Rudi came to Webb's side and reached for the telephone.

'Leave it,' Theo commanded sharply. Webb's heartbeat took off again. Rudi withdrew his hand and made his way back to his seat.

'What is your ailment, Captain?' asked Theo. 'The medicine?'

'Allergy, sir.' Webb had been ready for that one.

'It's all right, Theo,' said Rudi.

'Oberst,' Theo corrected, his eyes still on Webb.

Oh man, Webb thought. Oberst Theo and a mother pistol, asking questions. He busied himself fumbling at his cigarettes and lighter. Eric was still grinning at the telephone, Major Gunfighter was smoking a cigarette, and Major Bear was working vigorously on his ear with his little finger.

'Tomorrow,' Theo said then, 'I hope we're going to get the chance . . . to show you around. In the morning.'

'*Die Wolfe werden Morgen wieder jagen*,' mumbled Major Five to no one in particular.

Theo raised his glass. 'To you, Captain.' Everyone took a good belt of iced vodka. Webb almost gagged.

'And . . .' Theo raised his glass again. 'To the US Air Force.'

'*Die Amerikanische Luftwaffe kann mich am Arsch lecken*,' muttered Major Five, not raising his glass.

'Haha,' Major Gunfighter snickered, turning to Webb. 'The Major said the Air Force can kiss—'

'*Die Amerikanische Luftwaffe* –' Major Five seemed to be talking to his vodka glass – '*hat die sechs alten Messerschmitts nicht gefunden*.'

'The Major says,' explained Major Gunfighter, 'that the whole US Air Force has not been able to find our Messerschmitts.'

383

'The US Air Force found your Messerschmitts shortly after noon today.' Webb raised his glass. 'The United States Air Force.'

Eric laughed first and then the others, except Major Five. Webb was relieved to see the Oberst grinning, but the pistol stayed. All of them drank, except Major Five.

'And,' said Webb, 'to Major Gustav Beissemann . . . and Major Franz Osterhoudt.'

The others stopped, glasses held still.

'They were taken good care of,' Webb said.

All drank, including Major Five.

'And,' said Theo, 'to the Colonel Lowen.'

'*Der Oberst Lowen kann mich am Arsch lecken,*' muttered Major Five.

All drank, except Major Five.

'And,' said Theo, 'to your Commander, Captain. What is his name?'

'Butler. Sir. Colonel Butler.'

'Yes, to Colonel Butler.' Theo raised his glass with the others.

'*Der Oberst Butler kann mich am Arsch lecken,*' muttered Major Five, not drinking.

Webb felt this latest shot of vodka turn incandescent in his gut.

'He will wonder where you went, Captain,' said Theo.

Got that right, Webb thought.

'Perhaps he will be . . . worried,' Theo said thickly.

'Good,' said Major Five. '*Darauf trinke ich, haha. Prosit*!' Major Five drank alone.

Webb wondered if he fell off his chair what side he would fall on. And he wondered why no one else had fallen yet. It was unbelievable.

'Call him, Captain,' Theo said tonelessly from the end of the table.

'Sir?' Webb was sure he had not heard right.

'The telephone. You will call your Commander.'

'Sir?' Webb tried to smile. Only half his face seemed to work.

'Call,' Theo repeated. 'He is responsible. Remember that command and responsibility, Captain, are inseparable. Call.'

'Haha,' Major Five began laughing, slumped forward, staring down the table at Webb. The cigarette fell out of his fingers and he picked it up with great care.

'Call?' said Webb. Oh man.

'Tell him,' said Theo slowly, 'that you are being . . . well treated. As an officer. Tell him . . . no jet fighters. When the Colonel Lowen . . . when the Colonel Lowen.' Theo shrugged. 'Not sporting, yes? Haha.' Then his expression hardened. '*No jet fighters*!'

'Yessir.'

'*Sag' ihm zum Teufel mich zeinem Dusenjagern*,' muttered Major Five, trying to light the cigarette with a weaving match.

'Tell him . . . no jets. Because you . . .' Theo paused thoughtfully. Seconds passed, a minute.

'Sir?'

Theo looked up. 'Because you, Captain, will be getting your wish. To fly the piston fighter.'

'Sir?'

'Yes. You fly. One of our Gustavs. To Texas.'

'Sir?'

'You are a pilot, yes?'

'Civilian, sir. Civilian.' Webb was feeling faint. 'Hey.'

'Tell him . . .' Theo went on, 'greetings, regards. From officers of 76 Staffel. Tell him . . . when we meet the Colonel Lowen, then we go home. Vanish. We will be gone. Gone home.'

'Gone home,' repeated Webb. 'Gone home . . . to Germany.'

'No no, haha. I did not say Germany. Haha. Argen*tina*. Call!'

'Sir, I don't think I could fly one—'

Theo's fist hit the table with such force that every pilot jerked in his seat. Webb distinctly saw the little pistol bounce, expecting momentary heart failure for fear the jolt would set off the weapon at him. He snatched up the receiver, dialed, and got the Base on the first ring.

'This is Captain Webb calling for the Base Commander.'

'The CO's gone home, sir. Shall I patch you through?'

'Please. This is . . . emergency.' Webb waited, glancing at the pistol.

'Hello?'

'Sir, this is Webb.' Webb took a deep breath.

'Well, where have you been, Captain?'

'Sir, I was able . . . to locate the Staffel field. This afternoon. Before they left. For Texas.'

Butler paused. 'Are you serious, Captain?'

'Serious. Yessir. Serious.'

'Well, ah, Jesus, that's wonderful. Where are you?'

'Well, sir. With them. I'm with them.'

'With them? What do you mean with them? With who?'

'Them, sir. The pilots. The Staffel. I, ah, found the field. And, ah, the pilots. And they found me. Is more like it. I'm their, ah, guest. Now.'

'Guest? Jesus, Webb, are you drunk? Drugged?'

'Yessir. Drunk. Champagne. Mumm's mostly.'

'Jesus, Captain. They're holding you prisoner?'

'Yessir. No sir. Guest. They are treating me very well.' Webb made his best effort to sound reassuring; it seemed to be the military way to explain it. 'They had me to dinner, sir. Guest. With the entire Staffel. Dress uniform for all. Very spiffy, sir.'

'Dinner? Are you serious?'

'Serious, sir. I'm fine. Fine.'

'Why – how are you able to call?'

'They suggestion, suggested, I call you, sir.'

'Jesus, suggested? Where are you? Where are they?'

'Negative on first question, sir. They are here, sir. Sitting right here.'

'They're sitting beside you? Now?'

'Yessir. They have, ah, asked me to assure you –' Webb lost it for a second – 'being well treated. Which is true. And . . . to express regards from the Commanding Officer and all other. Officers.'

'Jesus,' Butler whispered. 'What can you tell me?'

'You don't need to whisper, sir. Only me can hear you. They want me to tell you . . . that when they meet Colonel Lowen they'll vanish.'

'Vanish?'

'Yessir, vanish. Go home. They have asked me to request . . . that you do not send up the jets. Not, uh, sporting. As they say.'

'Jesus, sporting? Are you at the field?'

'Yessir, no sir, I mean. I promised.'

'Jesus, okay. What are they going to do with you?'

'Ah . . . going to Texas with them. To Texas.'

'Texas? How? When?'

'Fly, sir. With them. In a Messerschmitt.'

'That's impossible.' Butler was almost whispering again. 'No way those 109s will take a passenger, Webb.'

'Yessir. I'll be flying one.'

'What?'

Webb paused; he was dizzy. 'You see . . . if I'm flying one of the 109s, they figure they won't have to worry. About the jets. However . . . me worry about, I worried about, the jets. Sir.'

'Jesus.' Butler sighed. 'All right, Major.'

'Sir?' Had he heard right? *Major*?

'Yes, Major. Congratulations. That was the agreement, Major.'

'Yessir, thanks.'

Oh man, *Major* sounded so good. It gave him strength, gave him pleasure, gave him pride so good. He sat up straighter in the chair. Outstanding. 'I'm hanging in, sir. Really. Not to worry.'

'Jesus, I hope so. You did well, Major.' Butler hesitated. Webb sensed, to his surprise, an invisible concern. 'Can you fly that Messerschmitt, Major?'

'I don't think there's much choice, sir.'

'Well, good luck, Major. Just take care of yourself.'

'Yessir. I was going to mention that. I'll be in one of those 109s, sir. Serious. You won't send up the jets?'

'Major, we'll be very careful. And you tell those Krauts . . . ah—'

'Yessir, I'll tell them. Your regards. Goodnight, sir.'

'Goodnight, Major. And good luck.'

Webb put down the receiver, staring at it. Too much; he calls Lowen and the Germans make him call Butler. Too much. He looked up. The others were watching him. They all looked very amused and very drunk. As was he.

'Very good, Captain,' said Theo.

'Major,' Webb corrected. 'Major. I have just been promoted. To Major. Sir.'

'Splendid, Captain, Major!' Theo beamed, raised his hands. 'Splendid! Clearly you deserved to be! Gentlemen, now we have the champagne!'

'You are now the Major, Captain?' Major Bear smiled, bobbing his head up and down, unlighted cigar clenched in his teeth. 'Very good. Drink to that. *Prosit*.'

'Congratulations, Captain Major,' said Major Gunfighter, raising his vodka glass. '*Prosit*.'

Across the table Eric nodded mechanically. 'Hey, Captain Major. All right.'

Major Five said nothing. But he poured the champagne. And drank with them all.

CHAPTER TWENTY-FOUR

Lowen's bedside clock read 12:42 a.m. when the telephone raised him from his sleep. He got to his feet and hitched up his pajama bottoms and padded barefoot downstairs to the telephone.

'Hello?'

'Roger, this is Ed, over at Williams. Sorry to disturb you.'

'It's okay. What's up?'

'We have a new, ah, development over here, Roger. It looks like Captain Webb found the Kraut field.'

'At this hour?' Lowen was both irritated and surprised. Webb, that gold-plated gung-ho sonofagun.

'We just found out a couple of hours ago.'

'So our Captain Webb is now Major Webb?'

'Our Major Webb also managed to get himself captured at the same time; early this afternoon.'

'Captured?'

'By the damned Krauts, Roger. He's okay apparently. They let him call me on the telephone, sitting there with them, drunk as a skunk. Jesus.'

'They let him call you on the telephone?'

'Yes yes. You ought to know about that. Jesus, those Krauts call you up all the time, don't they?'

Lowen wanted to laugh.

'Listen, Roger. The Krauts are going to put him in one of their 109s and make him fly . . . so when they go up we won't hit them with jets.'

'Makes sense.' Lowen scratched his head. Godamighty, more madness. 'Do you think Webb could fly a Messerschmitt?'

'Jesus, I don't know. But I don't think they're bluffing. He also said they'd leave, go home, after they met you. Now what the hell's going on down there I don't know about? My goddamned Exec goes running off into the goddamned desert without telling anyone and calls me up stinking drunk to tell me not to worry! And the damned Krauts are telling him to give me their best regards. Jesus. This is just not *acceptable*. Now I want to know what you know, Roger, and I want to know what you think.'

'Well, Ed . . . I think Captain, Major, Webb kept his part of the deal. Take it easy, now. It's coming together. Any idea where he is, where the field is?'

'They've got to be within a couple of hundred miles from here because he left the base about ten-thirty this morning. I just found out he ordered a bunch of aerial photoprints from the lab, so we're checking that out now. I'm pulling everything in to about 200 miles and we're going over those aerials with a microscope. And I'll put everything in the air at first light. We'll find them now.'

'Let's just see how it goes,' Lowen said soothingly. 'We got Captain, Major, Webb sitting right on top of them. So now it's their move.'

'Yeah, I realize that. Okay. Webb also turned up a witness who saw four of their aircraft last week on a low-level strafing practice up north about eighty miles. And the FBI turned up a trucker who delivered a crated German fighter about two years ago to a guy with a hangar up at Skyharbor. These people may be right in our backyard over here, Roger.'

'I'd like to see you keep the hardware on the ground, Ed, until we know what's going on. We've made more progress in the last twenty-four hours than we have in a week.'

'Yeah, don't worry. How are you doing? How do you like my boys?'

'A good group. We're buttoned up pretty tight as of today and I think we're ready. I have another volunteer, a genuine RAF Wing Commander in a genuine Spitfire, from Milwaukee.'

'Jesus, I don't want to hear about it. You just keep your damned hardware on the ground, Roger. You told me you'd let me know if the Krauts called you. Have they?'

'Still waiting, Ed. Still waiting. They said today. We'll see.'

'Webb said they were going to fly to Texas.'

'Relax, Ed. That's a thousand miles.'

'Yeah. Well, they won't get to the state line, now.'

'Unless Webb's flying with them.'

'Jesus . . . Well, you're right. We'll see what develops. Stay in touch, Roger, and I'll do the same if we get anything.'

When Lowen hung up he stood in the darkness thinking about the Captain – Major – Webb getting drunk with the Kraut pilots. More madness. Godamighty, he'd never have imagined such madness.

Lowen felt a trickle of perspiration run cool down his bare side. He was wide awake now and he went over and sat down at his desk in the corner of the dining room without turning on any light. He realized then that he was angry with Webb. And that he – yes, it was true – was probably angry because he envied him his youth and his energy and his enthusiasm. And there was some anger and some envy whenever he blathered on about the Kraut pilots, like they were damned heroes. Hell, Webb thought all fighter pilots were some sort of damned heroes. Himself included. Not to discount that, he reminded himself.

He wondered what Webb's life was like off duty. Probably he had a lot of free sex, screwing himself cross-eyed every night. Hard to imagine him sitting up reading books on the Daimler-Benz V-12 605 engine series. But the sonofagun knew his stuff, no argument there. And somehow he actually tracked down those damned Krauts.

Lowen lit up his pipe, watching the soft yellow flame turn upside down at the match-end as he drew in. Dinner and champagne and a telephone call to Butler. You had to laugh at that. Well, the damned Krauts were good fighter pilots, maybe the best ever, in a way. The Wing Commander was right: drink one for Jerry for a Good Show. Bastards . . .

Well, now Butler would read his map prints with a microscope and turn something up. Recon choppers and jet patrols at dawn. Lowen puffed rhythmically at his pipe, the tiny smoke clouds just palely visible in the semi-darkness. There was a part of him that was angry not only at Webb, but at much more. He never had quite been able to believe that rat-racing with the Krauts, a dogfight, could come off; it was too insane after all. Now the damned Air Force would get them. There'd be a phone call and he'd be sitting on his damned ass having breakfast and it would be all over.

But there was another part of him that persisted . . . in what? – persisted in warning him. To prepare carefully. Tomorrow. Right to the last moment. In the silence, the peace of night and dark, the Mustangs waited: fueled, tuned, armed, painted. In the morning they would have one final practice flight before New Mexico. They would be prepared. Barely.

He knocked out his pipe in the ashtray and then went upstairs and eased into bed, lying on his back.

'Roger?' Jean's whisper surprised him in the dark. 'Is something wrong?'

'It was the CO over at Williams. One of his officers located the German airstrip. And got himself captured.' He chuckled dryly. 'So we may not be going anywhere after all. They're gonna find those people pretty quick now.'

'Good.' Jean pulled the sheet over his bare chest. 'Can you sleep now?'

Lowen smiled to himself, thinking again of Webb drunk with the Kraut pilots; a damned dinner party. 'So . . . our Captain Webb is now a Major.'

'Who?'

'The officer who found the field. The CO said he'd make him a Major if he—'

'His name is Webb?'

'James Webb, why?'

'James Webb? Oh God!' Jean sat up.

'What is it?'

'Roger, about an hour before you got home, there was a call, a wrong number I thought. From a James Webb. I'm sure because he spelled it carefully. He said he had a prescription, to refill. I told him he had the wrong number but he went right on as if he hadn't heard me and read the numbers.'

Lowen sat up. 'What kind of numbers?'

'Like a prescription number. I didn't write it down.'

'Wait a moment.' Lowen pulled on the bedside lamp.

'It was an odd . . . numbers and letters.'

'Think,' he said, digging through the little nightstand drawer.

'He said it twice, carefully. It was three A's first. I remember because it was triple-A like the auto club. And then an A-and-W on the end like the root beer. And a fourteen in the middle.'

'Okay.' Lowen squinted at the paper as he wrote. 'What else?'

'There was a K . . . triple-K? No, triple-A and something

391

fourteen.' She rubbed at her throat. 'Damn, I'm sorry.'

'It's all right. Just think.'

'Does it sound like a prescription?'

'If James Webb called here, it's no prescription.' He held up the paper, handing her her glasses from the nightstand. 'Does that look right?'

'No. I'm sure of the triple-A . . . and then something fourteen and then A-and-W. Perhaps it was S-fourteen.'

'All right.' Lowen studied the paper, thinking of combinations.

She sighed, shrugged. 'I'm sorry. Oh fart.'

'Don't worry. Just keep thinking.'

'He was very short, quick. Almost rude.'

Lowen stared at the penciled numbers and letters. He knew it was Webb; he would have been quick because he had taken the risk to call. So there was a message. Ballsy sonofagun. Yeah, he'd do that.

He turned to Jean. 'What time did he call?'

'Almost nine, before. I'm sure.'

Lowen got up and went downstairs and sat down at the desk and lit up his pipe again. It was still warm. He studied the pad, then began writing out variations; there could only be so many.

Jean came down and began making coffee. As he fiddled with the A and the W and the S, he kept going back to the triple-A which kept nagging him because it was familiar, though he couldn't imagine what AAA could mean other than the auto club, which made no sense since all the auto club could mean was insurance and maps *map* – he dug down in his flight bag by the desk and pulled all the maps, everything, out because he recalled Webb giving him a blue road map marked up like the map on the wall at Willie. He found the map. It was blue and it was Triple-A.

'Jean,' he called. 'Put up a thermos for me, would you? And if we have a spare somewhere put that one up, too. Both black, okay?'

'We have three,' she called back.

'Three then.'

Lowen opened the map and smoothed it out on the desktop. The latitude sections were alphabetical on the right margin, A through T, and the longitude sections were numerical along the bottom margin, one through twenty. He looked back at the notepad. Jean was sure about the fourteen so he found fourteen at the bottom and traced it upward. It ran just east of Phoenix.

When he looked over to the letters on the right margin, the A was in Utah and the S was in Mexico so there was only the K. Which was north of Phoenix. Godamighty.

He was very pleased with Captain-Major Webb now. The Captain deserves to be a Major, he thought. With a pencil and ruler he crossed the coordinates and made a square. By the scale of the map the area was forty square miles just northeast of Phoenix, bisected by Route 87. Desolate country by the look of it, with only a single town – Sunflower. He looked back at the notepaper at the A-and-W, the S-and-W.

'Jean,' he called to the kitchen, 'does triple-A and K-fourteen sound right?'

'Yes. K-fourteen and then A-and-W.'

'Or S-and-W?'

There was no answer for a moment. 'Yes . . . yes, S-and-W. Yes.'

Of course. Southwest. 'Thank you, Rita.'

'What is it?' she spoke from the doorway.

'A map.' Lowen looked at his watch a moment and then took a fresh sheet of paper and a pencil and a pocket calculator.

'Was it a message?'

'Yes,' he said without looking up. 'Coffee, hon. Please?'

She turned away. Lowen opened an Arizona flight map, calculated it for a few minutes, and wrote more numbers on the paper. Then he got a flight map of New Mexico and studied the coordinates the Kraut Commander had given him. If the German field was where Webb said it was, the Krauts would merely have to fly an exact due-east heading and at 1400 hours – the time they'd agreed to meet – they'd have the sun high and behind them. Smart sonsabitches. He sat back, puffing his pipe with small noises like goldfish made in aquariums in the dark.

After a minute he stood up and went out in the hallway and dialed the telephone. It rang nine times before Fitzgerald mumbled hello.

'Major Fitzgerald. Listen carefully.'

'Roger?'

'Major, get our people up. Now. We're taking off at 0245 hours.'

'What?' Fitzgerald cleared his throat. 'That's – Roger, that's in fifty-five, an hour. You—'

'Listen to me, Major John Fitzgerald. We scramble at 0245 hours damnit Major we do not have one damned second to screw around. Do you hear me?'

'Ah. Yessir.'

'Now listen to me. My good friend Captain-Major Webb has found those damned Krauts. *He has found the Krauts.* And maybe, just maybe, we can catch them by surprise. Do you understand?'

'Hot damn. Yessir.'

'Now, Major, you get on that damned – are those kites ready?'

'Ready they are.'

'Now you get on that damned horn to that damned motel and call the ground crew first. And get five thermos bottles of coffee somehow. Then you call up to Holloman and clear us in for refueling about 0430 hours and tell 'em it's going to be like a pit stop at the damned Indianapolis 500; make that very clear, Major. And tell them to have some twenty millimeter, about 800 rounds. Got all that?'

'Yessir, yessir.'

'Haul ass, Major,' said Lowen quietly, then hung up.

When he turned, Jean was standing in the dining room door holding a mug. The front of her was in shadow and he could see the steam from the coffee mug against the light behind her; it was dark instead of light, the steam, and so was the form of her hips and legs in the thin nightgown.

'There are three thermos bottles, black,' she said.

'Good.' He got up, walking over to her and taking the coffee and heading up the stairs. 'Thank you.'

She followed him without saying anything. He shaved and then went into the bedroom to dress. She watched him from the chair, her feet tucked under her legs, while he put on the two pairs of socks and a long-sleeved undershirt and his flight suit and the soft lace-up high-tops. He kept waiting for her to say something but she didn't, though he wished she would because he didn't know anything to say to her. He tied the scarf – scarlet silk – carefully so there was plenty of it higher than his collar and then he zipped up. He glanced at Jean in the mirror. He noticed the freckles on her arms even in the poor light.

When he took the plastic-wrapped package from the closet shelf, and then the leather shoulder holster, he thought she'd say something but she didn't, not even when he unwrapped the plastic and took out the .45 automatic and three clips and then inserted one clip up inside the grip and then put the .45 in the holster and fastened it closed. She just watched. He prayed she'd ask nothing about the gun. He never remembered telling her. Fire was worse than anything and if you couldn't get the damned canopy back there was the blessed .45 right there.

He put the holster in the flight bag and looked at his watch for the fifth time in as many minutes.

'Handkerchief,' she said finally.

'Yeah.'

He got a handkerchief from the drawer and stuffed it in his pocket then smoothed both hands down his chest. He looked up, thinking again how she never complained about anything, ever. Hell, they had another good ten years easy, with luck.

'They may need us over there early today,' he said. She unfolded her legs and stood up and came over to him with her arms across her chest, hands on opposite shoulders, came up close and looked up. Her peaceful expression pleased him.

'You know,' she said, 'if you were doing this for another reason, I could understand it a little better.'

'Another reason?'

'Like for me, in some way. Isn't that silly?'

He studied her face for a moment. Her lips still had a little lipstick left on them. 'Well, maybe I am.'

She seemed to study him back. 'You're a good man.'

'I want something,' he whispered. 'Something of yours. A sort of . . . token. Good luck. Anything small, a scarf or something.'

She kept looking, her expression unchanged and her arms still crossed up over her bosom, as if she hadn't heard. Then she reached up and unzipped the chest pocket of his flight suit and put her hand back to her breasts into the gown and slipped out a white handkerchief and put it in his pocket and zipped it up.

'You've already got a fine scarf, Colonel. But now you have two handkerchiefs. One smells better than the other.'

He pulled her a little closer, not tightly, and she kept her arms crossed when he kissed her. There was a green taste of toothpaste and the scent of her sleeping, but he realized that he had already left her – down the stairs and down the road, to an airfield and an airplane.

✱ ✱ ✱

In the bedroom Marta had stripped down, leaving a trail of her clothing across the carpet. She had brushed her teeth, leaning against the wall to keep her balance and watching the movement of her breasts back and forth in the opposite direction of her brushing. Then she had gone over to the bed and yanked the spread off onto the floor and thrown herself sprawled naked on the cool sheets.

The room was air-conditioned and nearly dark except for the tiny orange night light. She kept her eyes open to keep her head from spinning. All she could see, lying on her back, was the dim textured ceiling. She wished there was something she could do or take to keep her mind from spinning, too. Being drunk had its compensations because you could more easily shift from thinking to feeling. What she wanted was just to feel, to forget everything that was happening. And everything she was afraid was going to happen.

God, they were all crazy, crazy in the way men were crazy. Surely they were born with it, that unique madness. Certainly no one taught them – Eric was proof enough of that. And now that Captain. If it was courage they were so obsessed with, how much did they think they had to have before it was enough? When did it stop?

But when they were crazy like that they were exciting; no way to deny that. All they ever worried about was having balls, it seemed, not so much for any woman but for each other. Even the pretty little Captain in his pretty blue uniform with the starched creases and his *Yes ma'am* and *No ma'am* routine, sitting there shaking in his shiny shoes and trading clever lines with that manic bastard Theo and amusing the Major – she giggled from calling him an ape. And Eric, stoned witless as usual. All out-braving each other.

Such a party. She wanted to stand up and put her heels back on and walk out naked, right now. And dance around the goddamned table, watching the pretty Captain watching, watching that prick Theo watching. How she wanted to hate that man and what a perverse horror to find herself unable to decide whether she would rather screw him or shoot him, to find herself unable to ignore the *truth* that he had that *power* – however cruel or manipulative – over men. That power . . . that prevailed.

What would a shrink say about this fantasy of aiming a gun at him, of seeing his expression, of pulling the trigger? What would that feel like, a pistol?

Or of somehow trapping him, imagining him tied down some way, of turning him on crazy and fucking him until he was weak . . . unless he was too old, his weakness for flesh transformed to power-tripping instead. She wondered if that was the subversion such men made of their lust.

Why damnit *damnit* did she think of such things? Perhaps, she decided drowsily, because her body was the best weapon she knew how to use. Was that why? Surely there was power there, power in the remarkable way that men came apart when you did something so silly as let your boobs show. She put her hands on her breasts and began kneading both nipples. Stuff these in the Herr General's face . . . and the pretty Captain's face, she thought, remembering his quick glances down the front of her dress, remembering Eric and the Major dragging him from the pool dripping wet and barely conscious with his pretty pecker barely veiled in his white wet shorts.

And the good Major – she slid one hand down between her opened legs – the good Major shirtless and wet, holding up the pretty Captain. From the kitchen she had watched, pushing herself secretly against the sink ledge, raising that lovely warmth. Eric and the Major and the Captain, all of them brown and wet and half-naked. Yum. Take on all three of them. God how perverse; it was wonderful. She moved her forefinger. Perverse. Wonderful.

The Major . . . the Major who loved her. Astonishing that he had fallen like that. There was no way you could mistake the way he sometimes looked; it was always in the eyes. Wonderful. For that alone she wanted him, wanted him. And had he not fallen for her, she might have had him. Pity.

But it was sticking in Eric's throat – she knew that – so it was really just fine after all. Just fine whenever she imagined him kneeled humping over some little twat cocktail waitress or counter clerk. She hated these visions. And loved them. That bastard, screwing around, confusing her with these erotic jealousies – no, not jealousy so much as anger – for it made her feel . . . less than valuable, less than perfect. Something to diddle.

There was once a pact, an agreement, and what was it worth if it had no value to him? When you made love with someone often enough, after a time there grew a very intimate kind of bond that took on value, like money, like an investment. And because of that agreement – mere words were all that held you – you felt safe and trusting enough to assume that whatever you shared then – from the most lascivious of fantasies to the most hideous of nightmares to the most beatific of dreams – would never be abused. It took a long time to build that.

And now it seemed wrong, perverse, that she could love him and hate him both at once. Wrong and perverse. Oh God. Oh God, she wanted him right now pushing it in her right now and she wanted the Major right now pushing it in her right now and she felt stupid so stupid for missing what little chance there had been. She wondered if she were gone, dead, how they would grieve. Would the good Major grieve, be drunk for months, perhaps even weep over her casket? Or would he fly away on the jetliner with a vodka in his hand, smoking a cigarette, staring at the ankles of the stewardess?

Eric would grieve, be drunk for months, and weep over her casket, yes. Because in his craziness, his pig-dog lust, there was still that truth to him, to his heart. She moved her fingers, aroused not by the thought of his flesh but by the memory of his words, loving words whispered in the night when he was opened honest from drinking or being stoned. What had they both come to be? Husband, wife, promise, need, lust, anger. None of it ever got simpler, as she had once expected.

She had always wondered what he had been like before Vietnam. Being in Vietnam had done something to him, but it took years to see. And she was still seeing, because whatever it was it just kept coming out. And being around the older pilots seemed to bring it out more, faster. It seemed to be an obsession that hollowed him out bit by bit, until he grew lighter and more transparent and more physical and more angry. Because of this, was he to be forgiven for disloyalty?

She knew he was in some way broken inside, disconnected. And crazy in ways you couldn't tell by looking; you'd hardly ever know except for those times when he was drunk enough to talk about it, when he told her stories after love-making when they rested naked and talked about things that could only be told in the dark. It just kept coming then.

He said that the helicopters – he called them 'slicks' – took off under fire and came in under fire very often, and he said the

He drifted, making sounds of pleasure like sighs trapped in his throat. He was like a child then – her child, her only child.

PopBang the starter fired up the huge Merlin V-12 of Lowen's Mustang, blasting a cloud of transparent blue-brown smoke out of the exhaust stacks as the four-bladed eleven-foot prop jerked, slowed, jerked again into spinning.

The P-51 was half out of the hangar into the dark but there was enough light to see by. Lowen sat in the cockpit, feeling the quiver of raw power tremble through the airframe and set up a humming whine in the instrument panel. The pistol was bulky under his arm and the parachute was bulky under his butt and he subconsciously moved his body around, adjusting pistol and chute while going through pressure checks; regulator, oil, oxygen, manifold. When he was satisfied, he looked over to his right where the other seven P-51s and the Spitfire were *popbanging* into life and warming up. He could smell the exhaust; he liked it.

Fitz was suddenly on the wing to his left, leaning in over the cockpit to help him with his harness.

Lowen looked up. 'You got all those guns charged?' he shouted.

'Roger, I went over each check for each ship, personally.'

Lowen could see that every pilot was in his cockpit, every prop was spinning. Blue exhaust haze floated in the hangar light. Wingtip navigation lights winked on red and green like Christmas lights among the cluster of aircraft. Ground crewmen scooted under the wings, disconnecting booster batteries and removing wheel chocks. The noise, eight 12-cylinder power-houses with open exhausts, rumbling at high idle, swelled to a reassuringly malevolent harmonic thunder.

'What do I tell that CO over at Williams if he calls over here?' Fitz's face glowed weirdly in the reflection of the cockpit lights.

'Call him first. About 0700. Tell him we're on our way over.' He gave Fitz a half-smile. 'To help him look.'

'What?' Fitz leaned closer, his hand cupped to his ear.

'To help him look!' Lowen shouted.

He saw a crewman coming over. He moved the battery switch to ON, set the supercharger at HIGH. The crewman shouted something up to Fitz, who then came back to the cockpit.

'Roger, we have no oil pressure in Five and it's heating up fast. Goddamnit!'

'Give it thirty seconds, Major. The scrub. Who is it?'

Fitz craned his neck. 'Colonel Recchio.'

'Check your roster,' Lowen yelled. 'If Recchio has more kills than any other pilot, yank the other pilot and put Recchio in his ship.'

Fitz clambered down and moved away. Lowen looked over the temperature gauges again. When he finished, he spoke into the R/T mike, 'This is Rebel Leader checking. Ready to roll. Acknowledge by name, Two.'

'Two, Polk here, Leader. All set,' came the voice in his headset.

'Acknowledge by name, Three.'

'Three, Willett here, Leader. Ready when you are.'

'Acknowledge by name, Four.'

'Four, Redmond-Donleavy here, Leader. Ready then.'

'Acknowledge by name, Five.'

Nothing. He looked over at the other aircraft. The prop on one of them was winding down and the pilot was climbing out, clumsy in his chute.

'Five is out, Leader,' came another pilot's voice.

'Acknowledge by name, Six,' Lowen went on.

As he contacted each of the others – cockpit silhouettes in the half-light – Lowen felt the adrenaline start to kick in. He wanted to get the damned show on the damned road now. He looked at his watch: 0258 hours. During the first leg to Holloman they'd have plenty of time in the air for briefing. And for him to warn them that one of the Messerschmitts might be piloted by the good Captain-Major Webb. He wondered if it was a bluff; they said Webb would have his wheels down. He glanced over at the dead P-51; crewmen were swarming around the nose. Damn the luck. Now they were seven. Against six. If they found them.

'Here we go,' he said into the R/T, releasing brakes.

Lowen taxied out, the noise of the Merlin rumbling smooth and strong, his landing lights glaring out across the pavement like a car's headlights, the green and blue-white glow of the instrument panel reflecting dully in the plexiglas bubble he pulled over his head and slammed closed. He flexed his control surfaces, irked because it was hard to see them in the dark.

At the end of the strip he braked the port wheel and swung

the P-51 around and straightened it out neatly. Behind to his left he saw the other six aircraft creeping in a line, illuminated by each other's lights, red bullet noses ominous in the whirling propeller circles. He could pick out the smaller Spit two planes back and he was once again very glad to have the Wing Commander along. Good show. In the tight solitude of the closed cockpit Lowen felt, rather than heard, the chorus of their engines.

Before him stretched the parallel lines of tiny yellow runway lights that converged in the dark. His eyes picked out several gauges for final check. Pushing the R/T mike away from his mouth he spoke aloud, his voice audible only in his throat.

'Well Lord, if there's any divine help for us . . . If there's the reality . . . of such things as good and evil . . . these men are good and brave. Please fly with us . . . Keep us from harm, for we seek victory in the name of good . . . in the cause of good. And the perpetuation of good.'

He eased the throttle forward and the P-51 gathered power, straining at the leash of its brakes, shaking from side to side. The Merlin's roar swelled in the cockpit, blurring the dim-lit panel gauges. He released the brakes and the Mustang surged forward, pressing him back in his seat. Nothing in front but the great hump of engine cowling spitting blue-yellow flame from both sides, the prop circle fading, the tiny yellow lights – rocket fireflies – whizzing past his wingtips gaining speed. And above, ahead, just blackness.

CHAPTER TWENTY-FIVE

'Now listen up.' Eric was leaning over the cockpit at Webb's shoulder. Webb could smell the fresh starched-washed smell of their flight suits, and the pervasive scents of fuel and fiberglass.

Watching and listening to Eric going over the gauges and switches on the instrument panel – most of which he thankfully found familiar – Webb was trying to overcome the uncomfortable feeling of tightness in the narrow cockpit; he felt as if he were sitting on the plane rather than in it.

'Gettin' into this mother is like stepping from a Volkswagen into a Grand Prix racer, but it's still an airplane and it works the same way as the stuff you been flying. It just has *boocoo* more horses. You understand?'

Webb nodded. His heart was clipping right along.

'All you gotta do is get the fucker off the ground. Flying it once you're up is a piece of cake; in fact it's a rush.'

Webb's knees were high in front of him, chest level, and the angle of the plane put him in a reclining position that reminded him of some carnival ride from his youth.

'The toughest part,' Eric went on, 'is taking off. It can get away from you if you aren't careful. Keep it stable – don't overcorrect – pour on the juice and just *launch* the sonofabitch.'

'And landing?'

'Another story altogether. We'll get to that. If you do what I tell you, you'll be okay. Don't sweat it.'

'Don't sweat it,' Webb repeated. Oh man.

'The thing is, you must keep it *absolutely stable* in one direction when you're taking off, even if you don't go as straight as you want. You got lots of room out there and you can run over some bushes, no sweat.

Webb could already feel sweat, running down the small of his back. When he glanced out the open hangar doors he saw the first blue-gray light of morning.

'Now we'll go over the panel once more and then we'll fire it up and you can run up and down the field a few times to get the hang of it. You'll do it, man. No sweat.' Eric patted him roughly on the shoulder.

Webb wondered whether what he was doing would be construed as acting in the defense of his country. He decided it sort of was.

Rudi stood by the hangar door alone, looking out. When Webb had taxied back from his practice runs out on the strip they had pushed the 109 back inside the hangar and helped him down and gathered around him to congratulate him. Then they had started and run up the other five engines. They had also removed the auxiliary fuel tank from Webb's Number Seven aircraft because of the high risk of his takeoff with the extra weight.

It was quiet now and Rudi decided not to worry about Webb getting the Gustav up in the air. There were other things to think about.

There was enough light to make out some of the distant mountains. He looked at his watch: 0548 hours. They had plenty of time, since takeoff at 1130 hours was scheduled for the rendezvous at 1400.

He wondered what Lowen was doing and he wondered how many planes he would have and he wondered what Lowen's pilots were like. The Staffel had many advantages, but they would need all of them against those devastating .50 caliber Brownings. Experience was the key, no matter how many planes Lowen had mustered.

Rudi lit up his pipe, peaceful in the dawn that lightened the desert. He was ready and he was feeling particularly good in spite of the hangover. What they were about to do seemed progressively more unlikely as the minutes ticked off. There was a good chance the Mustang group wouldn't show for some reason, most likely because the Air Force would muscle in one way or another. He resolved not to panic when he saw the jets, and to lower his wheels immediately. This time, he knew, they would shoot.

He glanced again at his watch. The waiting was always difficult. He remembered the war and the tension of lounging around dispersal waiting waiting waiting for the ringing of the telephone, bundled into flying suits and heavy boots with flares strapped around the legs, sweating in the flying jacket, bound by the parachute harness. Waiting. It was surprising when he remembered that he was so young then and that the feeling he was having now could be almost identical. So many years.

It was curious that some mechanism of his mind prevented him from thinking beyond this day, this sunrise coming, the dogfight if it happened. He knew how it would go; it would go crazy in ways he could never have foreseen or expected, as most warfare did. He didn't, really didn't feel afraid.

Whenever he thought of death he thought of Linda. He had the image often, like a dream. Now and again there were some things that would trigger it, but then just as often it came without being triggered. He had been wearing a new yellow windbreaker that the Goodyear people had given him and he was driving very fast in the new yellow 911 Targa with Linda at his side. Her wheat-colored hair whipped behind in the green-gold evening light. He was the happiest he thought it was possible to be, at forty-six. A beautiful woman was a treasure and his, he was sure, was more beautiful than any other in the world – white teeth shining in the forest dusk, tanned throat and white sweater – more beautiful than any other in the world.

There were a lot of leaves on the road and it was still wet in places, he remembered that. And he remembered the tail of the Porsche jerking once and he remembered losing it and seeing the trees, mostly pines. And he remembered, as the Porsche looped the first time, that he thought they might be lucky and miss the trees. But that was all he remembered. Until the hospital.

He never saw what was left of the car. It was suggested that it would be better for him to sign the papers without seeing her body, and he agreed. While he was in the hospital he gave up on Porsches forever. And love.

It had been a long time since he had seen death close up but he knew all the feelings. Death was just roulette unless you went looking for it. Then it was a different matter. Like today, he thought, when all of us are going looking for it.

* * *

At 0730 hours. Theo called them together in the first hangar. The sun was bright outside the open doors and the heat rolled in across the concrete floor to be sucked upward by the vent fans. Theo stood by the wingtip of Number Seven, sweating in his undershirt, with his flying suit unzipped and pulled down with the sleeves tied around his waist, wiping at his face with a towel. Eric and the pilots gathered in a loose rank while Webb stood hesitantly behind them. Marta leaned against the doorjamb of the briefing room with her arms folded.

'In order to meet the Colonel Lowen at the rendezvous –' Theo studied his watch – 'we will take off three hours from now. There is the possibility that before that time we may have visitors, if I was wrong about the Colonel Lowen . . . if he would alert the Air Force. So we must be prepared, yes?'

Theo zipped up his flying suit while he spoke. He had placed five plastic-wrapped packages on the wing and now he held one up. 'These packets contain your personal items: money, wallet papers . . . and a key for a luggage locker at the air terminal. If we should become separated you will find your luggage waiting there.'

He put one of the packages in the zippered pocket of his flight suit and then took a position of attention. The pilots lined up evenly and came to attention. Webb stood straight, too.

Theo studied them for a moment. 'Zip up your suits. The vacation is not over yet.'

The pilots followed his order quietly, quickly, and resumed their positions of attention.

'It has been a pleasure . . . an honor . . . to be your Commander.' He paused for a very long time, then lifted his chin. 'Oberstleutnant Felbeck.'

Rudi stepped forward and saluted. Theo whispered something to him, smiled, and handed him his packet. Rudi returned to the line. Marta and Webb watched as Theo repeated the ceremony with each pilot, including Eric last, who had no packet.

'I do not need to tell you to keep your elements tight. I do not need to say that the wingman must always be close. Especially if we are outnumbered. We are probably a little faster than they are. We have the cannon and the fuel injection, remember. And we are, I am sure, the better pilots. Good hunting.

'We will run up the engines every forty-five minutes. Put on the fire garments and suit up and help each other to adjust the parachutes. Do this now. And then, then we will wait. Like the war, yes? That is all.'

Marta watched the pilots slipping on white garments like long underwear, which made her sweat more heavily. Rudi had insisted that she come out to the hangars to be a driver for one of the vehicles if she was needed. And if some of them returned injured. She was not happy about waiting at the field half the day but the briefing room was air-conditioned and she knew that staying at home all day would have been unbearable, but now she was thinking that it could hardly be more unbearable than the heat, the hard wide lump in her mid-section.

No one was paying any attention whatsoever to her. Neither Eric nor the Major had even looked at her. Rendel had smiled once. She paced back and forth, smoking a cigarette in quick infrequent puffs, trailing her hand along the Captain-Major's sedan. They had plenty of vehicles; there was the sedan, which Eric had fixed and filled with aircraft coolant, and the Jeep, and the van. Rudi had made a point to show her that all three vehicles had their ignition keys in place.

They had given one of Weinert's flight suits to the Captain-Major; the fit was very good and he looked like the rest of them, black gloves and all, except that he seemed to sweat more and to have nothing to do. Eric had told her that whenever the Staffel got up in the air Webb would lower his wheels as a signal to—

The thunder came then, not far in the distance so that it sounded like the thunder of clouds, but much closer. And it had none of the whining noise one expected from any sort of engine. She had no idea of what it was. Then it seemed to be a double thunder, deep and wrathfully powerful – the ground trembled, resonant under her feet. And then it passed.

'Mustangs,' said Rudi flatly in the tense vacuum of silence.

Now not only the noise but the very word *Mustangs* struck terror in her throat. She was frozen in place like the others.

'Two of them,' Schilling called from the doorway. 'Very low. They have found us.'

There suddenly seemed to be a scent of danger in the air – like ozone. Everything seemed suspended. She wondered how to extinguish her cigarette; it seemed the thing to do.

'*Eric*!' Rudi yelled. 'Get the fuel truck away from the other hangar!' Eric sprinted away.

'Listen to me!' Theo barked. 'Be certain your parachutes are secure. Make your belts tight. Start these craft first, then the other three. Do not bunch up on the runway. Be calm and move quickly! Quickly!'

The others broke into action. Marta had still not moved. What did the Mustangs mean? Surely it was a mistake, a bad dream. The pilots were swarming over the three aircraft and yet it was so quiet she could hear their soles scraping on the wings as they scrambled aboard.

'Clear!' someone shouted.

Bang, one engine fired. She jerked in fright, backing against the Captain-Major's sedan. Rudi was in the cockpit, Rendel helping him with the harness, Kesler under the nose.

'Clear!' someone shouted.

Bang, the second engine fired, belching blue-gray smoke into the air. It smelled of oil and fire. Theo was in the cockpit, shouting to Kesler below. She then saw Schilling helping the Captain-Major into the cockpit of the closest aircraft, not twenty feet away. He was struggling, looking clumsy with the parachute bobbing under his butt.

'Clear!' someone shouted.

Bang, the third engine fired. The hangar was clouded in a blue haze of exhaust. Marta clamped her hands over both ears, trembling. The roar of all three aircraft in the hangar filled her body and numbed her feet. Dust rose from the floor. Rendel and Kesler were yanking wheel chocks away from the wheels. Schilling sprinted out the hangar door.

Then Eric appeared, his face glistening with sweat, his hands covered by the heavy work gloves, the Captain-Major's pistol holster at his waist. He ran up to the closest plane, the Captain-Major's, and jumped up on the wing by the cockpit. She was glad that Eric was helping the Captain-Major.

Rudi's 109 jerked forward and rolled outside the hangar and stopped. She could see the flaps and the tail flexing. Then the Number One – Theo's – jerked and rolled forward a few yards. The roar of engines deafened her. Prop wash swirled away the haze around her and lifted more blinding dust. She clung to the Captain-Major's car. Eric was still on the wing of the Captain-Major's plane and he was shouting at the Captain-Major, who was looking up blankly. She thought she heard Eric screaming 'Get out, goddamnit!'

'*Out?*' She saw the Captain-Major's mouth form the word.

Eric jerked the pistol out of the holster and put the barrel to the Captain-Major's face. With his other hand he was yanking the seat harness up and back. The Captain-Major stood up in the cockpit. Eric climbed down. There was a parachute on the wing and, unbelieving, she saw Eric putting it on. The Captain-Major was climbing down. Her eyes stung in the dust. She moved toward Eric.

As the Captain-Major touched his foot to the ground, Eric lifted the pistol and waved the Captain-Major back away, along the fuselage. The Captain-Major held his hands up. She was behind Eric now, several feet. He turned.

'*What are you doing?*' she screamed.

'Here!' he shouted, grabbing her hand and wrapping her fingers around the handle of the pistol. 'You must watch him, hold him! It won't fire until the pull this, the hammer, back all the way! Then you squeeze the grip, the handle, to fire! The second shot is automatic!'

'*What are you doing?*' she screamed again.

'Watch him, goddamnit!' Eric yelled in her face, struggling with the parachute buckle. 'If he gets away, we're screwed.'

'*What are you doing?*' she screamed again.

She saw Rudi's plane move away, the back of his head hidden by the spine of the aircraft. The pistol in her hands – squarish, dark gray – seemed to weigh ten pounds. She was terrified of it, of holding it, of dropping it, of it exploding in her hands. The Captain-Major was staring at her, his hands palms up. Eric turned and leaped up on the wing of the airplane.

'*Eric,*' Marta screamed, stepping closer, her hands frozen around the extended pistol. She looked at the Captain-Major, who backed in panic against the tailplane of the Messerschmitt. And then at Theo's plane, moving now. And then at Eric standing on the wing.

'*Eric,*' she screamed again over the roar of engines.

Eric turned, pulling at a strap under his thigh. '*Him*, you idiot,' he yelled back, pointing at Webb.

'Get down, *Eric*!' she screamed again. She cocked the hammer with her thumb, felt it *click* back into place.

Eric paused, one arm on the windscreen, his teeth bared white like a dog snarl. '*No time,*' he yelled. '*No time*! It's all the same. *It's all the same*!' His free fist went to his chest. 'I *like* it!'

What a stupid thing to say, Marta thought, watching him turn

410

and raise his leg to the cockpit. When she pulled the trigger, keeping the barrel low, the .45 jerked in her hands and made a very loud solid *bang* that she could hear over the engine noise. A fat little gold-colored cylinder popped out of the gun. Eric jerked, collapsed heavily on the wing, and rolled off to the floor nearly at her feet.

She was absolutely sure that she had not fired the gun. It was a mistake, an unthinkable act she could never have committed. She felt that if she somehow did something very quickly, the horror could be made right, reversed. *No! I did not mean to hit him.* There was a pink red wet smear *Oh my God* on the airplane. Eric on his back. The Captain-Major frozen flattened against the airplane, his mouth open. The dust whipping, noise thundering, sand stinging.

There was a movement to her left; Theo climbing out of his plane *Oh my God*, his gray thin hair fluttering in the sandstorm. *Rudi help me*, she thought. *Major help me.* How could this horror be? No one, no one, but Theo, now down off the wing crouched, running to the side, snatching up a wheel chock, returning to the airplane with it. Then turning to her, his hand in his suit, the other lifting his sunglasses, and now, a pistol. She could see the tiny hole of the muzzle. *God, he is going kill me.*

Theo crouching, coming forward. *Eric had said the second shot was automatic.* In the corner of her vision, Eric moving. She nearly fainted. A finger of gleaming red creeping out from under him. Theo's black-gloved hand wrenching the gun from her. Theo dropping to one knee beside Eric, yanking the orange scarf from him, opening his flying suit, yelling at the Captain-Major to help. The red finger widening creeping, its soft shining contours coated with dust. They were tying Eric around the chest. Her stomach turned, tightened. Theo's face in hers, his gloves gripping her upper arms.

'Can you drive?' Theo was shaking her.

She could not speak, staring at Eric.

'*Frau Malzahn*, you must drive this automobile,' Theo yelled in her face. His gloves were wet. 'You must get him to the hospital, quickly!'

Theo jerking her up by the front of her shirt. Gloved wet fingers clamping her jaws, jerking her face upward to his, to his squinting dark eyes. Feeling the slickness of Eric's blood on the leather vise squeezing her cheeks.

'He will not die,' Theo saying. 'But you must hurry! Get in now! *Get in*!' He shoved her into the Air Force sedan.

She watched as he and the Captain-Major lifted Eric – beneath him the shiny red pool seemed a yard wide – and placed him gently in the back seat.

Theo's face at hers again. 'Calm yourself, do you hear me? You must drive carefully to the highway.'

'Yes.' Gripping the wheel. Starting the engine.

Theo yelling to the Captain-Major, who stood slack-mouthed, pale. 'Get your aircraft moving, Captain-Major! It will overheat! Once you are moving, do not stop. You have but one chance. Move!'

The Captain-Major scrambled onto the wing.

Theo turned back to her. 'You must return. Do you understand? You must—' he was interrupted by a fiendish sound, like hail stones striking the hangar, snapping, cracking.

Marta shrieked, felt herself shoved down on the seat. The car windows *cracked* around her, fragments of glass spraying over the dash, the strange stones whacking whining, huge spider web cracks blossoming across the windshield. The car quivered, rocked on its suspension. She heard her own distant scream again. And then the thunder vibrating everything. Wood slivers showered over the windshield. Her next scream gagged in her throat. A rolling *boom* from somewhere outside shook the hangar. The thunder passed.

Theo jerking her upright, screaming 'Go go go!'

Marta shifted to reverse, launched the sedan backwards out of the hangar, and jammed it into low gear before it stopped. She saw the fuel truck out on the strip burning under a boiling column of orange flame and charcoal smoke. And the Captain-Major's plane rolling. And Theo crawling into his cockpit. She pulled away in the dust.

Webb's aircraft rolled forward across the sand, lurching with such violence that the harness belts bit into his shoulders and hips. His stomach churned with nausea; Eric's blood was all over his gloves, suit.

He had no forward vision, only the instrument panel and the armor glass windscreen and the huge rounded engine cowling. The great Daimler-Benz V-12 roaring just beyond his feet, vibrating through his feet, his legs, his gloved hand slippery on the stick. To the sides, desert bush whisking under the tan-brown wings that flexed with each jarring bump. He heard another engine howling, Theo's 109 alongside, their wingtips nearly touching, the Oberst pumping his hand up and down in the air signaling Webb to go faster.

More throttle. The tail slewed to the left. In panic, he corrected more cautiously, easing on more throttle. The engine howled higher, jerking the plane forward.

Just launch the sonofabitch. Now he was bouncing roaring ahead with such terrifying force that he yelled aloud to control his fright. The 109 was pitching, yawing, creaking, flexing, shuddering as if it would momentarily disintegrate. He concentrated on keeping it in a straight path, keeping the rudder pedals even, feeling them push and recede under his feet. The engine was deafening, dust swirled in his eyes. He felt the clump and scrape of bushes beneath his wheels.

Whatever you do, don't back off on throttle once you're rolling or you're dead. Faster, bouncing horribly, his stomach lifting, the aircraft dropping, he saw Theo's 109 roaring alongside, fifty yards, throwing a tornado of dust. *Whack* piece of green saguaro sailed over his wing. *Oh man.* Theo's 109 leaping up, lifting. More throttle, back on the stick. He could feel the tail lifting. *God, give me lift. Keep it straight.* Like skating on ice. *Whack* another piece of cactus. The plane see-sawing, a lightness lifting from the rear. More throttle, stick back, engine howling. *Oh man.* He was off the ground, no bumps. More throttle, stick back, nose rising. Theo above and ahead, bright blue undersurface with big black-and-white wing crosses. Oh man, *he was up*, easing back stick, sweat in his eyes, clean air rushing in, salt-dust taste in his dry mouth, heart tripping, his body pressed more and more into the seat. *Thank you, God.* The desert floor receding tipping tipping, Webb climbed for the sky.

Above him, Theo drawing close, pointing at his own headset. Webb nodded, hands trembling pulling the headset into place over both ears. Theo pumping his hand faster, climbing even more steeply, his voice over the R/T: 'Can you hear me, Major Webb?'

'Yessir. Yes,' Webb rasped.

'Very good, Major! Very good! More throttle, Major, more throttle. Faster, do you hear? More climb!'

Webb pushed more throttle, hauled back the stick.

'Close your canopy, Major!'

Webb yanked the canopy closed with his left hand.

'Now get your wheels up, Major! Quickly! Check radiator shutter open.'

Calmed somewhat by Theo's direction, Webb snapped his left hand from throttle to undercarriage control switch, then to the stick while he pulled the radiator shutter lever with his right.

'Now follow me, Major. And climb!'

Webb saw Theo pull away nearly straight up, sooty exhaust trailing back. His own wheels whined upward into place and he felt the immediate reduction in drag.

'Oberst to Staffel.' Theo's calm voice over the R/T. 'Keep your eyes open, especially astern. Form up at 10,000 feet. Gun switches on and test fire.'

Still too frightened to look about the sky, Webb hunched belted in the steel seat, head pressed against the padded armor plate, stomach knotted in nausea, hands trembling, watching the altimeter revolve like a berserk clock, seeing with relief the temp needles edging back away from red. The 109 seemed smoother now and his terror subsided.

As he heard each pilot in turn respond to Theo in German, it came to on Webb that he was in a German fighter – the Messerschmitt was real – and that the voices in his ears – the German of Luftwaffe aces – were real, and that the fantasy of his life, thought to be buried irretrievably in time, was unfolding around him. And that the price could easily be his life. He hung on, rocketing upward.

'Acknowledge Major Three.' Theo's voice in Schilling's headset.

'Three here, Oberst. Climbing at—' Schilling watched the sweeping altimeter needle – '4500. Over.'

His ears ached, popped. He swallowed, watching for Mustangs and for the other 109s. His gloved thumb lifting cannon button shield and pressing *bambam* cannon breach vibrating under the cover below his knees, now test firing machine guns in a short burst, filling the cockpit with cordite smell. He could feel the jerk of recoil against his momentum.

The sky around him was clear and pale blue. Above at 3 o'clock he picked out another 109 and then a second, both nearly vertical, trailing exhaust. He thought of Webb but he shut it out of his mind for the moment. The Staffel was in a bad place. They'd have a few hellish minutes trying to get formed up. And if the Mustangs caught them separately like this . . .

He ruddered to starboard to close with the two 109s he could see on his right. Barely able to move from the relentless vertical thrust of the aircraft, Schilling forced himself to concentrate. The 109 was climbing at 3000 feet per minute. The altimeter needle came around to 5000. All gauges seemed normal. He turned his head methodically left and right, scanning sections of sky, spotting another vertical exhaust trail well below to port. Damn, they were strung out!

He was shaking, and he tried to control it, surprised at it, angry at it. The ground strafing had rattled him a little but the take-off had nearly unnerved him. The damned Mustangs, back for a second pass, two mad hornets tearing up the strip, blowing the fuel truck. And yet not hitting any of the 109s on take-off; whether by accident or design he was unsure. But when one of them had thundered over him, as he lifted off, roaring like a freight train, he had truly thought he was a dead man.

Five thousand four hundred feet. The Messerschmitt climbed strong and smooth, the power of twelve cylinders flowing like electricity through the steel seat, along his spine and the nerves of his legs and arms. He was now tuned to his aircraft, sensing each movement, each force at work. He went into a slow vertical roll, revolving the 109 on its axis to gain visibility on all sides. Now he spotted two more 109s rising below on dirty exhaust ribbons.

'Three to Staffel,' he called over the R/T. 'Watch the sun. They'll come from the sun.'

6000 feet now. His ears again clogged, ached, popped. On he climbed, above the sand and above the mesas and above the mountains and above the haze and above the heat, higher higher higher where there was nothing – not even the lace of cloud – but blue.

Lowen and Meredith had almost completed their low-level search of the northern third of the rectangle when Willett and Spangler had hit the jackpot to the south. With Meredith tight on his wing Lowen turned south, incredulous that they had found the strip. Godamighty.

'Get up here fast, Three. Eight, get your element up here.

Repeat get upstairs to 11,000.' Lowen was not comfortable about having his whole damned flight beyond his sight.

'Eight here, Leader,' Recchio called. 'We're climbing at 3,000. On our way. Over.'

'Leader to Five. What happened down there?'

'After our first pass they came haulin' ass out of two hangars tucked away by a hill. We went around again to shake'm up. Counted six. Worked over the strip, took out a fuel truck, air-conditioned the hangar a little.'

'Did you hit any aircraft, Three? Over.'

'Negative. Just kept'em on their toes taking off.'

Lowen grinned. The Krauts would be rattled now, but he had not missed the fact that they had gotten out and up in moments; they were ready, the bastards. His eyes swept ahead, picking up three craft rising: the Wing Commander, Recchio and Polk. He was breathing a little harder and getting warm.

He went back to watching for Spangler and Willett, glancing curiously at seven o'clock where a distant smoke column was rising. That's where the Krauts would come up. He knew the 109s left a visible exhaust trail when they turned up the wick. It would take them well over five minutes to get up to 10,000 and they'd come up with their pants in a bunch. Perfect. *How's that for tactics, Oberst Kraut?* The bastard would be going nuts trying to get his people formed up.

'This is Leader to Flight. Change fuel to main tanks. Repeat change to main tanks.' Lowen reached down between his knees and tugged the fuel selector lever to MAIN L.H. He listened to the Merlin for any sign of missing. Nothing.

Then he spotted the canopy reflections from Three and Six climbing fast. Good. Now he had all five in sight.

'Leader to Flight, let's drop the tanks. Repeat, drop tanks. And form up.' Lowen pulled both release knobs at once. The Mustang jumped, lifted, freed of the weight and drag of the twin fuel pods. Ahead he saw jettisoned tanks falling away from the other three planes; like dully-shining fish they sailed down and back, turning end over end.

'This is Rebel Leader to Rebel Two, Four, Seven and Eight. Arm guns and test fire if you haven't. Over.' Lowen pressed the fire button on the stick, banging out a short burst that jolted the Mustang in its climbing flight. He watched Spangler and Willett joining the other three about one mile ahead and level. He looked at his watch; two minutes gone. Altitude 7,600 feet now. He was closing on the others.

'Looking good, Rebels. Making left turn forty-five degrees and continue to 11,000 feet. We'll give the Krauts just enough time to get to 10,000 like we agreed. We'll get the sun behind us and stay in formation until we know they see us.'

He adjusted his sunglasses, glanced again at the smoke column, now a dark rising smudge in the pink haze below. 'Leader to Four. What do you think they'll do, Wing Commander?'

'Four here, Leader. With six ships Jerry will spread out, Finger Four or Vee. One element might try to get up for top cover, I'd say.'

Hell, thought Lowen, we won't let anybody get on top of anything. He glanced at the panel clock. Four minutes. He was sweating. Where the hell were they?

'Leader to Flight. If they get up here in a group we'll stick tight and hit them together. If they spread out line abreast then – listen up, now – we *wait*, repeat wait, until we are in range, repeat *in range* and then stack up vertically – under me – and hit their left end. If we can take a couple of them out on the first pass, we'll have the edge. And remember, if one of those 109s has his wheels down, don't fire. But be careful. What do you think, Wing Commander?'

'We'd better be goin' in bloody fast, Leader.'

Bloody fast indeed, thought Lowen. In their rising turn at 11,000 feet he looked out at the other six fighters formed in echelon off his starboard wing. Like steps on a staircase. (Like Europe.) Oh they were beautiful these Mustangs, so clean and sharp, red bullet noses gleaming, silver-gray blade wings shining against the pure blue. As they edged closer he could almost hear their engines over his own, in chorus, in time, in deadly harmony. And how he proudly loved their great insignia, dark blue discs and white sharp stars.

And the green-brown Spit down there, slim swallow bird all alone on the end. *And one for the RAF now*, he thought. 'This is Leader to Four. Come on up here, Wing Commander. Off my port wing.'

'Roger, Leader. Coming up.'

417

Lowen watched the Spit rise smoothly around behind. 'Wing Commander, we would be honored if you would lead the attack. Do you copy?'

'Roger that, Leader. Splendid. And thank you.'

'Okay. When we get in position, I'll call it and it's all yours.'

'Hey there, we've got trade,' called Polk. 'Exhaust trails at seven o'clock low.'

Lowen didn't even look down. He knew they still had about two minutes. He was calculating their path ahead, a wide descending turn to put them over the sun and right at 10,000 at about the time the 109s got up.

'Counting three bandits at eight o'clock,' called Polk again.

Lowen dipped his port wing slightly, straining to see. There, three little pencil lines drawn against soft pink haze. Like Germany. Absurd. His adrenalin kicked in like a supercharger.

'Okay, Gentlemen,' he called. 'We have the firepower. And plenty of ammunition, so hose'm when you get anywhere close.' It was a subtle way, he hoped, of saying that the brutal fifties would compensate in some way for the Kraut's experience.

'Counting four bandits,' Polk called. 'Now five.'

'Leader to Flight. Okay, let's ease on down.' Lowen edged the stick forward. He looked out. Their formation was good.

'One more bandit,' called Recchio. 'Six now.'

Lowen fingered the trigger button on the stick grip, focused his eyes on the three concentric orange circles of his gunsight. Another glance over the gauges. All in order. He was ready. He looked out at eight o'clock. Tiny black gnats, the first three topping out at about four miles.

'Leader to Flight. Do those aircraft look familiar?'

'Jesus,' someone said.

'There's the lot of them then,' muttered Redmond-Donleavy. 'Bloody hell!'

The fourth 109 was topping out now.

'Hey now,' said Spangler. '*Déjà vu* and World War Two.'

The last two 109s were almost up. Lowen eased the flight tighter on their descending turn at 10,500. Their timing looked to be perfect. He watched the gnats.

'Fuckers don't look too organized,' said Spangler.

'Let's hit'em, Leader,' called Recchio. 'Come on, before they get pulled together.'

'Hold station, damnit,' Lowen snapped. Those damned

Krauts wanted this match. See who's got the biggest pair. We're gonna show them how to do this again. Fair and square. Stay tight now, for a half-roll to starboard on my signal. Tighter. Tighter.'

He saw the gnats trying to pair up, one crossing over another. The last two were still coming, curving up out of their climb. Three miles.

'Steady now, Chaps,' said the Wing Commander pleasantly.

Lowen's gloved left hand flexed once around the fat ribbed throttle handle. 'Begin run,' he said, pushing it. 'It's all yours, Wing Commander.'

'Tally ho,' called Redmond-Donleavy.

At 8800 feet Schilling was catching the two highest 109s, identifying them as Five and Two. As Rudi's wingman, he was glad to spot Two. He turned to watch two more of the Staffel rising below on their dark trails. Five; where was the last one? He slow-rolled his 109 again – very nervous about the Mustangs and very glad that the sky was so clear – paying special attention to the direction of the sun. He wondered how many there would be. Surely more than two.

Nine thousand two hundred feet. Sweating profusely, he shivered once from the cool air blasting in the cockpit vents at his knees. He closed the vents, checked his gauges, returned to scanning. At 9500 he eased the stick forward and banked right so that he would come up to Rudi. Freed of the pressing force of his climb, his body seemed to lighten. Sweat ran in his eyes and he snatched off his sunglasses and wiped his sleeve across his face. His gut ached. His mouth was dry. Then he closed on Rudi from below at about 50 yards. Again his eyes swept tensely along the hazed pink horizon sunward. The Mustangs could be—

'Achtung!' Kesler's voice over the R/T. 'Wolves at one o'clock high.'

Schilling snapped his eyes high and right, squinting, picking up several silver specks against the pale flat blue, sunlight flashing off canopies at three miles. He was surprised to see them there instead of low in the sun or very high and behind.

'Counting Wolves now, five . . . six,' Rudi's voice.

'Leader to Staffel.' Theo's voice. 'Form up quickly. Quickly! I'm coming up the middle.'

'Seven Wolves at one o'clock,' called Rudi. 'Steering right, Leader.'

Schilling strained to count the Wolves, seeing only six. The Staffel was trying to form up, flying parallel to the Mustangs which were now about 500 feet higher. And toward the sun, damn them. They were flying in very close formation, turning now, three pairs in perfect order and the one dark-colored fighter – it looked like a Spit – all in a cluster. Damned if they weren't tight. Christ, they were doing tricks. *Tricks*! They could have slaughtered us on takeoff and here they are waiting, squaring off and showing off. How insanely grand! And here the fuck we are scattered all over the fucking sky. This is it; nobody would back out now.

He made a calm assessment of their situation. Seven Wolves on a wide turn. That Colonel Lowen had got his act together all right. Not bad; he had faced worse odds than seven to five.

'Closer now! Closer now!' Theo called. 'Can you hear me, Major Webb? Get your wheels down! Get your wheels down!'

Their line was still strung out, Schilling saw. He boosted throttle, sticking to Rudi at 50 yards as they leveled out. Now the Wolves were turning at about two miles, still in perfect formation. And coming faster than he expected.

'Get'em down, Webb,' Schilling shouted. 'Get your damned wheels down!' He locked his eyes on the silver specks, keeping Rudi in his peripheral vision, cursing the sun swinging under the Wolves. The red eye of his gun switch light gleamed on the panel. He flipped back the cannon button shield. More throttle. He glanced out to see Theo and Kesler still a half-mile out. And, damnit, beyond them the last two still closing. He looked up. The Wolves were turning into them head-on.

'Calmly now,' came Theo's voice.

Schilling could feel his heart. He leveled out at full throttle and placed the specks in his sights. *Just like the war.* A mile now . . . less. His gloved fingers sought the gun trigger and cannon button of the stick grip. Then, disbelieving, he saw the specks shift, lift, climb over each other in pairs vertically.

Rendel had not seen the Wolves – he cursed his eyes – even when Theo had called them at one o'clock. He was topping out now, nervous because he was on the end. Theo's order for the Captain-Major to lower wheels came over the R/T and Rendel made his choice to overfly the American and place himself in front. He saw the Wolves then.

Webb, soaked in sweat, chilled, his ears clogged painfully, confused by the German in his earphones, was leveling off when he heard Theo's order to lower his wheels. Above him he could see the other 109s strung out in a ragged climbing line. His sunglasses slid down his sweat-slippery nose and he pushed them back quickly.

'Get'em down, Webb!' came a voice in his headset. 'Get your damned wheels down!'

He grabbed the undercarriage switch. With the pulsing roar of the engine Webb heard no hydraulic whine, had no sensation of the switch activating the undercarriage. He panicked. In the space of a second he considered then the emergency undercarriage release lever on his right, then abandoned the idea, loath to release the stick and trust a lever. In the space of the next second he chose instead to drop his left hand to turn the emergency undercarriage lowering wheel – something sturdy he could trust – at his left hip. He looked up then to see white dots bright dots whizzing silently by outside, dozens of them, beautiful glowing fireflies.

There is some mistake, he thought, furiously cranking the wheel. Then a sound as if his airplane had been struck by a hundred rocks. He jerked in fright. A terrible hail of flying things came banging punching into the fuselage. A fury of steel and glass and Plexiglas shards slashed over him. He shriveled instinctively in the seat. Instrument gauges popped and sparked on the panel. He felt himself struck, as if by sharp stones. *Please God*. His left arm numb. Pain cracking like fire through his left leg. His face and neck lashed. The canopy spraying sparkling fragments over his arms and lap. Cool air rushing in on a wave of pain.

Then the hail passed. As if in a dream, within the blink of an eye, he saw a red-nosed Mustang streak past so close he could see the rivets.

Rendel had caught and passed the Captain-Major and placed the Wolves in his gunsight when he saw to his horror that the Americans all seemed to be heading for him. A blizzard of glowing white fireballs stormed at him. He crouched blindly in the seat, knowing he was completely bracketed, doomed.

The sound was horrendous. The 109 shook left and right. Steel and glass thrashed through the cockpit over his head. A loud crack, cold air, and he sensed the canopy gone. Crouching lower, he realized that there was only the massive iron block of the Daimler-Benz between him and his death. For a moment he would be saved. The bullets passed. He jerked up in the seat, blinking. *Get out.* The 109 had become so much useless junk, preparing to fall. No control in stick or rudder pedals. It would disintegrate around him. Or, in a moment, explode.

Schilling, taken by surprise when the Mustangs shifted to vertical and hit the Staffel line on the far end, was not without admiration for the maneuver. Then he was firing. Bold or not, the P-51s still showed themselves as three-quarter targets, moving like rockets. He banked hard right, catching one in his sights, trying to lead, pouring out shells and bullets.

A flash to the right. Two fighters colliding, ripping each other apart, wings sailing, one fuselage rolling spewing debris and the other coming apart in an orange-white flash, its dark engine mass smoking white, arcing out and down. *Christ.*

The P-51s were gone. By reflex, he hauled back on the stick and swooped upward, beginning a vertical loop in perfect coordination with Rudi.

Now that the two groups had passed each other they would kick over and try to get the edge, looping up and over or turning, skidding at wing-tearing force to get each other in their sights. The image of the collision flashed back in replay. He had seen such things before and he remembered how he had felt about such things before, but this time he was jolted, sick. Stupid bastards all of them. All of us.

In the seconds it took to haul the 109 up on its back to the top of the loop, as he hung upside down with the pink flat earth above his head, he thought *Am I German or American?*

Rendel unbuckled his harness. There was no canopy to slide back. *Get out.* The engine shuddered pounded into self-distruct. Gray smoke streamed over the open cockpit, choking him. *Get out.* Move. Port wing ripped in a dozen places. Aileron gone, flap undulating up and down like a hand waving. *Get out.* Then the engine cowling lifted like the dark hood of an automobile, snapped away back over his head. Sparks swept up between his knees and it seemed he could smell the green blood of severed hydraulic arteries. *Get out.*

He put both gloved hands on the edges of the cockpit, placed his feet in the seat and leaped over the left side, drawing his legs up and grasping them cannon-ball fashion. He struck the trailing edge of the wing with his hip. The flap tore loose at the impact of his body and sailed alongside him spinning. Plunging downward, he looked up to see the port wing separate from the riddled fuselage, its blue belly a sheet of flame streaming thick smoke. Then it blew apart.

Rendel closed his eyes, still falling, the wind fluttering his flight suit, debris raining around him crackling sighing as it rushed by. He forced himself to be patient enough to fall clear of any other aircraft, having done this eleven times before. He fell and he prayed and fell and prayed, holding the metal D-ring. When he pulled it, he heard the pop and silken hiss of the chute streaming smoothly behind him. It seemed the most wondrous of blessings that he was still alive. And with two cigars in his zippered pocket.

Webb, in shock and momentarily paralyzed, slumped in the cockpit. Steamy smoke slipped from under the instrument panel, smelling of rubber and glycol. The engine was making a clunking noise that shook the entire aircraft. Then it stopped – silence except for rushing wind and metallic creaking. *Something very terrible has happened,* he thought. Like a bad car crash.

In the whistling silence he began to comprehend, with maddening slowness, that he had been hit. Looking up, he saw that the gunsight had been blown away from the top edge of the instrument panel, the windscreen twisted, armor glass pulverized. Oh man. His left leg was numb. Looking down, he examined a furrow across the top of his thigh, a wound oozing. He tried to move his left arm but it wouldn't work. Blood spattered everywhere; sleeves and thighs, panel gauges – it couldn't be his blood – and the maroon stain crawling to his knee. *Oh God. Wounded. Truly messed up.*

Now he was seized by nausea and terror. Raising his gloved hand to clear his vision – he was half-blind – he found two fingers gone – middle and forefinger. *This is not happening,* he thought. Mistake. Where were his fingers? Should he look for them? He'd heard that sometimes they could put them back on. *Mother help me.*

The plane began to tip, yaw. He was losing the sensation of moving forward. Smoke was gagging him. The aircraft crackling under him. *Sitting in a tin can.* Oh man. He was getting cold and he wondered why he had no strength. *Get out.* He stared a moment at the cockpit wall where the metal was chewed through, ragged edges showing light. The horizon lifted up below him, tilted left. *This is your Bingo,* he thought. *This is your Bingo, Motherfucker.* Bitter fumes swept his face. Heat waves shimmering around the nose cowling. *Jesus Christ God save me.*

Now he understood that there was no one to save him, except himself. *Just turn it upside down and pull the harness release,* he remembered Malzahn telling him. Yes. He willed his right hand to unsnap the harness release. Nothing on his left side worked; not his arm, not his leg, not his eye. Flames appeared outside around the cowling. He could feel the heat. *Get out.* He pulled the red emergency release pin. The canopy made a cracking noise, then vanished. Cool cool air. The horizon tilted more and he could feel the airplane sliding sideways. It would slip a little more, he knew. Then just fall out of the sky. *Get out.* He turned, was astounded to see a huge billowing trail of black smoke from underneath the trailing edge of the wing. Panicked, he threw himself back and forth from the waist. He couldn't stand. He pulled back on the stick and the nose lifted but he felt the side-slip increase. The nose dipped, lifted, dipped.

Fool, you can't roll without power. He pushed the stick forward, crashed against the instrument panel. The horizon swung upward. He was catapulted outward. He closed his eyes. With his two good fingers and thumb he found the metal ring and pulled it.

The chute fluttered out and jerked open with a tremendous yank that flung him horizontally like a rag doll.

When Lowen charged through the gauntlet of tracers he was stunned that the 109s had managed to return so much fire. He had taken hits, feeling them rattle over his fuselage. He remembered raking two of the 109s, one of which had its landing gear slightly opened.

Now that he was through the Kraut line he glanced back, appalled to see the descending wreckage of a mid-air collision.

'Two, Leader. I'm hit!' came a voice over the R/T.

Below and to his right Lowen glimpsed a P-51 winging over streaming white vapor from its belly. He checked for Meredith, saw him underneath. He wondered who had collided. Two down, three, more? Godamighty. No time. The Krauts would be around and on top of them in seconds.

'Tighten up, lads,' called the Wing Commander. 'Climb right. Climb right.'

Pulling back on the stick Lowen twisted in his seat, looking back and up to see three 109s climbing together into a vertical loop. Bastards were wasting no time. *Climb climb and turn into them*. He knew they had gotten the edge and would come around before his flight could. Too late, too late.

'Three and Six,' called the Wing Commander, 'prepare to split right on my signal. Steady now.'

Good show, thought Lowen. Let one element loose and maybe we can pinch the Krauts; they would stick together, be forced to choose Three and Six, or him and Meredith and the Wing Commander. Climbing hard, he again glanced back at the three dark 109s to see them closing, noses winking flashes, firing early, still upside down.

'Three and Six break right.'

The Wing Commander's order would balance the battle, buy them a few minutes. Lowen saw Spangler and Willett wing over and split. Again he looked back to see how the Krauts would go; he saw them twisting over, head-on. *Godamighty*, the bastards had chosen him. And Meredith. Lowen glanced over, reassured to see his wingman tight.

Climb baby climb. The howling Merlin hauled him upward. He half-rolled right to present a thinner target. There was nothing they could do except climb until the 109s got the range; if they broke too early they were dead. More glowing tracers; the Krauts were getting the range.

'On your tail, Leader,' Spangler called. 'We're coming.'

More glowing orange dots whizzed past his canopy into the blue. They were level targets now. Time to split again.

'Seven, break right!' Lowen barked.

Bullets whacked into his tail section. He hunched instinctively, banking left, boosting throttle. Now he and Meredith were separate targets. A hollow *bang* from the rear. He threw the Mustang into a snap-roll that nearly yanked him out of his seat.

A red cylinder bounced cracking off the instrument panel – his unsecured thermos. *Idiot*.

'On your tail, Leader. *Break*!' Spangler on the R/T.

Schilling, tight on Rudi's wing at fifty yards, came out of the vertical loop in pursuit of the five Wolves.

One was the Spit, smaller and slimmer, on the outside of the five. He had spotted it flashing past high on the right end of the Staffel line, its twin cannon flashing. He didn't like the Spit being there and he cursed it as he had years before. Fucking Brits, the only two machines they ever got right were the Spitfire and the Mini-Cooper and now the bizarre appearance of this Spit seemed an omen. He wondered if the Staffel was up against some hard-ass veterans.

Now he and Rudi were gaining on the Wolves, climbing hard. He half-rolled, held right rudder, seeing that they would close the gap in seconds. He looked over his gunsight, trying to bring his nose over in line with the Wolves.

Then they split; one pair right, the other three – including the Spit – to the left. Already bearing right, he and Rudi bore down on the pair. Schilling tried to put the left one in his sights, closing, closing, still too far to fire. Movement to his right above. He saw Theo's One pulling overhead to cut off the Mustangs. Wary of the other three Wolves, Schilling checked them climbing to loop over and come around; they wouldn't take long, he knew.

Now he and Rudi and Theo were closing on the two P-51s at about 300 yards. One of them danced in his sights. Above he saw tracers streaming out, Theo firing early. Then Rudi opened up. Schilling followed. The tiny embers swarmed at the Mustangs which split again, flying out of their fire. *Damn*.

Schilling ruddered right, following Rudi, tracking the Mustang that broke right, focused on the silver fighter, punching out bursts as the P-51 twisted over, slipping left in his sight, showing its belly. Schilling hit the buttons, seeing Rudi's tracers mixing with his, smoking outward to storm around the Mustang, watching it slip into the hail of glowing dots, watching white flashes *hit hit hit*! The P-51 sprouting a white trail, pieces flying off. *Horrido*!

'Hit, Leader. This is Seven; I'm hit!' Meredith's voice in Lowen's headset. *Damn this can't be*, Lowen thinking in a flash, coming out of the snap-roll, standing the Mustang on its port wing, feeling the fighter slew around as if caught on a wire. Pain squeezed his neck as the maneuver pulled him against the harness. More tracers outside. Feeling the Mustang slipping loose, he leveled out a second for the prop to get a bite and stabilize, got on the throttle, and pulled the stick back to climb. Snapping a glance below he saw Meredith upside down trailing smoke, its wings savaged with dark holes, the belly scoop torn open, the rear fuselage ripped so badly he saw the tail wheel assembly hanging out.

'Get out, Bob,' called Lowen, rolling over. 'Get—'

Bang. Lowen saw sparks burst on his starboard wing surface. Shrapnel clattered like BBs against the cockpit, *pop*-cracked his canopy. Then there were secondary explosions. And flame. He winced, rammed stick left to roll, continuing his climb, hunched in his seat, holding his breath, waiting for more, blessing the armor plate at his back.

Climbing. No tracers. Max throttle. There were holes in the cockpit wall. Something had struck his leg below the knee. The canopy was whistling from holes that spread webbed cracks outward. He glanced left and back, looking at the bulging snout of a Messerschmitt at fifty yards, seeing in one brain-blinding fraction of a second the dark cannon port dead center in the nose.

Without thinking Lowen rammed stick left, pulled throttle back, and let out full flaps; the braking effect seemed to tear him out of his harness. Praying for the 109 to overfly. Hits sparking off his wingtip.

The 109 overflew, a monster shadow, its mottled brown shape inverted as if swept silently above his head, tracers sailing around it like incandescent pilot fish following a shark. The 109 took hits that sparked and danced across the fuselage and tail. Lowen shivered, turned after the 109 which rolled again to escape the tracers swarming like bees.

Godamighty thanks guys. Lowen resisted the impulse to see who had saved him, keeping the climbing 109 above his nose. *Now the tables are turned, Kraut.* His heart was pounding its way up his throat. He glanced out at his damaged wing; the cannon shell had hit the gun assembly and ammunition boxes, and the sparks and staccato detonations had been his own rounds exploding. Now he saw orange embers glowing, spitting backward, and as he watched, the embers went out.

He turned his attention to the climbing Messerschmitt straight ahead, its path marked by a dirty shadow of exhaust.

Schilling, breaking away from the stricken P-51 with Rudi, turned to deal with the other three Wolves closing on them. He had seen Theo bank away to attack the other Mustang and lost sight of him. Now more tracers, fireballs everywhere in all directions like great snowflakes. The Wolves had caught up.

'Three, break right!' Rudi's voice sharp in his headset.

Automatically Schilling obeyed, hauling the 109 over, conscious of his neck aching from the ceaseless whipping back and forth, conscious that fatigue was already shaving his reaction times, draining his strength. It seemed that whatever he did, wherever he looked, tracers were in the air. He felt his skin crawl at his neck, expecting bullets to slam into the back of his seat at any second. The tracers had come downward, so the Wolves were above them. He and Rudi fled in a shallow dive at full throttle into the glare of the sun.

'Major Three.' Rudi's voice above the roar of the cockpit. 'Prepare to split right at my signal.'

'Roger that, Two. On your signal.'

Schilling knew there was little choice. They were being forced down, on the defense, chased – the worst place to be if you had tough pilots on your tail. Only if they split and turned to fight could they break out. He twisted in his seat, seeing the three fighters behind at 500 yards. Rudi would wait until they were closer, until they had the range.

Schilling then made an unorthodox decision; he would wait just a moment after Rudi split left and then, instead of breaking right, he would split-S and be up and over, high and behind Rudi. The P-51s would stay together, so Rudi's break would either suck them after him – in which case Schilling would be in a position to attack – or they would anticipate his break to the right, and perhaps be fooled into breaking right early.

'*Now!*' Rudi snapped.

Schilling barreled ahead for a two-second count and then lifted the 109 up, stick hard left *lovely fuel injection*, sailing over upside down. He glanced back, exhilarated to see that the Mustangs had gone right. Still inverted, he saw Rudi a quarter-mile off – with the bastard Tommy Spit on his tail.

'Two, on your tail! *On your tail!*' Schilling locked his eyes on the Spitfire, willing his guns closer, watching Rudi bank right.

The Spit twisted after him. Schilling was closing with agonizing slowness . . . 500 yards . . . 450 yards . . . 400 yards . . . The two fighters danced in and out of his sights like dark frantic moths . . . 350 yards . . . a little more. *Get away from him, you bastard.*

'On your tail, *Two. Climb climb*!' called Schilling.

The Spit opened fire then. Schilling saw the muzzle flashes from the twin wing cannon, gritting his teeth as he saw strikes on Rudi's fuselage. The 109 swooped upward out of the Spit's fire, streaming exhaust, and then a thin trail of white. The Spit swept through Schilling's gunsight and he ruddered left to lead it, firing early, watching his cannon tracers smoke out to chase the Spit. The bastard was not letting go of Rudi but now Schilling was in range.

He fired again. Rudi's 109 climbed, rolled right. The Spit rolled left. Schilling closed, following the Spit around. *Lovely Limey bastard* its wide thin pointed green-brown wings with red-and-blue roundels rocking in his sights. As he turned tighter and tighter, the Spit turned tighter yet, just by a hair, just the round rudder with red-blue-white bars teasing him in and out of the gunsight reflector. In frustration Schilling fired several cannon rounds, then the guns, sending tracers searching, hoping for a lucky hit. The Spit, he realized, was bringing him back around. To the other Wolves. Sweat ran in his eyes . . . 150 yards . . . more of the Spit's slender fuselage weaved in his sight. *Now*! As was his habit in the war, Schilling instinctively snapped a glance backward before firing; nothing left or high, then to the right. His heart seemed to seize; both P-51s, red bullet noses gleaming, were over his right shoulder at 200 yards. Even as he looked he saw the flash of their blade-wing guns, the winking fire of his death.

By reflex he jammed the stick forward and jammed himself down in the seat. The hits came, that strange thrown-stone sound of .50s punching in. His gunsight exploded away, stinging his face and arm. Bright sparks spewed off the engine cowling. He could feel the steel lasing the fuselage aft. They were going to kill him. The 109 dropped forward, quivering as the slugs tore at the tail section. Schilling wanted to be a stone, a rocket, a missile aimed earthward. He wanted to live.

In his dogged pursuit of the Messerschmitt, Lowen found a moment to be curious that the pilot was simply climbing, with no attempt to fight.

No oxygen up there for you, Kraut, he thought, fumbling at his own mask, checking the altitude; the needle was revolving full-tilt coming up on 13,000. He glanced out at his starboard wing, thankful that the fire had gone out, praying that the main spar had not been weakened. The climb would not severely tax the spar – unlike a full dive or the wrenching maneuvers of dogfighting – but when it let go, the whole wing went snap and there would be no escape; he would be instantly pinned paralyzed by G-forces as the fuselage fell in violently whipping turns. He had seen it more than once.

He glanced around to all quarters; no one near. *Godamighty, gonna get this Kraut now.* Thirteen thousand eight hundred feet. Crazy Kraut would have to breathe. Lowen found his own breathing labored as he watched the 109 hover out of range of his gunsight circles, dimmed by the dirty exhaust that whipped past his canopy; was it smoke? He could smell burning oil. He punched out a short burst – only his port wing guns fired – hoping a few might hit. White dots sailed out and diminished in the sooty wake. *Come on, Kraut.*

He glanced at the altimeter; 14,200 feet. He could taste oil, rubber. His chest ached. Breathing seemed more difficult. He checked the oxygen pressure gauge at lower right panel; on the money at 400 psi. Then he saw a glowing ember sail silently by his canopy in the 109s trail. Then another. *Fire,* the Kraut was on fire! He could taste the smoke; he was *breathing* smoke. Damn. He ran his gloved fingertips along the black-ribbed oxygen tube at his right knee. And found the rent near the connecting ring. *Godamighty damn.*

He sucked in deeper. The Mustang rocked in the slipstream of the burning Messerschmitt. Fifteen thousand feet. The smoke was thicker now, dotted with orange embers. He kept his eyes locked on the 109, tasting its smoke, watching it grow larger. A sharp pain now, then gone, then back. He eased right rudder, sliding the P-51 out into clear air, then yanked the useless oxygen mask away.

He turned the canopy crank, opening it a few inches, gasping at cool air. He was startled to see the Messerschmitt clearly at about 100 yards . . . eighty . . . sixty . . . fifty yards now.

The image of the 109 was spectacular: its tan-brown camouflage paint against the flawless azure sky, the great black-and-white crosses on wing and fuselage, the white numeral 1 on the flank behind the cockpit. Closer he came. He could hear his own heaving hissing breath. His vision seemed to dim.

Drawing up with the Messerschmitt low on the port side, he could see a thin stream of flame slipping back and over and under the wing root, joined by flame from other seams along the pale blue under-surface where they ran together as thin as translucent glowing ice. Most of the midsection of the fuselage was punctured, the bullet holes circled by bare metal rings bright against the giant black cross. *Godamighty*. Lowen knew what had happened; a severed fuel line or punctured tank was releasing high-octane fuel that burned as fast as it leaked, running along the hollow ribbed tunnel of the rear fuselage, eating away the aluminum skin, consuming the aircraft as it flew on, gouting brilliant orange flame and dense black smoke.

Lowen was almost alongside. He knew he could jink once and fire but there was no need. He blinked; his eyes stung, watered. His hand on the stick was growing numb. He thought perhaps he was dreaming. *Get out* he thought to the Kraut pilot, and as if on Lowen's order the 109s canopy popped up and off. The pilot, wearing sunglasses, was looking over at him. White smoke slipped up out of the open cockpit around his tan-fabric shoulders and the wind whipped off his cap and fluttered his white hair.

Godamighty, it's my Kraut, it's my man, Number One Oberst Kraut. Lowen heaved forward against his harness, sucking in cold air, edging on panic. Then the German pilot raised his arm and saluted, his black-gloved hand rigid. Transfixed, tortured by his straining lungs, Lowen had a terrible moment when he had no control. Vision dimming, he was blacking out. Then his own hand came up in salute. *Please get out*, he thought.

As if in a dream, the only sound his own roaring engine Lowen saw the great mottled metal bird ease over in a roll, showing the blue bottom, the ripped-out riddled wings streaking black oil, the aft fuselage a mass of orange fire. The 109 slowed as it rolled. Lowen could hardly see. He eased back on throttle, turned the stick over and forward. He saw the German pilot drop out.

Schilling aimed earthward at full throttle. Tracers sailed past on both sides, some tearing at his wings. Now one two cracking *bangs*

431

by his head, jarring him senseless as two rounds caromed off the armor plate headrest, striking sparks that ricocheted around the cockpit. The 109 gained momentum as it plunged; two and one-half tons of metal and fuel and ammunition. He willed himself lower and smaller in the seat. The tracers had stopped. He summoned his courage to glance backward. One of the red-nosed P-51s was behind at less than 400 yards, slightly to starboard, and his wingman high and behind at about 500 yards.

They had him. He was screwed now. The Mustangs would merely follow, wait to get close enough to blow him to pieces, wait for him to choose when there was no choice. Whatever he did – turn right, turn left, roll, loop – they would have him. Those .50s would rip him apart like buzz-saws.

The ground rose in a great pink wall toward him. He estimated his altitude at 3,000 feet, saw the altimeter revolve madly trying to catch up. The closer he got to the ground the sooner the P-51s could expect him to do something. He knew he was in the leader's sights, with the wingman ready to cover if he missed, and that when the closer Mustang had him in range he would fire. In seconds now.

Schilling was only slightly less terrified of attempting a negative-G diving turn – his last card – than he was of being chewed into a disintegrating fireball. Without thinking he hauled back on the stick and pressed left rudder pedal, expecting bullets to rain in. Forced out of its trajectory, the Messerschmitt began to shudder horribly as it strained into a curve. He expected it to snap in half, shed its wings.

He fought to hold the skidding plunging fighter, felt it stabilize for a moment, then jammed the stick forward, applying bottom rudder and more throttle, nosing under and curving into an outside loop – thus placing the pull of centrifugal force from the outside top rather than the inside bottom, sucking him up out of his seat, pressing his head against the fractured canopy, stuffing his guts up into his ribcage. His harness belts bit into his hips and shoulders. His knees began to float. Vertigo and centrifugal pull robbed his vision. He knew neither up nor down, caught helpless in the jarring maneuver that could tear the aircraft apart as it shuddered in the teeth of terminal physical forces.

Please. Blur of blue sky, the black instrument panel vibrating. He sensed the deathly thunder of the Mustangs over him, gray

shadows streaking by. The horizon came into focus [...]
vertical wall to his left. The 109 was coming out of t[...]
would expend its momentum and drop out of the sky. Pa[...]
Schilling felt the loss of movement, that moment of tr[...]
from being flung to being free to fall.

Hanging on the starboard wing he pushed on throttle a[...]
pulled the stick right, feeling the 109 tip level and charge out [...]
its sideways slide and become controllable. Rudi's voice calling
in his headset: *Major Three, Major Three.* Dazed, incredulous
that he had survived, Schilling searched for the Mustangs. His
vision snapped into focus. Up, back, left, right, below – he saw
no Mustangs.

'Major Three,' Rudi's voice again. 'Three, acknowledge.'

Schilling then saw aircraft at one o'clock, counting six dark
darts moving in pairs, in perfect formation. He blinked. The
aircraft were closing on him.

Then he saw they were jet fighters. They swept into a circling
turn, then tightened. They were F-5s, mottled blue and gray.
They were circling him. *Oh Christ,* he thought, *I am an American.*

'Major Three, acknowledge!' Rudi's voice, calm, tired.

'Three to Oberstleutnant,' Schilling called. He was confused.
Did Rudi see the jets? Now he had leveled the 109.

'Major, listen to me. *Lower your wheels.* Lower your wheels
and change to channel six repeat channel six. Do you copy?'

'Six,' Schilling said, 'Affirmative.'

He actuated the undercarriage switch and he felt and heard
the hydraulic mechanism whine, clunk, whine, clunk. No
indicator lights came on. He stared at the instrument panel;
junk. He looked up. The jets were coming for him.

He reached down with his left hand to turn the emergency
undercarriage hand wheel. It moved, stuck, moved; the muscles
of his arm and shoulder hurt so viciously that he nearly cried
out. There was blood on his right thigh and his lap was full of
glass fragments.

'Are you on six, Major?' Rudi's voice was urgent.

The wheel moved. He felt the drag of his lowered wheels
now. 'Oberstleutnant, where are you?' It sounded foolish.

'Overhead. High, behind you. *Change to six*!'

Schilling set the channel selector. The static crackle in his
headset vanished, became a new voice, a young voice: '–
repeating. Do you copy, Bandit Number Three?' Behind the

the unmistakable jet whine.

'...mative. This is Three.' Schilling picked out the blue
...nape of Rudi's 109 above. Now two pairs of jets were
...away. The other pair was behind him at a half mile and
...ng.

'...Bandit Numbah Three,' said the new voice. 'This is Air
...orce Cobra Leader. Do you copy? Over.'

'Affirmative, Cobra Leader,' replied Schilling. 'Are my
wheels down?'

'Your wheels are down, Bandit Three. You are directed to
follow all instructions. Or you will be fired upon. Do you copy?
Over.'

'Roger that. Loud and clear.' Schilling was soaking wet.
Sweat ran in his mouth. He looked back to see the two F-5s; in
the space of a second or two they had drawn up behind and high
at less than 100 feet. Uncontrollably he shivered. The closest jet
was cruising slightly nose-up with the speed brake flaps hanging
down. Above the pointed black nose-cone he saw twin cannon
barrels. And above that, the pilot; white helmet, black visor.
Robot-like. At each of the wingtips a long slender blue dart of a
missile. He could read the word RESCUE stenciled in black on
the fuselage below the cockpit. *Easy* now, he told himself. He
waved at the pilot, a single gesture. The pilot did not wave back.

'Bandit Numbah Three from Cobra Leader,' came the voice
so casually. 'Climb to 3000 and maintain airspeed two-five-
zero.'

'Affirmative. Two-five-zero.'

'Get your ass on up there, Numbah Three.'

The jet lifted away silently, followed by his wingman, as if
snatched by invisible hands. Schilling could smell their kerosene
fuel.

'Now all repeat *all* you warbirds listen up.' The voice was like
a disc jockey's, Schilling thought. 'Form up at 3000. We're
going back to Willie. Bearing is south southeast. Colonel Lowen
do you read? Over.'

'Affirmative Leader,' came another new voice in Schilling's
headset.

'What is your situation, Colonel? Can you maintain two-five-
zero? Over.'

Schilling climbed, closing on Rudi and the Spit and the three
P-51s from underneath, listening.

'Not sure. I've got three P-51s down.'

'Don't worry, Colonel. We have recon and Medevac choppers all over the place down there by now.'

As Schilling drew closer to Lowen's fighters he could see their battle damage. The three Mustangs, stacked in echelon, were pretty well shot up. The lowest aircraft was trailing a long thin line of white vapor and the top P-51 was throwing dark exhaust. The Spit was relatively undamaged.

'Rebel Six to Leader,' came another voice. 'I've got trouble.'

'Go ahead, Six.'

'We're gonna lose this Spam-can if I don't get it down, Leader. It's starting to cook.'

Boosting throttle to come up behind Rudi, Schilling heard his own engine stutter. He smelled electrical smoke; rubber, plastic, wiring.

'Mustang Leader to Cobra Leader. My other ship has no radio. The pilot is wounded and indicating he's going downstairs. We're not going to make Willie. Over.'

Now Schilling could see Rudi's 109 clearly from below and behind; it was trailing gray smoke and there were dozens of holes in the fuselage, tail, and wings. And he was falling back. The bottom P-51 began slipping lower as well. He looked up to see the jets circling vigilantly. He was sweating hot, drained. He thought about popping the canopy and going over the side. He lifted up beside Rudi.

Schilling could see Rudi's cockpit now. Rudi was slumped over, his head resting back on one shoulder.

'*Oberstleutnant*,' Schilling said. '*Are you wounded?*'

Rudi moved his head. His aircraft slipped downward a little. Schilling followed.

'Hold station, Bandits,' came the warning.

Schilling wondered what the jets would do if all the fighters reduced speed drastically. His own engine stuttered again and he sensed some loss of cadence in the exhaust note. His manifold pressure gauge and coolant/oil temp gauge were both dead.

'This is Mustang Leader Colonel Roger Lowing Bandits. I am in command ... of all warbird aircraft. Warbirds, reduce airspeed to at Willie. Over.' Cobra Leader, you and yo fight, not yours. Rel- home now. This is our descend. and

435

Uh-oh, thought Schilling. Static crackled in his headset.

'Cobra Leader to Mustang Leader. Sir, you are not in command. You are ordered to maintain station and follow escort. Do you copy?'

'Mustang Leader to Bandit Two. We will follow you. Let's get downstairs. Do you copy?'

'Affirmative,' said Rudi, dropping lower.

'Cobra Leader to all warbirds; you are ordered to follow escort or you will be fired upon.'

'Horsecrap, Cobra Leader.' Lowen's voice was so lazy that Schilling smiled. 'We're putting down on the Kraut field. Go ahead, Bandit Two. We are following.'

Schilling saw Rudi's nose drop and he followed. The P-51s and the Spit slowed and began to descend overhead, their wheels hanging down like bird's legs.

'Cobra Leader to Flight. Arm guns and form on me.'

'Mustang Leader to Rebels Four, Six, Three. Get above and around the Krauts. *Quickly*, damnit! Four, take the port side. Three to starboard. Six get underneath. Let's show these jet jockeys some formation flying.'

Christ, thought Schilling.

'Mustang Leader this is Cobra Leader. You are ordered to maintain heading to Willie or we will fire repeat fire.'

'Take your rockets home, Cobra. The party's over.'

Schilling saw the Spit settle downward off his port wing. He could see bullet holes in its small rounded tail, and more scattered across the aft fuselage. Its flat brown-green colors and bright red-blue-white-orange roundel seemed dazzling in the bright sun. And the gruesome skull painted below the cockpit. He could see the Tommy pilot looking at him through large dark glasses. Schilling nodded. The Tommy gave him the finger. Schilling nearly laughed. He wondered if the jets were going to shoot and he decided they wouldn't, not now. He and Rudi were completely protected.

Schilling watched the four jets sweep out ahead about a mile and a half.

'Tigh...

Krauts. I was now, Rebels.' Lowen's voice. 'Tighten up, you

'Jesus Christ, bastards to kiss wingtips.'

Schilling peered ... another P-51 pilot.

huge underside of the ...hrough his fractured canopy at the

...his head – Lowen's. He could

see inside the fuselage through the wheel wells. The starboard wing was ripped open and darkened black.

Then he watched the four jets. His heartbeat quickened. They were banking around about two miles out and level. *Christ*.

'Tighter, tighter,' Lowen's voice easy over the R/T.

'Steady now, chaps,' the Tommy sounded easy, too.

Christ, Schilling thought again. *Christ, Christ, Christ*. He decided not to watch the jets, but he found himself unable to resist. Those guys wouldn't hit the P-51s. The jets turned, head-on, level at one mile.

Please. Schilling froze in his seat.

'Steady, chaps.'

The twenty millimeter cannon fire came in a great storm, streaking silently in such mind boggling quantity that Schilling braced himself for instant death. The blurred orange lines rushed in horizontal bands of fire overhead and in front of the six warbirds, so close that sparks fell away. Schilling trembled. No one was hit. The F-5s streaked past in front of them – metal monster rocketships – and banked over so quickly that the image of their pale gray under-surfaces was no more than an instant's impression in Schilling's vision, like that of a camera shutter tripped.

Then they were gone, leaving a hazy wake that buffeted the six warbirds as they flew through it. The scent of kerosene and cordite, like Fourth of July, rose in Schilling's cockpit.

'Fuckin' hell,' muttered the Tommy.

Roger that, thought Schilling.

'Six to Leader . . . Jesus. Leader, I'm really in the red.'

'Hang on Six. This is Mustang Leader to Bandit Two. How close are we?'

'Five minutes, less,' replied Rudi.

'All right. Get us down. Open up a little now.'

Schilling looked below. The mountains were familiar.

Rudi dropped forward, still trailing gray smoke. 'Where is the Air Force, Leader?' he said in a thin voice.

'The Air Force,' replied Lowen, 'the United States Air Force, is a hundred feet behind you, Kraut.'

Schilling watched Rudi; he was rocking a little and the smoke had turned more white now. Oil. He could see the ridge where the strip was, below at eight o'clock.

'On approach,' said Rudi.

'Bandit Three, you follow Two,' ordered Lowen. 'Six, you—'

'I've got fire, Leader!' a voice cut in.

Schilling turned to see a P-51 behind and above blossom white flame out of its lower nose panels.

'Get out,' called Lowen. The P-51 lifted, climbed. The fire was astonishingly smokeless and bright.

'Get out,' Lowen repeated.

Schilling watched the Mustang climb higher. *Get out*, Schilling pleaded silently. The Mustang seemed to reach the apex of its vertical trajectory, seemed to pause. He knew it would blow apart. It rolled over with peculiar slowness. Then a dark figure dropped out.

Releasing his breath, Schilling turned back to follow Rudi. Altitude 800 feet. Rudi was turning left.

'Three to Oberstleutnant. Are you all right?' called Schilling. Rudi was right on line.

'I'll live,' Rudi answered as if he were short of breath.

Schilling felt his rudder pedals react strangely when he pressed left; there was pressure, then he lost it. The plane jerked when he tried to turn. Alarmed, he banked left, looking out to see his right aileron waggling up and down in the slipstream – without the tension of control cables. The wings rocked and he felt the 109 pitch and weave in the hot air currents that swam invisibly at low altitudes. His own landing would not be so simple.

He pushed back the canopy. A wash of warm air swirled around him with the promise of survival. He looked to see Rudi almost touching down. He then heard a flat *whump* underneath and forward. Fumes and heat boiled up from under the instrument panel. The cowling surface shimmered, undulated. Heat waves. Now smoke streaming past his windscreen. *Get the nose up!*

He pulled back the stick, pulled the radiator cut-off handle. His gloved fingers darted over switches. *Fuel selector valve to off. Mixture to idle. Throttle back to reduce airspeed. Retard pitch control to minimum.* The engine coughed once. The tail lifted. The plane tilted on its axis, dropping the port wing. He corrected with stick right and the plane tilted, wallowed the other way.

Now the nose dropped. Stick back. The nose lifted. Altitude 100 feet. Heat on his shins and knees. Bitter white smoke slipped up around his legs. The 109 tilted left again. Stick back and right. He could feel the increasing weight of the 109 as it settled with decreasing control; he needed power only a little longer. He glanced down to see the knees of his flight suit turning dark. The fire was being sucked up and out by the opened canopy.

He choked, gagged. He was losing control. No way to retract wheels, release the emergency fire extinguisher. No way to release stick. The pain was like electic shock, continuous. He knew the Nomex fire fabric would last about twenty seconds. Altitude fifty feet, less. *Shut off pump, leave ignition on to burn out residual fuel.* Hold, hold – thirty feet – to the last moment. The nose dipped. He gave it enough throttle to lift it once more, pulled back again on the stick, then shut off the ignition and yanked the extinguisher release, giving up control. He was now a passenger.

White foam burst out from behind his seat, hissing up around his waist and blinding him. He felt the dead weight of the 109 settle silently. He shoved his sunglasses away, wiped his sleeve over his eyes. The 109 sailed forward at what seemed like terrible speed. Pink sand swept by underneath. There was nothing to do but hang on to the heaving monster beneath him.

His 109 hit the ground, wheels first, then tail. The impact jarred him nearly blind, jerked his head forward, whipped his gloved hands against the instrument panel. The plane bounced, was airborne a moment, then slammed into the gound, the metal shrieking, rivets popping. He felt the landing gear collapse. The 109 slewed ahead, throwing him left then right. The harness felt as if it was dismembering him. It seemed impossible that the 109 could plow along for so long, grating, grinding, creaking. Then he felt it slowing, moving sideways. Still blinded, he yanked the harness release, gripped the cockpit sides as the hulk came to a stop.

He tried to stand, couldn't. He wiped at his eyes, gagging from sand, fire foam. He pushed upward from the seat with one arm, grabbed the windscreen with the other. *Get out.* He pulled himself over the side. It was so quiet. He heard the scraping thump of his own body sliding down and hitting the wing. Dazed, he got to his knees, clinging to the flank of the plane, staring a moment at the insignia – orange sun and gray eagle –

painted below the cockpit. The nose section was nearly buried, and there was no fire. From underneath, he heard the hot metal ticking and hissing.

He staggered away from the wreckage, blinking as his vision cleared, trying to spit. Looking down, he saw himself covered with sand dust and the white residue from the fire foam. The scorched fabric of his flight suit was shredded away from his forearms but he found the pain more numb than biting. He held up his gloved hands, flexing the fingers.

Then ahead, as if in a mirage, he saw Rudi's 109 sitting motionless about a hundred feet away, smoking, its prop slowly turning to a stop. He staggered forward, saw the hangars then. Overhead he heard other aircraft but he did not look up.

He shuffled up to Rudi's 109. The fire was growing, feeding on oil lines and wiring. Tongues of flame licked out of the panel seams. There were terrible bullet holes everywhere. Schilling clambered over the wing and up to the cockpit.

Rudi, still strapped in place, was looking up at him. His sunglasses were gone and his cap was gone and his blue eyes seemed unusually bright against the marble paleness of his face. His mouth moved and a thin dark red line spilled down from the corner of his lip and curved under his jaw. Schilling reached for the release buckle and found all of Rudi, from chest to waist, soaked in wet red everywhere.

'Get out,' Schilling whispered, as if he could somehow will Rudi to rise without help. He reached again for the release buckle; Rudi's gloved hands lifted and clamped both his wrists.

'Don't touch me,' Rudi said clearly, more thick red spilling from his mouth.

Heat blew against Schilling's side from the engine fire. Rudi's grip relaxed. Confused, Schilling was aware of an automobile drawing close and of other airplanes landing nearby, both as distant, as unreal, as a dream. Now there was flame under the instrument panel. He looked up at Rudi; his eyes were blue and dull now, his expression peaceful and vacant, his head back against the armor headrest. Schilling's knees began to buckle. Someone scrambling onto the wing behind him, rocking the plane, now crashing into him, knocking him to his knees on the sloping wing. Marta.

She sucked in her breath and clasped one hand over her

440

mouth, her eyes wide and fixed on her brother. '*Ahhhhhhhh*,' she breathed.

The sound of her agony pierced Schilling through. He took her arm. There was blood – dried, he was certain – all over her hands and shirt and white slacks.

'Come away,' he said, pulling at her arm.

'That's my brother,' she spoke with no inflection, staring in the cockpit, frozen.

'Come away,' he said again. Heat and fumes whipped around them. Smoke rose from the cockpit. Someone was running across the strip toward them.

'That's my *brother*.'

'It will explode.' Schilling struggled to get up.

'My brother!' she screamed, striking Schilling across the face. He clutched the edge of the cockpit, seeing little jets of smoke hissing from inside as if under pressure. He lunged into the cockpit from the waist and pulled the emergency extinguisher release. White foam burst up. Then he launched himself against Marta, grabbing her hair with one hand, her upper arm with the other, carrying them both off the wing onto the sand.

He struggled to his knees. '*Move*, goddamnit; it's going to blow!'

He began dragging her away by the belt of her slacks. He looked back to see two men lifting Rudi out. He shuffled forward, pulling Marta. She was making a strange noise, a terrible rhythmic keening, as he dragged her stumbling. They fell in a heap on the sand. Now he crawled, dragging her by the shirt, gasping, grunting in pain. When the 109 blew apart the shock wave pushed them down, rolling. The heat wave followed. Face down, he heard debris raining around them, hissing overhead, then the crackling of the burning plane. He did not want to open his eyes. Even in the war the ground had never felt so good. He just wanted to lie still, lie still forever. Hot sand against his cheek and chest, he felt his heart pumping at his sternum, his wrists, his temples. His arms hurt too much to move them.

'Peter,' Marta's whispered warning.

He opened his eyes. The two pilots were walking toward them; one was limping. Schilling struggled to sit up, gritting his teeth with pain. He felt Marta helping him. He watched the two men approaching. One was obviously a Mustang pilot and the other – he could tell from the uniform – was the Spit pilot. The Tommy pulled off his flying helmet, replaced it with an RAF officer's cap, and then drew a pistol from his shoulder holster. The Mustang pilot had the leg wound.

When they were close enough, the Tommy held the pistol barrel-up very casually and cocked it. Schilling, looking up at the opaque sunglasses, could hear the hammer click back. The Mustang pilot was unzipping the neck of his flying suit. He had a crimson scarf, and when he stood over them he pulled off his sunglasses, and just stared. The 109 cracked and sizzled in the quiet heat behind them. The Tommy lowered the pistol a little, enough for Schilling to see the muzzle.

'Do you speak English?' asked the Mustang pilot.

'I speak English,' he answered, licking his lips.

The Mustang pilot wiped his face, then looked over at the burning skeleton of Rudi's 109. Smoke rolled along the ground and past the parked P-51 and the Spit. The Mustang pilot shook his head. Exploding ammunition from Rudi's plane popped and cracked in the silence.

'He was gone,' said the pilot as if he were speaking to himself. 'We got him out.' He nodded at the burning wreckage. 'Number Two. Your Exec?'

'Affirmative.' Schilling wondered if the Tommy was going to shoot him. He wondered if it would be preferable to prison. The pain in his arms was fierce and he could feel his pulse in both of them. He quivered from a peculiar chill.

'Becker.' The Mustang pilot was shaking his head again. He turned to Schilling. 'Who are you?'

'Major Three.'

'Major Three. You don't look too good.' He paused, looking at Marta. 'Ma'am?'

Marta said nothing.

'This –' the Mustang pilot gestured to the Tommy – 'is Wing Commander Redmond-Donleavy.'

'Hallo Jerry.' The Tommy touched his cap brim. 'Ma'am.'

'Are you Lowen?' asked Schilling, ignoring the Wing Commander.

The Mustang pilot moved his head with the absent manner of cowboys in Western films, then sat down on the sand. He pulled at his bloodied pant leg, then took the scarf from his neck and began tying it above his calf. The flat whickering sound of a helicopter beat a staccato rhythm to the snapping of the burning 109. The Tommy looked up, shading his eyes, still holding the pistol. Schilling felt Marta touch his back.

'Godamighty,' Lowen said tiredly. 'Well, Kraut ... Major Three ... the war's over. Again.' He paused and looked up from wrapping his leg. 'Those were beautiful airplanes ...' The helicopter was closer now. 'Crazy.' Lowen sighed with a slightly pained expression at Schilling, as if he were explaining something very difficult and important. 'Crazy.'

Schilling stared at him, nearly faint from pain.

'You people,' Lowen said thoughtfully, 'have been starting wars ... before both of us were even born. Are you all crazy?' He emphasized the word *all*.

'It's a thought,' Schilling replied. It seemed so stupid, he and Lowen and Marta sitting in the sand, like some bizarre picnic, with the Tommy standing over them. He looked down at himself. He was dusty white, as if coated with flour. The knees and forearms of his flight suit were toasted, tatters, but he could see the textured Nomex fabric.

'Well.' Lowen was studying Schilling as if he didn't know what else to say. He seemed weary and his tanned lined sweaty face held no murder. Lowen then looked up at the Tommy. 'Well, Wing Commander. What do we do now?'

'If he's all that's left ... send the bugger packing then.' He put the pistol away.

Lowen looked back at Schilling. The helicopter came over low. No one looked at it.

'Well, Major Three,' said Lowen. 'When you get back to Germany ... if you get back ... you give them the message ... the message that we won it again, okay? Have you got that message, Major?'

Schilling managed to fix his mouth into a neutral grin.

Lowen looked up at Marta. 'Can you get him to a hospital?'

Schilling sensed Marta nodding.

'Or you can get on that chopper,' Lowen said. 'Take your choice. And you'd better hurry. We'll see to your Exec.'

Schilling saw the chopper descending beside the parked P-51 and the Spit. It had a white panel on its olive side, with a large red cross. Marta was on her feet, pulling at his arm. Schilling groaned from the pain. Lowen sat in the sand watching. The

443

Tommy came over and took Schilling's other arm, lifting him. His legs were numb, nearly useless. They half-dragged half-carried him toward the sedan.

'Major,' Lowen called out.

Schilling stopped, turned, supported by Marta and the Tommy. His arms hung limp. Lowen sat up straighter in the sand and threw a salute, sharp but not fast. Schilling nodded. He could not lift his arms.

'Sir,' he said.

Marta and the Tommy helped him into the front seat of the van. Schilling thought he was dreaming now, drowning in pain and fatigue. He even thought the Tommy patted him on the shoulder before he slammed the door.

CHAPTER TWENTY-SIX

When Schilling came slowly awake and decided he was truly seeing, eyes opened, he was puzzled; he saw a surface, textured ceiling, beige – nothing more. It seemed to extend beyond his vision to each side, but when he looked downward over his chest he saw the top of a gold-rimmed mirror and the dark Spanish dresser. Marta and Eric's bedroom.

Both of his arms tingled with a deep heavy pain, as present as stone, unmoving and continuous, the kind of pain you had to meet head-on, and endure. Another little test, he thought. When he turned his head – his neck muscles contracted in such pain that his breath caught – he saw Marta sitting beside the bed in a chair, watching him. She wore black and she held a drink and she was smoking a cigarette. He thought he heard music, yes, from the den.

'What time is it?' His voice sounded like sandpaper to him.

'Twelve-fifteen.'

She was tearing open a small white paper sack.

His heart beat faster. He had escaped death, but he had not escaped. 'Are we alone?' he asked, not looking over.

'More than you know, Major.' The dullness in her voice surprised him. She was reading from a small white tube. 'Myci . . . tracin. For your arms. And codeine.'

'Where's Eric?'

'In the hospital.'

This confused him. He went to something different. 'I'm sorry . . . truly sorry. About Rudi.' He remembered the pale face and flat blue eyes, lifeless. And Marta's cries, more painful than Rudi's death.

She seemed not to have heard. He decided not to say any more about it. Now she was reading from a piece of note paper. 'I have good instructions. From my doctor.'

'What did you tell him?'

'Party guest. Barbeque. Lighter fluid. A common hazard around here.'

Schilling was remembering more. The Texas Colonel, Lowen, had let them go. He could see Lowen sitting in the sand with his face cut, his leg bleeding, calling to him and then saluting. Then he remembered riding in the van, Marta crying as she drove, his tattered arms held palms up in his lap. He remembered turning to see the two Mustangs on him, the muzzle blast from their wings. And crashing, as the fabric of his flight suit turned black.

He looked down at his arms; they were numb from the ice-packed towels wrapped in plastic. He flexed his fingers, which hurt his forearms, but they worked. There was a sheet over him and underneath he realized he wore nothing. His knees and upper thighs hurt as if from severe sunburn but he felt no bandages. Where was Webb? Theo? Rendel? Why was Eric in the hospital? His mouth was so dry.

'Drink,' he said. 'Please.'

She came around the bed to pour him ice water from a pitcher on the night table. He noticed then that she looked very dressed up; the black dress had three-quarter sleeves and it looked, in its plainness of style, expensive. Her stockings were dark and, though he could not see her feet, he knew from her walk that she wore heels. Her hair was pulled back in a bun. She wore no jewelry, no makeup, and her eyes were red and puffed; he had missed the worst of her grieving.

He struggled to get up on one elbow. She lifted the glass to his lips; ice water that was wonderful all the way down. Every muscle he had was hurting. He held his breath in pain.

'Doctor said drink three times normal. And plenty of booze. And take these.'

'Good. Vodka, please.' He swallowed the two white tablets. 'I have to get out of here.'

'When you can walk. When I've dressed your arms. I've made reservations, at four-ten. Under Mr and Mrs, on a commuter flight to Denver. Does that meet your approval?'

He was confused again. 'Are you going with me?'

446

'No.' She handed him vodka and tomato juice.

The vodka was wonderful, too. He wanted to keep getting drunk, stay drunk. He was chilled and the vodka warmed him and he felt it going to work, spreading from his stomach to his legs and arms. He stared at the ceiling, thinking about Marta not coming with him. It occured to him that there were times when it was not difficult to imagine that there were no more women in the world to love. Or to love him. More stupid thinking, he thought.

He looked at the clock-radio again. Twelve-fifty. Marta had a drink on top of the bureau and she was sorting through her underclothing from one of the drawers, pulling slips out, selecting some. She tossed several of the slips on the bed, then reached for her drink, unsteadily it seemed.

'Are you drunk?' he asked.

'Of course I'm drunk.' She turned abruptly and left the room.

He listened to the music from the den. It was classical, melancholy and slow. He remembered staggering through the house. Drinking vodka. Then being in the shower, hanging his hands on the stall-door top while she stripped off her own bloody clothes and got in with him and washed him – even his hair – and then dried him and helped him to the bed. She had been crying much of the time and had never said anything, even while she packed the iced towels around his arms. He had drifted off in a stupor of fatigue and vodka, feeling very bad for her. And very helpless.

She came back carrying a fresh drink and a pair of shears. She sat down on the bed without looking at him and began unwrapping the plastic from his left arm.

'You look . . . fine. Dressed up,' he said.

'Thank you, Major.' She sounded very tired.

'Why are you dressed . . . that way?'

'It seemed . . . what to do, black. Rudi.' Her voice ran out.

She carried the wet towels to the bathroom and returned with fresh ones and began patting his arms dry. He looked down at his arms as she dried them. They were blistered badly, but his hands were unmarked. The gloves. He could not imagine getting up to walk. He looked again at the time, his pulse starting as another red digit clicked over.

'We've got to hurry,' he said.

'Relax, Major. We have time.'

She took up one of the blue-and-white tubes and squeezed out white gel into her palm and began applying it gently to his arm. 'Does it hurt?'

He grunted, took another swallow of his drink.

'Good. The doctor said it is worse when it doesn't hurt.'

'Thank you. For caring for me.'

'It is . . . what we – I can't remember. What Rudi said.' Her eyes filled. 'Yes, I remember, we are doing what must be done.'

'Yes,' he said lamely. Including, he thought, getting me out. He glanced at the clock-radio; one-ten.

'What will happen, to Rudi?'

'Don't worry. He'll be taken care of.'

'His goddamned airplanes. Oh goddamn goddamn *goddamn*.'

'Don't think of it. It can't be changed.'

Her expression never changed, though tears fell from her face unheeded as she continued to spread the gel over his arms. He could hear her swallow.

'Well . . .' She balanced, then caught, her grief. 'It's over, yes? The worst of it . . . is real. God forgive me, I am furious with him. It's his own fault.'

'Don't think of it.'

'How could he land the airplane?'

'I don't know. He was alive. He spoke to me.'

'What did he say?'

'He said, "Don't touch me." That's all. Then he was gone.' Schilling could feel again Rudi's grip on his wrists.

She began wiping her hands.

Schilling remembered the strafing, the terror of trying to get airborne as the two P-51s hit the fuel truck, but he could not remember what Eric had been doing. He had helped to start the planes, then . . .

'What happened to Eric?' he asked.

Again it seemed as if she was not hearing him. With her hands cleaned, she wiped her eyes. 'When the gun went off, there was this . . . pink stuff. On the airplane.'

Schilling had to work to put all this together. He became very apprehensive. 'What gun went off?' he asked carefully.

'I didn't mean to hit him.' She took a long drag from her cigarette, staring away.

Jesus Christ Almighty, he thought.

'I called the hospital. They said he was in a serious condition.

But guarded. I thought they meant that someone was guarding him.' She shook her head. 'Or maybe it was guarded but serious. I forget which.'

'Either way, the police are there.'

Schilling decided not to ask any more questions, not to say anything. It was more than he could handle. The pink stuff was probably lung tissue.

'When I drove him to the hospital ... he never stopped staring at me. I've never seen such an expression before, and it took me a long time to figure out what it was; he was looking at me as if he had never seen me before in his life.' She looked over at Schilling. 'When they took him in Emergency, I ran out. And came back.'

He took a long breath. 'Lucky for me.'

'Yes, lucky for you.'

She took up one of the slips and began to cut it with the scissors. 'So, Major . . . we are all alone. Finally. Isn't that nice?'

He was sure that it was something other than nice. He found it very disturbing that she had shot Eric. Never had he thought of women as physically dangerous.

'We are all alone,' she said in a childish sing-song voice, 'because my brother is dead. And because my husband is a . . . casualty.'

'He'll pull through. Don't worry. Anyway, it's all over.'

'Except for you and me.' Her voice turned indifferent. She had cut long strips from the slips. 'Where are the others, Major?'

'I don't know,' he replied, thinking, watching her wrapping the silk strips around his arm. He winced. The numbness from the ice was wearing off. He looked again at the time; one-thirty.

'Well, I know.' She kept wrapping. 'While you were sleeping I listened to the radio. Do you want to know what happened, Major? Do you want to know the score?'

Again he was apprehensive, not sure that he believed her. He said nothing, watching her.

'One of the Texas pilots was killed, one is not expected to live. Four were wounded, two seriously.'

The Tommy, thought Schilling, got out clean. He waited.

'Two of . . . ours were killed. They found two parachutes, presumed – as they said – to be German. They are searching.'

Theo, Rendel, Webb, he calculated. Which two?

Marta took another sip from her drink, then began to wrap

gauze strips snugly over the silk. 'The radio,' she continued, 'called the Captain-Major a fighter pilot. He would have liked to have heard that, yes? The Captain-Major may be dead now.' She shrugged. 'Or not. I called the hospital at the airbase. I told them I was his sister. When I cried, they believed me.' She paused. 'They said the Captain-Major was in critical, but stable condition. Or perhaps it was stable but critical. I forget which. He was wounded in the arm, the hand, the leg, and the eye. He will lose the eye. He had not regained consciousness.'

Schilling wished that he was somewhere else, anywhere. He checked the vodka bottle; there would be enough to get him to someplace else. But not fast enough.

'So, your "ultimate contest" is over. Yes, Major? And who won?'

She began wrapping his other arm. He lay staring at the ceiling again, thinking of Webb. And Eric. The clock-radio clicked over another glowing red ember.

'What is the music?' he asked.

'Berlioz. The piece Franz was practicing. Berlioz . . . was not German. I don't know what he is. Was. Do you like it?'

'It's not happy.'

'What would you prefer, Major?'

'Maybe the waltzes.'

'Ah, the waltzes, yes.' She cut loose several thin pieces of white tape from a roll. 'Well, we cannot dance this time, Major.'

'I was not thinking of dancing.'

'He was going to do it again, the fool. He was climbing into the Captain-Major's plane. There was no one to stop him.'

Schilling, caught again by surprise, said nothing.

'He gave me the fucking gun. To hold. On the Captain-Major. I told him . . .' Her shoulders slumped. 'He would have gotten hurt, wouldn't he? Perhaps killed?'

'Most certainly he would have been killed. Now he is alive.'

She finished wrapping his arm, then stood awkwardly. He wondered if she would be able to drive. After a moment, she walked from the room. 'The waltzes,' she called back.

When she returned she was holding a new pack of Eric's cigarettes. She stopped at the foot of the bed, swaying a little, looking at him.

'You bastards just go ahead and take,' she said. 'All of you.

You'll screw anything up just to get what you want. I wonder why we don't do that?'

Schilling closed his eyes.

'Are you in pain?'

'Yes.'

'There is some medication.' She continued to stare down on him. 'There is no medication for my pain. How inconvenient.'

She went over to the tray and poured a glass of water and gave him two more tablets. After he swallowed them he asked for a cigarette and she opened the pack, lit one for him, and reached over and put it in his mouth.

'How well,' she whispered over him, 'do you think the Captain-Major will be able to see? With one eye?'

Schilling watched her straighten and walk around the bed; clearly she did not expect an answer. The whisper haunted him. She went over and pulled the curtains closed, shutting out about half the light. Then she came back beside the bed.

'I remember,' she began as if telling a story, 'what Theo said at dinner last night: "We cause our own accidents." Do you remember . . . him saying that? He was talking about the Captain-Major.' She reached up and pulled at the neck of her dress, just below her throat, as if she was hot.

'Theo said, about the Captain-Major, "Here he is . . . so what is the difference?" That's what I've been thinking. About you, Major.' She looked down, taking a thoughtful drag from her cigarette. 'Somehow . . . the Major has arranged events . . . in a sequence where he finds himself naked in my bedroom, yes?'

'Had I been able to arrange this,' Schilling said, 'I would have done it differently.' He felt the medication working, a warm numbing sensation that traveled with alcoholic speed. The pain receded.

'You haven't called me Frau Malzahn, Major. Why not?'

'Frau Malzahn.'

'I like you to call me Frau Malzahn. It makes me . . . warm. And I like to call you Major. It kept you . . . where you were.' She walked over around the bed to her chair.

'I used to think that if there wasn't faith . . . fidelity – Are they the same? – then there wasn't love. Without . . . without love, trust, we all exist alone.' She looked down at him. 'Do you exist alone, Major?'

'Often.' Schilling wondered how she could talk so smoothly when she was so drunk.

She then sat down in the chair, crossing her legs. He breathed in that sound, the hiss of friction of her stockings. He watched her face. She was staring at him with no expression he could read. He was oddly apprehensive again. He could hear the waltz music, melodic and joyful, and he again wondered if Aneka would have looked like Marta. He could imagine that she would. He remembered – 1941 – her voice, only a fair voice, but earnest and clear, when she sang the Schubert lieder, still his favorites; *Auf Erden mir die Hoffnung wich, ich hier so einsam bin.* Upon the earth my hope has dwindled. I am so lonely here.

'Do you like my legs, Major?'

She raised her leg and rested her foot on the bed. She was wearing black shoes with little straps over the toes and one behind the heel, the kind of shoe that was better than no shoe at all. 'I like them. What do you think, Major?' She pulled back her skirt and the black lace hem of her slip a little.

'Yes. More.'

'More.' She hiked the slip back past the dark band of the stocking top. 'That's all of them there is. There are. Would you like to touch them, Major?'

He looked up from her leg to her eyes, not answering.

She drew her leg back and very gracefully put it down. She then raised the other one, parting her knees, and put her foot on the pillow by his face, touching her toe carefully to his cheek. He could feel the heat of her foot, could smell fine leather. After a moment she moved it down alongside his arm and hooked the spike of her heel on the sheet and pulled it down over his thighs in one sweep. There was a rush of anger at her. And of vulnerable embarrassment that he was not hard.

Marta leaned back in her chair, picked up her drink, looking at him. 'What do we do here? At the end. What is it – that is done?'

'I don't think—'

'Don't worry, Major. You don't have to – perform. Not a contest. This time. Not in this bed. This time, this is my – trip.' She raised her knee, tugged off one shoe, taking her time about it and watching him, still no expression.

Schilling's strengthened pulse hurt in his arms, his temples.

452

Then he slipped, just a little; he was sinking, as if he were fainting, a moment of balance lost, then serenity. She had moved, spoken, but whatever she had said went echoing away. He struggled to the surface, staring at her. She had opened her legs under the roof of black skirt and was covering herself with one hand – no, moving her hand. He had missed a moment or two. As if the film had been cut.

'Hold on to me, Major.' She slid her foot up over the edge of the bed and nudged her toes into his hand. His thumb closed over the high arch, fingers under her instep. Her flesh was soft and cool. He held on.

'Do you think,' she whispered, 'you could watch this. As well. With only one eye, Major?' Her breath caught then released, caught then released. In the shadow, with the angle of her thighs, he could not see her fingers. There was a moment of disbelief when he realized what she was doing.

'Is this – perverse?' When he didn't answer, she said, 'I hope it is. I don't care.'

Schilling, ignoring the pain in his arm, anchored his end of the tight-rope she was traveling.

'Hold on to me.' Her voice dry and thin as paper.

He held. The tendons in her foot flexed, quivered, in his grip.

'This is – what is done,' she breathed. 'Yes?'

He gave no answer.

'Perhaps —' Her eyes closed. 'Perhaps they are. All around the house. Now. With guns.' Her breath left her then. Her eyes opened, wide and liquid. 'Hold on to me hold *on* to me hold *on* to me.'

Schilling watched her fall, held the tension of her in his hand until it ebbed away.

When her breathing settled she was quiet, unmoving for a long minute, her eyes half-closed, lips parted as if hypnotized. Watching her eyes made his own grow heavy. He resisted. He waited. Her foot withdrew, left his hand, it felt like some life line, like the vital cables disconnected from an aircraft freed to fly. He heard the clock click over another digit, did not look at it.

Eventually she retrieved her shoe from the floor, slipped it on. He could tell that she had not yet come back. Then she stood and smoothed her dress at the hips and then picked up her drink and finished it, looking at him.

'Now, Major.' She placed the glass on the night table. 'I will help you dress.'

Marta looked straight ahead as she drove. Schilling sat with his hands in his lap, grateful for the comfortably cushioned seat of the air-conditioned Buick. He felt dopey and slow of speech from the codeine medication and Bloody Marys. He watched the passing of streets and traffic. It was like a film, a dull film, so strangely ordinary.

'How long will it take them to come, for me?'

'A day or two. I don't know.'

'Will we go to jail, do you think?'

'I don't think so.'

'What do you think will happen?'

'Nothing much, with the right lawyer. You didn't do anything, didn't know anything. Except that we were staying there. And going off to fly. The only time you ever went to the strip, the only time, was yesterday.'

'Oh God. I don't know how to twist the truth like that.'

'That's what lawyers are for.'

'And Eric?'

'The mechanic.' Schilling shrugged. 'Just the mechanic. Everyone's gone now. No witnesses.' These words depressed him and he hurried away from them.

Marta remained silent. Schilling looked down at her legs, wonderful legs; he could look at them all the way to the airport. He squirmed in the blue plush seat. He felt crawly. Nerves. He kept wanting to turn around to see if they were being followed. No, stupid thinking. He could expect that at the airport. They'd be checking all outbound passengers – no, more stupid thinking – they'd only be looking for German nationals.

'How do I look?' he asked.

'Ordinary.'

He nodded. Good. Actually he was satisfied with his appearance. The nylon jacket hid the bandages on his arms, though Marta had had to slit a few seams. His hands were unmarked, thanks to the gloves, and the bruises and scrapes on his face were minor enough.

'Rudi left me some papers,' Marta said. 'On the airplanes.'

'What kind of papers?'

'Titles or bill of sale or something. In my name and Eric's. In

454

case anything happened.' She lit another cigarette. 'He was like that.'

He looked over. 'Listen to me. When you drop me off, go home and get them and take them to a lawyer immediately. Those planes are worth a lot of money, even the pieces.'

'How much?'

'A lot. Hundreds of thousands. Even mine, the wrecked one. And there are parts in the hangar.'

'What do I do, run an ad in the paper under Used Planes?'

'I'm not sure. Find warbird people. Or you could call up that Colonel, Lowen, at the airbase. His Confederate Air Force might be very interested. You could make him and the Captain-Major, ah, joint owners of some kind.' Schilling smiled; it seemed like an excellent idea. 'They both might develop a terrible memory by the time they get to court.'

Marta said nothing, keeping her face straight ahead. Her eyes were hidden behind thick prescription sunglasses, as if she were there and not there at the same time, and he felt a hundred miles distant, more distant, he knew, than he could ever reach or fathom.

When they turned into the airport what he felt was time running out. He kept trying to make himself believe that she was secretly planning to leave with him and that she would pretend otherwise until the last moment. It would be just the sort of thing she would do.

Marta shut off the ignition and looked at her watch, then at him.

'How much time?' he asked.

'Plenty. I put the medication in your left pocket. Take two more in two hours.'

'I'm all right.'

'Do your arms hurt badly?'

He shrugged. As far as he knew, there were no words in his vocabulary to tell a woman you didn't want to leave her, couldn't bear to leave her. Unless you were drunk and desperate and doped.

'I don't want to leave . . . you,' he said, staring straight ahead. 'I don't know how to do anything more.' Ah, what weak words. How he hated them once said.

'I know. I know you don't. I'm sorry.'

Her words he hated even more.

She leaned on the steering wheel, her face turned toward him. Then she took off her sunglasses and reached over and took off his. They looked at each other for several long seconds. Her eyes were still swollen and she looked tired and a little older than before. 'I never knew a thing. Is that right?'

'Right.' He noticed for the first time that one of her eyes was green, the other gray.

'Never went to the airfied. Until yesterday.'

'Right.'

'And Eric never—'

'Right.'

'What else happened that I should pretend didn't happen, Major?'

'I guess you can pretend away whatever you choose.'

'Pretend away,' she repeated. 'I like that. I think I'll pretend it was only lust.'

'Maybe lust is better. Simpler.'

'It was lust.'

'Come with me.'

'I can't . . . won't, rather.'

'Why not?' He had never asked that of any woman before and he hated doing it.

'It was my agreement.'

He said nothing.

'And because, if it's all such a fucking gamble, I'd rather gamble with what I know. Do you understand?'

'I understand the agreement.'

'I thought you would, Major. I knew you would.' She put her sunglasses back on. 'Time to go.'

She got out and came around and opened the car door for him – it made him feel foolish – and when he got out and stood up she came up against him. 'We say good-bye here, okay?'

'Good-bye, *Frau* Malzahn.'

'Good-bye, Major,' she whispered, putting her mouth on his.

They locked the car and began walking. Reeling from the heat and the vodka, Schilling thought the terminal seemed a mile away. He glanced at Marta, lugging his bag. She didn't seem as tall as before, even in heels, tacking along, her loose hair tangling in the blast-furnace breeze. Looking at her was beginning to hurt. When you sober up a little, he thought, you'll cut out this crap.

In the terminal Schilling felt his gut tighten. He could believe that every passing male had been assigned to apprehend him. Marta bought two tickets, Mr and Mrs, with a credit card. The business of her buying the tickets – like carrying the bag and opening the car door – made him feel even more helpless than he was. Now all he wanted was to get on the airplane. They had twenty minutes.

They walked to the gate, saying nothing to each other, and then stood at the huge glass windows looking out over the acres of airport concrete. It was already a busy day; within his view four of the great passenger jets moved back and forth, deceivingly massive and slow as they lumbered into or away from their berths. With great effort Schilling kept himself from turning around to watch for police or APs or whatever the hell they might send out to watch the airport.

'Hold the tickets,' Marta said, putting them in his pocket. 'I have to go to the damned ladies' room.'

Schilling watched the airplanes until they called for boarding. He looked around first for police and then for Marta. He saw neither. There was always ten or fifteen minutes to board. He was now tense to the point of nausea. He watched the passengers line up until they were all through the doorway and he watched the dozens of travelers passing beyond the waiting area, scanning every woman he could see, until there was no more time. He turned and went through the doorway – his boarding pass receiving the usual quick glance from the attendant – and down the tunneled ramp to the airplane door.

She had done it on purpose, now he knew, and he admired her even more; it was a good smart thing to do.

He took an aisle seat towards the back of the plane and discovered that he couldn't buckle the seat belt. It would be fine to have the stewardess do it.

They closed the forward door with a soft slam; the sound of it echoed in his soul. It was the sound of his freedom – now he began to believe he might get away after all – and it was the sound of the last of her. Frau Malzahn. He kept his eyes to the front of the plane a few seconds longer, then he gave up.

He looked out the small squarish window, seeing nothing. It was more painful than he expected, leaving them all, and leaving alone.

He remembered Theo the night he spoke in the hangar, his

silver hair illuminated by the single small light above, and the Messerschmitts in their evil warpaint in the gloom. He remembered Rudi, his tense blue eyes wrinkled at the edges in the baking sun, chewing his ass out for forgetting to lower his wheels. He remembered Marta at the moment he took her waist to try the waltzes, and when she was barefoot by the pool in a white dress, tossing white flower petals on the blue-mirror surface.

The plane moved gently. He hadn't felt the engines start.

He remembered Eric sitting drunk by the pool with him, asking how it was to be fifty-two. And he thought how it was to be fifty-two and in this airplane and the answer was the same as always: pleasant and temporary.

He remembered Franz lovingly polishing his oversized violin, though it had already gleamed with the polish of a thousand hands.

One of the stewardesses was demonstrating the procedure for using oxygen masks. The aircraft was not half full.

He remembered Rendel telling the story of his trip to the airport while his great paw hands played so delicately with a wine glass. He remembered Kesler, drunk as he could be, mumbling *Die Amerikanishe Luftwaffe kann mich am Arsch lecken*. And he remembered Captain-Major Webb entering the dining room and staring at everyone as if they were ghosts.

Now the other stewardess – she looked so young – was starting the seat belt check. He watched her coming up the aisle, her hands skipping rhythmically along the tops of the seat backs. She had lovely ankles. He would ask for his vodka as she buckled the belt.

When she got to him she smiled, speaking at the same time. 'You are the Major? I was told you might need some help with your seat belt.' She leaned down and pulled the belts together *click*. He could smell her hair.

'Thank you,' he said, hesitating.

'Also' – she straightened and took something from her pocket – 'I was asked to give you this.'

He took the small square of folded paper. The stewardess moved on. He looked at the paper for a moment, then opened it. It was folded three times. How strange that he could so easily remember her saying – as if it were an echo – the very words she had written: Eat your carrots.